K. J. PARKER

This special signed edition is limited to 1000 numbered copies.

This is copy *349*.

SAVAGES

SAVAGES

K. J. PARKER

SUBTERRANEAN PRESS 2015

First Edition

ISBN
978-1-59606-615-1

Subterranean Press
PO Box 190106
Burton, MI 48519

subterraneanpress.com

Something nudged his toe, and he woke up. He saw a dozen men standing over him, one of whom he recognised. "Sighvat?" he mumbled.

"Get up."

A spearpoint touched the base of his neck, the hollow where the collarbones meet. It rested on its own weight, just enough to prick through the skin. A little pressure, such as a child would be capable of, would be enough to pierce his windpipe. "I can't," he said.

The spear lifted, just enough to allow him to move. He rolled out from under it, off the bed, onto his knees on the floor. There were spears all around him. "Sighvat," he said, "what the hell do you think you're playing at?"

"Sorry," Sighvat replied. "But I've had enough."

"What?" Made no sense. "I don't understand."

"I'm going to kill you," Sighvat said. "You're an intolerable nuisance, and I'm not putting up with it any longer."

Don't be so stupid, you don't mean that. But, in forty years of close, intimate contact, he'd never known Sighvat to say anything he didn't mean. "Oh come on," he heard himself say. "You can't really be serious."

"Sorry."

A spasm of terror; he smothered it, quickly and completely. I'm going to die now, he thought. Well, everyone dies. It's the defining characteristic of humans. He looked into Sighvat's eyes and saw nothing but distaste; a sensitive, intelligent, thoughtful man forced to do something he didn't want to, because it had to be done. Twelve men with spears, carefully placed around him in a ring. His nearest weapon, his beautiful and expensive sword, was on the far wall, dangling from a nail. Might as well have been hanging from the moon for all the good it'd do him.

"Outside," Sighvat said.

His arms were pulled behind his back and held firmly; whoever did it had done this sort of thing before. A hand gripped his beard and pulled him to his feet. No point in trying to resist. He spoke to himself inside his head; it doesn't matter, because nothing matters. What you can't do anything about doesn't count against you; what doesn't count against you doesn't count. The voice was strong, clear-headed, sensible. He trusted it.

Broad daylight outside in the yard; that's what you get for oversleeping. There were a lot of men he didn't recognise, standing about, leaning on spears and shields. Trust Sighvat to do the thing properly; enough men, careful planning, scrupulous attention to detail. He's won, he thought, and for a moment he was nearly swept away by anger, because Sighvat couldn't win, it couldn't be allowed, because if Sighvat won it'd mean he was the better man. But; it didn't matter. Irrelevant now. He stepped out of all that, the place and time and circumstances in which it mattered who was the better man; shedding it like a soaking wet coat when you come in out of the rain. Define *better*, he challenged himself. Or rather, don't bother. None of this is anything to do with me any more.

"Is everyone outside?" Someone must've nodded. "Right," Sighvat said. "Turn him round so he can see."

He saw his mother and his wife; their hands were tied, and there was a man standing next to each of them. Behind them, he saw three men with pitchforks loaded with hay, and a small brass brazier he didn't recognise. Sighvat must've brought it with him. The men held the hay over the brazier until it crackled and lit.

"I want you to know I'm taking nothing out of the house," Sighvat said. "I'm not a thief."

The men pitched the burning hay up onto the thatch. All his possessions were in there, and he'd always been so attached to things. Furniture, weapons, clothes; imported, most of them, he'd spent a great deal on things, and he loved them. The heat of the burning house would wreck them all; such a waste. But there, it didn't matter. He turned his back on it.

"The livestock and the hay I'm taking as compensation," Sighvat went on. "You cheated me over the water rights and the felling rights in Long Wood, and your men killed three of mine and you never paid me anything for them. I think that's perfectly fair."

He shrugged. "You think what you like," he said.

Sighvat frowned. "The land," he said, "naturally passes to your next of kin, but we'll come to that in a moment. However, I formally lay claim to the flood meadow and West Beech, which belonged to my grandfather and which you've been in unlawful possession of ever since my uncle died." He paused. "We've got sufficient witnesses. Are you going to challenge my claim?"

He shrugged again. "I can't be bothered."

"Fine. That's settled, then. Oh, sorry, I almost forgot. Pitland and Conegar Steep were part of your wife's dowry, so they revert to her father. I make no claim to them."

But she's still alive, he thought. Then; oh.

By way of confirmation, Sighvat smiled. "Quite," he said, then nodded once. The man standing next to Torild produced a knife and, with a neat, confident flick, cut her throat, then stepped smartly aside to keep from getting soaked in blood. Her mouth opened; no sound at all. Her knees folded and she dropped like a sack.

It doesn't matter, said the voice. Nothing matters. He checked himself to see if he'd moved, and was relieved to find he hadn't.

Sighvat nodded again. His mother, this time. He felt an intolerable pressure inside him, as though he was about to swell up and burst. He forced it to subside. Doesn't matter.

"Under other circumstances," Sighvat was saying, "that'd have been an entirely indefensible act. But I needed you to see it. You do understand, don't you?"

You can answer him, said the voice, or not. Makes no difference. Besides, they loved you. If they'd survived you, they'd have spent the rest of their lives grieving. That's what love does, why it's such a very bad thing. Now you can die knowing they won't suffer.

"Thank you," he said.

"What?"

"I said, thank you."

Sighvat was confused. Splendid. I've said the wrong thing, he thought. Sighvat had it all worked out in his mind; what he was going to do, what he'd say, what I'd say, his perfectly pitched replies, and I've spoilt it. Well. Hardly important, but, well.

"Your sons," Sighvat went on, "are away from home, of course. Luckily, I was able to catch them and bring them along." He snapped his fingers; the barn door opened, and Geiti and Reitung were bundled out, trussed up in ropes, stumbling, tripping over their own feet.

Oh, he thought.

"It was sort of inevitable," Sighvat said, "that one of your sons would disgrace my daughter. I guess I'd resigned myself to it, more or less from the day she was born. Both your sons, though. I confess, I hadn't prepared myself for that. Not really your fault, I suppose—"

Reitung yelled, "I didn't. I swear to God—" Someone kicked him in the face, and he stopped abruptly.

"For the record," Sighvat said, "she's admitted it. Both of them. I had to lock her up in the barn for five days, no food or water, before she confessed. Have you any idea what it felt like, having to do that to your own child? I'd rather have cut my arm off. Their fault," he added, "and therefore yours. It all comes back to you in the end. Everything."

Reitung was sobbing. He simply couldn't cope with pain. Sensitive, his mother called him; she'd said, well, why should he have to? There's nothing good about suffering. Quite right, of course. And Reitung could make a rock smile, and he worked so hard on the farm. Geiti, on the other hand, was thinking quietly, looking for a way—if I throw myself sideways, I could knock over that goon, which would give Reitung a gap to run through, except that that one'd have a clear stab at him as he passed; so, forget about that, what if—? He nearly smiled, but stopped himself in time. For Geiti the world was one enormous puzzle, riddle, intelligence test; every component of it challenging his mind and body to be resourceful, be imaginative, excel. It wore you out sometimes, just watching him think, but one time in four he'd figure it out and find a way; one in four is pretty good, when you think about it. And they'd always been on the same side, right from when Geiti was a little boy. That really was precious and rare. Geiti looked up and their eyes met; don't worry, Dad, I've got an idea, it'll be fine.

He looked away.

"There's still the matter of the chieftainship," Sighvat said. "We both know you beat me to it through bribery and undue influence, and by rights it should be mine. So, here's the deal. You transfer it to me, now, legally, due form and process. In return, one of your sons survives." He paused, then added. "You don't need to think about it, do you? Best offer you've ever had."

He nodded. "All right," he said. "Which one?"

"Ah." Sighvat smiled at him. "That's the good bit. You choose."

For a moment he was afraid it had all been in vain; that he'd cry out, weep, yell, struggle against the rope. The pressure inside him was so overwhelming he didn't know how to resist it. Somehow, from somewhere, he found the strength. "I can't do that," he said.

"No? Pity. In that case, the offer is withdrawn. Entirely up to you, of course, but—"

Up till then he'd managed, the voice had managed to persuade him that Sighvat didn't matter, that he was just the face Death had chosen to wear today; Sighvat, a disease, a fall from a horse, old age, so what? It's just death, death is unavoidable, now or later, who gives a damn? But the sheer horrifying malice of it—choose, Geiti or Reitung; don't choose, both of them. Despair is manageable. It's hope that tears you apart.

He looked at them. Reitung shouted out, "Dad, please." The words bubbled through the blood in his mouth. Geiti caught his eye and shrugged; he was saying, Don't be hard on him, Dad, you know what he's like. And choose him, not me.

That's my boy, he thought, always trying for the best possible outcome, always trying to *win*. Because, if Geiti *volunteers*, the choice is no choice and Sighvat's horrible scheme fails, and we've beaten him. All-conquering us, invincible even in defeat.

He thought; Geiti's the better man, but I think we've established, that doesn't matter. But Reitung would suffer more, he loves us so much; loves me. I will not allow love to hurt him with the greatest pain of all.

"Geiti," he said.

Reitung screamed, "No, Dad, please!" and tried to lunge forward; a hand grabbed his hair, jerked his head back, as another hand drew a sharp edge across his throat. Geiti was roaring like a bull. He closed his eyes, just for a moment.

"Good choice," Sighvat said. "The other one was pathetic." He paused for contradiction, was disappointed, continued; "Your turn. The chieftainship. Can you remember the words?"

Of course. He said them slowly and clearly; trying to remember, as he did so, why on earth it had mattered so much, once upon a time, to get this pointless thing he was now giving away to his enemy. How ridiculous. Meanwhile, he took care not to look in Geiti's direction, so as not to see the reproachful look on his face. I'll be spared all that, he thought; reproach, guilt, shame, pain. The thought made him feel almost cheerful, like when he was a boy and he'd been let off some dreaded chore; he'd somehow kidded poor Geiti into taking all that stuff on for him. Rather him than me, he thought. And Geiti will manage; he'll fight it, think it to a standstill and beat it, somehow, some day. I'd never be able to do that.

"Splendid." Sighvat was speaking again, which presumably meant he'd finished saying the magic words and the chieftainship was now duly and legally conveyed. In which case; any other business? He couldn't think of any. Sighvat turned to an older man on his left, who nodded. "That's that, then." He lifted a finger, and the man standing behind Geiti swung his hand-axe and buried it in the back of Geiti's head. He fell forward without a sound.

He looked at Sighvat, who shrugged. "Well," Sighvat said, "I think that's pretty much everything. That just leaves you."

Even now, after everything he'd seen, he still couldn't help feeling a terrible chill; like he'd felt that time when they'd had to pull the arrow out; and he'd known it was necessary, if they didn't he'd probably die, but there's no way you can really prepare for acute physical pain. He deliberately relaxed, every muscle and tendon. He could feel his heart beating fast. It doesn't matter, he told himself, because pain only matters if you survive it, and I won't be around to feel the throbbing and the ache. Or not for long, anyhow.

"Now then," Sighvat said briskly. "I've given this a great deal of careful thought, knowing you as well as I do. I thought; if I was in his shoes, what would I least want him to do to me? I guess I'll never know if I was right, but it's a chance I'll just have to take." Sighvat paused, and he thought; he's not enjoying this, the way he'd expected to. "I never wanted to be a cruel man," he went on. "But you bring out the worst in me."

Suddenly he thought; this is my last chance to say anything, my very last; now or never. So; anything? No, he decided. It's not important enough to warrant comment.

Sighvat did it with a slight twitch of the head, indicating time and direction. They pulled him to his feet, shoved his back hard to get him moving. For a moment he was mystified, until he recognised the direction; across the yard, south-east. They were going to—

It was very hard, but he caught it in time. He said nothing, and his face didn't move.

It took four of them to slide away the massive square slate well-cover. He'd forgotten that Sighvat was religious, or at least pragmatic enough not to take chances. If there really was a Great Sky-Father and a happy land beyond the setting sun, then it might also be true that a drowned man's soul was completely destroyed; and if not, well, no harm done.

He was standing on the edge of the well. No point in looking. He knew what was down there. "Well?" he heard Sighvat call out. "Is there anything you want to say?"

Three heartbeats; then something pushed hard against the small of his back. He toppled. Extreme and nauseating dizziness; then the shock as he hit the surface of the water, went under.

He kept perfectly still, allowing his body to float upwards. By the time his head emerged into the air, he was in total darkness; they'd slid back the slate. He kicked water for a moment. You bloody fool, he thought, and groped for the wall. It was smooth brick, slimy with green muck. You bloody fool.

Forty-three years ago, two days before he was born, his father had started the well. It had been his project, and he never did anything much after that; a quiet, peaceful man, content to do exactly the same thing every year. Died with a hoe in his hand, among the spring cabbages.

He raised his arm as high as he could reach, then slowly dragged his fingertips down the brickwork.

A careful man, too; careful to the point of being neurotic, particularly when it came to his only son. That was why he'd had the well-cover made so big and heavy, to make sure that no kid could shift it, not even with the exceptional ingenuity he stood to inherit from his grandfather, and a very long lever. Very hard indeed to shift from above; from below, absolutely impossible.

His fingers dipped into water. He thrashed his feet to keep his head and shoulders out, twisted round a quarter turn and raised his arm to try again.

Also, at great expense and inconvenience, his father had insisted on setting one brick in every fifth course out proud, so as to form a crude and terrifying ladder; the idea being, that if someone were to fall in, someone very brave could climb down and fish him out again. Mercifully, no-one had ever had to try it out. His fingers found a projection; he clamped his hand around it and let his full weight hang on it, like an anchor. Thanks, Dad.

Sighvat undoubtedly knew about the well, its depth, the massive nature of the cover; he'd seen it often enough, visiting the farm as a boy, before the falling-out. It was fairly obvious that he'd suborned one of the farm hands or servants, which was how he'd acquired the detailed knowledge of the daily routine necessary to execute his perfectly-planned raid. What the traitor hadn't told him—

(He reached up, found the next brick; scrabbled under the water with his feet; found a foothold)

—And why should he? Slipped his mind, or hadn't seemed relevant; or maybe a last vestigial trace of loyalty had made him leave out the relevant detail; that, three years after the well was finished, a landslip up on the mountain had changed the course of a stream, bringing floodwater down onto Conegar, the farm's second best pasture. Disaster; so Father had had a storm drain dug, at ruinous cost, no expense spared; he'd even had the drain lined with hard clay pipe, forty-eight inch inside diameter, big enough for a man to crawl through, if he was desperate enough. There was nowhere for that much water to soak away without causing muddy havoc, so Father had continued the trench right down into the yard and knocked through the wall of the well. If memory served, the drain mouth was about fifteen feet down, just to the right of the line of brick steps.

Bloody fool, he thought. All that effort, all that horrible, horrible waste, and Sighvat had failed, trying to be too clever.

Later, he asked the question. At the time, though, it never occurred to him not to clamber up the bricks until he found the drain mouth, swing himself into it and start to crawl.

It was a long, vile climb, but he refused to countenance stopping, suspecting that if he did, he wouldn't be able to start again. At least the pipe was wet; that told him that water was trickling down it, which suggested the mouth wasn't blocked. Ditching was a winter job, because that was when there was most risk of flooding, and clearing out the land drains was the last stage of ditching, so nobody would've been near the place where the drain head stuck out of the bank like a hungry fledgeling, not for months; there'd be nettles and cow parsley and all manner of garbage grown up in front of it, but nothing, he devoutly hoped, a desperate man couldn't burst through—

Devoutly hoped. Desperate man. Changed your tune somewhat, haven't you?

He took official notice of the evolution, but was too preoccupied with scrabbling to consider the issues in depth. Death in the abstract was one thing; he'd faced it, eye to eye, up there in the light, probably because none of it had sunk in properly yet. In the dark, in a confined space only just wider than his shoulders, death was absolutely out of the question as a viable option; something to be avoided at all costs, with every last fanatical breath and wriggle.

No light; should be seeing light by now, unless the stupid bank's caved in, or the pipe's silted up three feet thick—which had happened the year before last; they'd had to break through with a crowbar and fish the silt out a handful at a time, lying on their faces in the stink. His bare feet—hadn't noticed before, but they'd dragged him out of bed without giving him a chance to put his boots on; what does a dead man need with footwear, at that?—weren't getting much traction as the pipe got wetter and greasier. Hell, he thought; if I slip and slide back—Somehow, he made up for the lack of grip with sheer force and energy, feeling the skin go on his palms, fingertips and toes. There should be light by now, surely—

His left hand stopped in a soft, solid mass, so hard that he nearly broke his fingers. He clawed at it, recognising the texture of caked silt. The drains washed down a fine-grained sandy deposit, reddish brown, with the occasional small stone and clot of rotting leaf. He hooked his fingers into it and pulled out a gobbet; stopped, asked himself; where do I put this? No idea. Could be a few inches or two tons. He reached over his head and dumped it on the nape of his neck, and clawed out some more.

But his chest was soaking wet; there was water, a faint trickle but (he felt with his right hand) *moving*. If a gentle dribble of summer runoff could get through, so could he. He clawed with both hands, dumping the spoil on his neck and hair, wriggling to shuffle it down his back and out of the way. After an amount of time he had no way of quantifying, he realised he was having to reach almost the full extent of his arm to get his hand into the silt. He shuffled forward into the cleared space, thinking; air. I can breathe, so air's getting through as well as water. I can do this, if only—

He scrabbled a handful, and his hand went *through*; and at the same moment he was suddenly, overwhelmingly bathed in light; just like the Invincible Sun in an icon. It washed over him like victory, steeping him in silver and gold; *light*, for crying out loud, the most glorious, the most wonderful thing—

And of course it mattered. It all mattered, every damn thing. Saying otherwise was just being stupid.

He stuck his wrist out into the precious light, and the horror crashed down on him like a wave. Dead, killed, murdered, burnt, taken away from him, everyone, everything that mattered, all gone, lost, dead; and there he lay in the mouth of his father's drain, not dead, not buried, flooded and drenched in cruel, undeceivable light, and what the hell did he think he was playing at?

But his lungs were gasping in gallons of air, and his heart, he could feel it, was hammering, and if any doubt lingered there was so much pain, in every bit of him, to remind him that he was still very much alive. Well, he thought, you had your chance, but now it looks like you're stuck with it.

Thanks, Dad. You and your ridiculous bloody hydraulics.

Feeling incredibly stupid, he gouged away the rest of the silt and squeezed himself out of the hole, like a turd from the arse of a constipated man, and let his face drop forward into three quarters of an inch of liquid mud. Well, birth's always messy. He allowed himself the calf's ration of gasps of air, then wiggled and flopped his way out, until his legs were free and he was an autonomous, independent creature, a newborn, helpless as a blind kitten, bloody, barefoot and raw-palmed. He looked at his hands and thought, shit, what a mess. Then he looked up, for some reason, at the sky.

Think, he told himself.

Sighvat and his men; would they have any reason to hang around? Sighvat had said he wasn't a thief, so presumably they weren't still down there looting the place, and besides, they'd burnt the house, and the stuff in the barns was just commonplace, though still worth having, because everything is. Burying the dead; Sighvat might just do that if he thought it constituted common decency, but not if he'd decided leaving the carrion for the crows was a proper right and entitlement for the winner. More likely, he'd be concerned with rounding up and driving off the livestock, not a straightforward job and one that needed to be done and finished in time for him and his men to get back for afternoon milking. Life, after all, goes on.

In which case; what would he have done? Assuming the traitor had told him where the herd was, they'd have ridden out to the long meadow, with a view to driving the stock back along the river, the quickest way back to Sighvat's place. He'd also have sent a detachment—three men, possibly four—to fetch the sheep down from the moor. Most direct route for them would be along the top of the ridge, so if they chose to look down they'd see the house, possibly see a man in the yard. He realised he was making excuses; I don't want to go back, he admitted to himself, I really don't want to go back there ever again. And you don't have to. Means you can't sneak back to the barn for the stockman's old coat and boots; no possessions whatsoever. A price worth paying, he decided. And besides, there's still the linhay.

Suddenly it was intolerable to stay there a moment longer. He had to go somewhere—where? Unlimited choice, more or less. Consider the world, and how very little of it is taken up by one farm. The linhay first, because grand gestures are all very well but one must be sensible. Then everywhere.

His great-grandfather, who'd died before he was born, had built the linhay to store winter hay for the sheep. In really bad years, a shepherd could get snowed in up there for days at a time. Accordingly, his grandfather had decreed that there should always be a change of clothes, boots, firewood, basic tools and weapons up there, in the little loft, under the eaves where wandering layabouts wouldn't think to look. Father had honoured the decree to the extent of not actively removing anything, so, in theory, there should be a complete set of the equipment necessary for a man to be human, bundled away up there in the roof.

In theory.

The coat, when he dug it out from under a thriving community of spiders, was distinctly theoretical. It had sleeves but no back, and when he tried to wriggle into it, the frayed cloth disintegrated, leaving him with two clothed arms and a bare body. He dumped it and spent a minute or so scrabbling the cobwebs out of the mud he was caked with. The boots were as stiff as wood, but soaking would fix that. The shirt was rotten through, but curiously the trousers had made it, apart from a broad hole over the left knee. The woollen mittens and hat were a grey fuzzy pulp, but so what, it was summer. The horn mug and leather bottle were salvageable. The knife was a brown wafer of rust that crumpled in his hand like a dry leaf, but someone had loved the axe enough to wrap its head in greasy cloth; it would do, though the handle was woodwormed and rat-gnawed. The spearhead was rusted so thin he could push his finger through it. No matter. What possible use would he have had for a weapon, anyway?

He made the voice in his head repeat that, slowly and loudly.

No use whatsoever. If he'd had a weapon, he might possibly have felt obliged to walk down to Sighvat's house and get killed trying to do something pointless. Instead, he looked at the flakes of rust and thought; can I really be bothered? The answer, he was pleased to find, was no. Killing Sighvat would mean going back (because it would raise the implicit question, why are you doing this, and that question would put him right back in the hole, in the ground, out of the light). Much better to go away instead, and keep going, at least until he fell over. Let's do that, he thought. Let's run away.

Or rather walk; or, more realistically, hobble. Another splendid feature of the linhay was a big stone water trough. Its contents were green and stinking, but considerably cleaner than he was. He washed himself as best he could, until his whole body smelt of green slime, and dunked the boots in the trough to soften up.

They proved to be rather too big, so he stuffed them with bracken until they moved more or less in time with his foot. He washed the shirt and trousers he'd been wearing, squeezed out as much green water as he could, and put them back on; the trousers from the roof would do for best, he decided, in case he found himself attending any weddings or other formal occasions. He wrapped the axe, mug and bottle in one of the sleeves of the coat; something to carry, which gave him the illusion of still being a man of property. So, he thought. Time to go.

Half an hour's walking brought him to the boundary of his, what used to be his land. The idea was to go straight across the moor as quickly as possible and straight on into the wood. Because it was so long and narrow, occupying the whole uselessly steep side of the valley, by the time he came out the other side he'd be in places where people wouldn't know him and he wouldn't know them, unless he was unfortunate enough to run into a major landowner. From there; well, it didn't matter, but his inclination would be to keep going until he reached the coast; at which point, his unlimited choice would be somewhat restricted by the sea, and maybe he could stop, sit down and pull himself together. Or not, as the mood took him.

Now here's a proposition, he thought. Can something be untrue if no witnesses can be called to testify against it? No witnesses, no case. Can something be true if I'm the only witness? I'm a fallible man, God knows, with a less than perfect memory. Wasn't there that crazy old man once, other side of Bluegates, who was absolutely convinced he was the rightful king of the Vesani? If only I know something, how can it possibly be true?

The boundary was a low wall, neglected (but that wasn't his problem any more). He grazed his calf scrambling over it, as though it was determined to bite him before it let him go.

WHEN CALOJAN WAS a young lieutenant, two years out of the Institute, his unit was posted to northern Permia. Their function was simply to show strength on the border (who they were showing it to was never entirely clear) and most days were spent in camp, two miles outside the only settlement in those parts which could plausibly call itself a city. Usually when his fellow subalterns suggested that he join them in a trip to the city's one and only brothel—magnificently if obscurely named the College of Essential Arts and Sciences—he made excuses; partly because, left to himself, he'd rather read a book; partly because his family background made it more than likely that such invitations masked some laboured attempt at a practical joke at his expense. There came a point, however, when his evasions began to be talked about, prompting a degree of speculation which the colonel decided was potentially disruptive. Colonel Ortheric rather liked Calojan, though he was fairly sure he didn't understand him; but he knew from bitter experience how dangerous it could be to have an unpopular officer in the chain of command. Fortunately, as he saw it, the matter was susceptible to a simple and painless solution—

"To clarify." Calojan was giving him the look he'd perfected recently; comfortably the right side of dumb insolence, but easily achieving the same effect. "You're ordering me to go to the brothel."

"Yes," Ortheric replied.

"Sir."

Ortheric's face cracked into a grin. He'd cultivated it; the smile-in-spite-of-himself, military and human at the same time. "Don't give me all that," he said. "It's like my mother used to say about childrens' parties. You'll enjoy it when you get there."

"Sir."

It was a feature of Calojan's style (you had to use the word) that he never said *sir* except as a rebuke. He had a marvellous knack of phrasing things so as to be able to avoid the customary military civilities without actually infringing regulations. Ortheric had tried to figure out how he did it, so as to do the same himself, but the secret remained elusive and he didn't like to ask for instructions. Ortheric liked clever officers, in spite of the difficulties they caused.

"You know your trouble," he said. "You're in that awkward no-man's-land between leaving the Institute and getting your first command. In five years time you'll have your own outfit in some godforsaken remote corner somewhere, and you won't have to make yourself pleasant to anyone, and at that time I confidently predict you'll soar like a bird and leave the rest of us poor plodders for dead. Until then, I'm afraid, you need to make an effort and make people like you. I'm very sorry, but it's got to be done. Understood?"

For the first time since Ortheric had known him, Calojan replied with a broad, warm smile. "Permission to speak—"

"Oh, get on with it."

Calojan nodded; then he sat down on the edge of Ortheric's desk and poured them both a drink. Ortheric hesitated—like everything Calojan did, it was a gambit, a calculated tactical move—then took the glass Calojan had poured for him, muttered "Cheers", swallowed half of it and immediately felt better. "Well?" he said.

Calojan took a moment to marshal his words, then said, "It's not really that I think I'm better than everyone else. I know I come across that way sometimes."

"All the time," Ortheric said. "Except occasionally when you're asleep."

Calojan nodded. "The fact is," he went on, "I act that way because I've spent my life being made aware that I'm worse than everyone else, because of my father. Trying to redress the balance, I overdo it. When you're pushing a huge boulder uphill, it's hard to remember not to go too fast."

It was Ortheric's turn to choose his words carefully. "People respect you," he said, "because of your abilities. As far as the men are concerned, that's really all that matters. They'll follow you and love you because you'll win battles without getting them killed. Where your brother officers are concerned, that same ability will make you extremely unpopular. Once you've been promoted a few times it won't matter so much, because they won't be your brothers any more, they'll be your subordinates, and respect will do just fine. Until then, you have to make the effort. Battles, wars and cities have been lost because junior officers can't stand one another. It's a bloody stupid reason for getting men killed, and I don't want it happening here." He paused, and softened his voice a little. "You know all that perfectly well," he said. "You don't need to be told."

Calojan frowned, then nodded. "You're perfectly right," he said. "I should know better. Only—" He tried not to pull a face, almost succeeded. "Does it have to be the brothel? They'll make jokes—"

"Of course they will," Ortheric said. "And you'll give them every opportunity to do so. That's the point. Well, isn't it?"

"Of course it is. Sir," he added, and grinned.

So, the next time he was asked, Calojan said yes, why not, and his comrades in arms (who'd been expecting the usual prevarications) were slightly stunned, then mildly jubilant, as though they'd just won something. During the week before the scheduled expedition, Calojan also made a point of losing at chess (twice) and being late on parade (once). He did these things awkwardly, like a right-handed archer trying to shoot left-handed, so that nobody was in any doubt that he was making an effort. It was a gamble; like all Calojan's gambles, it worked.

"I recommend you try Eupraxia," Goltuhar said sagely. "She'd be just right for you. Nice easy pace and a good turn of speed for the finish." He poured himself another drink from the jug. "Or there's Joffa, if you fancy a challenge."

"Excuse me," Athanalaric objected. "She's mine. Besides, Joffa's strictly postgraduate stuff. You want something more entry-level, like Corduza, or that redhead, what's her name?"

"Brother Calojan's far more advanced than that," Ferrio said. "Expert, bound to be. After all, his dad wrote the book."

There was a very brief moment of extreme tension. Then Calojan frowned, and said, "Well, you know what they say about cobblers' children. Gentlemen, I'm entirely in your hands. Whatever you recommend will be just fine with me."

There followed ten minutes of lively debate; then Atzel, a quiet first lieutenant of sappers who hadn't spoken yet, said, "Surely it's obvious. Stothia. Only possible choice."

Dead silence; then everyone began to laugh. Then the motion was put to the vote and carried unanimously.

"Excuse me," Calojan said, and the slight panic in his voice was very probably genuine. "What's so special about—?"

They grinned at him. "You'll see," they said.

SAVAGES

AT FIRST HE assumed it was just that she was very, very tall; which made sense, since he was the shortest officer in the regiment. She was also ten years older than him and very beautiful. He sat down—the chair, not the bed—and made a show of wincing. "The thing is—" he said.

She smiled at him. "You've hurt your back," she said.

"Yes," he said gratefully, "actually it's killing me, but I didn't want to look like a wimp in front of the others, so—"

She nodded. "You must be Calojan," she said.

He blinked. "They—"

"Talk about you, yes."

"Ah."

"I can see why." She frowned analytically. "You get on their nerves."

"So I've been told."

"You do it on purpose."

He thought before answering. "I suppose I do, yes. Partly because—"

"Of your father, I know. Partly just because you can." She was looking at him with her head just a bit on one side, as though contemplating putting in a bid. "They say you're a genius."

"I'm not."

"No." It wasn't what he'd expected. "Or you wouldn't be here." She picked at a loose thread on the front of her dress. His mother had done that. "You don't approve."

"You know about my father?"

Smile. "Oh yes."

"My mother—"

"That too. Also," she added, "you don't agree with the strong taking advantage of the weak. That's because your family was poor and got pushed around a lot. That's understandable. And you have something of an artist's attitude to beauty. That's understandable too."

Calojan grinned. "Does that mean I've been let off?"

She shrugged. "Up to you," she said. "Of course, it doesn't work if we don't do it."

"Excuse me?"

She looked genuinely surprised. "They didn't tell you?"

"Tell me what?"

She burst out laughing, which surprised him. "Ah, right," she said. "Now, then. Your friends must like you rather more than they're prepared to admit. You don't know who I am."

21

"No."

"Actually, I'm nobody, it's what I can do." She smiled again. "I'm from Scona," she said. "Heard of it?"

"No."

She nodded. "Scona women—some of them—have a special gift. After sex, if everything's gone all right, they can tell your fortune for you. Really, really accurately. It's not just a myth," she added, "it's true. Trust me."

Calojan felt awkward. "I'm not sure I really believe in fortune-telling," he said. "No offence."

"Until three centuries ago, nobody believed in camels. They were wrong." She teased a tangle out of her hair without looking. She smelt of sweat and peaches. "Entirely up to you, I don't mind one way or the other. That said, I'm mildly curious. They do say all sorts of good things about you, how clever you are, what you're going to achieve one day. If we don't do it, I won't know. But—" She shrugged again. "It's no big deal."

Calojan leaned back a little in the chair. She had a slight bruise on one wrist, two or three days old. "Can you do the fortune-telling without, you know—"

She gave him a sour look. "In exceptional cases," she said drily, "it's possible to get a reading just from a kiss. But it'd make it very difficult for me."

"Sorry," Calojan said. "Only, I've hurt my back, you see."

"Of course you have."

Something about the way she said that—annoyed but forgiving, perhaps—made him want to kiss her after all. "Go on," he said. "Let's give it a try. You wouldn't mind an evening off, would you?"

"I'd love it," she replied. "But I've got my reputation to think of. If I can't prophesy for the famous Calojan, people will think I'm a fraud."

"You could make something up."

"I don't do that." She said it so savagely he apologised. She shook her head. "It's all right," she said. "You don't believe in fortune-telling. You think it's just a gimmick, so I get more tricks."

"Yes," Calojan said. "But I'm open minded."

That made her laugh; still laughing, she stood up, walked to the chair, bent down and kissed him. For a moment he forgot about the whole situation; then she broke off, walked back to the bed and sat down. When she lifted her head and looked at him, her face was dead-white. "Are you all right?" he asked.

"What? Oh, I'm fine."

"Well?"

She shook her head. "I'm sorry," she said, "I haven't been entirely straight with you. Lieutenant Atzel—he's a regular of mine—promised me three tremisses if I got a reading out of you. He wants to know if you're going to be a famous general. If so, he intends to be your best friend."

Calojan wiped his mouth on the back of his hand. "I see," he said. "So, what will you tell him?"

She brushed the hair away from her face. There were lines under her eyes he hadn't noticed before. "Up to you," she said. "I could tell him you'll never be anything special, you'll start off well but make a bad mistake in about six years' time, and then it'll be very bad for anyone who's close to you."

"Right," Calojan said, and his throat was curiously dry. "Is that true?"

"No."

"I thought you said—"

"I don't tell lies to the people I read for," she said calmly. "Atzel's a shit, I don't give a damn about him."

"All right," Calojan said. "What did you see?"

She took a moment to reply. "You won't become emperor," she said, "but that'll be your choice. You will rule the empire, but on behalf of someone else. You'll win all your battles except one, and you'll save the empire from being exterminated nine times. You'll always try and do the right thing, you'll mostly succeed, but in the end your actions will turn out badly, and you'll end up a bitter, disappointed man. You'll do a great deal of good, but on balance it would've been better for everyone if you'd never been born." She paused for breath, then said, "That's about all I can tell you. I'm sorry."

It was a while before Calojan could speak. Then he said, "I bet you say that to all the junior officers."

She didn't smile. "Of course I do. That's what they pay me for."

"I don't want to be emperor," he said, suddenly and with a degree of fury that surprised him. "I don't even want to be a general. I just want to be given a fort or an outpost somewhere, where there's nobody to order me about and I can do some painting."

His hand was in his pocket, identifying coins by the thickness of their rims. He found four silver tremisses; two months' pay, and he owed two tremisses thirty for mess bills and lodgings. "Thank you," he said, and looked for somewhere to put the coins down. "I don't believe in prophesy, but thanks all the same."

"Keep your money," she said, and he realised he'd offended her. "You pay Anticyra on the desk one tremissis thirty when you leave. Tipping is not encouraged."

There was nowhere except the floor, so he put three coins down by his feet. "I'm sorry," he said. "I didn't mean to sound rude. I'd better go."

"Wouldn't if I were you," she said coldly. "They'll be expecting you to be another half hour at least. That's the sort of thing they'll make jokes about until you're sixty."

He hadn't thought of that. "I'm sorry," he repeated. "I'm not used to people trying to help me. It makes me uncomfortable."

She shrugged. "No hard feelings," she said. "You don't believe in fortune-telling. It's not something you can choose to do." She sighed, then said abruptly, "Do you play chess?"

"What?"

"Well, of course you do, you're a master tactician. We've got half an hour. Would you like a game?"

She had one of those travelling chess sets that packs away into a small box, which unfolds so that the base becomes the board. The pieces were ebony and walrus ivory. It was quite valuable. He didn't ask where she'd got it from. They played four games; lost, drawn, won, lost. It was the first time he'd been beaten against his will for several years. "Don't tell me," he growled, as he pushed over his king with his fingertip at the end of the fourth game. "You can predict what moves I'm about to make."

She laughed. "You look at the pieces you're interested in," she replied. "You want to be careful about that."

"Thank you, I'll remember that." He hesitated, then stood up. "I enjoyed the games."

"You were trying too hard," she said. "Good luck, Calojan." Suddenly she gave him a beautiful smile, which took him completely off guard. "I'd make you promise to remember me when you're ruling the empire and send me a cartload of gold, but you won't be able to."

"What, remember?"

"Send a cart to Permia," she replied. "Goodbye."

He never found out what she told Atzel, but from then on, all the other subalterns treated him with a sort of terrified respect, which irritated Colonel Ortheric so much that he got him a transfer. A double-jump promotion went with it, so he didn't mind.

Fourteen years later, at the height of the Second Sashan War, when Calojan replaced Ortheric as commander of the Nineteenth Army, he went to see him in the guardhouse cells at Edista, the night before his court-martial.

"I'm sorry," he said. "I don't think I can get you out of this one."

Ortheric had got old; also, he'd lost a hand and an eye at the siege of Chastel Rosc. He looked away, then said, "You could, you know. You're the officer commanding the last viable army in the empire. You can do anything you damn well want."

"I'm sorry," Calojan repeated. "Is there anything I can get you?"

Ortheric shook his head. "You know what they'll do to me," he said. "They'll put out my good eye and pack me off to a monastery in the Feralia. I'll be dead in six months." He looked up. "I got you your first command," he said. "Or had you forgotten?"

"Only because you couldn't stand the sight of me."

Ortheric shrugged. "Does the motive really matter all that much? Yes," he added, "I guess it does. Get me a copy of the *Seven-Chambered House*, would you? I'd like to read it again, while I still can."

Calojan reached inside his coat. "Funny you should mention that," he said.

He stood up to go. Ortheric opened the book, then put it down. "You remember what the whore said."

The noun made him wince, for some reason. "Vaguely."

"You'll rule the empire, and win all your battles except one. So far, it's looking good."

"I've fought six battles," Calojan replied. "And we're this close to losing the war. Hardly conclusive."

"Promise me," Ortheric said. "When you're in charge, if I'm still alive, get me out of there. I hate monks and I hate religious music. All right?"

"Sorry," Calojan said. "I don't believe in prophesy."

He never saw Ortheric again. In the early hours of the following morning, as a result of a shameful lapse in security, someone managed to get past the guards and spirit the old man away. He was last heard of in the Vesani Republic, lecturing on strategic theory at a low-grade military crammer. The date of his death is not recorded; his will, however, was proved in the Vesani probate court on the same day that Calojan won his first major victory in the Sashan war. He named Calojan as his sole heir. There were a few clothes and trivial household goods, a rather fine sword (which was confiscated and destroyed by the Vesani authorities) and forty silver tremisses cash; the only valuable item was a comprehensive collection of the works of Roumain Dragash, the foremost erotic and pornographic artist of the post-Mannerist era, whose other claim to fame was that he was Calojan's father.

There was a certain amount of trouble about the bequest. For one thing, the estate was insolvent, which meant that the paintings and books had theoretically to be sold at auction; but that wasn't possible because of the Vesani obscenity laws, which required that such material be destroyed unless it exhibited genuine artistic content, in which case it was forfeited to the librarian of the Immaculate Hope temple. A little diplomatic activity solved the problem; Calojan discharged Ortheric's debts, and the librarian, on behalf of the Senate of the Republic, made a gift of the artwork to the Chancellor of the Studium, who sold it to Calojan for a nominal sum.

THEY CAUGHT THE Emperor trying to sneak out of the Crescent harbour on a fishing boat. Immediately, Admiral Sechimer gave orders for the boom to be lowered, sealing the harbour mouth. Then he ran down to the quay, where his galley stood ready, as always. He grabbed the captain by the shoulder, turned him around and pointed at the little blue sail in the middle of the harbour. "Quick as you can," he said.

Calojan arrived, out of breath, just as the galley was about to cast off. A dragoon sergeant helped him aboard. "Well?" Calojan snapped. "Is it him?"

"Looks like it," Sechimer said quietly.

The galley was the fastest ship in the world, and quite possibly the most manoeuvrable. The fishing boat tried to wobble out of the way, but the wash from the galley's three banks of oars stopped it dead in the water. They caught it with grappling hooks and dragged it alongside with the main winch. There were two men in the boat. One was the fisherman. The harbour master happened to be on board the galley, caught out by its unscheduled departure. "I know him," he said.

Sechimer frowned. "Let him go."

They put him back in his boat and released the hooks. The other man was a giant; nearly seven feet tall and ridiculously broad and fat; next to him, even the magnificent Sechimer looked small and oddly irrelevant. He had red hair down to his shoulders, a flat red face with a white scar just below his left eye. He was missing two front teeth.

"That's him," the captain of the guard said, but they knew that already.

Two sergeants were holding his arms behind his back. "Get him a chair," Sechimer said. "After all, he's the emperor."

It took a while; the nearest chair was in Sechimer's cabin, two decks down. They got the emperor into it by treading on the backs of his knees. "Watch him," the captain of the guard said, superfluously. They tied his arms tight behind his back. Fifteen marines stood around him in a three-quarter circle, arms linked.

"Hello, Hodda," Sechimer said. "That's your real name, isn't it?"

The emperor grinned at him. "Done your homework," he said.

Sechimer nodded. "Hodda son of Matto," he said. "Your father was a wheelwright."

"That's right," Hodda said. "Skilled man. Politician, wasn't he, your dad?"

Sechimer didn't flinch, bless him. Calojan had been there when Sechimer got the news of what the emperor had done to Sechimer's father. He couldn't help glancing at Sechimer's face, which didn't move.

"That reminds me," Hodda said. "Got something for you. On a string, round my neck."

Calojan could see Sechimer hesitate, just for a moment; as though whatever it was could defeat him, even now. Then he nodded. A guard pulled up the lapels of Hodda's shirt, found the string and lifted it carefully up over the neck and the torrent of hair.

Oh God, Calojan thought. The guard handed the thing to his captain, who stood holding it, not knowing what to do with it.

"Well?" Hodda said. "Don't you want it?"

"Get rid of it," Sechimer said quietly.

Calojan looked at it, before the captain threw it over the side into the sea. A small, shrivelled thing, the stub of a human finger; the famous sixth finger, from Sechimer's father's left hand.

"They told me it'd bring me luck," Hodda said. "Ah well."

Calojan watched Sechimer keep control of himself. It was an impressive sight. "Just the one question," he said. He was looking directly into Hodda's eyes, as if nothing else existed. "Are you proud of the way you've run the empire?"

Hodda laughed. "Trick question," he said.

"I'll answer it for you," Sechimer said. "You achieved the throne by mutiny and murder."

"Yes." Hodda nodded. "The old emperor was a lunatic. They kept him in a cage. He bit people."

Sechimer shrugged, conceding the point. "You broke your oath."

"Sure." Hodda smiled at him. "I worked my way up from the ranks, I was a damn good soldier. The old man was a joke. If it hadn't been me it'd have been someone else. Some toff. Someone like you, probably."

"Indeed," Sechimer said. "But when you took the throne, we had a six billion surplus in the Treasury, the provinces were loyal and we were at peace with the Sashan. Now we're bankrupt, Scheria and Permia have broken away and they tell me you can see the Sashan camp from the top of the Winter Temple tower. Your fault, Hodda."

"Maybe." Hodda was matching him stare for stare. "But all that was coming anyway, you know that. Let's face it, you're no different. Only difference between us is, *he* went to work for you."

Calojan felt a slight shiver as the emperor's head nodded in his direction. "Not really," he heard himself saying. "Why I chose him instead of you, that's the difference."

Hodda ignored him. Well, he would. "You got lucky," he went on. "You got the military genius there, I didn't. Just luck. Otherwise, we're the same."

"You executed something in the order of nine hundred people, including half the Senate."

"Had to," Hodda said. "Political. It's a nasty business. I expect you'll do the same."

"You murdered my father," Sechimer said.

"Yes," Hodda replied. "Didn't I just."

Sechimer looked away. "That's enough," he said. "Did anyone think to bring an axe?"

Apparently not. "Fine," Sechimer said. His hand moved to his belt, but there was no sword there. "Captain."

The captain of the guard was wearing a yatagan; short, wide blade, concave edge with a convex flick at the end, like a flattened S. The sight of it made Hodda go pale. They untied his hands, pushed him down the deck; a soldier planted a boot between his shoulder blades. "We need something for a block," the captain said, looking round. "That'll do."

They fetched one of those wooden things the ropes go through; what's the proper word, Calojan tried to remember. Block, as in block and tackle. Coincidence. They dragged Hodda's head up by the back hair and tucked the wooden thing under his chin.

"Please." Hodda sounded terrified. "My hair."

Sechimer frowned, then laughed. "Sorry, I forgot. He's a Ruddite." The captain looked at him. "It's his religion," Sechimer explained. "They think, if you cut their hair, you damage the soul." He smiled. "Can't have that, can we? Captain."

The captain nodded to a sergeant, who knelt down and gathered Hodda's hair, twisted it around his hands and pulled back, exposing the nape of the neck. He looked up at Sechimer.

"That's fine," Sechimer said.

The other sergeant bent his knees and swung the yatagan in a fine circular flourish. As he brought it down, Hodda arched his back and jerked his whole body backwards, dragging the arms of the sergeant under the sword's edge. The sergeant screamed and let go. Hodda back-somersaulted, landed on his hands, did a handstand and a cartwheel across the deck and flopped over the rail like a fish. At the last moment, a guard grabbed his ankle; he was pulled forward but managed to brace himself against the rail and cling on. "For crying out loud," Sechimer yelled. Two more guards reached the rail, grabbed Hodda's trouser leg in handfuls and hauled him back onto the deck. He was thrashing and wriggling like an eel, and bellowing. Two guards had to sit on his chest.

"Look after that man, for God's sake," Sechimer said. They lifted up the sergeant and twisted their scarves tight round his wrists; he was streaming blood and crying. They bundled him to the hatch and down below deck. Hodda was still struggling, moving the men sitting on him. Sechimer was looking away, the scene too revolting for words. It occurred to Calojan that he was the senior military officer present, and so it was probably up to him to deal with it. "Cut his throat," he said. "Go on, do it."

"Sir."

Wrong. Never give an order you know they aren't able to obey. Hodda was twisting and writhing so much, you wouldn't dare introduce a sharp instrument for fear of getting cut with it yourself, or carving up one of your own people. Hands and arms everywhere, grappling and grabbing, legs kicking, a mess and out of control. Can't have that. Calojan walked over, located Hodda's head in the jumble, waited for the moment and kicked it hard. No effect. He did it again. Hodda went limp; the tangle collapsed around him. A sergeant put his left hand on Hodda's neck, feeling for the jugular vein, pressed down hard with his palm like a butcher jointing ribs, drew his short knife with his right hand and made a slow, careful slice. Blood hit him square in the face and he flinched out of the way. Job done.

Calojan looked across at Sechimer. "What should we—?"

"Get rid of it," Sechimer said quietly. Calojan had forgotten for the moment. Sechimer wasn't good with the sight of blood.

"Is he dead?" Calojan asked the sergeant.

"Yes, sir."

Calojan looked for himself, to make sure. Quite dead. The eyes and mouth were open, empty, ownerless. Nobody home. He gestured with his head. It took five of them to drag the body up and over the rail, and there was a loud splash, almost comic.

Job done.

Slowly and deliberately, Sechimer sat down on a coil of rope and slumped forward, weight on his elbows, head lolling. It suddenly occurred to Calojan that this was as far as he'd planned; that in his mind he'd reached the end. Not good at all. He walked over, trying to be quiet, waited for a few moments. Sechimer didn't move.

"Well," Calojan said quietly. "I suppose you're the emperor."

Sechimer lifted his head. He looked exhausted. "What?"

"I said, you're the emperor now. Aren't you?"

"I suppose I must be."

"You don't sound exactly thrilled."

"I'm not."

Fair enough, Calojan thought. Who in his right mind would be? The empire was in ruins, one battle away from being exterminated by the Sashan. The new emperor could reasonably expect a reign of about a month, and then the end of a thousand years of glorious history would for ever be his fault. Not a job you'd choose, given the choice. He tried to think of something to say.

"Well," he said. "At least we've got rid of him."

Sechimer smiled painfully. "You mean," he said, "I just murdered my predecessor. Just like he did."

"I wouldn't call it murder," Calojan said mildly.

Sechimer sighed wearily. "He was unarmed, so it wasn't a fair fight," he said. "And there wasn't a trial, so it wasn't due process. And you couldn't call that shambles a formal execution. I guess assassination sounds marginally better than plain ordinary murder, but it amounts to the same thing."

"He had to go."

"So did Gendomer." Sechimer stood up, straightened his back, like an old man in the middle of a day's haymaking. "Not that it matters particularly. All we've done is save the Great King a job. Don't suppose he'll thank us for it."

Long live Sechimer the First, Calojan thought; though right now he doesn't look like he'll last five minutes.

"I suppose we'd better get back to the palace," Sechimer said. "It's going to be a long day."

Look at him, Calojan thought. Twenty-nine years old, the most handsome man on the continent, and now emperor. He'd seen happier refugees in the camps. "The staff meeting," Calojan reminded him.

"What? Oh God, I'd forgotten all about it. Yes, straight away, that's far more important." He looked round for the captain, gave orders. "You know what I'm like," he said with a grin. "Any little thing distracts me."

The staff meeting first; then, presumably, some sort of coronation—except that nobody seemed to know where Hodda had hidden the triple crown, the lorus and the divitision, sacred regalia without which no legitimate coronation could take place. So Calojan sent a couple of his best men down to the theatre, where they had a big wicker hamper stuffed with crowns, loroi and divitisia, impeccably authentic in every detail. They smelt strongly of damp and the lives and deaths of mice. Fortunately, during the coronation ceremony, only the Patriarch and the three archdeacons stand close enough to the throne to notice, and the archdeacons carry thuribles of steaming incense, and the Patriarch happened to have a heavy cold.

(THEY DID, HOWEVER, find Hodda's will. Most of it was irrelevant, since both his sons and one of his three brothers had been killed in the civil war (the other two had died fighting the Sashan), and the bequests to his loyal supporters obviously couldn't be allowed on political grounds. That left a few minor gifts of personal property to palace servants—shoes to a valet, bedlinen to a chambermaid (appropriate and well-earned, by all accounts), a ceremonial sword and helmet to his batman, seventy angels and a pair of silk slippers to his barber and so on. Also one item which, for some reason, nobody thought to query; to general Calojan, the contents of my sandal-wood book box, to be found in my bedchamber; with all due respect.

Calojan had a pretty good idea what it would be, and he was right; an almost complete set of his father's major works, impressively bound in brown calf, the collectors' edition, together with some of the lesser works, including some rarities, which he kept. The rest he donated to the widows-and-orphans fund, with strict and sincere instructions about anonymity.)

"IT DOESN'T SEEM to be moving," Guaritz said.

The head of the faculty of rhetoric wasn't in the habit of visiting the *Chastity & Forbearance*; a pity, because he'd have recognised Guaritz' last remark as a perfect example of the Self-Evident Observation Best Left Unmade, as outlined in Demodocus' *Interlocutories*, XIV, 27c. Although his attention was focussed firmly on the ring in the centre of the room, Aimeric couldn't help congratulating himself on remembering the reference. After all, only yesterday the Junior Tutor had hinted quite strongly that it would be coming up in the exam.

"Quiet, for pity's sake," Dargoin hissed.

Dead silence is the required protocol for watching the Grand Lesser Herpetilude (that's lizard-fighting to you and me). Any sort of noise from the spectators is likely to send the combatants into a mild form of shock, leading them to freeze solid and sit completely still for up to an hour. Since they were both already doing that, however, the magnitude of the offence was slightly diminished. Even so.

The long periods of dead quiet inactivity are, of course, an integral part of the lizard-fighting experience. They serve to ratchet up the tension, already considerable when a Town reigning champion is fighting a University challenger in the finals of the Hilary Tournament. Aimeric, whose interest in the proceedings was primarily financial rather than sporting or aesthetic, just wanted them to get on with it, but he was sensitive enough to appreciate the unique atmosphere. On what other occasion, after all, would you find the main room of the *Chastity* packed with equal numbers of Golden Spire students and junior members of the Coppersmiths' Guild, both sides quite adequately armed within the letter of the law, and sitting perfectly still and quiet on their respective sides of the hall? To a man who had some time ago resolved to devote his life to the abolition of war and the peaceful resolution of all conflict, it was an eloquent paradigm of what could be, if only—

In the ring, something moved, very fast.

The Coppersmiths' Big Old Sandy was a six-year-old marsh skink, a huge creature (four pounds, two ounces) who had won three successive Hilaries through sheer bulk and neck-muscle power. The students' White Death of the Vesani was a rare and valuable imported Desert Muiraptor; small and slight, but devilish quick and equipped with three superimposed rows of ridiculously sharp herringbone teeth. In the previous round it had dealt with the Watermen's Blue Glory by ripping its throat out in a single pass, and so far in the tournament hadn't suffered more than a few trivial scratches. All that, however, had just changed. Guaritz was groaning, Dargoin looked completely stunned. Aimeric's expression didn't change, but in his heart he was deeply troubled. All that was visible of the White Death was its hind legs and tail, still twitching feebly, sticking out of the skink's monstrously swollen mouth.

"Politically," Aimeric pointed out, as they trooped sadly back into the tap room, "it was a good result. If we'd won, they'd have been furious, and there'd almost certainly have been a fight, which, on past form—"

"There may still be one," Dargoin muttered darkly. "No way was that match honest. I think they must've given it something."

Guaritz looked at him. "Ours or theirs?"

Dargoin shrugged. "I don't know. Both, probably. I say we wait outside and give them a good smacking on their way out. They'll be so pissed they won't be any bother. For the honour of the university, you understand."

Aimeric sighed. "If you care to stand outside in the rain for two hours, you go ahead. I'll bring you out a beer if you give me the money."

Guaritz frowned. "I thought it was your—"

"Yes," Aimeric said. "But my entire hospitality budget for the rest of the month just got eaten by a sort of green sluggy thing with tiny little legs. Accordingly, I'm forced to depend on the charity of my dear friends."

Dargoin winced. "For crying out loud, Aimeric—"

"Well, don't blame me. You told me it couldn't lose."

Dargoin sighed, and felt in his pocket. The immutable rule was that all drinks consumed on Hilary finals night were paid for by the losing team's supporters. Given the legendary thirst of the junior Coppersmiths, that was liable to run into serious money.

"You'll have to write home," Guaritz said grimly.

"Can't," Aimeric replied with feeling, "not three times in one term. That'd be diplomatically inappropriate."

"Your old man's loaded," Guaritz pointed out. "Especially—"

"Yes, thank you." Dangerously close to his least favourite topic. He raised his voice just a little; it came out louder, but higher and sharper. "But there are limits, even to such a morally laudable course as diminishing my loathsome father's obscene wealth. In fact, I rather think I exceeded them the last time. That was the impression I got from his letter, anyway."

"Hell," Dargoin said simply. "In that case, we're definitely going to beat up at least one Coppersmith before we go home tonight." He paused, and considered his beer. "A small one, naturally."

Aimeric decided he hadn't heard that. "Apparently," he said, "in Merpelleuse they fight rats instead of lizards, which makes much more sense to me. I mean, you can train a rat, to a certain extent. You'd be dealing with more of a known quantity."

"Pity you didn't go there, then." Aimeric winced slightly. He hadn't noticed Jauvaiz slipping in quietly on his blind side. "Oh, no, wait, I'm sorry, I forgot. If you'd gone to a university in your own country, you wouldn't have been able to dodge the draft."

"Indeed." He turned his head a little and gave Jauvaiz a friendly smile. "Here, do join us. There's an empty seat, look."

"No, thanks. Call me picky, but—" Jauvais grinned and walked away. Guaritz frowned. "I don't know why he does that."

"What?"

"Pick on you like that."

Aimeric shrugged. "Helps pass the time, I guess."

"Next time," Dargoin said, "you ought to smash his face in."

"That would be violence," Aimeric pointed out. "Which I don't do, remember. If I did, I wouldn't have had to dodge the draft. I'd be in Merpelleuse, making a fortune betting on rats."

Dargoin seemed to have forgotten about beating up coppersmiths, for the time being at least, but Aimeric decided it'd be a good time to withdraw. Quite apart from the military-political situation, he didn't really want to drink tonight; he was presenting an argument in front of the Junior Tutor in the morning, and he'd need a clear head if he wanted to make any sort of showing in his Disputation. Announcing his departure would lead to further comments about his inability to pay his share of the bar tab; much better to wander off for a piss and not come back. He counted to twenty, then got up and headed for the door.

Outside, a knot of Junior Coppersmiths were leaning against a wall, passing round a big brown jug of moonshine. They looked at him, decided against it and ignored him. Splendid. That was the one good thing about being six foot seven and broad as an ox. It's so much easier being a pacifist when it's obvious you can pick people up in one hand and throw them across the street.

Forty-seven angels, abruptly snuffed out by a lizard. So much for gambling as a profession. The thought of them, no longer his, now the property of a bunch of semi-literate apprentices (but not for long; they'd blow the lot in the *Chastity* and the brothel inside of a week) made him feel horribly depressed; so, since he was passing the door of the *Moderation*, he decided to award himself just one drink, to be paid for out of the education and arts budget. After all, he wouldn't be able to concentrate on his work if he was dead miserable.

One drink led to three; the third drink inspired him to challenge a couple of first years from Constitution Hall to a game of blind man's donkey; an easy victory netted him nine angels sixty, enough to drink on through to mid-term if he was careful. The moral; gamble on your own abilities, not those of expensive foreign reptiles. He went back to College, and found two of the proctors' men waiting outside his door.

Bloody Dargoin and his insensate love of violence; presumably he'd had his fight after all, and something bad had happened. Mercifully, he had the two Constitution Hall suckers for an alibi, except that he'd neglected to find out their names. "Good evening, gentlemen," he said, as calmly as he could manage. "Something I can do for you?"

They had that awkward look, and he was suddenly very scared. "The Dean would like a word, please, sir."

Not good. The proctor, not the Dean, dealt with all breaches of discipline, up to and including murder. "If it's about the Hilary match—"

"Nothing like that, sir. If you wouldn't mind."

The old saying; it's when they're polite that you really need to worry. "Can't it wait?"

"Not really, sir."

Ah, he thought, so I was right. Somebody's died, at home. And then, the words slipping into his mind before he could stop them, *hope to God it's dad, not mother or Gesel.* Too late. Immediately, he pictured his father; *lie to other people, son, but not to yourself.*

"Are you all right, sir?"

"Fine." He'd barked the word out like a drill-sergeant. "Sorry," he added. "Maybe just a drop too much at the *Moderation* on the way home. You know how it is."

"Yes, sir. If you're ready."

There were, he told himself as he proceeded behind his escort across Middle Yard, other possibilities. The Vesani Republic has formed an alliance with the Sashan, and I'm to be interned as an enemy alien. They're so impressed with my last dissertation that they're going to offer me the chair of Formal Logic. The Dean's wife is hopelessly in love with me, and the Dean's been unexpectedly called away to a full ecumenical council. Loads of other reasons why I've been hauled out here in the middle of the night, in the rain, to see the boss.

The Dean lived in what had once been the main cistern for the entire citadel. The high, curved walls were now entirely covered with bookshelves; over a thousand pigeonholes, and from each projected the cap end of a brass or silver tube. They said the Dean owned more books than any one else in the world, except possibly the King of Sashan—but he cheated, because his collection was made up of one example each of every known edition of the Fire Gospel, and they were all sealed, to make sure nobody read them.

At the base of that enormous cylinder, on the small three-legged stool which was the only seat in the room, sat a man in a big coat. The Dean stood a few yards away, reading (he always read the old-fashioned way, standing up). He frowned and lowered the scroll as Aimeric entered the room. Aimeric looked at him, then at the man on the stool.

"If you'll excuse me," the Dean said. He took a step back and pressed the shelving behind him with the tips of his fingers; the shelf revolved, revealing a door. He slipped through it sideways, and it closed behind him.

"Hello, Hosculd," Aimeric said.

The man in the coat started to get up, but Aimeric stopped him with a small shake of his head. "So, what are you doing here?"

"Your father's dead, Aimeric."

A flood of relief; it seemed to start in his chest, and reach his knees and elbows simultaneously. His head, by contrast, felt completely numb. "I guessed it was something like that," he mumbled. "What—?"

"His heart," Hosculd said, and Aimeric noticed that the top of his head was now almost completely bald. "It was all very sudden. We found him at his desk. I thought he'd dozed off, but—"

Aimeric lowered his head a little. His father often fell asleep in the middle of the afternoon. "Well, then," he said. "So, what else is new?"

Hosculd knew him well enough to ignore that. "The funeral was the day before yesterday," he said. "I came as quick as I could, but you know what it's like trying to get anywhere these days, with the war and everything."

Aimeric drew a deep breath. "Does she want me to come home?"

Hosculd nodded. "Better had," he said. "Things aren't—well, they could be better."

For the first time, it occurred to Aimeric that his father's death might not be the whole story. He put the thought firmly back where it had come from. "I've got mid-term Collections in three days," he said, "so I can be ready to leave, say, this time next week."

"Sorry," Hosculd said. "She'd rather you came on straight away, if that's all right."

Clearly he didn't understand. "No," Aimeric said, "mid-term Collections are quite important, the results are part of my degree. I can't just not—"

"I'm sorry," Hosculd repeated. "You've got to come home straight away. You're needed at home."

"For the first time ever." Aimeric hesitated. There were a great many people in the world he wanted to shout at; Hosculd wasn't one of them. "It's just so bloody inconvenient," he said. "It'll mean I'll have to repeat the whole year." As he said it, he realised he wouldn't mind that, not at all. Another year at the university, away from his family, among his sort of people, away from the war. At the rate things were going—Butcher Calojan slaughtering the enemy on all fronts—in a year's time it might even be over, and it'd be safe to come home for good.

Hosculd was one of those people who know when not to say anything. Aimeric looked at him, but for once he wasn't quite sure he was reading him quite right. "Fine," he said. "I'll come. I'll need to explain, and pack a few things. Have you got somewhere to stay?"

"We really ought to get going straight away."

"Hosculd, it's the middle of the night." He stopped. Hosculd knew that. He tried to catch his breath, found it surprisingly difficult. "What's going on?"

THE EVENING BEFORE the battle, Calojan was in his tent, staring at a chessboard. On it were two white knights, one red bishop and a red pawn. He was concentrating so intently that he didn't notice the deputation until the senior deacon cleared his throat.

Calojan looked up. "Gentlemen," he said.

The senior deacon was dressed all in white. There were tiny traces of blood under the fingernails of his left hand. He looked happy. Calojan tipped over the red bishop with the tip of his forefinger. "You've taken the auspices."

"We have."

"And?"

"Excellent," the deacon said. "Primary indications in the front east chamber of the heart, and corroborative features in the corresponding quarters of the liver. I think I can safely say that victory is inevitable."

Calojan gave him a big smile. Since the last time, he'd taken the trouble to read the standard text on haruspicy. Primary indications was augury-speak for nothing out of the ordinary. Corroborative features meant a buildup of fat. Since they force-fed the sacred goats brewers' mash, that wasn't all that surprising. "I'm so glad," he said. "Thank you."

The deacon hadn't finished. "Also," he said, "there's been a portent."

Calojan maintained the smile. "How exciting."

The deacon beamed at him. "Not only will you win the battle, you'll also take the city."

"Ah."

"Quite so. This morning, when the junior suffragan lector went to unlock the cubiculum to fetch the sacrament, he found a snake coiled around the key." He paused, then went on, "The fifth book of Gennadius' *Omens*—"

"Excuse me." Calojan was still smiling, but there was a hint of that slight weariness at the corners of his mouth that warned experienced staff officers to make excuses and leave. "That's not a portent."

"I beg your—"

"Now if the key had been coiled round the snake, that'd be a portent. Or even if the snake had coiled round a key that hadn't previously been smeared with honey. Those little midges," he went on, as kindly as he could, "the ones you find around stagnant water. They get their legs stuck in the honey, and the snake licks them off." He picked up the red bishop and dropped it back in the box. "Thank you so much, and don't let me keep you from your duties."

When they'd gone, he set the pieces out again; four white knights on one side, two red bishops and five pawns facing them. He used an ebony ruler for the river, and his hat for the mountains.

FIELD-MARSHAL MARDONIUS—THAT wasn't his name; they couldn't pronounce it, so they took the first four consonants and added their own vowels—had drawn up his heavy cavalry in four rectangular squadrons on the north bank of the river. Each squadron was just over ten thousand men. Two hundred yards behind them stood the heavy infantry, in three continuous lines. Light infantry and archers guarded the wings, and thirty thousand light cavalry formed the mobile reserve, five hundred yards away on the lower slopes of the mountain.

"Retreat," one of the staff officers said. "Nothing else for it."

Calojan turned his head slightly. "You think so?"

"Well." The staff officer thought for a moment. "As soon as we start to pull back, he'll throw his light cavalry across that ford over there. They'll make a real mess of our rearguard, but with any luck, we ought to be able to salvage at least some of the Seventh and the Thirteenth. Better than nothing."

"Right," Calojan said. "We'll do that, then."

There was a moment of silence so profound that its like can't have been heard since the beginning of the world. "You agree."

"Why not? See to it, would you?" Calojan added. "I need to take a leak."

He heard the words, "Who, me?" shouted after him as he walked away. He made it look as though he hadn't heard. Instead, he walked up the slight rise and sat down behind the easel he'd had set up, at the point that gave the best view of the field. It had belonged to his father, but he'd had the frame with the grid of thin wires added. If you looked through it, you saw the field divided into squares, like a chessboard. Artists use something similar to gauge perspective.

He watched the courier galloping down the hill with the order to withdraw; a short delay—he could imagine the colonel of the Ninth saying, "He said *what?*"—and then the shuffle rippling through the ranks as the unit started to turn. He lined himself up so that the whole of the first company fitted inside one square.

He thought; how ridiculous, how utterly absurd, that the mind, the will, the *cleverness* of just one man can shape the future of the world. It's unfair, it's barbaric, it's hideously precarious—for example, what if I'd woken up this morning with a headache, and couldn't think? There really should be proper procedures for this sort of thing; a grand committee, perhaps, recruited from the wisest men in every nation, chosen by the people and constrained by a rigidly defined mandate, all important decisions requiring a seventy-five per cent majority. And if that was how it worked, what would I do? Easy. I'd blockade the council chamber with two companies of Aram Cosseilhatz, and not let the delegates out to use the latrine until they agreed to do what I wanted. My justification? If I didn't do it, someone else would, and quite possibly he wouldn't be as enlightened and benign as me. So, instead we have wars.

He raised his hand, and immediately an aide materialised two steps away on his left.

"Go to the Fifteenth," he said. "Tell the colonel, exactly how we planned it. Repeat that for me."

"Exactly how we planned it, sir."

Calojan nodded; the aide vanished. A few seconds later, he crossed a square diagonally, riding recklessly fast. Calojan frowned. He'd allowed plenty of time for the courier to get there at a sensible pace. If his horse stumbled and fell, that'd be the battle lost, the war, civilisation as we know it. Why do people insist on *gestures*?

The Ninth had begun its withdrawal. It wasn't going well. Everybody knows that heavy infantry are at their most vulnerable when manoeuvering in the face of the enemy. Every infantryman relies for protection on the shield of his right-hand neighbour, just as he shelters the man on his left with his own—a fine metaphor for the well-ordered body politic, but a hopeless liability on the battlefield. The man on the extreme right of the front line will always try and keep his exposed side away from the enemy. The result is a lot of edging and shuffling, with the right wing getting over-extended. Bad enough in a straightforward face-to-face collision of shield-walls; when you're trying to do something complex and sophisticated, like a hundred-eighty degree turn, it's a recipe for catastrophe—

And now the Sixth, on the Ninth's immediate left, began their own manoeuvre; a slight advance to fill the gap left by the Ninth's withdrawal. It was quite painful to watch, as the two units appeared to drift helplessly toward each other on an inevitable collision course. Calojan looked away for a moment; when he looked back, he saw the Ninth's bunched left crash into and get tangled up in the Sixth's straggling right. The foul-up immediately became the fulcrum for the Ninth's over-extended line, which swung wildly forward on the right until the river blocked its way and it could go no further. Stuck, like a cart in the mud.

It's moments like this, Calojan reflected, that decide the course of human history. Pathetic.

From where he was sitting, he couldn't see Mardonius. He didn't have to. He could picture him so clearly in his mind's eye; the look on his face as he recognises the perfect mistake, the perfect opportunity. From what he'd gathered about his opponent's command style, he felt safe in assuming that Mardonius would be astride his milk-white stallion, with the divisional commanders on his left and his six trusted advisers on his right. Mardonius points; look, the bloody fool's got himself all jammed up. A moment of doubt; but he can see for himself, that's no ruse, it's a genuine godawful balls-up. He now has seven minutes to end the war. He's given to huge arm movements, so he flings his left arm out to the side; that means, get the light cavalry across the ford, ignore the Twelfth, hit those clowns before they can untangle themselves. Now he's thinking hard, three, four moves ahead; the Twelfth will fall back and wheel to close the door, so they'll be in flank to the river. Take them out of the picture, the whole of that side collapses. Calojan's got reserves, but not enough. He'll have to abandon the Ninth and Sixth, he'll try and save what he can, he'll draw everything back—in which case...

He doesn't want to do it. Swimming his heavy cavalry across the river is the only conceivable way he could lose the battle. No, he reassures himself, there's no danger, because by then Calojan's front line won't be there any more, it'll be a hundred yards back and still retreating. There's no serious danger, and we'll win, I'll win the war. His mouth is suddenly dry; he has to swallow a couple of times before he can say the words and give the order.

He says it quite calmly; everything across the river, now (or words to that effect). Then he takes a moment to consider what he's just done; changed the world, permanently; destroyed the greatest empire the human race has ever known—

INDEED, CALOJAN THOUGHT. Lucky for us we're the *second* greatest empire. Up till now.

"Piece of cake," Calojan said.

He couldn't see the river any more. It was so thoroughly clogged with bodies that it was no longer distinguishable as a geographical feature. They'd have to clear it out in the morning, or there'd be flooding down on the plains.

"I knew I couldn't win the battle, not from that position," he went on. "So I had to make the other lot lose it."

He was putting on a performance, and he was ashamed of himself for it. But he'd gradually allowed the after-battle briefing to become an established part of the Calojan style; and the style was all he was. The First Minister's man was staring at him with the sort of awe usually reserved for talking pillars of fire. Get a grip, for pity's sake.

"Luckily," he went on, "practically any battle can be lost, if you really set your mind to it. So I thought; if I was him, what would I most want me to do? Easy, I thought. So I did it."

The First Minister's aide's aide was writing it all down. Calojan winced, but spoke slightly more slowly.

"That's why I couldn't tell the Ninth and the Sixth what I had in mind," he went on. "When you're lying to someone, there's nothing better for giving the essential illusion of authenticity than the real thing. If Mardonius had suspected for one moment that I was having him on, we'd have been screwed. As it was—"

He didn't finish the sentence. He could see the tall, lame captain approaching, the man he'd sent to get the enemy casualty figures. For a variety of valid strategic reasons, he needed the number to be more than seventeen thousand. Less than that, and the whole exercise would be pointless—

"The men," the aide was saying, "are calling you the Miracle-Worker."

Calojan closed his eyes for a moment. "No," he said, "not me. Can I help it if the enemy's an idiot?"

The interim provisional figure was nineteen thousand, seven hundred and forty-six, as against two thousand, one hundred and fifteen. Field-marshal Mardonius was found at the bottom of a heap of corpses, his gilded helmet and breastplate squashed flat, his body still inside it with nearly every bone broken; he'd tried to stop them running away, and they'd ridden over him, and then the Aram Cosseilhatz penned them up and slaughtered them.

So, RATHER THAN join the general staff for the customary after-battle mutual congratulation session, he wandered down to the small hollow where the Cosseilhatz had pitched their tents. Before the battle there had been five thousand of them—fewer now, of course, but still, it was remarkable how they'd managed to find a patch of dead ground that could hide every trace of them from sight on what was essentially a prairie. *You'd never have known they were there* was the usual comment by travellers, geographers and diplomats; for over a century, the civilised world had believed the western steppes were completely uninhabited, until the Aram Cosseilhatz suddenly appeared in East Permia, burning cities and driving off livestock.

The sight of the tents made him smile; they looked like dozens of fresh cheeses lying in the grass, or maybe some kind of particularly graceful fungus. Amazing, how such sophisticated structures (each one consisted of a dozen woven spar frame panels, covered by a two-inch layer of chalk-white felt) could be assembled and disassembled in an hour, and packed away on the backs of mules. Once you were inside, you could believe you were in a prosperous middle-class house in Tragus or Oeaea; rugs on the floor, icons on the wall, a three-legged bronze stove and elegant little occasional tables with brass jugs and pot-pourri bowls. I'll retire from the army, he thought, and set up in business importing this stuff; I'll start a fashion, and make a fortune, and—

And there'll be nobody to buy it, because if I retire they'll give the command to Plotinus, we'll lose the war and the City will be ashes. Ah well. Nice to have something to daydream about.

He recognised the tall, slim middle-aged woman as the king's mother. She smiled at him. "Tea," she said; a prediction of the inevitable rather than an offer.

"Thank you," Calojan said. He hated the stuff; to start with it tasted of hot water, then like the foul stuff that collects in the bottom of your canteen when you're crossing the desert. He looked round for something to sit down on. Usually they had a stool, for visitors.

"My son will be home shortly." She made it sound like he was late back from the office, rather than returning from battle. At least, he assumed he'd be returning (but surely they'd have told him if the commander of the auxiliaries hadn't made it. Well, not necessarily). He squatted awkwardly on the floor, and a thirteen-year-old boy in a long silk gown handed him his tea, in a tiny bone cup.

Protocol, he thought. "Thanks," he said.

The boy looked at him thoughtfully, as though he was an optical illusion; one of those puzzles where, if you hold your head slightly to one side, the two faces in profile turn into a goblet. "You're welcome," the boy said.

"My grandson," the woman said. "His name is Chauzida."

"Ah." Calojan was one of those people who have no idea what to say to children. "Well, thank you, Chauzida."

The boy appeared to have solved him; at least, the look of scientific curiosity had gone, replaced by understanding and mild disappointment. "Did we win?" the boy asked.

"Excuse me?"

"The battle. Did we win?"

Oh, that. "Yes. Yes, we tricked them into crossing the river, and your father—"

"His uncle," the woman murmured.

"Sorry." Calojan smiled weakly. "Your uncle Joiauz hit them in flank and rear, and they broke and ran. Quite a good outcome, actually."

The boy nodded. "Is my uncle all right?"

"Yes, of course," Calojan said quickly, very much hoping he was telling the truth. "He and all your people did marvellously well today. You can be very proud."

The compliment sort of drained away into the boy's fixed expression, making Calojan feel more than a little foolish, though he wasn't quite sure why. To cover his discomfort he nibbled at his tea, which was still boiling hot. He felt the roof of his mouth turn raw. What sort of people, he wondered, deliberately burn themselves with hot liquids, for pleasure? Or maybe their mouths were lined with scales of horn. Of course, you'd have to dissect one to find out.

"I think the general would prefer some wine," the woman said.

"No, really, I'm fine." The Aram Cosseilhatz classified strong liquor as the Third Great Abomination, the First and Second being homosexuality and shellfish. Why shellfish, he wondered, they live six hundred miles from the sea. Presumably there had been a time when they'd lived somewhere else. "Actually," he went on, "I don't touch the stuff, myself."

"Ah."

True, as a matter of fact, but he'd managed to make it sound like a lie to curry favour. Well done. "Yes, as I was saying," he went on, "once again we left all the hard work to your people, and once again they did an outstanding job. It makes my life so much easier having allies I can rely on to do as they're told."

That had come out all wrong, of course, but the woman didn't seem to have noticed. The boy was standing perfectly still. Presumably his duty was to stand there until the teacup was empty, and then take it away. Calojan smiled and glugged down the rest of it in two heroic swallows. "Thanks," he said, and handed back the cup. The boy took it, nodded and went away, leaving Calojan alone with the woman. He felt a fierce need to keep the conversation going, but couldn't think of anything to say.

"Excuse my asking," he heard himself saying, "but I've often wondered. The felt you make these tents from—"

His gambit got him a brief, clear and comprehensive lecture on felt-making, a complex and horribly labour-intensive process that sounded as if it occupied most of the waking hours of the entire community. He smiled and made listening noises until the talk was over. "Thank you," he said gravely. "That was fascinating. Well, I won't hold you up any longer—"

"My son should be here any minute."

"Sorry." Calojan smiled, deliberately stretching his mouth. "But if I'm away for more than a few minutes, everything goes to pieces. Tell the king I'm really grateful, and I'll catch up with him later."

Outside it was raining. Calojan looked up at the sky, not wincing as the raindrops hit him squarely on the face. An hour or so earlier, the rain would have changed everything, deprived him of his only manoeuvre, lost him the battle and the war. But it made the air smell wonderfully fresh. He thought of the clogged river, and the danger of flooding; if the river came up over its banks, they'd catch it hard in Moesatz, and it'd be his fault. There was a remote possibility that the danger might have occurred to someone else, someone in a position to do something; far too remote to rely on. He sighed, and broke into a run.

THE THING ABOUT being perfectly free, he'd discovered in the forest—the keynote, the dominant quality of freedom—is that you're always hungry. Getting food is all you think about and all you do, and it's never ever enough.

He'd discovered a sort of fungus. It was milky white with a faint yellow tinge, and it grew on the trunks of dead trees. It was big, like a shelf, and crumbly, like new cheese. It had no discernable taste, which was probably just as well. If you ate it all day—start at dawn and keep on stuffing it into your face until it's too dark to see—it kept you alive, just about.

Luckily, there was a lot of it. He'd been eating the stuff for—what, four, five, six, seven, ninety days now—and there was still plenty (maybe it grew back) in this still, quiet hollow in the bottom of the forest, where it was never particularly hot or cold, and the high canopy kept the rain off, and there seemed to be no other living creatures except him. The leaf mould was soft to lie on, almost as good as a bed, and it didn't seem to get damp. His jaws ached from chewing.

Yes, he thought, but I was a human being once. I was a (unfamiliar concepts made him frown, the effort of handling them, heavy and sharp edges) farmer, a landowner, I was a husband and a father, I was chieftain of my district. He smiled, and crumbs of half-chewed fungus spilled out of his mouth. Yes, of course you were. Fairy stories.

He broke off another slab of fungus and stuffed it into his mouth, which was still three quarters full. When he was a boy he'd occasionally gone and just sat in the field where the cows were grazing. If you kept perfectly still and you didn't look at them, because eye contact spooks them, they'd come right up to you (eventually; one step a minute), sniff at you, lick you to see if you were edible. But you weren't, so they'd go back to eating grass, which they had to do all day long, to get enough.

He sat up. Just sitting among the cows had got him yelled at; his father for idleness, his mother for sitting on the wet grass, which would undoubtedly lead to fevers, consumption and death. He'd given it up at some point between his ninth and tenth birthdays, though he'd always claimed it had made him a better stockman. He scowled, trying to remember, as though a memory is something you can force out by muscular exertion. I was a good stockman. I was calm, patient and decisive and I didn't stand for any nonsense. I controlled animals, I made them do what I wanted. He looked up at the leaves overhead, over which, very occasionally, a rook or a pigeon soared in a purposeful hurry. Just think of that, he thought, and went on chewing.

He heard a twig snap. He didn't move, but suddenly every part of him was alive. Twigs don't just break themselves. Anything big enough and careless enough to break a twig as it moves about is to be considered dangerous until proven otherwise. He didn't move, because movement is what a predator sees. He sat perfectly still, not chewing, listened, sniffed.

Voices, as in people, talking out loud in the forest, where nothing makes a noise if it can possibly help it. He froze, mouth still half full, only his eyes moving as he assessed possible escape routes. Would they come down the path? If so—no, bad, because the short holly was thick on three sides and the fourth was the wet ground, up to his knees, stuck. Climb the tree. Brilliant, except he wasn't a squirrel. Sit tight and don't get seen. Yes, let's do that.

The voices were close. He could hear the words. He understood what they were saying—well, something of an exaggeration; they were talking about the differences in prices of some commodity at various markets, which was ridiculous, almost as though the old world hadn't ended and people still did that sort of thing. He closed his eyes, because the only white thing in a wood is an eye.

The voices stopped. Then someone said, "Hello?"

Oh, he thought.

He opened his eyes, spat out the fungus and turned to look. Two men; one about his age, one younger. They wore clean, plain clothes and good boots. Chances were, therefore, they weren't here to steal his fungus.

"Hello?" the older man repeated. "Are you all right?"

The cornered prey pretends it's something else—a stone, twig, log. He decided to pretend to be a man. "Fine," he said.

The older man frowned, as if his answer hadn't been quite right. He thinks I'm not all right, but is reluctant to call me a liar to my face. Accordingly, he doesn't know what to say, but still feels compelled to say something. "Excuse me, but are we on the right road for Eucris?"

Where? "Yes," he said. "Just keep on following the track and you'll come out on the old cart road. Just on my way back from there myself, as a matter of fact."

"Ah, right." The older man seemed relieved. He was unarmed; the younger man had an axe in his belt (but then again, he remembered, so do I). He was also carrying a bag that might contain food. "Never been this far before, see."

"Ah," he replied, and smiled.

"Mind if we join you?"

He thought; my fungus. But they had their own food. Indeed, they might be inclined to share. "Be my guest," he said, and managed not to laugh at his own joke.

They sat down. The younger man shivered; not a spontaneous action, he was exaggerating, to persuade the older man that he was cold. Any minute now he'll suggest they light a fire. Why? It's warm enough.

"I'm Donda and this is my nephew Otkel," the older man said. He waited, expecting some reciprocal response. "Sorry, you're—?"

Name. He wants to know my name. Just then, a black bird sailed the small blue ocean between two continents of branches. A raven. "Raffen," he lied. "I'm a charcoal burner."

"Ah." Good answer. Charcoal burners sit around in woods; it's what they do. "We're on our way to the levy, Otkel and me."

Levy. A meeting, organised by the district chieftains, to raise an army. But these two had no weapons. "Is that right?" said Raffen. "We at war with someone, then?"

The young man laughed. His uncle grinned. "Not that I know of," he said. "Not that sort of a levy."

"Is there any other sort?"

"Hiring levy," Donda explained. "Men wanted to go and work in the Big City, making swords for the Emperor. Good pay for skilled men." He smiled. "Well, the boy and me, we thought we'd give it a go. Cousin of ours went to the City, what, seven years ago, came back and you never saw the like. Blue coat with a fur collar, felt hat, red shoes, and a gut on him like he was expecting. And he was just what they call a day labourer, hauling logs in some machine place. They got a huge round saw powered by a wheel driven by water. Cuts a tree that size—" he pointed; some tree or other "—into planks in three minutes. Marvellous people they must be, thinking of things like that. So we thought, good pay, fat of the land, so to speak, and see some rare old sights while we're at it. And we're skilled men, blacksmiths, so we ought to do all right, wouldn't you say?"

The Big City. Raffen had heard of it, but—"Skilled men," he repeated.

"That's right. Men with a trade." Clearly, Donda reckoned he could guess what he was thinking. "Not sure they'd want charcoal burners, mind."

"Oh, I'm a skilled man," Raffen replied easily. "I haven't always done this, you know. Before that, I was a fletcher." First thing that had come into his head; still, he'd watched a fletcher once. "Do you think there'd be any call for that?"

Donda was managing not to laugh. "With the war on? Oh, I should think so."

War. Come to think of it, someone had said something about a war, a long time ago, somewhere else. None of his business, of course. "Good pay, you said."

"Cousin Bollo said he was getting eighty trachy a day," the young man said.

"That's not bad." Trachy. What in God's name is a trachy? "Got to be better than this game, anyhow." He realised he was copying them, accent, phrases, way of putting words together. They hadn't noticed. Of course, all he wanted was for them to go away and leave him in peace with his fungus. "Been piss-poor lately," he went on. "No call for charcoal, this time of year."

Donda looked at him oddly, but didn't comment. "You thinking of going, then?"

"I might be." He sat up a little. He could feel himself changing, from prey to predator. He decided to ride with it. "Trouble is, getting there. Like I said, trade's been pretty bad. A man's got to eat on the road."

Awkward silence. "It's, what, three days to Eucris?" Donda said.

Raffen remembered hearing himself say, I'm just on my way back from there. "Thereabouts," he said.

They were looking at each other. "We got a bit to spare," Donda said. "Not a lot, mind."

"Oh, I'll pay you back, of course," Raffen said quickly. "Once we get to the City. You've got my word on that."

Young Otkel wasn't happy. That just made his uncle more determined. "Fletcher, you say."

"Damn good one, too. But there was trouble. A man called Sighvat. Heard of him?"

"Vaguely."

"Sighvat," Raffen repeated. It felt very strange saying the name. "He had a quarrel with our lot, there was a bit of trouble. Time to move on."

"Ah."

"But it'd be good to go back fletching again," Raffen said. "I always say, if a man's got a trade, he ought to use it. You'd say the same, I'm sure."

Another silence. Raffen tried not to stare at the satchel that almost certainly contained food. Bread, quite likely; a fist-sized chunk of that keeps you going for a whole morning. Just think of all the things you could do in that time. Then Otkel said, "Isn't Sighvat's place that big spread down in the Mere valley?"

"No, that's Segibert," Donda replied. "Sighvat's up over Whitestones, surely. Easthanger district."

"That's right," Raffen said, though they were both quite wrong. But he felt Donda would like to be proved more knowledgeable than his nephew. "Other side of the moors from here."

Donda nodded. For some reason, his small victory had helped him make up his mind. "You can come with us if you like," he said. "I've heard they're more likely to take men in groups rather than ones and twos, so it'd be good for all of us."

The City, Raffen thought. Who'd have ever imagined I'd go there? Still, why not? Or, better still, walk along with them a little way, then when they're asleep, steal their food. *I'm not a thief*, that man had said, like it was some big grand thing. But everything steals; the hawk from the fox, the cow from her calf, the old dog from the young dogs, it's how you can tell who's the best. And they'd have stolen my fungus, if I'd let them.

"I've never been to the City," he said, meanwhile. "What's it like?"

AIMERIC LOVED NEW places, but hated getting to them. Particularly by road; ships were cramped, terrifying, nauseating and wet, but you were on them for a matter of hours, after which they either arrived or sank. Coaches, however, take days.

Going home was, therefore, the worst possible thing; three days in a small wooden box, every rut in the road a punch or a kick; can't possibly sleep while you're being beaten up, ditto reading—the book dances about in front of your eyes, catching a word's like trying to catch flies one-handed. Can't even talk, because you have to yell to make yourself heard over the groaning of the springs, rattle of the wheels, thumps, bangs. Nights in the coach, or the fleabag *Quality of Mercy* at Phio, always jampacked with smelly couriers, graziers, soldiers, so you have to sleep on nine inches' width of a communal mattress, serenaded by drunks, trodden on by midnight urinators. The reward for enduring all this; to end up back home, his least favourite place in the whole world.

The main road was blocked off, for some reason, so they had to drag into Town through the eastern suburbs, where the river runs fat and slow beside the Eastway; mile after mile of long wooden sheds, whose waterwheels drove mills and drophammers; horrible noise, foul bitter smoke from a thousand charcoal forges and furnaces. The family business had started here, one shed among hundreds, but Father had moved it up West, to be close to the docks. At least they had the sea breeze there, to clear away the stink and smooth out the noise. We ought to do something about all these small independents, he caught himself thinking, as the lines of sheds rolled past the coach window; buy them up or undercut them out of business. They're killing profitability.

Not that that was any concern of his, because the one thing he would never do was dirty his hands with the business. So far, all he'd managed to drag out of Hosculd was that things weren't going well, and that his mother needed to talk to him about the future; she wanted to explain it to him herself, so Hosculd wouldn't say any more. Fine; he could extrapolate. His father had built the business up from nothing, he was a legend in the arms trade, and it was well known that his son had no taste for commerce, particularly in instruments of death. A woman couldn't run a business empire, obviously. Therefore, the whole thing would have to be sold, simple as that. No problem. Even if, as he suspected, the death of his father had wiped out a substantial percentage of the value of the business, there would still be enough for all of them to be ridiculously wealthy, from now until the end of time. All in all, a very satisfactory outcome. He could see why he'd be needed, in person, for quite a while. As sole male heir, he'd have to sign all the documents, swear the oaths and the indemnities, register the transfer of undertakings; meetings with buyers, suppliers, all the different government agencies; Senate committees, most likely, since everything they made these days was restricted war supplies. He had no idea how long it would all take—six months, a year, longer. But at least when it was all over he'd be rid of all that. Free.

Traffic gridlocked at the Undergate; munitions carts going down, a column of soldiers coming up. He leaned out of the window and swore.

"The hell with this," he told Hosculd. "I'll walk from here."

"Better not."

Hosculd was right, of course. The streets around Undergate were no place for a civilian pedestrian these days. If you weren't robbed, stabbed or run over, you'd still have to face an hour queuing at the checkpoint on New Bridge (and, he remembered, he didn't have current papers, so he couldn't leave the coach in the City, not even to piss against a wall). He sighed, pressed his back into the seat and closed his eyes. At least the pummelling had stopped, and he could converse without shouting.

"Hosculd," he said. "What's going on?"

Hosculd gave him that sad, shifty look. "Your mother—"

"I want to hear it from you first."

"I'm sorry."

He felt a little spike of irritation; after all, he was now the head of the family, therefore head of the company, therefore Hosculd's lord and master. In theory. "I know," he said. "She wants to explain it to me herself. Fine." He smiled. "Little hint?"

Hosculd looked away. "It's bad, Aimeric. That's all I can say."

"Fine." He reached into his coat pocket and found his copy of Clovian's *Triumph of Peace*. Maybe it wasn't the ideal book for sitting in traffic; Clovian was a passionate and committed pacifist but a somewhat turgid poet; he'd put the book in his pocket as a sort of statement to the world, but on balance something like the *Private Histories* would've been better for passing the time. Hosculd just sat and stared out of the window, which he found disconcerting.

It was dark by the time they arrived at the house, and all Aimeric wanted to do was dissolve in a warm bath and go to bed. Instead, he was told that his mother was waiting for him in the upstairs room.

"Mother," he said.

She turned her head and looked at him. "You're too late for dinner," she said. "You'll have to have something cold on a tray."

For seven years, until she married Father, she'd been the principal soubrette at the Comedy theatre. The Golden Butterfly, they'd called her. Certain death to mention that nowadays, of course. A little of that ethereal beauty still remained, almost detached, like a pool of rainwater stranded in mud as the floods recede. His father had believed he was marrying a beautiful airhead. Best mistake he ever made, people said.

He supposed he ought to say something. "Mother," he said. "I'm so sorry—"

She looked at him. "Did Hosculd explain?"

"No."

"Good. I told him not to. Sit down."

He sat. The upstairs room was Mother's territory. Accordingly, the furnishings were sparse, severe, uncomfortable and obscenely expensive. He perched on a three-legged ivory stool, folded his hands in his lap, and waited.

"The business is bankrupt," she said.

He frowned. "Sorry?"

"You heard me. We're on the point of collapse. There's no money."

A very odd feeling. The closest he'd ever been was a bad moment in the *Compassion*, end of the term before last, when a man he'd ben having a political discussion with very nearly succeeded in strangling him. A sort of vagueness, inability to think; a floating sensation in a moment of total numb stupidity. It occurred to him that he might be having a stroke, except there was no pain. "What do you mean?" he heard himself say.

"There's no money," his mother repeated. "To be precise, we have twenty-six thousand four hundred in the current account, as at close of business this evening. Tomorrow morning I have to pay out twenty-four thousand nine hundred for the wages. The day after tomorrow, I have to pay the steel bill, which is eighteen thousand two hundred and fifty. We're owed forty-six thousand by the Armoury Board, payable in six weeks time, but by then we need to have found five hundred and eighty-six thousand for bills and overheads, plus fifty-four thousand interest on loans. There's also the penalties on contracts we won't be able to honour, which will be something in the order of five hundred thousand." She paused to draw breath, then went on, "The assets of the business, at valuation as at your father's death, stood at five million three. Loans and mortgages charged on those assets, seven million nine. Value of contracts—"

"I don't understand." He wanted to laugh, because it was a really good joke. "How can we go bust making weapons for the government in the middle of a war?"

She gave him her famous non-smile. "Good question," she said. "Somehow, your father managed it. Mostly, I gather, by ruinous under-bidding to offer the lowest price on large-scale contracts. For the last three years we've been equipping the armies of the Empire at twenty per cent below cost, apparently. Tremendously patriotic of us, but really rather stupid. Also, he was paying well over the odds for labour, when everyone else was hiring foreigners and savages. I knew about that," she added briskly, "but not about the under-bidding. Stupid of me. I assumed he'd have more sense."

Aimeric stared at her. "But we're winning the war," he said.

"Quite," she said. "Which, of course, makes matters worse. About the only thing that could have saved us—presumably he was counting on it—would've been a major defeat, the loss of an entire division, a whole army. Then there'd have had to be new contracts for equipping new recruits, and presumably he was hoping he'd have the Board over a barrel and a chance to renegotiate the old contracts and bleed them white on the new ones. Instead, we've got Calojan driving the Sashan into the sea, and the end of the war possibly only a matter of months away. After which, the entire civilised world will be awash with surplus armaments, and nobody will want to buy new for a generation. We're finished."

Aimeric shook his head. "The government won't let us go bust," he said. "They need what we make. They can't fight a war without us."

She made a faint tutting noise, as though he'd made an elementary mistake in his long division. "The government is our biggest creditor," she said. "They'll take over everything and run it themselves. It's what they've been wanting to do since the outbreak. Your father—" She stopped. Some things are diminished by being confined in words. "They'll take everything and there won't be anything left. There it is."

Saloninus, in the *Exceptional Dialogues*, speculates about the end of the world. Will it be a great sundering, the sky falling on the land, or a great inundation, the sea gradually rising until the last treetop is drowned, or a great fire, or—Wrong. The end of the world is like this, and a deaf man who couldn't lipread wouldn't even realise what had just happened. "So," Aimeric said. "What will we do?"

"I don't know."

She must have failed to understand the question. He repeated it.

"I don't *know.*" She never raised her voice. "It's not like I can go back on the stage again. You're useless. Your sister knows how to wear clothes and hold still while they do her hair. We aren't on speaking terms with your uncle Hilderic. I really don't know. This house will have to go, obviously. I don't know if your father put anything aside for something like this, though I doubt it. If he did, the secret died with him. I'm sorry, Aimeric, I really don't know. I don't suppose any of your college friends has a father who needs a clerk and a housekeeper."

Not meant as a joke. He looked at her. All his life, she'd always known what to do, in every circumstance. No money. *Think.*

"How much did you say was in—?"

She laughed. "The twenty-six thousand? The same thought did cross my mind. But we can't get at it until the bank opens in the morning, and by then the news will be all round the town. We wouldn't get past the City gate."

"Isn't there anyone you could talk to?"

"I tried," she said. "Stupidly. I went to see Senator Luitprand on the Ways and Means committee. He owed your father enough favours, God knows."

"And?"

"Luitprand alerted the Armoury Board, the bank and our principal suppliers. National security. Serves me right for thinking someone might actually be inclined to help us." She examined a fingernail, picked at it, looked away. "Hosculd wanted to help. He offered me his life savings. I told him not to be so stupid."

"How much has he—?"

She looked at him. "There's nothing we can do, Aimeric. I for one am simply too tired to bother any more. I propose sitting here still and quiet and waiting to find out what they intend to do with us. It's not ideal, but I don't see that we have much say in the matter any more."

The way she'd phrased that made him shiver. "What do you mean, do with us?"

She smiled coldly at him. "One line of argument would be that your father was the business, so its debts and malfeasances died with him. An alternative view would be that you're his heir, the company is still in being, therefore you should be held liable. I don't think they'd be able to make out a case against you in the criminal courts, but a civil action's quite different, I understand. And a debtors' prison's more or less the same as any other sort of prison, though I imagine you get a slightly better class of people."

"That's—" The way she'd said it. "That's not fair."

"No, not really. After all, you made it abundantly clear that you never wanted anything to do with the business, apart from the luxuries its proceeds bought you. Of course, if you'd taken a little bit more of an interest, we might not find ourselves in this ghastly situation, but that's all past history, isn't it? No, I don't suppose for one moment that what's going to happen to us will be the least bit fair. That's life, Aimeric. It's a pity they didn't teach you that at that expensive university."

He felt as though she'd just stabbed him. He'd always assumed—He drew a line in his mind. "There must be something we can do," his voice said. She didn't bother to reply. Instead, she said, "Gesel's downstairs, if there's anything you want to say to her." She was quite right; he'd forgotten all about his sister. Most people did. Even so. "She'll have heard you arrive."

She picked up her embroidery frame. He had no idea what had become of all the cushions, centrepieces, gloves, screens, pillowcases she'd embroidered over the years; she worked at it for four hours a day, every day without fail, but there wasn't a single thing to be seen anywhere in the house, never had been. He wondered; if you took the frame away from her (the bailiffs would do just that), would she still sit there, from supper till bedtime, her hands moving without frame, thread or needle? She didn't like people looking, but the glances he'd managed to steal over the years suggested she was very good at it. As she should be, after so long.

The frame told him he was supposed to go now. He got up without a word and lumbered down the stairs into the main room. Gesel was sitting on a stool beside the shuttered window. "Hello," he said.

"You're back, then."

Almost an accusation; as if he was a fellow-prisoner who'd escaped and been recaptured, and now they were going to double the guard and build extra watchtowers. "Looks like it," he said, went to pour himself a drink. The decanter was empty.

"She had Gathia pour it all away," Gesel said.

He nodded. "Probably wise," he said. "We all need to keep a clear head if we're going to get out of this mess." He stopped. "You do know—?"

She nodded. Oh yes, she knew.

"I asked her what we're going to do. She said she didn't know."

Gesel shrugged. "You don't know," she said. "You weren't here."

"Yes, thank you, that fact hadn't escaped my attention. For crying out loud," he snapped, "what was everybody thinking of? Letting it get in such a state."

She frowned; breach of good taste. "He thought very highly of you, you know."

"Balls."

"He was very proud of you, going to the University."

"He did his damnedest to stop me going."

She looked at him. "Really," she said. "Do you honestly think, if he hadn't wanted you to go, he'd have let you?"

Once again, that stunned feeling. He'd never thought of it in those terms before. The answer to her question, quite obviously, was, No.

"He'd read out bits from your letters," she went on. "Not the bits where you asked for more money, of course."

Which was the only reason he'd ever written. With little descriptive interludes between the heartfelt pleas, for padding and to create a general feeling of goodwill and benevolence. He'd copied those bits out of a book; *The Student's Scrivener*, letters home for all occasions for young gentlemen of good family in temporarily embarrassed circumstances. And he'd always thought of his father as part enemy, part prey; to be beguiled, deceived, ambushed, punished, forced to pay reparations. Maybe he'd only spent all that money so as to have a reason to gouge some more.

But there was no time for any of that. "She seems to have decided," he said, "that all we can do is sit quietly and wait for the bailiffs." He waited, to see how she reacted. Like the scorers said at archery practice when you missed the target completely; nothing seen. "Well? What do you think?"

Quite possibly the first time he'd ever asked her that.

"It's not up to me, is it?"

For a very short moment he wanted to hit her for that. No, not up to her, or to Mother, or Hosculd. Which leaves—

"I'm going to bed," he announced. "See you in the morning."

He lay in the dark and tried to remember the seventeen principal elements of the reductive syllogism; he got as far as twelve, lost his place and had to start over again. No good; time was running out, the exam was— No, not even in the dark. That foolish young man was gone for ever. No great loss, either.

At some point, he fell asleep. He woke up, opened his eyes, thought, What am I doing here? His neck and back ached as though he'd just spent three days digging peat. He dragged on yesterday's clothes and blundered into the main room. Gesel was there, and his mother. They were putting things in boxes.

"I'm going to see general Calojan," he said.

"Don't be stupid," his mother said, not looking up.

"No, really. My father came to me in a dream. He said go and see Calojan. I may be back for dinner."

"It's rather unlikely that we'll be here when you get back," his mother replied. "If I find out where we're being taken, I'll try and leave a note on the door."

HE'D TAKEN A book—two, actually; but the one he'd brought to read was Saloninus' *Great Engine* and *Art of War*, students' economy omnibus edition—so the three-hour wait wasn't so bad, though the window-seat in the anteroom was hard, with a sharp edge that cut into the backs of his thighs. He even took ten minutes off from contemplating the finest mind the world had ever known to stare up at the painted ceiling, on which a rather portly, red-faced Destiny entrusted some emperor with authority over the entire world (a small yellow thing like a pie-dish) while various gods and heroes stood around looking like they wished they were somewhere else. He was reading the famous passage about the relative merits of strength and weakness when a miserable-looking character in uniform came to tell him that the general would see him now.

He tucked Saloninus away in his pocket, took out the other book and followed the sad officer into the next room.

General Calojan wasn't what he'd been expecting; in fact, his first thought was that the great man wasn't there after all, and had deputised some clerk to see him. But a clerk probably wouldn't have been sitting with his feet up on the general's priceless Interregnum gilded burr walnut and ivory escritoire. The confusion was, however, warranted. The general, the last, best hope of the empire, Butcher Calojan, the White Death of the Sashan, was a small, thin, pale, rather rat-like man, with gossamer-fine white-blond hair, a narrow, pointed face, enormous eyes, a weak mouth and chin, soft lips, little girly hands; out of uniform, except he was wearing artillery boots. He hadn't shaved his chin, and his moustache was music-hall-stereotype Permian immigrant. Strengths and weaknesses, he thought, mentally thanking Saloninus for bringing the issues to his attention. You looked at the general and you thought; if a pathetic creature like this has managed to rise to his pre-eminent position in spite of all his natural disadvantages, he must have a mind like a razor. Strengths and weaknesses indeed.

"Hello," Calojan said. "What can I do for you?"

Aimeric hesitated; and in that moment of silence, Calojan saw the book in his hand. His face hardened, just a little. "I see you've brought me a present," he said.

Maybe not such a good idea after all. Still, he was committed to it now. He held it out. Calojan hesitated, just for a moment, then took it without looking and put it on the desk. "That's a rarity," he said. "Quite valuable."

"Is it?"

Calojan grinned at him. "Between six and eight thousand, depending on condition. Limited edition of seventy, Dad's middle period, which is very collectable these days, with hand-coloured plates. Ten out of ten for generosity," he went on, sliding a sheet of parchment over the book. "About minus four for tact. Unless you're trying to make some sort of clever statement."

"It belonged to my father," Aimeric said.

"Ah."

And in Aimeric's mind, trumpets sounded. In with a chance, after all. "He kept it by his bed. He used to read it, last thing at night."

"I see. Your mother—" Calojan shook his head; we won't go there. "Well," he said, "thank you for that. As it happens, it's one I haven't got."

"You collect your father's work."

Calojan frowned. "I sort of feel I have to," he said. "Even though the only model he ever used was my mother. But I guess he was an artist, in his way. Never thought of himself as one, but people nowadays say it's art, so—" He folded his hands and leaned back in his chair. "Your point, I take it, is that we have something in common."

Aimeric nodded.

"Namely, we aren't to blame for the transgressions of our fathers. Well, you would say that, wouldn't you?"

"Yes."

"And quite right too. Fine, you've got my sympathy. Trouble is, I don't see that there's very much I can do for you."

"Don't say that," Aimeric said gently. "After all, you're the most important man in the empire."

"I think you'll find that's the emperor," Calojan said. "All right, what did you have in mind?"

"Let's not talk about me. What do you need?"

Too early; tactical error. He looked at Calojan and saw a faint twinkle in his eyes. *He knows I've made a mistake and he's forgiven me. Prey complicit in its own capture; I have his permission to keep going.* "What I mean is," he went on, "how can I prove to you that our company is essential to the war effort, by supplying you with exactly what you need, when you need it."

"Oh come on." Calojan was trying to be kind. "You're bankrupt, everybody knows that. You can't pay your suppliers—"

"We'll come to that in a moment," Aimeric said calmly. "What do you need?"

"Right now?" Calojan smiled at him. "I need one million bodkin-head dogwood-shaft medium spine arrows. Tanged, not socketed. Since you asked."

"Bodkin—?"

"You're new to all this, of course," Calojan said pleasantly. "Let me explain." He settled himself comfortably in his chair. "I've got a million arrows, of course I have. Four million, actually. But they're the wrong sort. They've got heavy ash shafts, which means they're just right for the issue infantry longbow, but rather inefficient for the short composites used by the Aram Cosseilhatz. Not bendy enough. They don't shoot as far or as fast, and they're a tad too long to draw easily from the quiver on horseback. Also, they're socketed."

"Socketed," Aimeric repeated.

"Exactly. They're made with a socket that fits over the end of the arrowshaft. The Aram Cosseilhatz prefer them tanged. That means," he went on with a smile, "they're made with a tang instead of a socket—like a nail sticking out the back, which fits in a hole drilled in the end of the shaft. It's a bit naughty, actually. The Aram Cosseilhatz don't glue the tang into the shaft, they just press it in. Then, when some poor devil's got an arrow stuck in him and his mates try and pull it out, the arrowhead parts company from the shaft and stays in the wound. Since the Aram Cosseilhatz soak their arrows overnight before a battle, their arrowheads are always rusty. Death by blood poisoning, even from a relatively minor wound. Horrible way to go, believe me, I've seen it often enough. Since the Sashan pride themselves, quite rightly, on their military medical service, it means they've got a huge amount of manpower and resources tied up in treating wounded men in agonising pain who'll die anyway. I calculate it reduces the efficiency of their army by at least sixteen per cent. Hence, you see, tanged rather than socketed."

Aimeric felt sick, but he made a show of ignoring it. "I understand."

"Our suppliers," Calojan went on, "won't make tanged dogwood arrows. Partly, they say, on ethical grounds, which may actually be partly true. Mostly because it's more expensive. Actually, it shouldn't be, it should be cheaper, but they won't listen when I explain. Now, the only real difference between us and the Sashan is, we've got the Aram Cosseilhatz and they haven't. If I'm to win this war, I need to use them to maximum effect, which means I need to keep them happy. They've been moaning at me about arrows ever since we started. They're having to use their own personal arrows, because they won't use the standard issue, which costs them time and money. If I could give them a supply of the sort they like to use, they'd be happy and I'd be happy. That happiness would be worth a lot to me." He paused, then added, "Well, you did ask."

"One million," Aimeric said.

"Yes. An Aram Cosseilhatz horse archer can loose twelve aimed shots a minute from the saddle. Twenty thousand archers will loose off a million arrows in four minutes. That, approximately, is how long it takes to win a battle. Two million would be nice, but I'm a realist. Well?"

Aimeric took a deep breath. "No problem."

It pleased him to see that he'd managed to disturb the great man's composure. "What?"

"No problem. When do you need them by?"

"Six weeks?"

"Eight." He had, of course, absolutely no idea. But that didn't matter right now.

"All right, eight weeks. How can you possibly—?"

"That's my business. Now, let's talk about money."

Calojan looked at him for a moment, then nodded. "All right. What did you have in mind?"

Nothing, to be honest, because I never thought I'd get this far. "I'd like to renegotiate all our existing contracts with the government," he heard a voice say, and was surprised and amused to recognise it as his own. It seemed to have some plan in mind, so he let it have its head. "All liabilities for supplies of raw materials, past, present and future, to pass from us to the Treasury. In effect, you pay our suppliers direct."

"What a novel approach. Go on."

"Including outstanding bills which we should already have paid but haven't."

Calojan gave him a happy smile. "You're insane," he said.

"Quite possibly. Next, we'd like payment in advance. Fifty per cent," he amended quickly. "We need it to pay our workforce what we owe them."

Calojan nodded. "I see. And?"

"The unit price for a—" He floundered and stalled.

"The standard is per barrel of ten dozen arrows."

"Per barrel," Aimeric said gratefully. "The actual cost of labour and overheads, plus five per cent."

Calojan laughed; a joyful sound. Possibly the first time he'd been genuinely amused in years. "To recap," he said, when he'd finished laughing. "We pay for the steel, wood, feathers and glue. We pay for the labour. You get five per cent of the labour cost. Or have I missed something?"

"No, I think that's about it."

"And we pay off all your outstanding debts."

"Yes, thank you, I'd forgotten that. Yes, you do."

Calojan's face changed a little. Serious. "And you'll make me a million tanged arrows in eight weeks."

"Yes."

"And you want to me to do all this for you just because your father was an arsehole too."

"Partly," Aimeric said (and he felt like he was on the very end of a slender branch, reaching for an apple). "But mostly because I'll make you what you need, not what the Armoury Board thinks you ought to have. And then you'll win the war."

"Eight weeks."

"That bit," Aimeric said pleasantly, "isn't the part that I'm concerned about."

"Fine." Calojan ran his fingertips down the edge of his jaw. "I'd sort of got the impression you're a pacifist. Against war in general, that kind of thing."

"I am. I guess."

Calojan nodded. "Me too. But it's an imperfect world, and I take the view that the best thing to do with wars is get them over with as quickly as possible. Doesn't Saloninus say that somewhere?"

The clerk told him what I was reading. "*Art of War*, book one, chapter six. But he wasn't a pacifist."

"Nobody's perfect," Calojan replied. "All right, I'll see what I can do. Mostly I'm doing this because it'll have those turds on the Armoury Board in tears. I'd like that."

"Splendid," Aimeric said. "Thank you for your time."

"Thank you," Calojan replied. "For the book."

Aimeric left the building, walked round the corner into Clothiers' Yard, and threw up violently against a wall. The convulsions were so bad he could barely stand. He only just managed to pull himself together and get moving again before the watch arrived.

He went home. The house was empty, bare, even the threadbare rug in the kitchen gone. There was a note on the door.

HIS MOTHER HAD been wrong about one thing. The debtors' prison wasn't quite so bad as the regular prisons, or at least not the ones in the Vesani Republic, where he'd had to go occasionally to visit fellow students arrested for various public order offences. There was a wall with battlements and a gatehouse, making it a walled city inside a city; the impression was that at any moment, some enemy might assault it with siege engines and battering rams. If so, it'd be ready. It was a small masterpiece of military architecture. You'd feel really safe in there.

But bored. There was a large central courtyard, swept perfectly clean, surrounded by buildings where people lived. The resemblance to the University was too striking to ignore; the prison was slightly more modern, and the sloping slate roofs were interrupted by chimneys at regular intervals, suggesting that the place was heated in winter, to some extent. Another difference. And that was all; courtyard, buildings. No hall, chapel, refectory or master's lodgings. The yard was deserted when he walked in through the main gate, which was perplexingly wide open.

He tried the porter's lodge, where a broad, bald man looked down a list of names and gave him directions; staircase seventeen, room nine.

"I can just go up there, can I?"

"Sure. Why not?"

Also, no smell of cheese and boiled cabbage; therefore, no kitchens. He crossed the yard, found where the staircase numbers were painted on the arches, located number seventeen and climbed the stairs. In due course he was confronted by a big grey oak door with the number 9 carved on it in Mezentine cursive. He knocked, and waited. The door opened, and there was Gesel, staring at him.

"There you are," he said cheerfully. "Can I come in?"

"You've got a—" she said; he slid carefully past her and into the room. It was rather like the one he'd just left, at home; empty, not a single man-made object to be seen. No table or chairs, no bed. Just his mother, sitting on the floor.

"Oh," she said. "It's you."

Under other circumstances, it was a picture he'd have liked to contemplate, just for a moment or so. "It's all right," he said. "I've fixed everything."

His mother gave him a look that would have sterilised yoghurt. "You know, I doubt that."

"Suit yourself. But I went to see Calojan. We've got an order for two million arrows, they'll write off the old contracts and pay all the suppliers. I've saved the company."

"You idiot."

Not the first time she'd said that, but this time it didn't seem appropriate. "What did you say?"

"I called you an idiot, because you are one. You stupid, stupid fool. The company doesn't make arrows."

He frowned. "You're joking."

"Your father always kept us out of the arrow trade. He said it was impossible to make money at it. Therefore, we have no machinery, no skilled tradesmen—"

He wasn't sure he wanted to hear any of this. "Not to worry," he said. "We've got eight weeks."

"*Eight weeks.*"

"Exactly. Plenty of time."

He'd managed to shut her up, which was remarkable. He took the opportunity to make a show of looking round. "Could be worse," he said. "It's clean and dry, at any rate."

"Aimeric."

He smiled at her. "I imagine that once Calojan's people have drawn up the new agreements and paid off the suppliers, we'll be able to get you out of here. Until then, just sit tight. What's the arrangement about food?"

Gesel's voice, behind him. "We were going to ask you that."

"It's the responsibility of prisoners' families," his mother said bitterly. "So I suppose that means your sister and I will starve."

"Don't be silly," he said. "I'll have something sent round."

"How? You haven't got any money."

No, but Hosculd did; and at some point he'd pay Hosculd back, and everything would be fine. "Leave everything to me," he said. "You'll be out of here in no time, trust me. Though I can't see why the people in here don't just walk out through the door. It's not locked."

"And go where?"

He shrugged. "It'll all be sorted out before you know it," he said. "Meanwhile, cheer up. We're back in business."

"You moron. Two million arrows in eight weeks."

"Don't worry about that," he said. "I know exactly what I'm going to do."

Hosculd gave him a bed for the night. It was the first time any member of the de Peguilhan family had set foot in his house. His wife (surprisingly young and pretty; he realised he didn't know her name) looked terrified as she dished up some sort of grey semi-liquid in pewter dishes. When she'd escaped into the back, he told Hosculd what he'd done. Hosculd looked at him.

"Well?" Aimeric demanded.

"We don't make arrows."

"I know. Doesn't matter."

"I think it does, actually."

"No it doesn't." As he said the words, the first glimmer of an idea formed in his mind, and suddenly he knew what he was going to do. Simple. Problem solved. "You leave the grand strategy to me, and everything will be just fine."

"Well." Hosculd straightened his back against his chair—rather a nice old piece, quite valuable; but when Hosculd's great-great-great grandfather had bought it, it had been just a chair. "Normally I'd say no, you haven't got a clue about the business and I wouldn't be inclined to trust you an inch." Aimeric froze. He'd never imagined Hosculd would talk to him like this. "On the other hand," he went on, "this time yesterday, De Peguilhan Brothers was dead. Now—" He shrugged. "Listen, Aimeric. I worked all my life for your father, and the old man before him. Your dad was almost as smart as he thought he was, and look where it got us. You I don't know about."

Aimeric found it hard to speak. "Come on, Hosculd," he said. "You've known me all my life."

Hosculd nodded. "I knew a stuck-up kid who thought he was a cut above trade and reckoned the arms business was dirty and disgusting. I thought, so what? When his dad goes on, they'll sell the business and I'll be working for someone with half a brain, someone who values it enough to pay good money for it. Never thought I'd be working for you, so never bothered to take any notice; just stayed polite and kept out of your way, so to speak. Truth is, I don't know you from a hole in the ground."

Aimeric actually thought about that, for a moment. "You know what," he said, "neither do I." He smiled, but only a reflex. "It's when Mother said, there's no money. I was *terrified*, Hosculd."

"Fair enough. Who wouldn't be?"

"No." Aimeric shook his head. "Not sad, or angry or miserable. I was so damn scared. Having no money would be like not being able to breathe. I couldn't be poor, Hosculd, I don't know how it's done, I don't know the rules. I wouldn't last two minutes. I realised I'd do anything, anything at all, to save myself from that. And then—" He hesitated; he wasn't quite sure for a moment what came next. "Then it was almost like someone I didn't know barged into my head, elbowed me out of the way and said, leave this to me, I'll fix it. I don't know who he is, Hosculd, and I don't think I like him very much, but he does seem to know what he's doing."

Hosculd laughed. "Being poor's easy," he said. "You think, if it was hard, all those millions of people out there would be able to do it?" He made a small, vague gesture with his hands. "I don't know," he said. "There's some people who can only think straight when they're scared. Had a cousin like that. Small time thief, burglar. Couldn't he ever think on his feet, when the kettlehats were after him."

"An appropriate example," Aimeric said. "I feel like that right now, actually; like the watch is kicking down the door and I've got one leg out of the window. You're right. It refines the mental processes better than second-year formal logic ever did."

Hosculd shrugged at that and wished him goodnight. Much to his surprise he slept well, and just after dawn set off to walk to East Town.

He could have afforded a cab or a chair, just about, but he decided to walk instead, so as to be able to look about at the right pace. He arrived at his destination just as the men were filing in to work; a slow brown and grey stream, like floodwater, men who saw each other all day every day talking quietly while they could still hear themselves think. Anything you wanted to say once you were inside the gates would have to be worth the effort of shouting.

Someone told him where the office was; a small, square grey stone building in the corner of a yard formed by three long, low wooden sheds. There was no door, for some reason. He went in, and a young, round-faced clerk gave him a professional smile. He told him his name. The clerk had heard of him, no doubt about that. He was quite certain that Mister Huneric would be able to spare him a minute or so.

Aimeric sat down on a stool to wait, but didn't have time to settle comfortably. The clerk was back. Would he care to step this way?

He'd never met Huneric, but he knew what he'd look like; a solid man, running comfortably to fat after a slim, lean youth. He was a head shorter than Aimeric but probably weighed a little more. Good teeth.

"So you're Gaiseric de Peguilhan's son," he said, rocking back slightly in a huge, ornately carved chair. "Sorry to hear about your father. He'll be missed."

"Thanks," Aimeric said crisply. "Now, then. I expect you've heard about the trouble we're in."

"Some of it."

"Oh, there's not much to it, really. Anyway, all that's changed. I have a confirmed order from general Calojan for arrows, and I want to talk to you about sub-contracting some of it out to you."

Huneric frowned. "You don't make arrows."

"We do now. Anyway, the good thing about it is, from your point of view, I won't be trying to squeeze you on price, and there's no risk on your part, because you're guaranteed payment by the government."

There was a long pause; presumably, Huneric was deciding whether to have him thrown out or not. "Go on."

He explained, briefly and selectively, the deal he'd made with Calojan and what was so special about tanged arrowheads. Huneric's face didn't move at all. Eventually, Huneric said, "He agreed to that?"

Aimeric shrugged. "He's a soldier, not a businessman. Or a politician, come to that. He knows what he wants, and he's not the one who has to find the money."

"They won't let him."

Aimeric shook his head slowly. "This is general Calojan," he said. "But for whom, right now this city would be nothing but rubble and cold cinders. Instead, he's about to win the war. Do you honestly think, if he asks for something, anybody in his right mind's going to turn round and tell him, No, you can't have it? Except, of course," he added, "the Armoury Board. Which is precisely why he needs me. Us."

Huneric gave him a faintly wounded look. It was saying; but that's so simple and obvious, when you put it like that. Just go direct to the general, don't bother pissing around with the bureaucrats. Yes, Aimeric thought, simple and obvious. You could've thought of it yourself. But you didn't, and I did. "We can't make two million shafts in six weeks," Huneric said. "We don't have the capacity."

"Fine," Aimeric replied. Guessing time. He had a mental image of the size of the sheds, from when he'd walked through them just now. "But you could do half a million. We both know that."

Huneric thought long and hard. "Yes," he said. "I suppose we could."

"Of course you could. Let me refresh your memory. Before the war, you were the biggest supplier of wooden dowels in the empire, mostly for joinery and cabinet-making. You built this site to carry out a contract for ash dowels for the shipyards, but the war at sea is pretty well over now, that contract's nearly finished and when it's over you'll be sitting on your hands. Arrowshafts are just lengths of dowel; dogwood instead of ash, but so what? I don't actually know what a dogwood tree looks like—"

"It's not a tree. More a large bush."

"Is that right? Easier for you, then, less sawing up. And the joy of it is, all you need to worry about is getting it done on time. Not meeting a price, not getting screwed on a couple of percentage points. The government will pay my suppliers direct. You supply me with arrowshafts, you're a supplier. So long as you're sensible, you can name your own price."

Huneric looked at him as though he'd just turned water into wine.

"Oh, and while you're at it," he went on, "I'll get you to drill the hole in one end, for the tang to go in. You can do it easier than we can, and of course you'll get paid for it."

Huneric blinked. "And what will you lot be doing?"

"We'll stick the feathers on, fit the arrowhead and pack them in barrels. And deliver them, of course. On time, wherever the general tells us to. That's all he wants, and then he'll be happy." Aimeric smiled. "Most things in life can be simple, if only you let them."

He could tell that Huneric was annoyed about something, probably didn't like him very much. He also had no alternative but to agree. They haggled half-heartedly over terms and details—Huneric proved to be one of those awkward people who won't take Yes for an answer—and then there was nothing more to discuss. He had a deal.

"Pleasure doing business with you," he said, and got out fast.

There were six more factories just like Huneric's within a twenty-minute walk. Aimeric went to all of them and struck the same deal. Three million arrowshafts, where he'd agreed one million with Calojan. But Calojan had said, two million would be nice, never expecting he'd get them. It made a lot of sense to arrange a pleasant surprise for the only man in the world who actually mattered—curious, in fact, that nobody else had thought to do it, but never mind. No matter how simple the idea, someone's always got to be first to have it. As for the extra million, well; if he contracted for three million in six weeks, he was pretty sure to get two. If he got stuck with an extra million, that'd be a problem for another day, or an opportunity. He decided he'd done well enough, and went to see the drop-forge people at Underway.

"THAT'S INSANE," HOSCULD told him, when he explained what he'd been doing all day.

Aimeric shrugged. "Maybe," he said. "But they've agreed to do it, so—"

"They must be mad."

Hosculd was beginning to get on his nerves. "A week ago, I could've given you a perfectly reasoned discourse on why no sane man would be in the arms business anyway. Weapons lead to wars, war is the worst possible thing. Therefore, no sane man, et cetera. I'm a bit rusty now, of course, so I don't suppose I could do justice to the material. Does it matter if everybody in this loathsome business is stupid except for me?"

Quite soon, he thought, I'll go too far and lose him, and that'd be a stupid waste. Not yet, though; and when he's furiously angry he says what he thinks. "All right," Hosculd said. "I'm sorry, I shouldn't have spoken to you like that. It's just—"

"Yes," Aimeric said. "Meanwhile, we've got to do something about getting my sister and mother out of jail. Did you—?"

Hosculd nodded. "I took it down there myself."

"Well, at least they'll have something to eat. How about books, embroidery stuff, that sort of thing? They must be bored out of their minds."

Hosculd shook his head. "Debtors aren't allowed personal property," he said, "except for two changes of clothes and some bedlinen. If I took anything else down there, it'd just be confiscated."

That could have been me in there, Aimeric thought. And without anything to read, even—No. Death first. Of course, his mother would say exactly the same thing. "I want you to go to the Board office, first thing. There's got to be something we can do to hurry things along."

Something occurred to Hosculd that troubled him. "Have you been to see them today?"

"What? Me? No, no time, I'll go tomorrow. After I've seen the gangmasters." He felt sure he was wearing a hunted look, though of course he had no way of knowing. "Oh, while I think of it. Carpenters. Do we know any?"

"We've got some."

"Have we? Oh, that's handy. Tell them, I want ten thousand equilateral triangles cut out of three-quarter inch pine board—"

"What triangles?"

Aimeric blinked. "Triangles whose sides are all the same length," he said. "Sorry, thought you'd have—Anyway, three-quarter inch thick, sides seven inches long. Oh, and a hole drilled in the exact centre, precisely three-eighths. *Precisely.* Got that?"

Hosculd was frowning. "The same diameter as the arrowshafts."

"Yes. Got to be a push fit, you see."

"What do you want ten thousand—?"

"See the Board man about a chit for materials," Aimeric went on, raising his voice just a little. "Take on more men if you need to, we need them in five weeks. Oh, and get five thousand glue kettles. Small ones, nothing fancy."

"Five thousand glue kettles," Hosculd repeated. "Where the hell from?"

"The glue kettle people, of course. I don't know, do I? You may have to get them made. Five weeks. And brushes, and small charcoal stoves. Should be able to get them off the shelf somewhere."

"Five thousand?"

Aimeric thought for a moment. "Twenty-five hundred. Two men can share. Now then, let's see. Oh, barrels. We've got barrels, presumably."

"Not enough for two million—"

"Then get some more. Right, I think that's about it. No, last thing. How many men have we got?"

Hosculd looked at him. "Full-time, you mean? Nine hundred."

"Splendid."

"You didn't know—"

"But I do now. And that really is it." He grinned. "You know, it makes me wonder what the hell people do all day. I've just set in motion two million arrows, and it's only taken me about twelve hours."

JUST BEFORE DAWN he was shaken awake by Hosculd, who told him there were soldiers at the door.

"What?"

"Soldiers," Hosculd repeated grimly. "A sergeant and two kettlehats. You'd better come and see what they want."

"For crying out loud," Aimeric groaned. He rolled out of bed, grabbed his shirt and tied it round his waist.

"Just make sure you leave me and my family out of it," Hosculd growled in his ear. He nodded vaguely and blundered to the front door.

The sergeant looked at him with the total lack of expression soldiers use for dissolute civilians. "Aimeric de Peguilhan?"

"That's me."

"Letter for you, sir. From general Calojan."

Aimeric stared at him for a moment, then held out his hand. The letter came in a standard issue bronze message tube, embossed with the eagle-grasping-thunderbolt and the number 20. "Thanks," Aimeric mumbled.

"Would you like us to wait for a reply, sir?"

"No, that's fine."

Impeccable salute, precise to within half a minute of angle. "Sir."

Aimeric staggered back indoors and spent the best part of two minutes trying to poke the rolled-up letter out of the tube. In the end he had to wander into the kitchen and use the back of a wooden spoon.

Calojan to Aimeric de Peguilhan, greetings.

I hope you know what you're playing at. I've had a succession of grubby little men trooping through my office with bits of paper signed by you, wanting money. The Armoury Board is hopping mad, yelling and scream-ing—which is probably why I've countersigned everything and told them to get on with it.

My time, however, is not without value; so I've appointed an officer i/c all your little bits of signed paper. His name is major Gundohad, at Central Supply. Please direct your vultures to him, not me. Enclosed please find a war-rant, with all the relevant scrambled egg, to show to your grubby little men.

By scrambled egg, Calojan apparently meant the Imperial seal, affixed to the bottom of a magnificent example of illuminated calligraphy. The warrant—he read it, then read it again. As far as he could tell—in second year you could do either Law or Logic but not both; he'd opted for Logic—the warrant authorised him to do *anything*.

He grinned like an idiot. His poor father; forty years in the business, going through channels, wrestling with the Board, never occurred to him to take one big stride and step over all of that, go directly to the man himself. True, by all accounts Calojan was unique, a one-off, a phenomenon. Even so.

There's never a bit of paper when you need one. He was forced to cut the flyleaf out of Hosculd's copy of the *Offices* (luckily, Hosculd's family didn't follow the practice of using the flyleaf to record births, marriages and deaths). He found the ink and wrote—

Aimeric de Peguilhan to His Excellency general Calojan, greetings.

Noted, and thank you.

He rolled up the note and stuffed it into the tube; reluctantly, because it was a pretty thing and he'd have liked to have kept it. But the scrambled-egg warrant was prettier still, and he was definitely keeping that.

He rummaged about in Hosculd's kitchen cupboard and eventually found a silver-gilt napkin ring, a cut above the rest of Hosculd's junk, prob-ably a family heirloom of some sort. He rolled up the warrant and slipped the ring over it. It'd do, till he could find something more suitable.

THE NEWS EVERYONE had been waiting for arrived; the snow in the Jehec mountains had finally thawed, the Mair was in spate and unfordable, and the Blue Comb pass was open. Calojan mustered the Third Army on the parade ground in the Ropewalks. He had sixteen thousand regular infantry, nine thousand heavy cavalry and fifteen thousand Aram Cosseilhatz auxiliaries. It was the largest army the empire had been able to put into the field for quite some time. It was also, according to the best informed opinions, not enough.

"I'm not sure how long I'll be gone," he told the emperor, at a private briefing at dawn on the day of his departure. "It'll be either three weeks or for ever. As I used to tell my mother, don't wait up."

Sechimer smiled. "It's not looking good, is it?"

For a moment, Calojan's grin wavered. "The bloody thing is," he said, "there's so *many* of them. You slaughter them like sheep one day, a week later they're back and there's three times the number. I have this horrible dream where we finally win, and we set off to take possession of our new territories, and we cross the frontier and travel for days and days and never see a living soul, because we killed them all. It's ridiculous, really."

"You get that one too, do you?"

"Unfortunately," Calojan went on, "we simply don't have those sort of resources."

Sechimer looked at him. "It's true, then. I wasn't sure. You can't always believe—"

"It's true. They can afford at least four more defeats on the scale of Greenwater. If we lose one battle, that's it. Time to pack. There'll be nothing left."

Sechimer gently massaged the scar where the stub of the sixth finger had been. He'd had it discreetly removed by a defecting Sashan surgeon, because tradition insisted that the emperor must be without visible physical defect. "Your friends the Aram Cosseilhatz—"

"Have a curious aversion to getting killed," Calojan said. "Which complicates things further. I can foresee a scenario where we win a glorious victory, wipe out all five of the Sashan field armies, and still end up losing the war because the Cosseilhatz take casualties at a level they consider unacceptable. If that happens, they're just gone, like that. No amount of money would persuade them to stay." He shook his head. "If I was the Sashan, I'd concentrate everything on killing as many Cosseilhatz as possible, no matter what the cost, even if it meant losing ten major cities and three armies." He looked away, and his grin returned. "The really stupid thing is, they could have had the Cosseilhatz instead of us. The clan council gave them first refusal, but the Great King wouldn't meet their price. They'd rather have fought for him, all things being equal. Similar religion, for one thing."

"Just as well he's an idiot," Sechimer said.

"He's an idiot with something in the region of two hundred thousand men in the field," Calojan said. "And I'd still bet my money on him, if I could get decent odds anywhere."

THE PRESIDENT OF the college of augurs took the usual auspices. The ceremony was irregular, because the army had already left (for some reason, Calojan chose to leave just after dawn, though the schedule he'd sent the president clearly said noon); however, there were precedents, so they carried on as usual.

When the ceremony was over and the president had thoroughly washed his hands and scrubbed under his fingernails, he sent a herald to the palace urgently requiring an audience with the emperor—

"*Require*," Sechimer said. "Now that's a truly priestly word."

"It's how they always phrase it," somebody told him.

"Of course," Sechimer said. "Well, I suppose I'd better see what he wants."

He received the president in the Long Gallery. To reach the throne from the door, you had to walk the length of the hall, passing underneath a hundred and twenty-seven life-sized portraits of dead emperors, beginning with Florian I. Only seventeen of the portraits had faces; the other hundred and ten were practically identical representations of a man's body, dressed in the same lorus, chlamys and divitision that Florian had worn a thousand and twenty years ago and which now—except that Hodda had disposed of them somewhere; they hadn't turned up yet, so Sechimer was still wearing theatrical props. Where their faces should have been, however, there was a crude oval of bare wood, where the paint had been scraped away when the subject of the portrait had been formally anathematised by his supplanter, or a later successor wishing to distance himself from the policies of his predecessors.

"Majesty," the president said. "Thank you so much for seeing me at such short notice."

Sechimer gave him such a pleasant smile. "Is something the matter?"

"I'm afraid so, yes." The president explained, and Sechimer, who hadn't done any background reading, nodded and mumbled politely to give the impression he was following it all. "So you see," the president concluded, "we have a problem."

Sechimer frowned. "This isn't supposed to happen," he said.

"Indeed," the president said. "We take all necessary steps. Nevertheless—"

Suddenly Sechimer smiled. "You know," he said, "I've never been what you'd call a regular templegoer, but something like this is enough to restore a man's faith in the Almighty. If, in spite of all the trouble you people go to, He can still somehow contrive to get a bad reading past you, then it's pretty damn convincing proof that He exists, don't you think? Thank you, you've made my day."

"Majesty—"

"I'm being flippant, do forgive me. So, these are really bad omens."

"Yes." The president hesitated, then added, "About as bad as they could possibly be."

"I see. What do you want me to do?"

"Recall general Calojan immediately. If he engages the enemy under these auspices, the outcome is unavoidable. The empire will be irreparably damaged."

Sechimer nodded. "This empire?" he asked. "Only, it's that old chestnut again, isn't it? *If you cross the Astleir, a mighty empire will fall.* And the fool assumed they were referring to the enemy, but in fact it was his own."

"This empire, Majesty," the president said. "The eagle-with-thunderbolt was clearly visible in the lesions on the upper third quartile. The omen clearly indicates us."

Sechimer was perfectly still for a moment. "Thank you," he said. "It was good of you to bring this to my attention. I trust you've not—"

"Of course not, Majesty."

"Of course not. The last thing we need is alarm and despondency. Well, I won't keep you. Thank you again."

The president retired, looking vaguely bewildered. When he'd gone, secretary Gulfilas leaned across the throne, close to Sechimer's ear, and said, "Well?"

"Load of old nonsense."

"Yes," Gulfilas said, "but if we lose, the first thing the old fool will do is pin up his load of old nonsense on the temple doors, and suddenly it'll all be your fault."

"If we lose," Sechimer replied, "it *will* be all my fault. Besides, it'll be somewhat academic by then. Of mild interest to the Sashan, maybe, if they can be bothered to read it. We won't be here. We'll be dead."

Gulfilas nodded. "Understood. So, no action."

"No action. And find some way to keep that clown out of my hair, will you? I've got enough on my mind right now as it is."

Sechimer retired to his chambers, where he took off the lorus, chlamys and divitision, laid them neatly on the bed, like you do with your uniform, and knelt on the floor under the icon. It was the one he'd brought from home, a basic village Accession to Glory, with yellow paint instead of gold leaf, the faces brown with age and wood smoke. He said three stages of the Office of Penance, the Beneficence and the General Confession, and then a special plea for forgiveness, because he'd spoken offensively to a priest. Then he looked up, and looked away. He'd met the eyes of the Invincible Sun, as he'd done twice a day every day of his life, and today they were cold and empty; nobody home. He drew his hand across his face, as if trying to wipe something off. It didn't seem to help. He rocked back on his heels and tried to think what to do.

My fault, he thought. It's anathema for a deformed man to presume to sit on Florian's throne, and no good will come of it. He rubbed the scar on his left hand. That was why, when a new emperor was crowned, they rounded up all the other possible claimants to the throne and blinded them, castrated them, cut off their ears or noses. I was only trying to help, he told himself, I never thought they'd make me be emperor; and then, when it turned out there was nobody else left, I somehow assumed—He'd had the Patriarch write him a special confession, and the Patriarch had assured him it'd do the trick, but obviously not. Besseric had had a prosthetic nose made by the finest goldsmith in the empire; pure gold, painted flesh-colour, said to be so convincing that even his wife never knew. Cordumer had made them sew the old emperor's ear onto his head—preserved in myrrh and honey, and he'd started the fashion of shoulder-length hair. Atho and Florian VI had simply sat defiantly on the throne, not even bothering with glass eyes or eyepatches. And Sechimer; how many times, they'll ask in years to come, do we have to go through all this before they finally get the message? A deformed man can't be emperor. Break the rule and you're asking for a disaster. Simple as that.

He grinned, in spite of himself. It was obvious what should happen now, to save the day and make everything all right. Calojan; Calojan wins the battle, comes storming home at the head of his victorious army, has himself proclaimed emperor (the old tradition of being lifted up on a shield), kills the unworthy occupant of the throne and takes it for himself. More than enough precedents, God knows, and Calojan would be a good emperor. And I could live with that. Well, so to speak. It'd solve everything.

He looked hopefully up at the icon, then looked away again. No dice.

Besides, the omens had been clear; the empire will be irreparably damaged, and if Calojan was in charge, he wouldn't let that happen. So; back to *my fault*, no clever way of sidestepping it. Let's just hope that, when He's finished kicking the shit out of His chosen people for their own good, there'll be some pieces left for somebody to pick up.

IT WASN'T, THEY said later, one of Calojan's best battles. The odds against him were enormous but not overwhelming. The enemy commander wasn't a master tactician—a bit of a plodder, in fact; a deputy, a safe pair of hands given charge of the Southern Army, because it'd be the Eastern Army that caught up with the Imperials and brought them to battle; so, some marks to Calojan there for doing what nobody had anticipated. But the battle itself was commonplace, dull even, and the Sashan had broken off early, as soon as they'd realised they were in for a drubbing if they stuck around. There hadn't been a sudden swooping envelopment, fish in a barrel, the rivers running red; no masterful deployment of the Aram Cosseilhatz, who spent most of the battle watching from a nearby wood; just a businesslike rout, hardly followed up at all. The Eastern Army, suddenly aware that Calojan was between them and their only source of supply, broke off their triumphant march on the City and scuttled back to Dura Ceniotis, relinquishing the whole of the Mair valley, so dearly bought the year before last, but more or less intact, with their morale still reasonably good and their best general undisgraced and therefore permitted by the Great King to keep his head on his shoulders. Of course the Empire didn't have men to spare to garrison the Mair valley towns, so presumably at some point the Sashan would come quietly back and dig in, again.

A bit of a disappointment, really. Something and nothing.

"WELL," SECHIMER SAID. "You won, didn't you?"

"Oh yes, I won. That wasn't the point." Calojan arched his back against the chair. He was still wearing the same clothes he'd fought the battle in. "The point is, I could've exterminated the Eastern Army. Only I couldn't, if you see what I mean."

"Not really."

Calojan made an effort. He didn't want to have to explain. He wanted a hot bath, white bread and cheese and clean sheets. He was, however, talking to the emperor. "The Easterners were too far advanced," he said. "What I'd have liked to have done was draw them in even further, cut their supply lines and force them to come to me, somewhere in the Mesoge. It's lovely and open there, and I'd have had the chance to play games with them, get them all strung out and open, and then send in the Cosseilhatz."

"But you didn't."

"No." Calojan pressed his fist to his mouth for a moment. "The Cosseilhatz aren't happy. They don't feel sufficiently loved and wanted, I guess. I need to do something for them, to show them I respect and value them as they deserve. Until I can do that, I can't expect them to perform a hundred per cent. They'll follow orders, but they won't—"

"I know what you mean," Sechimer said. "So instead—"

"Instead," Calojan replied, "I sneaked past the Easterners, beat up on the Southerners, basically just persuaded them all to go home and sort themselves out, try again later. I haven't actually achieved—"

"The Eastern Army was three days' march from the City and we're in no fit state to withstand a siege. You accomplished something."

Calojan shrugged. "It's the wasted opportunity, really," he said. "Take out the Easterners, end the war. I can picture future historians saying, this was where Calojan made his mistake. It's frustrating."

Sechimer's face didn't change. "Or you could have engaged the enemy when you weren't at your very best, lost the battle and brought about the end of the empire. On balance, I think you made the right decision. Besides, even if you'd wiped out the Eastern Army, we know what would've happened next. They'd pull back to the Summer Line and start recruiting, we'd have four years to catch our breath, and then the whole miserable job to do again. Things aren't going to be any better around here in four years' time, I can promise you that. Quite the opposite."

Calojan grinned. "Thank you so much for that. It's reassuring to know that even miracles won't quite cut it any more."

"One big miracle," Sechimer said seriously. "One very big miracle indeed. So," he went on, moving the hem of the lorus so it didn't cut into his neck. He had a sore patch there, Calojan noticed; the stupid thing must chafe like hell. A hundred and twenty-seven emperors since Florian, all uncomfortable all of the time. "What do you need to do for these savages of yours, to make them happy?"

"Says here you're a cooper," the gangmaster said. "Well?"

"No."

The gangmaster gave him a sour look. "You're not a cooper."

"No," Raffen said. "I pretended I was a wheelwright, but I never said anything about being a cooper."

"Pretended—"

Raffen nodded. "At the border. You had to have a skill or they wouldn't let you through."

The gangmaster was an elderly man, bald on top, bushy clumps of white hair over his ears, as though he'd split and the stuffing was coming out. "Bloody hell," he said. "So what can you do?"

"I don't know," Raffen replied. "Most things, I should imagine."

"I ought to have you sent back." The gangmaster scratched his ear. "Still, you're here now. Listen, do you think you could drill holes in bits of wood?"

"Could you do it?"

"What? Yes, I suppose so."

"In that case, so could I."

The gangmaster looked over Raffen's shoulder and counted under his breath. "Sod it," he said, "we need to get the numbers up. You're in. But if anyone asks, you swore blind you're a cooper, all right?"

"Wheelwright," Raffen corrected him gently.

"Cooper," the gangmaster said firmly. "Bloody savages. All right, next."

Grinning, Raffen turned his back on him and walked slowly across the yard to join the others who'd already been enlisted. They were standing, or sitting on barrels, in front of the tall double doors of a long wooden shed. It made a change to see a proper wooden building again, after all the strange, faintly unnatural stone and brick. Although the sky was clear and the sun was shining, stone buildings made him feel cold and faintly uneasy.

"All right?" he asked the group. A few of them looked at him.

Uneasy, probably, because the only stonework he'd seen before he came to this strange place had been the ruins, which the giants had built, before they were wiped out by the gods in the Great War. Raffen wasn't sure he believed in gods or giants, though it had always seemed perfectly reasonable to accept that only creatures of superhuman size and strength could have hauled the yard-long stone blocks of the ruined towers up in the air and slotted them neatly into place. But the people here were, on average, a head shorter than him, and if they were that strong, why did they need to hire foreign workers? So, he told himself, they're not giants, therefore there never were any giants; no giants, no gods. The conclusion troubled him far less than he'd have imagined.

"What happens now, then?" he asked.

Someone shrugged. "We stay here and someone comes and tells us what to do, I guess."

"Fine." He found a low barrel, pulled it across and sat down on it. "My name's Raffen," he said. "I used to be a ropemaker, but then I went charcoal burning. Where are you from?"

The man frowned slightly. "Laxriver," he replied. "What's it to you?"

"Laxriver," Raffen repeated. "That's over the West Dales, isn't it?"

"That's right."

"You know a man called Sighvat?"

The man thought for a moment. "Can't say I do. Why?"

"Good grazing in Laxriverdale, I heard."

"Not bad. Where are you from?"

"Eastmarch."

"Never heard of it."

Raffen nodded. "It's a small place," he said. "You go up the Skell road from Belmouth and bear east. What do you do, then?"

"Wainwright."

"That's an interesting trade."

"Is it?"

"We had a wainwright in Eastmarch. Torbert, his name was. Heard of him?"

"No."

"Ah well. Old chap, about five two, squint in one eye."

"No, sorry."

Raffen smiled, tapped his fingers on his knees. "The food here's not bad."

"It's all right."

"I was worried the food would be all different and funny, but it's quite like home."

"It's whatever's cheapest," the man replied. "So I guess it would be."

"No beer, though. Not that I'm all that bothered. I'm not a great drinker."

"Chance'd be a fine thing, round here."

"And at least the water's clean. Amazing how they do that, clean water, just comes out of a bit of pipe in a wall. They're clever people here, all right."

"Talk a lot, don't you?"

Raffen laughed. "My dad used to say that," he said. "You married? I'm not. Never have been."

"Is that right?"

"Never found time. Always moving about, nothing to keep me in one place. There's been women, of course there has, but nothing—well, you know. If there's nothing keeping you nailed down, you can do anything, really. That's always been my philosophy, anyway."

The man got up and walked away. Raffen shrugged, and sat on the barrel he'd just vacated. It was wider, therefore more comfortable. Lesson learned, he noted; the tiresome man gets the best seats.

Some time later, a man in a leather apron turned up, muttered, "This way," and headed off without looking back. Raffen jumped up and followed him. Gradually, the rest of the group fell in behind. *This way* proved to be a narrow path between two of the long sheds, eventually leading to a third shed. Inside there was a workbench running the entire length of the building, with a toolrack up the middle.

"All right," the man in the leather apron said wearily, "listen carefully. I'm going to tell you what you have to do. If you get it wrong, you don't get paid. If you aren't quick enough, you don't get paid. If you steal tools or materials or you make trouble in any way, you're out of here and back where you came from, is that clear?"

Silence, so presumably it was. The man in the leather apron reached into the toolrack. "This," he said, holding up a wooden triangle, "is your pattern. You trace round it—" he mimed, to explain the difficult new word "—with your stick of charcoal—" He showed them a stick of charcoal "—onto a length of plank, then you cut it out of the plank with the saw." He lifted up a saw, so they'd know what he was talking about. "The triangle you've just made will be exactly the same as the pattern, or you don't get paid. Now then, in the dead centre of the pattern you'll see there's a hole. Mark through this hole with your stick of charcoal onto the triangle you've just made, making sure the two are exactly lined up. Then you put the triangle you've made on the side here, until someone comes round and collects it. The you do it again, and so on, till I tell you to stop." He paused. "That's it, any questions?"

Raffen wouldn't have minded asking *why are we doing this, what are the triangles for,* but the look on the man's face suggested that that wouldn't be a good idea. Nobody spoke. The man nodded.

"Right," he said. "Space out down the bench, an arm's length apart. They'll be along with the planks shortly. No talking," he added and walked away.

Raffen picked up the saw and examined it. At home, a saw was a great big thing for planking logs, or else six inches of thin steel tape in a boxwood frame, tensioned with wedges or (more usually) bits of twine wound tight with a stick. These saws were two feet long, wide as a handspan at the handle, tapering; who on earth had so much steel that they could afford to use it so extravagantly? He remembered that he couldn't saw a straight line to save his life. Well, maybe that had changed too.

They brought the planks. The man on his left set to straight away, drawing with the charcoal, then bracing the plank against the bench with his left hand, carefully aligning the saw with his right. Raffen watched him for a while. It was very impressive.

"Excuse me," he said.

The man looked at him. "What?"

"I don't know how to do this. Can you show me?"

The man stared at him for a moment as though he was something horrible and offensive. Then he moved into Raffen's space (he stepped back so as not to get trodden on) and picked up the pattern and the charcoal. "Like this, all right?" he said, extending his hand so that Raffen could see how the charcoal was to be gripped, in a sort of collar formed by the thumb and two fingertips. "You draw your lines," he went on, "nice and steady. See? Right, now you do it."

Raffen concentrated. "Like that?"

The man nodded. "That'll do. Take it slow to start with, you'll speed up when you get the hang of it. Now." He took the saw; hand through the elongated hole in the wooden handle. "Hold it like this," he said. "Then, you press down with your left, like I'm showing you. Got that?"

"I think so."

"Marvellous. Now, you look at the back of your saw, you'll see it's a straight line, right? That's if you're holding it properly. So, you line up the back of your saw with your charcoal line, and you push on your saw so you can feel it's cutting clean, don't force it, don't try and cut on the pull stroke, and that's it. Do it like I just told you, it's so simple even you can manage. Got that?"

"Yes," Raffen said. "Thanks."

"Don't mention it. Any questions, problems, anything at all, ask somebody else." He moved back to his own space, hesitated, looked back. "How'd you get in here, then? They're only supposed to be taking skilled men."

"I lied," Raffen said.

He turned the plank over, so as not to cheat by using the triangle his neighbour had drawn, and picked up the charcoal. Here begins the great lesson, he thought; simplicity, which makes the rough places plain and levels the mountains and the sea. Everything yearns to be simple. The trick is, to let it.

Some time later, there wasn't enough plank left for another triangle, and he had a stack of freshly-cut copies sitting on the edge of the bench, each exactly superimposed on the one below; he ran a finger down the side and felt no ledge. The man on his right, his mentor, still had two triangles' worth of plank to go. Well, Raffen thought. Nobody's perfect.

He looked round for someone to bring him another plank, but there wasn't anybody about. Hypothesis; I can cut straighter and quicker than they can, because there's nothing in my life except the charcoal line; nothing in the way. The other one, the man I used to be, wasn't like that. When his father tried to teach him to saw a straight line, there were all sorts of things; expectation, wanting to excel, not wanting to fail, fear of failing, disappointment, irritation, resentment; the other one never stood a chance. Now me, all I wanted to know was how to saw a straight line. Nothing in the way. Easy. Piece of cake.

They brought him another plank, and another one, and another one after that. He could feel himself getting tired, so he slowed down a little, applied a little less strength to the saw, which cut faster and easier as a result. He thought that was rather funny, and laughed; the man next to him on his left stared, and he made himself stop. But it was distinctly amusing; the less effort you put in, the easier it gets. He wanted to tell someone, but decided he'd better not.

He wasn't particularly conscious of the passage of time, but at some point the light coming in through the unshuttered windows changed its slant, falling on his right instead of his left. They kept taking away his triangles. Tomorrow, he promised himself, he'd try and keep score. His feet ached a little from standing. He wondered what they'd be given to eat that night, and if they'd be sleeping in the same shed.

It was getting dark; soon it'd be too dark to see the charcoal line clearly, and then he'd stop, because he didn't want to spoil things by doing bad work. He realised that a man had been watching him for a while, though he couldn't say how long. A while, though. Someone with nothing better to do. He decided he didn't mind.

The man in the leather apron came back and called out, "Right, that's it." Everyone else put down their charcoal sticks and their saws, but Raffen was three-quarters of the way through a cut, and didn't want to stop. He heard his saw against a wall of silence, which made him feel a bit silly; but two more strokes of the saw finished the job and he put the completed triangle on top of the pile and stepped back from the bench. The kind man on his right, who'd taught him all he knew about carpentry, was scowling at him.

"All right, clear off," said the man in the leather apron. "Not you."

Not-you was Raffen. He stayed where he was; the rest of the shift walked round him, as though he was a rock in the sea with the tide going out. One or two of them looked at him; curiosity, hatred, pity. When they'd all gone, the man who'd been staring and the leather-apron man came up to him.

"You're good at this," the staring man said.

"Thanks," Raffen replied.

"And quick," said the leather apron man.

"Am I?"

"I was counting," the watcher said. "In the time it took for the rest of them to do two planks, you did three."

Raffen frowned. "That's all right, isn't it?"

The leather apron man pulled a face Raffen wasn't supposed to have seen and couldn't quite parse. "It's fine," the watcher said. "No problem with that. Like I said, you're a good worker."

"Ah well," Raffen said. "Back home I was a wainwright, see. You had to be handy with a saw in my line of work."

"They were supposed to send us only skilled men," leather apron said mournfully. "Half these monkeys don't know one end of a saw from the other."

"You fancy something a bit more interesting than cutting out triangles all day?" the watcher said. "There's more money. A bit."

"Sure," Raffen said. "What have I got to do?"

"Planing and facing, a bit of jointing. Right up your street, I should imagine."

Raffen had a vague idea what planing and jointing would be; he'd never heard of facing. "If you like," he said. "How much more money?"

The two men looked at each other. "Thirty trachy," the watcher said.

Trachy? The men in the woods had talked about trachy, but hadn't explained what they were. Still, thirty of anything sounded good. "That'll be fine," he replied, which seemed to surprise the two men, though they tried not to show it. "Thing is, I'm not used to the sort of tools you people use here. They're all different, back home. Cruder."

Leather apron laughed. The watcher grinned. "Like the saw, you mean?"

"Exactly, yes."

"Don't worry about it. Ulfilas here'll give you a crash course in the morning. You'll get used to them in no time, smart man like you. What did you say your name was?"

"Raffen."

"Good man. Be here, seven sharp, and we'll show you where to go." They started to walk away. "Excuse me," Raffen said.

"Sorry, what?"

"Where do I go now?" he asked. "Only, I didn't happen to see which way the others went."

Leather apron seemed to find that mildly amusing. "You haven't got lodgings, then," the watcher said.

"Lodgings? No. Should I?"

The two men looked at each other again. "Out of the gates," the watcher said, "turn left, keep on going down the hill till you come to a big archway. Through that, and you should see a load of your lot milling about. They'll tell you where to go. And if you reach the river, you've gone too far. That's odd," he went on, talking to leather apron, "I thought Ledulf was sorting out billeting arrangements."

"Oh, him," leather apron grunted. "He's no bloody good. Gone home early, I'll bet, and doesn't give a damn."

They seemed to have lost interest in him, so he started to walk away. He hadn't got far when the watcher called him back. "Haven't you forgotten something?"

"Have I?"

"Your wages," the watcher said slowly, as to a child. "You want them, don't you?"

"Well, yes. Where do I—?"

"Office. Out of here, turn right, it's a little shed thing. Hurry up, or she'll have gone home."

He hurried. The woman in the shed ticked his name off a long list, then handed him a little cloth bag.

"What's this?"

She didn't seem inclined to reply. He thanked her, left the shed, walked a dozen yards until he reached some steps, sat down and opened the bag. He peered into it, then spilled its contents out into his hand. He found his palm filled with a heap of tiny thin copper discs, irregular in size and shape and slightly dished. The biggest one was the size of his thumbnail. He peered at it and could just make out two little human figures, stick men holding objects too stylised to identify. He counted the bits of copper. There were a hundred and six.

Coins, presumably. He thought he knew about coins. They were silver, about three-quarters of an inch in diameter and a sixteenth-inch or thereabouts thick, with a man's profile stamped on one side, some sort of bird on the back. That man, the other one, had had a big pot full of the things, in among the rest of the silver, though of course he'd measured silver by weight, like any other commodity. Nine ounces of good silver paid compensation for a day labourer; twelve for a stockman; fifty for a free man's sister, ninety for a son or a brother. The other one had received a hundred and thirty ounces for his father, killed by a single axe cut to the head while counting sheep beside the river, but that was a special case, because he was a man of considerable importance and standing in the community, therefore much more expensive. When the other one killed the men who'd ordered his father's death, he only paid a hundred and ten for the pair, though of course there'd been trouble about that—

He shovelled the bits of copper foil around the palm of his hand with his fingertip. A hundred and six. Well. Then he put them back in the bag and went where he'd been told to go.

Turned out he wasn't rich after all. A bed for the night (eighteen inches of a sort of shelf sticking out of a wall, shared with twelve other men) cost him forty-six trachy. Some sort of soup with bits in was twenty-five. Beer was twelve trachy a jug, but he couldn't be bothered.

"*Two* million."

Aimeric smiled at him.

Calojan looked vaguely stunned. "But the order was for one million. Look, here in the contract."

"You said two million would be nice." Aimeric shrugged. "So."

Calojan leaned back in his chair, and Aimeric felt the full force of his attention. It was like looking directly into the sun; don't ever do it, his father had told him once, so of course he had. He'd counted up to six before his nerve failed him, and here he was, still able to see. "So this is by way of being a nice surprise."

"I suppose you could call it that, yes."

"Even though it's not my birthday."

Aimeric felt cold. It was just possible that he'd misread this man completely, in which case everything would soon start collapsing around his ears. He realised he was holding his breath.

"Don't ever do anything like that again," Calojan said. "Understood?"

Aimeric nodded. He nearly said something—an apology, something of the kind—but decided at the last moment that silence would be better. He waited.

"That said," Calojan went on, "*two* million. That opens up a certain number of possibilities I hadn't even bothered to consider." He shook himself, like a wet dog. "How the hell did you manage it, just out of interest?"

Aimeric nerved himself and smiled. "Trade secret."

"Not from me."

Fine. "I simplified things," he went on. "Like, for example, it's a skilled job applying the fletchings. You're apprenticed seven years to a master fletcher, who teaches you how to space the feathers evenly around the end of the shaft, all by eye. But then all you do is dab on a bit of glue and press the feather down."

"So?"

"So I had these jigs made up, lots of them. Two wooden triangles, with a hole in the middle. You stick the shaft through the hole. You glue a feather on the top. Then you turn both triangles onto their second side, if you see what I mean. Stick a feather on the top. Third side, stick on a feather. Job done. You could train monkeys to do it. The whole mystery and craft of the fletcher rendered irrelevant in one easy step."

Calojan frowned. "And that works, does it?"

Aimeric nodded at the arrow lying on Calojan's desk. "Judge for yourself."

"I might just do that." Calojan stood up, crossed the room, opened a cupboard in the panelled wall that you'd never have seen if you didn't know it was there. From it he took a long red lacquered case, hinged down one side, which he laid on the desk. Inside was a beautiful Aram no Vei horn-and-sinew composite bow, its back dappled and deeply shining, unstrung, so that it bend backwards like a half-moon. Calojan strung it effortlessly, with a movement Aimeric didn't quite follow; it was supposed to take two men and a special jig, though of course the savages had some clever knack they never showed anyone.

"Stand up," Calojan said.

Aimeric did as he was told, though he could barely move for sheer cold terror. "Short-range accuracy is a notoriously poor indication of long-range stability," he said, "but we haven't got time to traipse out to the Artillery Yards, and besides, I'm not that good a shot. Now, I'd like you to stand perfectly still."

He's playing a game with me, Aimeric told himself. Calojan was rubbing a little block of beeswax up and down the bowstring. "On the desk," he said, not looking up, "you'll see a copy of *Essays on Military Logistics*. I want you to pick it up. Go on."

The book was roughly the size of a roof tile. Aimeric took hold of it, dropped it, picked it up again.

"Splendid. Now, holding it by the edges, rest it upright on the top of your head."

"I don't—"

Calojan looked at him. He did as he was told.

"That's the idea. Now, keep absolutely still. If you flinch, assuming you survive, we'll just have to do it all over again."

He felt as though there was something big and cold inside him, right in his centre. Calojan took the arrow and clipped the notch onto the bow-string, drew back half an inch against the string, walked backwards five paces, lifted the bow. He could see Calojan's right eye directly over the arrowhead. He knew he had to watch the eye, because if he looked away for a split second, he'd flinch, move, fall down; the eye knew what it was doing; the eye gave him strength. He heard a faint sigh and a creak, the ox-horn belly of the bow compressing as Calojan drew. He had his feet wide apart, and his shoulders were splayed like the wings of a panicky chicken.

Oh well, Aimeric thought. His hands, fingertips on the edges of the book, were perfectly still.

The book was snatched away from him and then he heard a whack-ing noise; later he realised, like his mother beating the carpet. He stayed exactly where he was.

Calojan held his position for a full second, then slowly lowered the bow. "Always wanted to do that," he said, "never found anyone stupid enough to let me try. Now, let's see."

Aimeric felt so fragile that, if he tried to move, he'd break a bone. Calojan walked past him, stooped to pick something up. Very carefully he turned to look.

Calojan was examining the book. It had a hole torn right through it, top left but comfortably inside the rectangle. Bits of feather stuck out of the hole. A few yards further on, five feet or so from the panelled wall, the arrowshaft lay on the ground, lacking head and feathers. Calojan was examining the wall.

"Not bad," he said. "It's gone in the full length of the head and a quarter-inch of the tang. Mind you, that's a hundred-and-ten pound bow. Not a great shot," he added sadly. "After all, ten yards, it's a pretty big aiming mark. On a regulation target, that'd have scored me four out of a possible six."

Aimeric said quietly, "Did you have to do that?"

Calojan had his back to him. "Traditional way of proving arrows among the Aram Cosseilhatz. Actually, they don't do it as a matter of routine. But the purchaser has the right. I shall, of course, have to offer myself as a target when I deliver these arrows of yours; they may take me up on it or they may not, depends on what mood they're in." Now he turned to face Aimeric. "Just so you appreciate," he said. "Supplying the government may be no big deal. Supplying *me* is different. All right?"

"I don't suppose you ever made my father—"

"No," Calojan replied, "I didn't. I never met him. He dealt with the Armoury Board. You chose to deal with me. I'm a rather different proposition." He smiled. "Drink?"

"Yes, please."

Calojan put the bow down carefully on the desk and poured two glasses from a decanter. "It's all about the spine of the arrow, you see; that's how stiff it is, the degree to which it bends. Well, you know that, obviously. Spine too weak or too strong, shot goes high or low, or it flounders or fishtails, could go anywhere. I'm really pleased you got the spine just right."

Aimeric had forgotten about spine; most definitely hadn't mentioned it to the suppliers. "The Cosseilhatz have these tall cylindrical felt hats," Calojan said. "Rather smaller target than the book there, but of course they're much better shots than me. Wish me luck."

Aimeric tried not to gobble the drink all at once, but didn't quite manage it. "So you're happy with the order."

"Bloody ecstatic," Calojan said. "I can now fight two major battles back to back. Lucky me." He shrugged. "Seriously, you may have won us the war. Or I might lose a battle and then we're all dead. In any event, I'll see to it you get paid before I leave."

"Do you mind if I sit down now? My legs are a bit wobbly."

"Sure, help yourself. It does that to you, the first time. Actually, first time I did that, I pissed myself good and proper. You're clearly a man of steel. Another?"

"No, thank you."

"Then you might as well go home. We'll talk about the next contract when you're feeling a bit less fraught. Want the book? As a souvenir?"

"No, thank you."

"Suit yourself. Thanks for calling in."

Aimeric walked quite normally from the palace to the corner of Coppergate and Straight Acre. Then he had to sit down on a low wall, and stayed there for some time until he got the use of his legs back. Among the thoughts that crossed his mind; just as well, as things turned out, that the arrow he'd taken with him had been the original one Calojan had given him as a sample.

SAVAGES

Tradition required that the Great King of the Sashan should be a man of unpredictable moods and volatile temper, as reluctant to forgive failure as to neglect to reward success. Consequently, he had already been obliged to execute three of his four genuinely talented generals, and promote worthy but uninspired thirty-year men to take their places. He was uncomfortably aware that he now had only one man left capable of giving Butcher Calojan a run for his money. So, although the Sashan army still outnumbered the Imperials eight to one, his territories were still largely intact, his treasury tolerably full and his front line still only sixty miles from the gates of the Imperial City, the Great King had no option but to regard the immense expeditionary force that left Limes Sasani the day after the autumn Fire Festival as his last serious chance of winning the war and avoiding a generation's worth of miserable attrition. He sent Atrabanes, the expedition's commander, the usual commission. It was inscribed on silk in gold ink, and the immaculate Classical calligraphy set out the King's demands; seek out the enemy and destroy them, burn their cities, enslave their women and children, drive off their herds and flocks; above all, do not fail. With the commission inside the message tube (ivory, with gold filigree decoration) was another, shorter message, written on a scrap of linen paper in the King's own handwriting; *You will be careful, won't you? We're all depending on you. I simply don't know what'll happen otherwise.*

Atrabanes had a pretty idea of what would happen. If he lost, he could predict at least one consequence with absolute certainty. He tried not to think about that. Instead, he concentrated his remarkable mind on the problems facing him, not the least of which was the quite ridiculous size of the army he now commanded.

It was the traditional proud boast of the Sashan that, wherever they went, their armies drank rivers dry. In this case, unfortunately, it was quite true. Small rivers, anyway; and most of the few rivers between the frontier and the Imperial City were small. True, the Macour and the Quento were in spate; more than enough water there, in fact rather too much, since he had to find some way of getting just over a hundred thousand men, forty thousand animals and an unascertained number of carts and wagons across them without disaster or excessive delay. His reward for doing so, should he get that far, would be the chance to play chess for his life with Calojan, the White Death of the Sashan, somewhere on the moors or in the cabbage-fields beyond them. No pressure.

Calojan, he knew, would already know the full size and nature of his army, and of course he'd be familiar with every inch of terrain westwards from the City to the frontier. Thus informed, he would by now have predicted every step of the invasion and worked out foolproof strategies, based on what any good Sashan commander would be most likely to do. A man like that, with his unparalleled record, didn't just make it up as he went along. Therefore—

Instead of marching west on the main coach road, Atrabanes headed north, following the Quento until he reached the coast. He moved quickly, covering the seventy miles in four days. He then went west, methodically sacking the north-coast ports; their governors made no effort to resist, but concentrated their efforts on evacuating the civilian populations by sea. All eight of the String of Pearls were entered, looted and burnt to the ground inside a fortnight, and as yet Atrabanes hadn't shot an arrow or seen an Imperial soldier. He hated to think of what it would cost the Great King to rebuild all that, once it was his; by some educated estimates, a fifth of the Imperial economy was now ashes, rubble and junk. There was also the small matter of where a third of a million refugees had been taken to; his reports said, the City, but that didn't make sense. The last thing the emperor needed, with the very real prospect of a siege, was yet more hungry mouths to feed inside Florian's Wall. What was Calojan playing at? He called staff meetings, set up think-tanks and working parties, the best minds in the King's dominions. They reported back with a wide range of hypotheses, none of which made any sense at all. He moved on, until he was in sight of the golden spire of the Lesser Studium at Mondhem, the second city and second greatest port in the empire. It was utterly inconceivable, he was sure, that Calojan would simply evacuate and let him destroy it. Wrong again.

Rumours began to filter through. The emperor, they said, wasn't happy. Calojan's strategy was to lure the Sashan to a certain carefully chosen location, where he'd prepared a stroke-of-genius trap that would neutralise all Atrabanes' advantages and turn them into insuperable difficulties (Atrabanes, struggling to find fodder for his horses in spite of having looted the second biggest grain store in the empire, reckoned it wouldn't take a genius or a special place to do that). As far as Calojan was concerned, the loss, disgrace and human misery was a small price to pay for the crowning victory of his career. Emperor Sechimer, however, wasn't so sure. He'd sent urgent messages to Calojan urging him to save Mondhem, was furiously angry that they'd been ignored; had threatened to recall Calojan, who'd replied with words to the effect of, *You and whose army?*

Whose army indeed. It had long been suspected that Sechimer was wildly jealous of Calojan, or terrified in case the great general deposed him and took the throne for himself; who wouldn't be, after all? It was possible verging on likely that the disastrous loss of Mondhem would give Sechimer the justification he needed to cut his over-mighty lieutenant down to size, with the soldiers too horrified by the shame of losing one of the empire's most valuable assets to maintain their loyalty to their charismatic general.

Only rumours; but Atrabanes decided to sit down in the ashes of Mondhem and see what happened next. As far as he was concerned, the only man in the world who mattered was Calojan; if there was any chance that Sechimer might deal with that insuperable problem for him, he was determined not to spoil it by interfering. While he was there, feeding his men and horses on supplies freighted across the sea from the King's North Sea ports, he began to hear other stories, equally exciting. The Aram Cosseilhatz, Calojan's invincible savages, were unhappy. They didn't like the way they were being treated, cooped up in camp outside the City like domestic poultry, and there was some sort of stupid fuss about some religious rite they'd been forbidden to perform—it included something that could be interpreted as human sacrifice, and the priesthood were up in arms. It was just possible that they might be open to a better offer, if a better offer happened to come along.

A voice in his head warned Atrabanes that all this seemed just a little bit too good to be true. On the other hand, it was also distinctly plausible. He decided to wait a little longer. While he was waiting, a deputation arrived from the elders of the Aram no Vei.

Atrabanes had heard of them. They were savages, roughly the same sort as the Cosseilhatz but further north, in that vague, huge expanse of flat grassland where it was murderously hot in summer, lethally cold in winter. The Cosseilhatz and the no Vei and the Chantat and the Rosinholet, according to the book he had rushed down to him from the Capital library, were all basically the same apart from the differences; being so similar yet so different, naturally they hated each other like poison. Every thirty years or so there was a horrendous, vast war—Chantat against no Vei, or Cosseilhatz against Chantat, or Chantat against Rosinholet; the impression he got was there was some sort of roster, with elements of a league table. The rest of the time, they got on passably well, but the wars were violent enough to keep the numbers down and the four clans irrevocably separate, which was just as well for the rest of Mankind.

The no Vei had come to him with a proposition. For a modest consideration, they would be happy to extend their sacred war against the Cosseilhatz into a new southern theatre. If the Sashan could see their way to helping them out with provisions, materiel and a certain level of logistical support, they would engage the Cosseilhatz, who would undoubtedly abandon their strictly commercial loyalty to Calojan in order to fight for clan and honour. Furthermore, assuming the no Vei were successful against the Cosseilhatz (which they would be; there would be a lot of them) they would be open to offers to continue in the Great King's service after the empire had been dealt with, as a shield against all his future enemies.

Needless to say, Atrabanes made the fullest enquiries possible. The results were very encouraging; the no Vei were who they said they were, and there was no reason to suppose they weren't deadly serious and entirely capable of delivering what they promised. There was indeed a great war going on in the north; amber-traders operating along the Old North Road had seen the aftermath of appalling battles, and the amber price had doubled in consequence on the Sashan exchanges. It was entirely plausible that the combatants were the Cosseilhatz and the no Vei. Informed sources had reason to believe that the no Vei were under extreme pressure from a new race of savages, wagon-riders rather than horsemen, expanding eastwards across the great lakes and the Rooftree mountains in search of land, plunder, sanctuary from invaders, something of the sort. Typically the no Vei would respond to such pressure by attacking the Cosseilhatz, who would then either fight back or attack either the Rosinholet or the Chantat, depending on the niceties of the balance of power. As for the idea of a southern front, it made sense. If the Cosseilhatz in Imperial service were recalled to defend the clan, they could easily turn the tide of the war. Sensible, therefore, to cut them off down here and make sure they never made it back home.

Atrabanes wasn't a religious man, but it did occur to him to wonder. If there was such a thing as divine intervention, he told his close advisers, surely it'd look something like this. Remove both Calojan and his tame savages, and look at what would be left; thirty-five thousand regular infantry, nine or so thousand cavalry, a few ragged and unreliable auxiliaries. Thanks to a decade of misrule exceptional even by the standards of the Empire, that was all they could afford, and the Sashan could walk through them to the City without slowing down. For the first time since he'd been handed his commission, Atrabanes was inclined to see the size of his army as a possible benefit. Without Calojan and the Cosseilhatz, overwhelming force would probably be enough to get him to the City gates and institute a siege. Once he was there, the additional half million refugees inside the walls would do his job for him.

Scepticism and caution have their uses, but they should be a man's tools, not his master. Atrabanes gave the no Vei sixty thousand mancus as a down payment and advanced on Coal Harbour, the last surviving major port on the north coast. If there truly was a serious rift between Calojan and Sechimer, Calojan would let the Sashan take Coal Harbour, and Sechimer would recall him, or try to. Calojan would either go meekly to his disgrace or stage his own impromptu coronation; at which point, under the terms of the deal, the no Vei would attack the Cosseilhatz. And the joy of it was, if the pieces of the miracle somehow didn't fall into place, Atrabanes could still fall back, in good order and at his leisure, to supervise the setting of garrisons in the ruined shells of the north coast ports. There was no danger, either way. No battle; therefore no opportunity for losing. He arrived in front of the walls of Coal Harbour at the head of his army to find the gates open and the streets deserted.

The wording of the commission was unequivocally clear; burn their cities, enslave their women and children, so on and so forth. Relectantly, therefore, he gave the order to destroy Coal Harbour. Rather a shame; it was an old city with some unique architectural features dating right back to the Third Kingdom and some outstanding neo-Rescensionist frescos, together with probably the best and most efficient freight handling systems in the world. But, so long as there was a chance that the empire might come back fighting, it'd be a serious mistake to leave the city intact, given its strategic position. Besides, its real importance now lay in its potential to give Sechimer a pretext to move against Calojan. The order was passed back to the sappers, who trundled their heavy plant through the massive, redundant gates and set resignedly to work.

Six days smashing down a thousand years of history and achievement; and then Atrabanes got the news he'd been praying for. Calojan had been recalled to the City for an urgent meeting with the emperor; and, by all accounts, he'd gone off as meek as a lamb, with only a secretary and two Cosseilhatz as escort. Like a man in a dream, Atrabanes wrote a letter to the no Vei. It was short; the no Vei never bothered to read more than the first three lines. It said, *Calojan recalled in disgrace. Attack now.*

THEY WERE KICKING his door. He opened his eyes and rubbed them. No call for that sort of thing.

He dragged himself out of bed, grabbed his gown and stumbled across the room. He'd only been in the house three days, so navigating through it in the dark wasn't easy. He found the front door and opened it.

"Aimeric de Peguilhan?"

Two kettlehats; imperial guard, no less, gilded breastplates (supplied by his father, a special order that ended up costing him money) and drawn swords. "That's right," Aimeric mumbled. "Please don't kick the door. This place is only rented."

"You're with us."

"What?" It dawned on Aimeric that he was in trouble. "Oh, all right. I'll just get some clothes on."

"No time for that."

Oh. Fortunately, he'd left his shoes just inside the door, so he was able to stuff his feet into them without needing anybody's permission. Then one of the kettlehats grabbed his elbow, and he was no longer in charge of his own movements.

"Where are we going?" he asked. No reply. They couldn't have heard him.

Not far, it turned out. Aimeric's new home was on the corner of Stoneyard and Five Acres, two minutes' walk from the palace. They walked for two minutes. When they got to the palace, they didn't go in through the tall, ever so slightly vulgar Eagle Gate. Instead, they went round the north side, to the door in the wall that led directly into the watch house yard. Across the yard, down a flight of spiral stairs, down a long, dark corridor. A door opened; it was heavy oak, with a very small window. He went through the door into pitch darkness. They closed it behind him, and he heard a key turn.

Thanks to his father's robust views on parental discipline, for most of his life Aimeric had always been able to reassure himself that, no matter how bad things seemed, he'd been in worse places or worse scrapes before. This time, though, he was in entirely new territory. It was darker than the cupboard in the game larder, and colder; possibly slightly smaller, though he needed light to be categorical about that. Also, his father had never left him locked up for more than a couple of hours (and if his father forgot he was there, his mother let him out). No way of marking the passage of time, naturally, but definitely longer than two hours. He couldn't feel anything to sit on except the floor, which was hard stone and damp. He waited for it to get light. It didn't.

Unbelievably, he must have fallen asleep at some point; he woke up in a blaze of hot white light, flooding in through the inch-wide gap between door and frame. A kettlehat grabbed his arm and hauled him to his feet; he staggered—feet numb, not under his control—and was towed like a stone-barge into the searing brightness of the corridor, lit by two lanterns.

"Excuse me," he said. The kettlehat upped the pace a little. The numbness had turned into the most excruciating pins and needles he'd ever experienced. He considered pointing that out to the guard, but decided against it.

Up the spiral staircase, into the yard, the light still painful; across the yard and through a low doorway; along a corridor, then another. A door. The kettlehat tapped on it—remarkable that so brutal a man could tap so delicately. "Yes," said a voice. Through the door, into a room. He was folded and compressed down into a chair. There was another chair facing. In it sat another soldier, officer (were they still issuing the Type 7 officers' small-ring mailshirts? He remembered that contract going through when he was seven). He heard the door close.

The officer lifted his head and noticed him. "Aimeric de Peguilhan."

"Yes."

The officer smiled. "You're in so much trouble."

Not what he wanted to hear. "I'm sorry," he mumbled. "What did I do?"

The officer was a big, broad man, good-looking, good haircut, beard trimmed to a needle-sharp point. He had a scar on his left forearm, a pink shiny patch as big as Aimeric's hand, and a single gold earring. "Here's the latest news, in case you hadn't heard. General Calojan has been recalled and placed in custody pending formal charges. Well?"

Made no sense. "Calojan? What did he do?"

"Oh, lots of things," the officer replied. "About midway down the charge sheet, we've got corruption, misappropriation of funds, misappropriation of supplies, unauthorised trading in government property, failing to declare an interest in a commercial enterprise supplying goods to the government." He paused for breath. "Stuff like that. You look surprised. Maybe you should've gone on the stage."

"I'm sorry," Aimeric said. "I don't know anything about any of this."

"Really? Let's see." The officer took a roll of paper from the desk and spread it out with both hands. He leaned forward, then back a little. Short-sighted. "You secured a contract to supply arrows."

"Yes, that's right."

"One million."

"Yes, but—"

"You supplied two million. And were paid for them. And the government paid off all your substantial debts."

"Yes."

"None of this went through the Armoury Board."

"No."

Another smile; warm and happy, but not friendly. "Thank you."

"Sorry?"

"For confessing. Sensible of you. I don't think you'd have enjoyed standard procedures for obtaining a confession from a recalcitrent witness. Right, we'll jot down something for you to sign and then you can go."

Then I can go. An explosion of joy and relief; but then he heard himself say, "Excuse me, but I don't understand."

"You don't need to. Just sign and go home."

"But I didn't do anything wrong."

The officer looked earnestly at him. "You did, you know. You conspired with general Calojan to defraud the treasury of twelve million solidi. Since you've turned state's evidence, you won't be prosecuted." He paused, then said, "That's right, isn't it?"

"I made Calojan two million arrows," Aimeric said. "But I don't think I *conspired*."

The officer looked very sad. "Maybe you're just unusually stupid," he said. "So I'll say it again. You conspired with general Calojan to defraud the treasury of twelve million. You now bitterly regret your actions and are pleased to assist the authorities in bringing Calojan to justice. Is that clear?"

"That's not—"

The officer looked at him. "Fine," he said. "You have a choice. You can walk out of here physically intact and go home. Or bad things can happen to you. Calojan's a dead man whatever you decide. Please don't let me influence your decision in any way."

There was a knock at the door. A clerk came in, with a piece of paper, an inkwell and a pen.

"Why are you doing this?" Aimeric asked. "Calojan's winning the war, isn't he?"

No reply. The paper was put in front of him. The inkwell was about four inches from his right hand. He shot a book off my head, Aimeric thought; he could have killed me. Made no difference. Don't lie to yourself. You can't—

"My time," the officer said gently, "is not without value."

He picked up the pen. "Where do I sign?"

ONE OF THE kettlehats who'd escorted Aimeric to this interview went off duty an hour or so afterwards. He took off his armour, put an old coat over his regulation habergeon and went down to the Old Town, where he stopped at the *Flawless Diamonds of Orthodoxy* for a beer. While he was there, he collided with another man carrying a tray of drinks. They exchanged apologies, and the soldier stooped to help the man pick up the dropped crockery. Very soon after that, the man who'd been carrying the tray left the *Diamonds*, walked quickly to the livery stables on Short Cross, took out a fast, expensive post horse and left the City in a hurry. He rode as far as the *Seven Tears of Mercy* at Mercovic, where he happened to meet up with an old friend who bought him a drink. He then returned to the City. His friend rode fast for the rest of the day and through the night until he reached the frontier at Escatoy, just before dawn. He climbed in through the collapsed roof of a derelict barn, just on the Imperial side of the line, stayed there for a minute or so, then left quickly. Not long afterwards, someone crossed the frontier and rode to the Sashan mail station at Erymees, from which a Royal courier set off shortly afterwards. The courier took the Great Post Road north and handed over his message at Relay Seven. Twenty-three hours and five changes of rider later, the message was placed in the hand of general Atrabanes, who opened it, blinked twice and sat down. A little later, he sent for his general staff and issued a great many orders.

It was a beautiful day for the time of year. Below the hill where Atrabanes had set up his standard lay a meadow, prime fat grazing land, richly embroidered with red and blue flowers. On the far side, he could see a long black line. Not a copse or a bank or a wall, and there was nothing marked on the map he'd had drawn. Therefore, inevitably, the enemy.

Pity the general with weak eyesight. The bright sun helped. He looked out for light flashing on steel, but the Imperials knew better than that; paint or rust. He sent out a dozen scouts. They weren't away long. The Imperials were advancing in a straight line, infantry in the centre, cavalry on the wings, the eagle-and-thunderbolt standard just to the left of the exact middle of the line.

He leaned forward in the saddle to ask; was the background of the standard red or purple? Purple. He nodded and took a deep breath. He could smell the flowers in the meadow below. So Sechimer was leading his troops in person. He chose a reliable scout and sent him to get as close as he possibly could.

As planned, then; good. Atrabanes could make it up as he went along with the best of them, but he preferred not to have to. He also loved simplicity. Today, he fervently hoped, would be perfectly straightforward. Three to one, and a massive advantage in cavalry. No river this time, no adjacent woods, no dead or broken ground, no marshes, no sunken road, no deceptive open ground waterlogged by recent heavy rain. At the back of his mind he couldn't help asking, why has the idiot allowed me to make him fight me here? But the only answer he could come up with was, because I'm smarter than him and I've forced him to do it. It was a dangerous answer, but sometimes the dangerous ones are true. He closed his eyes, opened them and tried to imagine he was looking at the field for the first time. Well, he thought; a plain open battlefield, no junk, no Calojan. I give up.

The scout came back, breathless and excited. He'd got close enough to take a really good look and yes, it was Sechimer himself, at the front, in golden armour. He knew it was Sechimer because he'd seen him once, before he was famous. He'd been a junior adjutant to his father, and on one occasion there'd been a parlay, and the scout had happened to be close enough to see them both clearly, and curious to see the two celebrated six-fingered men.

There was something wrong; Atrabanes could feel it, like a pip lodged between his teeth, but however hard he tried he couldn't figure out what it was. Something very slight, a tiny thing; he drew in breath to order his men to fall back. No, he thought, I can't do that. We're here first, we outnumber them three to one, if I'd been asked to design a battlefield to my own personal specifications, this is what it'd look like. I've got myself worked up into a state, and I'm imagining problems where there aren't any.

He asked; where are the Aram Cosseilhatz? Right and left wings, extreme ends. Fine; how many? About seven thousand each side; ten squadrons, seven rows of ten men per squadron.

So few—But there had been rumours about desertions, whole family groups simply packing up and riding away. Six thousand fewer than he'd anticipated, and really, he wasn't bothered about the rest of the Imperial army. He stood up in his stirrups and craned his neck. They were still coming on, in good order but their lines were starting to look thin, like too little hair combed over the top of a man's head. Time to go and greet our guests.

IT WAS SOME time later, just after he'd sent a rider to move out his centre against the Imperial heavy infantry for the hammer-blow charge on which all his plans hinged, that he realised what was wrong. Sechimer was in the front line. No commander-in-chief would put himself there, not unless he was a vainglorious idiot. A commander plants his standard where he can see everything; and from where he was, Sechimer was blind to his own wings. Sechimer wasn't an idiot. Therefore, he wasn't commanding the army.

Therefore, someone else was.

He howled for a rider to recall the advance he'd just ordered. A young staff lieutenant thundered away on a white horse, scattering men like wheels rolling through a flooded rut. Too late.

FROM HIS VANTAGE point on the slight rise on the far side of the meadow, Calojan saw a white horse going rather too fast towards the centre of the Sashan line. He smiled. The white horse was like a stone thrown in a pool. From where it stopped, ripples of uncertainty and confusion began to spread. He could almost see the point where they turned into panic; men hesitating, getting under each other's feet; a conflict of orders, a clash of seniorities as junior officers yelled contradictions over the heads of their men. It was a bonus, not part of the plan, but it was beautifully opportune. He lifted his left hand level with his shoulder, counted to five and pointed to the left wing.

"As good a time as any," he said.

A rider burst into motion, and Calojan stood up in his stirrups to watch him go. When he was half way, he sent the other rider to the right wing; a shorter distance. Not essential, but helpful if both riders arrived at the same time, so that both wings would make their move simultaneously. Atrabanes would waste a second or two trying to decide which way to look.

The riders paused to deliver their messages; the Aram Cosseilhatz advanced towards the enemy cavalry at a gentle trot. The messengers sailed out past them, riding straight at the enemy, two shooting stars against a green sky. A wide parabolic trajectory around the Sashan heavy dragoons—a few outriders were despatched to cut them off, but they wouldn't reach them in time. The riders hurtled on in to deep green space, heading directly for the Sashan mobile reserve, comprised of fifteen thousand Aram no Vei—

Well, not quite. No Vei, Chantat, Cosseilhatz; bloody savages. They all look the same, don't they?

FISTS RATHER THAN boots against his door this time. As it happened, Aimeric was awake, even though it was the middle of the night. Lately he hadn't been sleeping, for some reason.

Kettlehats; steel breastplates, so a line regiment rather than the Guards. "Aimeric de Peguilhan?"

He nodded. He'd already put his shoes on, on the way to the door.

Four of them. They fell in precisely around him, one behind, one on either side, one in front. "It's all right," he said, "I know the way." No reply. Well.

In through the front gate this time; up the grand stairs, in through the gold-sheathed double doors embossed with the eagle-and-thunderbolt, across the vast lobby, up the main staircase itself; left at the top landing, down an endless corridor with mosaic walls, marble floor, fresco ceiling. The doors bore no name or number and were identical. The guards stopped in front of one, and the leader knocked softly. "Yes, come in," faintly through the closed door. The guard opened it. They went in.

"Thank you," Calojan said. He had his feet up on the desk. "You can leave us to it, sergeant, thanks." The door closed. There was only one chair, and Calojan was sitting in it.

He looked exhausted, drained, as though he'd just crossed the desert. "Thanks for coming," he said. "Sorry, you can't sit down. If I've asked for another chair once I've done it a dozen times, but this is the palace. Probably a chair will arrive here in a hundred years time, and nobody will remember why. You can sit on the desk, if you like."

Aimeric looked at him. He wanted to say something—I'm sorry, they made me do it—but he was too scared to make any noise at all.

"First things first," Calojan said. "The latest news is, the emperor is making good progress. The Chief Surgeon says they've got the arrow out— just as well it wasn't one of yours, right?—and there's a bit of infection there but it's responding well. Apparently they were able to get a grip on the edge of the socket with a really good pair of forceps, and just kept on wiggling it from side to side very gently, and suddenly it just came away like that. There," he added with a smile. "That's wonderful news, isn't it?"

Aimeric nodded. He'd forgotten the emperor had been wounded. He certainly hadn't realised the injury was serious.

"Anyway," Calojan went on, "while his Majesty is indisposed, there's a sort of committee of us running the show. I got badgered into joining, so I'm rushed off my feet here, so this'll have to be quick. I just wanted to apologize."

What for? For ordering my execution, presumably. Decent of him, in the circumstances.

"The whole thing," Calojan went on, "was a necessary charade. We knew they'd got spies somewhere right in the thick of things, and everything depended on our being able to make Atrabanes believe I'd been arrested and disgraced. So I had you arrested and bullied into bearing false witness against me." He smiled. "I knew I could count on you. I hope you don't mind."

Aimeric could feel himself shaking. No surprise there; but he was intrigued to find so much anger in among the terrified relief. He opened his mouth, but no hope of getting any words to come out.

"Anyhow," Calojan went on, "worked like a charm. It even made it possible for us to identify who the traitor was; nice little bonus. I find that when things start going right for you, it all sort of snowballs. Look, are you sure you don't want to sit on the desk? You look like you're about to fall over."

"Thank you," Aimeric whispered, "but I'm fine."

"Suit yourself. Anyway, it all went beautifully, start to finish. The bit I was worried about was making the Sashan think the Cosseilhatz we'd sent over to them were really no Vei. Can they really be that stupid, I wondered. But apparently they were. I honestly do believe, the first Atrabanes knew about it was when his so-called no Vei auxiliaries rode up behind his heavy dragoons and started shooting. Of course, all that was all thanks to you. It'd never have occurred to me to try that if you hadn't sent me the extra million arrows; I simply wouldn't have had the tools for the job. Oh, that reminds me. Reason I sent for you, actually. I need another two million, quick as you like. You can manage that, can't you?"

"Of course."

"Splendid. Truth is, we've only got about two shots per man left for the whole Cosseilhatz contingent, and there's still a certain amount of mopping up to be done before we march on their capital. Remarkable, isn't it, when you think about it. Two million arrows loosed off in just under fifteen minutes. The poor bastards just sat there in their saddles, didn't have a clue what was going on. Eighty thousand dead." He stopped talking, so abruptly that Aimeric looked to see if anything was wrong. Nothing to see, though. Nothing at all. Nobody home.

Aimeric felt an urgent need to say something, just to break the silence. He cleared his throat. "So," he said. "Two million arrows. Same terms?"

Calojan nodded. "They're claiming," he said, "that it's the second single biggest loss of human life on one day in the history of the world, and that's including natural disasters. And the only one beating it's the earthquake and tidal wave off Ap' Escatoy in AUC 877, and, you know, I'm not really inclined to count that. That was ninety thousand, estimated, and I don't think you can count an earthquake *and* a tidal wave as one event, because Ap' Escatoy's about ninety miles inland. So, properly speaking, that's, what, thirty thousand for the city and sixty odd for the tidal wave;

I mean, compared to us, that's *nothing*." He stopped again, for about three seconds. "You agree with me, don't you? I really do feel quite strongly about this. There ought to be someone keeping proper score, someone you can write to for a definitive decision. I want it confirmed by someone that I've killed more people even than God. Well?"

Aimeric looked away. I didn't sign up to this, he was thinking; and then, Just as well nobody else is seeing him in this state. I don't matter, of course. Lucky me.

"Same terms?" he repeated.

"Yes, why not? Expect some aggravation, by the way. They're saying you made the last lot so the heads would come off and we wouldn't be able to pick them up and use them again, therefore we'd have to buy new stock from you. Have you noticed, incidentally, that once money comes into it, people will believe the most amazing rubbish?"

"I could glue the heads in," Aimeric said. "Just a drop of glue. That way, the head would still come off in the wound, but not if the arrow missed or glanced off something."

Calojan gave him a horrible smile. Someone was home now, but not the usual tenant. "Yes, why not?" he said. "I can announce that to the Armoury Board, make them think they've made me do something." He took his feet off the desk and moved the inkwell about an inch. "Well, I think that just about covers it from my end. How long for the arrows? Not such a rush this time. Ten weeks?"

"Eight. Same terms as before."

"That's fine. See you in eight weeks, then."

He turned round and walked out without looking back; like when he was a small boy, and if you looked back, the monster would get you. Of course, it was a bit late for that now.

SOMEONE COINED THE name, "the battle of the Field of Red and Blue Flowers", and for some reason or other it stuck, even though it was a bit of a mouthful. The public holiday in its honour, to be celebrated in perpetuity, would be Red and Blue Flowers Day, and people would be encouraged to wear a red or a blue flower; one enterprising grower on the northern outskirts of the City immediately put down ten acres of prime land to poppies and cornflowers, so as to get an early jump on the market.

Reports on the emperor's health were frequent and wildly contradictory. He was gravely ill but out of danger; he was up and walking about;

he had survived a horrific operation to remove an arrowhead from his left cheekbone, was weak but making exceptional progress, all things considered; he was conscious and directing the affairs of state from his bed; a regency council had been formed to manage the affairs of state until he recovered, which could be as soon as three months' time; there was no infection; there was a slight but manageable infection; the fever had finally broken and he was expected to recover; since the emperor, although well and already taking regular exercise in the palace grounds, was too weak to supervise matters personally, the grand victory celebrations would be organised in his absence by the purely temporary Board of Control, who were not (it should be stressed) in any sense a formal regency council.

Aimeric de Peguilhan delivered his second order of arrows, which were assessed by the Armoury Board and passed as acceptable, following a slight modification to the design specifications. No more arrows were likely to be needed for the foreseeable future, but the Board was pleased to announce a substantial contract for new livery for the palace guard; five hundred suits of the very best quality Type 7 formal and ceremonial harness, richly decorated in the latest style. De Peguilhan was therefore able to lay off his substantial workforce of casual and itinerant unskilled labour and recruit established specialists, thereby providing employment for a substantial number of refugees from Mondhem, who'd previously worked in the White Crown atelier. This was seen as an encouraging start to the regency council's Imperial-jobs-for-Imperial-citizens initiative, a key part of the post-war economic restructuring program.

The victory celebrations, it was announced, would be the greatest and most elaborate spectacle ever staged in the thousand-year history of the City. They would reassure the people of the Empire that, in spite of recent events, because of them, the empire had never been stronger or more secure; its values reinforced, its vigour undiminished, its ability to achieve and excel greater than ever. The victory would be portrayed as a victory over war itself, since now that the Sashan had been utterly destroyed—the Great King had been captured, disguised as a salt miner, on the Great Caravan Road leading east to the end of the world; there was no longer any place on earth where the empire's enemies could hide—there was, quite literally, nobody left to fight; no race anywhere powerful and sophisticated enough to pose a realistic threat to the nation that had made good its assertion to be the natural leader and master of Mankind.

THE REGENCY COUNCIL met in the Old Cloister of the Golden Spire Temple to vote on the proposals for the victory celebrations. The first item on the agenda was the formal resignation of general Calojan. In a letter read out to the council, he said that his presence was required at the front for the final assault on the Sashan capital; he was confident of early success but clearly couldn't predict a specific date; accordingly, since he would not be able to attend meetings for quite some time, he felt it would be inappropriate and counterproductive for him to retain his seat on the council. His last act as a councillor would, therefore, be to propose the co-option of Aimeric de Peguilhan as his replacement. In recommending Aimeric to his former colleagues, he wished to draw to their attention the six decades of unwavering loyal support shown by three generations of the Peguilhan family to the empire, culminating in Aimeric's invaluable contribution to the victory they were preparing to celebrate. Furthermore, Aimeric had proved that he had a keen and practical mind, a talent for designing innovative solutions to apparently insoluble problems, a finger on the pulse of commerce and, most important, the best interests of the empire at heart. The chair then recognised Aimeric de Peguilhan, who confirmed that he would be willing to be co-opted, on the strict understanding that he would relinquish his seat in favour of general Calojan once the latter had completed the conquest of the Sashan and was in a position to resume his duties, should the emperor still be indisposed at that time. A vote was taken and Aimeric de Peguilhan was declared co-opted, nine votes to three; Aimeric himself, as Calojan's proxy, abstaining.

Next, the committee moved on, with barely disguised impatience, to the celebrations themselves. Archdeacon Vorsiger of the Lesser Studium proposed that an official victory ode, not less than one thousand and not exceeding two thousand lines of dactylic hexameters, be commissioned from the leading poet of the empire and recited to the public on the steps of the Golden Spire on three consecutive mornings. There was general agreement in principle, but some dissent over specifics. The archdeacon recommended approaching Senator Liutprand, surely the greatest living poet, and suggested a thousand solidi as a suitable fee. Commissioner Astigern dissented; Liutprand's work was bland and derivative, he said; Bessas would be a far more exciting, modern and popular choice, and he would do the job for five hundred and be glad of the money. Representative Carloman pointed out that Bessas was Astigern's nephew; he suggested Poliorcetes, whose *Fall of Perimadeia* demonstrated grandeur and pathos blended with a uniquely patriotic sensibility. Archdeacon Vorsiger objected that Poliorcetes was a Scherian, therefore not a citizen of the empire; also, his recent works demonstrated a sadly casual approach to such fundamentals as scansion and classical form, which in the archdeacon's view offered a poor example to aspiring young poets. Chancellor Maerving expressed the view that a thousand lines was too much and a thousand solidi far too expensive. Instead, why not hold a competition for the best (short) ode, with a first prize of four hundred solidi, one hundred for second place, fifty each for two runners-up? That way, they'd get at least four times as much poetry for rather less money, and the operation of market forces would ensure that what they got was the very best stuff. Formally proposed by Chancellor Maerving, seconded by Aimeric de Peguilhan; passed, eleven votes to two.

City Prefect Hunfort then set out the sub-committee's proposals for the victory games, which would be the core event of the celebrations.

On the first day, to highlight the glorious achievements of the Imperial military, there would be a grand procession of the Imperial guard, starting at Northgate, down Three Acre to Florian's Column. The Guard would then perform a mock battle in the Perfect Square, with incidental music provided by the orchestra of the Lesser Studium. Soldiers from the Home regiments would then compete in a full day of athletics, to include running, jumping, wrestling in full armour, timed and freestyle javelin, armed combat in the pit, man-against-horse racing and mounted relay through obstacles. The day would conclude with a display of patriotic dances and the execution of war criminals and dissidents. The second day would be given over to a festival of theatre and music, staged in the courtyard of the Blue Star temple; dramatic companies and choirs from all parts of the empire would compete for a 1,000 solidi prize, to be awarded by a panel of judges made up of the faculty of the Lesser Studium and the regency council. In the evening, there would be a grand outdoor service of intercession for the health of the emperor, concluding with the beheading of the Great King of the Sashan (admission by ticket only). The main event would be reserved for the third day; a re-enactment of the great naval victory of Grain River, to be held on an artificial lake in the middle of the City, with at least a dozen full-size replicas of Second Kingdom warships crewed by condemned prisoners. The festivities would conclude with a banquet and reception at the palace for selected dignitaries, and a Five Thousand Feast—five thousand pigs and five thousand hogsheads of beer—in the Perfect Square for the populace at large, culminating in a scattering of largesse, say 5,000 solidi in gold quarters, by various elected officials.

"It's a lovely idea," someone said. "But where in God's name can we dig a lake in the centre of Town?"

"That's the beauty of it," replied Chancellor Maerving. "We temporarily divert the river at Eagle Bridge. The water will follow the course of the old canal and flood about two-thirds of Westponds. We clear the rest for stands and seating areas, stalls, what have you. A couple of days work and you'll have your lake, at minimal cost."

Silence. Then Aimeric said, "Excuse me, but that district's all residential, isn't it?"

Maerving smiled. "You could call it that, I suppose. I prefer the term 'slums'. That's the other good thing about this plan. Once the water drains off, we can go in there and start redeveloping from scratch. I mean to say, that whole end of Town's a disgrace. Should've been cleared out years ago. The only people who live down there now are the immigrant workers—" He looked up at Aimeric and grinned. "Your lot," he said, "the savages. Well, you won't be needing them any more, now you've gone up-market. It's not like they've got roots here. In fact, it's a nice, strong hint to them to go back where they came from. Now we've got all those poor devils from Mondhem and the north coast, we've got all the unskilled labour we need. We can build cheap housing for them in Westponds. It'll be a lasting legacy of the victory games—damn sight more use to the City than a racetrack or an auditorium."

"Legacy Park," said the archdeacon. "Nice ring to it."

"Yes, or Victory Estates," Maerving replied. "Anyway, I can't see there's anywhere else we could put a lake, what with commercial property as it is at the moment. You go and ask the Merchant Venturers if they'd mind us flooding Cornmarket and see what sort of an answer you'd get."

"Who owns all that land?" Carloman asked.

"It's nearly all ecclesiastical property," Hunfort replied, with a glance at the Archdeacon. "Golden Spire, the Studium, the College of Arms, North Inn. I don't see any objection coming from that quarter."

"You'd be doing us a favour," the Archdeacon said.

"The City would, of course, be happy to discuss the terms of a joint venture for redevelopment," Hunfort said smoothly. "Good investment for both of us. Rented accommodation for hard-working skilled manual workers. Safe as houses, literally." He looked back at Aimeric. "Sorry, were you about to say something?"

Aimeric hesitated, then shook his head, then added, "Have you got a timescale in mind? Presumably the tenants down there will have to be given notice to quit."

"Oh, I wouldn't worry too much about that," Hunfort said. "I imagine they can clear out fast enough. I mean, it's not like any of them own anything they can't carry with them when they leave."

"More to the point," put in Commissioner Astigern, "where are we going to get a dozen Second Kingdom warships from? And if anyone says build them from scratch—"

"Not a problem," Carloman said. "Calojan saw to that, bless him. Guess what he came across when he captured the loot the Sashan took out of Coal Harbour? One dozen full-scale replica Second Kingdom quinquiremes, in kit form, stolen from one of the fancy upmarket shipyards. Apparently they'd made them for some nut in the Vesani Republic who wanted to play at sea battles on the lake in the grounds of his country estate. They're official war loot now, of course, so we don't have to pay for them. All we need do is cart them back here and put them together. That's what gave me the idea in the first place."

JUST WHEN HE was starting to think he was in real trouble, Raffen managed to get two days work on the Games, uncrating and assembling the ships. Later it turned out that Prusimand, who'd been one of the foremen at Peguilhans and was now shift leader with one of the Games crews, had told the boss there what a good worker he was and how he could turn his hand to anything. Accordingly, he was summoned to the site office, where a tall, thin, very young clerk asked him if he knew anything about shipbuilding.

Raffen smiled. "I ought to," he said. "I worked for my uncle for fifteen years, and he was the best shipwright north of the mountains."

"Oh." The clerk looked confused. "I thought it was all landlocked up there."

"We do have rivers," Raffen explained patiently. "Great big ones. Furs, hides, grain, all that, it's got to go downriver on barges." He tried to remember; he'd seen a freight barge once, when he was a boy. "I was on laying keels, mostly. Got to get that exactly right, or the whole job's screwed."

The clerk nodded. "In that case you may be overqualified, if anything," he said. "We've got all the shipyard workers from Mondhem and Coal Harbour in Town queuing up for work. All I'm looking for is people who can knock a peg in straight."

"I can do that," Raffen said confidently.

He went back to Westponds and told her he'd got a job. She smiled at him, for the first time in days. "Doing what?" she asked.

"Carpentry," he replied. "On the Games."

"Oh. Not a permanent job, then."

He shrugged. "It'll do for now," he said. "I can look around for something better." He rested his hand on her shoulder. "That's what I like about this place," he said. "There's always work for a man with the right skills."

She didn't look convinced. "Pity you're not a foundryman," she said. "They're hiring at the bell foundry."

He made a mental note of that. A foundry is where they melt metal and pour it into moulds. Should be able to do that.

"They came round for the rent today," she went on. "It's gone up."

He frowned. "You had enough?"

She nodded. "Just about. It's up sixty trachy."

"We should find somewhere else," he said. She gave him a startled look and didn't reply.

Working on the ships was no trouble. They had skilled men who knew what to do; all he did was carry lengths of timber, hold them steady, occasionally knock in a wedge or a peg. He watched carefully, figuring out how a ship was constructed, what went where, the technical terms they used. The job got behind and he was needed for a third day. The next morning (he hadn't told her the job was finished) he walked down to the shipyards. He strolled for an hour, looking around, taking note. Then he went up to a man he'd identified as some sort of boss. "Excuse me."

The man (short, square, neck as wide as head) frowned at him. "What?"

"They say you're looking for skilled men."

The man shook his head. "Not here, son."

"Oh. This is the White Boar yard." He'd asked someone the name out in the street.

"That's right."

"Fine. Sorry, I must've got the wrong end of the stick." He turned his head slightly and made a show of watching three men nailing on strakes. Something wasn't quite right. Lucky. "Don't take this the wrong way, but your spacing's a bit wide, isn't it?"

"You what?"

"Those blokes down there," Raffen said. "They're spacing the nails, what, two foot apart. Where I come from, we nail every eighteen inches."

"So do we."

"They aren't."

The man shifted and followed his gaze. He waited patiently for five seconds or so, then added, "Place I used to work, the lads had a scam. Nail every two foot, keep back the leftover nails and sell them down the lumber yards. They made a bob or two, over time. Not a good idea, though. More chance of the strakes springing under heavy flex."

"Bastards," the man said. "I'll have them for that." He hesitated. "Where did you say you're from?"

"Oh, all over," Raffen replied. "North-west, originally. But I was in Coal Harbour, Mondhem before that, bunch of other places. I've just finished working on a job for the victory games. They brought me in to help with assembling those old warships."

Something was moving inside the man's head. "Someone told you there was a job here?"

Raffen nodded. "Stetigern," he said. "Supervisor. I expect you know him."

(A safe bet. There was indeed a Stetigern who'd overseen the assembly work; a very grand man in clean clothes who paced up and down pointing out mistakes to the foremen.)

"Oh, I know him," the man said, slightly uncomfortably. "Big pal of the boss. Come to think of it," he said abruptly, "they do need another pair of hands frame-laying."

"That's handy," Raffen said. "That's what I did at Coal Harbour."

It was touch and go for a while; much harder than anything else he'd done, and some of his early mistakes made the foremen angry. By the end of the day, though, he'd more or less got the hang of it, and the pay was twenty trachy more than he'd been getting at Peguilhans. Even so, he decided he'd better look around for something else.

He stayed late to finish off what he'd been doing—they liked that, he'd found, and it wasn't as though he had anything else to do. As he was putting the tools back on the racks, the foreman walked up.

"Been watching you," he said. "You do things a bloody funny way sometimes."

"Do I?"

"Say this for you, though, you stick at it." He lowered his voice, though there was nobody else in the huge, echoing shed. "You said you were on building the ships for the victory games."

"That's right."

"Live down Westponds, do you?"

"Yes. How did you—?"

The foreman gave him an odd look. "Lucky guess. Look," he went on, his voice now almost a whisper, "you do know what they want those old ships for, don't you?"

"THAT'S STUPID," SHE said. "We just paid the rent."

He told her again. "We need to find somewhere else straight away," he said, "before the others find out and start looking. You know what this city's like. As soon as there's demand, they'll jack the rent up."

"But there isn't anywhere else." She stopped and gazed at him. "You do know that, don't you? We aren't allowed to live anywhere else."

FLOODING THE WESTPONDS district proved to be, in the words of the Prefect's chief engineer, a piece of cake. Two rows of forty five-foot-diameter piles were driven into the river-bed, using a triphammer mounted on a grain barge. Nets of bricks were hoisted up on barge-mounted derricks and dropped between the rows. It wasn't enough to dam the river completely, but it sufficed to raise the water level enough to breach the judiciously weakened embankment walls at Cutlers Cross, sending a torrent of floodwater down the Old Cut. After forty minutes, the nets of bricks were lifted out again; the river subsided to its usual level, the embankment was repaired and reinforced. The piles were removed by the simple expedient of tethering fully-laden stone-floats to them and letting the current drag them out; the floats then carried on downstream to Florian's Wharf, where the giant granite blocks were needed for the triumphal arch that the regency council had commissioned for the north end of the Perfect Square.

The engineers had judged it perfectly. The flood level stopped just above the junction of Milegate and the Tanneries, so that the rows of stakes the surveyors had driven in to mark the site of the lake were about a quarter submerged. Come the day, seepage would bring the level down a foot or so, which would be about right. Demolition crews moved in to tear down the tenements and slum housing between the Tanneries and Fletchers Row. Carpenters from the Imperial Engineers followed on to raise the stands and bleachers. Finally, at sunset on the third day of the operation, the twelve replica ships were hauled down Oldgate on rollers and launched on the newly-formed lake, as crowds threw flowers and the Court choir sang a cantata specially composed for the occasion.

The migrant workers evicted from Westponds were given the old gravel workings outside South Foregate as a temporary campsite, though it was anticipated that they wouldn't be staying long. When District Representative Disimer raised the issue in the House, he was told that the City was paying the gravel consortium 750 solidi for the use of the gravel pits (which had been abandoned since the beginning of the War) but rents from the pitchholders were expected to exceed 125 solidi, so that was all right. Furthermore, the tenants would, in their own interests, clear out the gorse, briars, thorn saplings and other rubbish that had grown up there over the past seven years, so that when they moved on the site would be ready for development in accordance with the joint venture agreed between the gravel people and the City; a considerable saving in both time and money.

IT WOULD HAVE ruined everything if it had rained; but the armies of black cloud that marched on the City early in the morning of the third day of the victory games were driven off by a courageous south-easterly wind. The Invincible Sun put in an appearance late mid-morning, as the crowds began making their way down Oldgate. By midday, every seat in the auditorium was full. The City Prefect and the ecclesiastical dignitaries arrived in gilded State coaches by way of the Ropewalk and Riot Lane, which had been closed to civilian traffic since dawn. Shortly afterwards, closed wagons arrived from the Bridewell, bringing the prisoners and undesirables who would be rowing the warships. The cordon of Imperial kettlehats drew in tight around the stadium, turning away late arrivals. The palace orchestra set up and began playing the overture. At noon exactly, when his brother the Invincible Sun was directly overhead, the emperor finally made his entrance, riding in Florian's chariot, with a widow and a beggar standing behind him to remind him he was mortal. By proxy, of course; the emperor, though much improved, still wasn't quite up to the exertion of a major ceremony, so his place was taken by Chancellor Maerving, wearing the chlamys and divitision but not the lorus. The chlamys was too big for him and the divitision was far too small; he was bright red in the face by the time he reached the royal box and was able to take them off without anybody seeing and clamber into his usual loose-fitting monastic robes.

As soon as the chancellor had saluted the people and taken his seat, the orchestra began to play the specially commissioned symphonic fantasy by Orderic now universally known as the Sea Battle Music. During the brief pause between the second and third movements, the six warships representing the Vesani fleet launched from their dock on the east side of the lake, followed shortly afterwards by the Imperial fleet, emerging in column two abreast from their boathouse, formerly the Westmills public granary. As the third movement reached its stirring crescendo, the Imperial ships moved deftly from column to line to outflank the Vesani on the left—a slight liberty, since in the original battle it was the Vesani who outflanked the Empire; a more patriotic version of events had, however, been specified by the regency council. Lovers of fine music may find it hard to believe that on the occasion of its premiere, the glorious coda to the third movement would probably have been inaudible above the snapping of oars and the crunch of the rams, as the Imperials stove in the sides of the leftmost Vesani ships. Add the clash of steel as the Imperial marines boarded the stricken vessels, the shouts of the officers, the screams of the wounded and dying; it's practically certain that the end of the third movement and the first forty bars of the fourth would have been entirely drowned out.

WHEN THE BEAK of a ship suddenly burst through the planking three feet from where he was sitting, Teudel decided he'd had enough. He let go of his oar (which ripped out of the hands of the man next to him on the bench and slammed into the chest of the top man on the row behind) jumped to his feet and looked round for the paceman. No problem there; a fallen spar had got him at some point, and he wasn't going to be any trouble to anyone. Teudel took a deep breath and yelled, "It's all right, the screw's down, let's get out of here." If they heard him, they ignored him, carried on heaving on their oars; as though it mattered, as though surviving and winning might give them a chance. Idiots, he thought. Let them drown.

"You." A sergeant of marines, who quite definitely hadn't been there a moment ago. He was terrifying; six feet tall, parade armour polished to a blinding finish, a real soldier rather than a convict in fancy dress; had the lunatic *volunteered* for this, or was he here because he'd been given no choice by a court martial? Not that that mattered, either. He was very frightening, but not nearly as frightening as a billion gallons of water.

Teudel wasn't a fighter, never had been. But the sergeant was closing on him, and the dead paceman had a sword. He was lying on it, which didn't help, and he was no featherweight. Teudel hauled him out of the way just in time, drew the sword and took two long paces back. Water was spurting in through the hole in the side, from which the horrible iron beak had just withdrawn, but nobody seemed prepared to acknowledge the fact.

Old proverb; only idiots fight on board a sinking ship. Well.

The sergeant lashed out at him; a massive blow, propelled by the biggest arm he'd ever seen, an arm like a leg; negated and rendered entirely safe by taking a step backwards. The sword sliced the air in a whistling arc, just as the ship lurched and shifted, its balance compromised by the incoming water. Teudel dropped his sword, flung both arms in the air and managed to brace his hands against the decking overhead. The sergeant, recovering for another haymaker cut, toppled forward and brained himself against a vacant bench.

Time to go; all very well saying that, but how was he supposed to get out of this thing? His feet were under water. Obviously, you're not supposed to get out; they intend you to stay here, keep rowing, drown. He remembered; they'd come in through a hatch, which was closed, probably bolted or nailed down. No other way out, except for the monstrous gash in the side. No chance of getting through there. If he tried, the jet of water coming in through it would probably splatter him onto the bulkhead.

Why is nobody else panicking except me? But they weren't. They were still rowing, God help us all, with no paceman and no sergeant-at-arms, and the ship doing its best to roll onto its side, like a cow about to calve. Exact replica of a Second Kingdom man o'war, he'd heard them say. The bilge pump wasn't invented until the Fourth Kingdom. Indeed. Just possible that his fellow criminals hadn't done a year of military history at the Institute and didn't know that. But they had eyes, and possibly even brains. Ah well.

The ship lurched again. His hands slid nine inches before he could stop himself; he felt splinters go in to his palms, which made him flinch. The poor fools on the right were up to their knees now, barely able to row because they couldn't slide their arses on the bench. But the left side had lifted up quite some way; the left-side oarsmen were straining, presumably only their blades in the water. In which case—

He had to judge it just right, because if he got it wrong, he'd probably bash his own head in. Unfortunately, he had absolutely no data on which to base any form of geometrical calculations. The next lurch would break his grip. Hell. He let go, staggered, crouched and threw himself sideways.

He didn't see any of what came next. The idea was, to throw himself onto an oar, crawl along it out through the oar-port and then, since the left-side oars were lifted up and clear of the water, simply drop off, splash, start swimming. It can't have happened like that. Something hit his shoulder a terrific crack, so that his whole left arm went numb; but his head—his eyes were shut, but he knew by the movement of the air and the wet chill of spray on his cheek; his head was *outside*. Sod it, he thought, and kicked with his feet. He felt an unendurable pressure on his back, surely enough to snap his spine like a twig. It stopped. He was falling. Something whacked him. Water. Then he started to drown.

No, the hell with that, I can *swim*. One arm out of action hindered him, but not as much as he'd have thought. He kicked with both feet, clawed with his right arm. Something huge and horribly charged with momentum swished past very close to his head. Oar-blades, for crying out loud. Sure and sudden death, thrashing about trying to swat him. Wishing he had a little air in his lungs, he dived down out of the way.

It's not fair, he thought, I only want to stay alive. You've changed your tune, said a voice in his head. Well, yes.

A huge mass—an island, or a continent—loomed over him; swimming the wrong way, under the ship, stupid. An impartial mathematician inside his head carried out the necessary calculations and told him that, with no air in him, it was completely impossible for him to get to the surface before he either passed out or gave in and filled his lungs with water. Sorry, and all that. He jacknifed—his left arm was still dead; thank you so much— and flailed his legs. Accepted, that he wouldn't get there in time; but, just for a laugh, let's see how far he could get. Halfway? Two thirds? Bet you. He rose, the man who swallowed a volcano, through the roots of a forest, which turned out to be oars as he smashed through into the light.

For a period of time not susceptible of measurement he stood in the water, head in the air, and gasped. He felt like he was burning up, as though he'd just swallowed a gorse bush, as though each draught of air came wrapped in brambles, nettles and bees. An oar-blade swung over his head, dripping water in his eyes. The water, incidentally, was foul, slightly oily, tasted disgusting; he had a good mind to write to his Representative about it. He opened his eyes (he'd closed them against the dripping water and the cruelty of the light) and saw a steel beak coming straight at him.

Sledgehammer and nut, surely; that great big warship, just to ram insignificant him. It was horribly wide, with pulverising oars twelve feet long on either side. Its wake ran ahead of it like the way cloth tears. Nothing for it but to go back down there again. This time, he took a deep, deep breath.

So much better when you take some air with you. He let himself sink for two seconds, then did a few dance steps to hold station. Overhead, the ship cruised silently past—he wondered, would that be what a god looks like, vast, unstoppable, murderous, oblivious, going about its self-ordained purpose way up there where the important stuff happens? He took his best guess, then swam slowly up. His left arm was back in business; it had come to life again at some point, and he hadn't noticed. It probably hurt, but he wasn't sure.

He aimed for a floating plank of wood that turned out to be a dead man when he tried to climb onto it; the corpse bobbed and turned over, shedding him—thanks, you were a great help. He looked around. There were ships, one stuck deep in another, a safely long way away, thirty, forty yards. In the other direction, a clear, uncluttered line to the edge of the lake, and the solid wall of his fellow citizens, who'd come to eat pistachios and watch him die. He hesitated. If he swam to shore, he'd be—*safe* bubbled up in his mind, but a bubble is an illusion, you think it's solid and real but it pops, leaving nothing behind. *Not* safe. There had been a generally-accepted communal hope in the holding pen the night before; the survivors will get a free pardon and go home. Had anybody actually said as much? No, and if they had, you'd be crazy to believe them. An amnesty, in keeping with the spirit of goodwill and joy, was possible; so was a five-legged mule. Come on, Teudel, you're supposed to be clever. Think of something.

But he couldn't; and as he bobbed in the water trying and failing, a twenty-foot spar drifted up and nudged his thigh. He let it sidle past him, then threw his right arm over it and cuddled up grimly. They'd come round, of course, when it was all over, in boats; fish out the floaters who came quietly, bash the rest over the head. Try as he might, he couldn't think of a way round that; except—

He groaned. Do I really have to? Sorry, yes.

He peered over his spar. Sixty yards towards the centre of the lake was a ship. It looked in reasonable shape—not listing too much, moving rather than drifting. Its ensign was Imperial red, not Vesani white. Another survey suggested that the proceedings were winding down. He could only see four ships; three red, one white, and the white had a red grappled up on either side. The third red, the one he'd picked as his possible salvation, was hanging back, catching its breath. He let go of the spar, calculated an approximate bearing, and dived.

For a long time he was sure he'd gone astray and missed the bloody thing; then, just as he was about to give up and head for the surface, he saw it, belly of a leaf-shaped sea monster, up and left a bit. He headed up and broke water a yard or so off the stern, arm's length from the starboard rudder. He hooked his fingers round the rudder's blade and let it take responsibility for him.

At one point during the long drift that followed, he was sure a man on the ship saw him; identified him as alive, frowned, confused as to what to do (man overboard, yes, but did normal protocols apply?) decided it wasn't his problem, looked away. Other than that, just tedium and catching up on the pain, which he'd neglected for some time. Actually, the pain (more or less everything hurt) didn't seem to matter; it was an ocean of pain, and he floated on it, drawing reassurance from it that he was still alive. The only thing he objected to was the pounding headache, because it got in the way of thinking. Not much to think about right now, though, so no excessively big deal. The next bit, he knew, was going to be really hard, and he was in no hurry to start. Relax, therefore, enjoy the pull of the ship and the company of the pain, because quite soon enough it's going to be bloody.

The oars had been shipped and the galley was drifting gently to shore. Close enough now that the roar of the crowd was breaking up into different sounds—chanting, singing, a lot of general yelling; some laughter, which he was inclined to take personally. Twenty yards or so away, there were people drinking twelve-trachy-a-quart white wine, gobbling cashews and spitting out the shells, maybe so caught up in their conversations that they missed the good bits (ships colliding, wood splintering, men torn in half, men dying). At some later date he would definitely come back and slaughter the lot of them, cheerfully and deliberately, while eating a chicken salad. For now, though, he hoped with all his heart and soul that their attention was elsewhere. He let his feet trail, as though his legs were paralysed, until a bump against his toes told him he was practically there. Second Kingdom galleys were wonderful for the shallowness of their draught; float on a puddle of spit, the old builders used to say. They could sail in through the harbour and up the main canal practically to the watergate of the Old Palace. A gentle shudder. Close enough, he decided. He let go of the rudder, drew in as much air as he could, and dived one more time.

He followed the line of the keel and found the sternpost. It was all precision stuff from now on, and he'd be guessing all the way.

The idea was that the point where the sternpost meets the water was a blind spot. If he stayed right in close to it, the people on the shore couldn't see him, and neither could anyone aboard the ship. He'd be vulnerable to boats out on the lake, but a head is a fairly small object, easily lost against the dark wood of the ship or mistaken for some other kind of flotsam. Stay put until it gets dark, then go ashore. Simple. Simple but very difficult and dangerous. For one thing, there was nothing to hold on to, so he'd have to tread water for hours and hours. No tides on an artificial lake, but plenty of backwash from the ship, other ships, boats, which caused him to bob up and down when he particularly wanted to keep still, because a moving object is so much easier to notice. Also, he was horribly, horribly tired, and there was a very real danger he might drop off to sleep; only for a moment, but that could easily be enough for him to drift out where he could be seen. The more he thought about it, the greater the odds stacked against him—wouldn't it be so much more sensible to give in now, let himself be seen and picked up, or just sink down under the water and take a good, deep breath? He couldn't help but consider the value of the life he'd been fighting so long, so hard to save. Worth it? A joke. Teudel; son of a clerk, on the far periphery of a good family; an educated man, got into the Institute, but thrown out for petty theft and dishonesty; discovered quite by accident that he had a certain degree of artistic flair and manual dexterity, just enough to enable him to engrave a coining die with a passable copy of the emperor's head and the eagle-and-thunderbolt. Good money in counterfeit coins, excuse the pun. He'd learnt about standards and trussels, trefoils, martlets and die rotations. His mistake had been the understandable urge to improve on the original. The official portrait of the late unlamented emperor on the gold solidus had made him look like a constipated goat. Teudel's version was rather more flattering. At his trial the judge had joked that he wasn't sure whether to send him to the gallows or the Mint. Only kidding. Executions backed up nine months, shortage of qualified hangmen, typical government inefficiency. A life worth struggling for? Well, quite.

But then, he thought (terrible pain in his legs; if cramp were to set in, he'd be finished) what about money? Copper has its uses, but gold's no good for anything, too soft, too heavy; you could use it in plumbing, or flashing for roofs, but you'd have to work a lifetime up to your waist in a river to get enough to make two feet of water pipe. But roll it into a sheet, punch out a bucketful of discs, put the discs between two dies, whack the top die with a hammer; stoop to pick up the result, suddenly you're holding wealth equivalent to a small house or ten oxen or four carriage horses; the breathtaking miracle of reverse alchemy, which turns a small flattened blob of gold into any God's amount of mundane but useful dross. What makes gold valuable is the struggle, the effort you put in to get it, the two years your average working man would have to give you before you paid him one gold solidus. Well, mostly gold; six parts in ten these days, thanks to the war, or five parts if it's one of Teudel's (though the artwork would be better). On that basis; such a life is worthless, unless and until given value by the effort to keep it. Nice thinking, Teudel. Thank you.

The people were going home now, he could tell by the pitch and volume of their voices. He could picture them getting to their feet, looking around for their possessions, picking up their nutshells and apple cores and empty bottles. Far out to his right he could see a small boat. But it'd only take one over-observant bastard looking back just as he was climbing out of the water; a shout, a pointing finger, kettlehats running, and all that endurance and resourcefulness gone to waste. Unless—

Why the hell not? Taking a deep breath, he dived again, swum wearily under the hull until he found the anchor chain. It was nearly as thick as his waist—clearly they took no chances back in the Second Kingdom. There was a gap between the chain and the hull, easily enough to squeeze into. He started to climb, each link a convenient ladder-rung, the chain between him and the shore, hiding him almost perfectly from sight. A reckless swing, grab and heave to get him over the rail; he was banking on the ship being deserted, the survivors having been marched away, the regular navy not yet arrived to take charge. His luck was in; he hadn't been seen. Now for the imaginative part—

He scrambled up onto the rail, as if engaged in some authentic nautical task involving rigging; leaned back a little, waggled his arms, rocked on his heels until he lost his balance, fell backwards overboard with a pitiful wail. Hit the water head-first, nearly knocked himself out (careless), came up spitting water and cursing; trod water for a moment or so, then breaststroked to shore, squelched dejectedly onto dry land, head down. And what did they all see? A shamefaced sailor who's just fallen off his own ship with everybody looking.

He kept going—squelch, squelch, every water-seeping footstep now a witness for the defence rather than the prosecution—as far as the corner of Tanneries and Fletchers'. Left into Tanneries, left again into the first narrow ginnel. A wonderful place, the square quarter-mile just north of the Tanneries. You can do pretty much anything you want; a hundred people will see you do it, but if the kettlehats come asking, it'd be *never seen this man before in my life*. Provided you've got nothing worth stealing and you don't tread on someone's foot, it's one of the freest, safest places in the world.

But not for long. People move quickly there; they hardly ever run, but they walk fast and purposefully, eyes straight ahead, relying on peripheral vision to warn them of danger.

The trouble with your son (said the Governor of the Institute, when implored by his mother to give him another chance) is that he's thoroughly corrupt, right down to the core. Whenever he's called upon to choose a course of action, he'll always opt for dishonesty and deceit, even if the honest path would be easier and safer. He's not criminal through force of circumstance, but by inclination and choice.

Harsh words; mostly fair. Four blocks away, in the wall of an outhouse in the back yard of the *Integrity Rewarded*, there was a loose brick behind which he'd stashed twenty-seven best-quality reproduction solidi. The irony was that those coins contained eleven full ounces of pure, honest gold; a fortune, enough to set a man up for life. Not his gold, admittedly; it belonged to his backers, but two of them had been in the galley with him and were presumably now at the bottom of the lake, and the other three had to be long gone by now. They wouldn't begrudge him. Well, they would, but tough. It'd be a desperate waste of his courage and determination if his intention to start a new, better life was frustrated at the outset for want of a little liquidity.

He'd forgotten that the brick needed a lever to get it out. He sneaked into the kitchen of the *Integrity* and borrowed a spoon, which he somehow neglected to put back.

THE RECEPTION WAS held in the Royal Gallery, that awkward and unprofitable space that runs the entire length of the west wing of the palace. For a thousand years, the heirs of Florian haven't really known what to do with it. Florian III commissioned a series of narrative frescos for it, which were paid for but never finished. Gratian I had them panelled over and used the gallery to display his celebrated collection of erotic sculpture. Venseric sent the sculptures to the limekilns and turned the gallery into an indoor archery range. Mardimer simply dustsheeted it and closed it down. Heriman housed the Studium library in it for a while, until the New Building was completed. Florian VI kept his private menagerie there, until a tiger got loose and mauled the Mezentine ambassador. Clensimer lined it with portraits of himself. Hodda had it emptied, cleaned up and redecorated, then left it empty. So far, Sechimer hadn't set foot in it, though he'd talked about getting some icons and making it into a sort of fully-enclosed cloister, for meditation and silent prayer. Nobody else seemed particularly keen on the idea, and as yet no formal proposals had gone to the Works Committee.

For the victory reception, however, it was ideal. The guests came up the grand front staircase, past the portraits of the emperors and the death-masks of defeated kings, while the domestic staff had a clear run up and down the privy stair to the kitchens and the wine cellars. The weather was still pleasantly warm, so the nightmare issue of heating the dreadful place didn't arise. There were just enough tables in the whole palace to line the inside wall, allowing guests to stroll up and down the gallery or walk out onto the balconies for a breath of air and the undiscriminating adulation of the huge crowd gathered in Deacon's Yard.

As a member of the regency council, Aimeric had to be there half an hour before the start; he was rushed back from the sea-battle in a covered coach, scrambled to get changed into his robes of state—invented specially for the occasion, a tribute to rather than an imitation of the imperial regalia;

a massive black wool dressing-gown embroidered with a thousand baroque seed-pearls, a white ermine mantle and a cloth-of-gold sort-of-scarf-thing that had to be pinned ruthlessly to the mantle to keep it from escaping and winding itself round his feet. Then just enough time for a quart of water (essential not to get dehydrated on these occasions) before the stewards came to escort him to the gallery.

He met his fellow councillors in the Ivory ante-room. They looked up as he was shown in, then went on talking to each other. Aimeric leaned against a statue and tried to adjust his shoes, which were worth at least 500 solidi in materials alone and which didn't fit. Chancellor Maerving detached himself from the group, came over and smiled at him. "How do you like the fancy dress?" he asked.

"It's horrible."

"Quite," Maerving said. "Mind you, count yourself lucky, I had to wear the real thing. I now have a new theory."

"Oh yes?"

Maerving nodded. "The imperial regalia is expressly designed to deter people from becoming emperor. Trust me, it wouldn't be worth it." He ran a finger between his scarf and his neck. "This pale imitation's bad enough. We were just discussing how you're supposed to pee without taking the whole lot off."

"Did you reach a conclusion?"

"Not yet. We decided to appoint a sub-committee. Talking of which, would you like a drink before we go down?"

Aimeric shook his head. "You're the chancellor," he said. "I thought the empire was essentially bankrupt."

Maerving nodded cheerfully. "It is."

"Right. Then how can we afford all this *junk*?"

Maerving smiled. "No choice. All this junk is to give foreigners the impression we're not bankrupt. You wait till you see the dinner service. All solid gold, and everyone gets to keep his cup and plate and take it home with him. I had to close down the Ordnance Survey to pay for it, but it'll be worth it, I promise you."

Aimeric shrugged. "What about all the war loot? I read in despatches we'd captured the Great King's treasury."

"We did. Calojan gave it to his savages. I got the impression that if he hadn't, they'd have taken it anyway Believe me," he added with a smile, "whatever rumours you may have heard about the financial situation, the truth is much, much worse. Come and have a honeycake, before the ravening hordes descend on them."

Hordes was about right. Aimeric was in the front rank as the guests advanced; he wondered how the hell people like Calojan did it, stand and watch a wall of hostile strangers advancing. He knew without a shadow of a doubt that he'd squirm his way out and run for it, so fast that not even the Aram Cosseilhatz on their tall, slim warhorses would be able to catch him. In the gallery, however, there was nowhere to run to except a balcony, ten stories up. He anchored his feet to the floor and raised a smile, like a mighty shield.

Actually, it wasn't that bad, after a while. First chance he got, he drifted sideways towards the food (Carchedonius in his *Art of War* recommends a similar manoeuvre using marshland, broken scrub or scree; the principle was exactly the same). It wasn't fun, but it wasn't death by bastinado either. He hunkered down under the lee of the cold roast chicken and slugged it out like a man.

"Aimeric." The Archdeacon had crept up behind him. "Someone I'd like you to meet." He turned and found himself practically nose to nose with a small, slim, bald man, brown skin and eyes, dressed in a white gown with a raised gilded collar. "Aimeric de Peguilhan, Orseo Spatharius. Dr Spatharius is the Mezentine charge d'affaires. He knew your father quite well."

Which was more than I did. "Pleased to meet you," Aimeric said. "Presumably—"

"Your father and I did business together on a number of occasions," the Mezentine said. "I remember him fondly. I was most distressed to hear that he had passed away."

Aimeric had no idea what to say to that. "So you must be in the arms business."

The wrong thing. "Not really," the Mezentine said, while the Archdeacon frowned slightly. "As well as my diplomatic post, I hold the agency for the sheet metal workers' guild. We supplied your father with best quality brass and latten embossing stock, for decorative work. My country doesn't sell arms to foreigners, you see."

"No, you keep them all for yourselves," the Archbishop interrupted cheerfully. "Which is probably why his late majesty the Great King left you in peace and came pestering us; thank you so much. Not that we could afford any of your stuff anyway. It's way over-specified for the modern battlefield. I keep telling you, the days of small, highly-trained standing armies are long gone. I mean, look at this last scrap. The Great King had the best regular infantry in the world, marvellous chaps, brave as lions and do exactly what they're told. And what happened? Calojan's savages rode up behind them and shot them to hell. All that training, effort, discipline, esprit de corps, all that stuff, not worth a light. Three solidi; that's how much it cost to equip one Sashan heavy infantryman. Sixty thousand solidi in kit and weapons alone. Fat lot of good it did them."

The Mezentine smiled bleakly. "I would tend to agree that the armoured footsoldier has probably had his day. In Mezentia, we're very interested in exploring the potential of mobile field artillery."

The Archdeacon laughed. Could it possibly be that he wasn't quite as steady on his feet as he usually was? "Oh, that old chestnut. Why send a man where you can send catapult shot instead? They were saying that back in the Third Kingdom, and look what happened to them."

The Mezentine took a small but ostentatious step backwards, to just outside the range of the Archdeacon's breath. Aimeric smiled widely and tried to think of something else to talk about. "Doctor Spatharius," he said. "You're a medical man, then."

Weary smirk from the Mezentine. "Doctor of divinity," he said. "I have the honour to be a minister of the Central United Congregation. I also lecture on ethical theory and predictive science at the guild seminary. All of which means I couldn't set a broken arm if you paid me."

"Predictive science?" Aimeric asked.

"Fortune telling." The Archdeacon had a wonderful way with tolerant contempt. "The Mezentines still believe in all that stuff, but these days they have to dress it up in geometry and algebra. They draw these extraordinary charts—"

"It goes without saying," the Mezentine said firmly, "we do *not* purport to tell fortunes, predict the future, anything of the kind. It amuses our friends in the Studium to pretend that we do, but that's just their humour. What we actually do is use proven mathematical models to analyse patterns in human behaviour, looking for archetypes that might conceivably repeat under certain rigidly defined circumstances."

"Fortune telling," the Archdeacon muttered. "Bobbing for apples and cross my palm with silver. Still, we used to do it, six hundred years ago, so I guess we're in no position to criticise."

It was rather splendid to watch the Mezentine keeping his temper; like seeing a first-class sheepdog at work. "Funny you should mention that," he said. "A month or so ago we found some really quite fascinating manuscripts in the Congregation archives. I had them copied for you. I think you might find them amusing."

A waiter was hovering with a tray of canapes. Aimeric smiled at him and took a selection. For a moment he was sure he recognised the man's face. When he looked back, he was surprised to see the look on the Archdeacon's face. "You wouldn't happen to be talking about the Codex Synergicus, by any chance?"

"You heard about it, then." The Mezentine was enjoying himself.

"Rumours," the Archdeacon said. "But surely—"

"A complete copy," said the Mezentine. "Of the second collected rescension. We have a respectable provenance, before you ask."

"The *second* rescension—"

"Quite." Very smug. "At least seventy-five years earlier than any other recorded manuscript." Suddenly he smiled, or at least he opened his mouth and showed his teeth. An ambiguous gesture. "Such a shame that there are no surviving manuscripts inside the empire. Tell me, is possession of a copy still a criminal offence? If so, I wouldn't dream of compromising you with such an unwelcome gift."

"I have a special dispensation," the Archdeacon said, quickly and urgently.

"But no actual manuscripts?"

"No."

Aimeric could resist no longer. "Excuse me," he said. "What exactly are you talking about?"

He'd obviously made the Mezentine's day. "Perhaps you'd better tell him," he said to the Archdeacon. "One sceptic to another."

The archdeacon glowered briefly, then turned to Aimeric. "The Codex Synergeticus is a Second Kingdom collection of prophetic texts—"

"Fortune telling," murmured the Mezentine under his breath.

"Purporting," the archdeacon went on, "to predict a number of key events in the history of the empire. According to the sources, some of them were alleged to have proved uncannily accurate."

"Speculation and reconstruction," the Mezentine interrupted. "Your scholars don't actually know what was in the texts, because your emperor Florian V had them all called in and burned."

"Ah," Aimeric said.

"Apparently," the Mezentine went on, "he took the view that an obsessive level of interest and belief in the prophesies wasn't conducive to public order and good governance. Whenever there was a crisis, all anybody was interested in was, what do the prophecies say? Also, according to some commentators, most of them were so ambiguous and vague, they could be twisted to mean whatever you wanted them to. Florian V decided the empire would be better off without them." He paused and smiled. "Fortuitously, a number of copies, obtained by scholars and spies over the years, are believed to exist in other parts of the world. The Great King, for example, was rumoured to have a set, though as I understand it, general Calojan was unable to locate it."

"They burned it before he could get to it."

"Indeed. Most unfortunate. Our discovery is, therefore, quite a find. So, on the strict understanding that we aren't breaking any laws, or inadvertently encouraging His Majesty's loyal subjects to break them, we're delighted to be able to make a copy available to you. Free of charge," he added, "as a gesture of goodwill. Purely as a historical curiosity, of course, since we all know that predicting the future is impossible."

The Archdeacon had gone bright red in the face. He lowered his voice. "You've got to tell me," he said. "Does it really say—?"

"All in good time," the Mezentine replied briskly. "You can read it for yourself and see. Talking of which," he added smoothly, "how is the emperor?"

As if he'd slapped the Archdeacon across the face. "Recovering," he said. "Excellent progress."

"Ah." The Mezentine nodded. "I'm afraid I find the daily bulletins somewhat confusing, although," he continued with a smile, "I'm not a doctor of medicine. But I do have some slight acquaintance with the subject, and I have to say, his progress doesn't appear to conform to any recognised model of cranial injury or post-operative infection. One day he's nearly well and walking in his garden, the next he's recovering peacefully after a severe bout of fever. The danger, I can't help noticing, is always in the past, in the interval between bulletins. Perhaps if they were read out in the evening instead of the morning, we'd get a better idea."

"Excellent progress," the archdeacon repeated stiffly. "He's being attended by the Great King's personal physician, probably the finest doctor in the world."

"Whose late master's head you cut off only the other day." The Mezentine nodded. "I'm not sure our doctors would be so forgiving. But the Sashan are—sorry, were—such curious people. We never did get around to understanding them." He smiled. "Fortunately, we no longer need to try."

"The truth is," the Archdeacon hissed in Aimeric's ear, a bit later, when the Mezentine was talking to somebody else, "the emperor's perfectly fit now, but—" He lowered his voice even further. "The trouble's up here." He tapped his forehead. "Nobody home, as the saying goes. He doesn't recognise anybody, doesn't know who he is, just sits there all day staring out of the window. He'll talk to you perfectly rationally for an hour about some bird he's been watching or the different shapes of cloud, but if you tell him he's the emperor, he just laughs at you. The Sashan says it's a recognised condition and he should just snap out of it at some point; trouble is, there's no guarantee of that, and there's nothing anybody can do for him. It could be a week, or he could stay like it for the rest of his life. Terrible thing; to have won the war and saved civilisation, and not to be able to understand what you've achieved."

"I can imagine," Aimeric said.

"Can you? I can't. And of course, none of us has the faintest idea what to do. Maerving's all for putting him out of his misery and choosing a new emperor, but at the moment that's out of the question. The only candidate everyone would follow is Calojan, who's made it perfectly clear he doesn't want the job; furthermore, if anything happens to Sechimer—accident, illness, whatever—he'll personally see to it that the entire regency council will meet with similar misfortune. So, you see, we're in a dreadful mess."

Aimeric wasn't feeling well. "He is all right, isn't he? Sechimer."

"Like I said, fit as a flea, physically. Just—" He made a vague gesture. "Couldn't have picked a worse time, really. There's so much that needs to be done, and who's got to do it?" he pulled a face. "Us, God help us. It's an unprecedented state of affairs. Not even like a proper regency. At least then, you know that on a certain hour of a certain day, the little horror will come of age and from then on everything will be his fault, not yours. This—it's so open-ended, it's impossible to formulate a coherent policy. Nobody's really in charge, everyone's principally motivated by fear of the repercussions if they propose something risky or unpopular, you've no way of knowing if you'll be in office long enough to see anything through, and you've got twelve friends and colleagues desperate to see to it that you take the blame if anything goes wrong. It's hopeless. We might as well be a republic."

Aimeric frowned. "The Vesani manage."

"No, they don't. They lurch from one crisis to another, bribe their own people to stay quiet with constant handouts and stave off disaster by borrowing obscene amounts of money from gullible foreigners, which they then neglect to pay back. And the Mezentines—well, would you want to live like that?"

"No," Aimeric admitted.

"Nor me. So, we've got to think of a way of coping with this mess before anyone finds out what's going on. If you come up with anything, be sure to tell me."

Aimeric's mind was, of course, a complete blank. So he said, "These prophesies."

"Quite. Do you really believe it's a coincidence, a complete set turning up at this precise moment?"

Aimeric did, until the Archdeacon put it like that. "No, of course not." His brain was starting to work. "Presumably Calojan destroyed the Great King's copy."

"That's what he told us. Whether or not he did remains to be seen. Well, would you, in his shoes?"

"We can use them," Aimeric said.

"Thanks, but one thing we're not short of is toilet paper."

"We can use them," Aimeric repeated. "We can reveal that the Codex—"

"Synergicus."

"The Codex predicted the course and outcome of the war," Aimeric went on, "with quite uncanny accuracy, and goes on to say—what would we like it to say, do you think?"

The Archdeacon frowned. "Good question."

"I think," Aimeric said, "the Codex predicts that on the eve of battle, the Invincible Sun will appear to Sechimer in a dream and promise him victory in the place where the red and blue flowers grow, provided that once the Sashan are defeated, he'll retire to a contemplative order and live the life of a simple monk. For an unspecified period. In his absence, the empire should be governed jointly by the most senior representatives of the House and the Studium."

"Maerving and me." The Archdeacon covered his mouth with his hand for a moment. "We'd need a really good forger," he said.

"There's someone I've heard of in the Vesani Republic," Aimeric replied. "Works for the academics at the University. They're always wanting ancient manuscripts forged, to prove some point or other. Her work's got to be good, it has to get past the best scholars in the world. I believe she uses genuine old parchment, the right inks, everything."

"I don't know," the Archdeacon said. "The thing is, we're not a superstitious nation. You could pull something like that on the Sashan. I'm not sure how it'd go down here."

"It was just a thought," Aimeric replied.

"Leave it with me, let me talk to some of the others." Only some, Aimeric noted. "I think it could work, but we'd have to go about it exactly right, or it could all end in disaster."

The waiter was back again. Aimeric looked at him thoughtfully, then beckoned to him. "I know you," he said.

"Sir."

"Didn't you use to work for me?"

"Yes, sir."

"That's right." Aimeric nodded. "I remember the foreman pointing you out, said you were a hell of a good worker, turn your hand to anything."

"Yes, sir. Thank you, sir."

"What's your name?"

"Raffen, sir."

"That's right. What are you still doing here? I thought all you people had gone home."

"Not all of us, sir."

"Ah well. Good luck, anyway. Yes, I think I'll have one of the cheesy ones, and is that salmon?"

"I couldn't say, sir."

The waiter started to withdraw. On an impulse, Aimeric waved him back. "Look," he said, "if ever you're after a job, come and see me. I'm sure we can find you something."

"Thank you, sir."

The Archdeacon nudged his elbow. "All right," he said, "we'll try it." He took Aimeric's arm and towed him, like a barge, further out into the room. "Maerving'll be a bloody nuisance, as always, but I can deal with him later. Where's that bastard Mezentine got to? We need those documents."

Aimeric glanced across the room. The Mezentine wasn't hard to find, the only brown face in the room; but before he could point him out to the Archdeacon, a bell sounded and Chancellor Maerving strode out into an open space just under the rose window at the far end. Everyone was looking. Maerving held up his hand and smiled, and the room fell silent.

"Friends and honoured guests." He wasn't shouting, but his voice was perfectly clear. They'd understood about acoustics back in Florian's time. "I've just been handed a letter from the emperor, which I would like to read out to you." He paused, to give everyone time to settle into a posture of serious attention. "He says; I am sorry that my illness prevents me from being with you tonight. I would have liked to thank many of you personally for the important parts you played in ending the war and preserving the empire and our way of life."

(Aimeric leaned close to the Archdeacon. "Nicely put."

"Thank you.")

"The threat we faced," Maerving went on, "was nothing less than total annihilation. For three hundred years, it has been the avowed intention of the Sashan to wipe us off the face of the earth. The Great King boasted that he would stand on Gratian's Watchtower and review his troops marching through the Perfect Square. I can report that his prophesy came true, after a fashion. The few survivors of the Royal guard were paraded in the Square yesterday morning. The Great King's head hung by its hair from the tower battlements. I think it was Saloninus who warned that prophesies tend to take on a life of their own."

General laughter; during which Aimeric whispered; "Oh dear."

"We may have to leave that bit out of the published version."

"We didn't start the war," Maerving went on. "We did, however, finish it, once and for all. It has been a terrible ordeal. It is during such times, however, that we find out who we truly are. The ore goes into the fire, the dross burns away, the pure metal is left behind. We are left with the genius and devoted service of general Calojan, the courage and endurance of our citizens, the undiminished glory of the empire. By this dreadful and traumatic struggle, we have not only defeated the Sashan, we have also vanquished war itself. To the west, we see only loyal and steadfast friends. To the east, we see the former subjects of the Great King, freed from centuries of tyranny and oppression by our courage and sacrifice. Quite simply, there is no-one left to fight; no-one with any possible complaint against us, no-one strong enough to pose us a credible threat. To our glorious dead, and those who sadly but proudly mourn them, I say this. To have saved the empire is a marvellous thing. To have ended not just this war but war itself is a gift for which future generations will praise and honour you to the end of time. The night is over. A wonderful day waits for us. Humbly and gratefully, we accept that the world is ours. Thank you."

"Good stuff," Aimeric said, raising his voice over the general applause.

"Not all mine," the archdeacon confessed. "But who reads Didactylus these days? Quick, the Mezentine's getting away. Be a good fellow, run across and head him off at the door."

WHEN THE RECEPTION was over, the gallery had been cleared, the trash and uneaten food carted away, the floor scrubbed and waxed and the borrowed furniture put back where it came from, the deputy chief steward of the bedchamber sent a clerk and two kettlehats down to the back courtyard behind the stables, where the casual staff hired for the occasion had been rounded up and told to wait. They filed past a folding table, and each one was given a little twist of cloth holding fifty-five trachy, to include a five trachy bonus because everything went so well. "Don't spend it all at once," the clerk joked. Then the workers were herded out through the service gate, which was locked and bolted behind them.

Raffen sat down on the steps of the Recovery temple, unwrapped the cloth and spread the coins around on the palm of his hand. The sun was just rising. Yesterday afternoon, before reporting for work, he'd given her all the money he had left; four hundred trachy. You're sure you don't want to come with us, she'd said. He'd shaken his head. Then she walked away.

He looked up at the red edges of the clouds. All in all, he didn't think he liked the City very much. At first he'd assumed it was just the noise, the confined spaces, the quite ridiculous number of people, jammed together for no obvious purpose—and the smell, let's not forget that. But he hadn't been aware of the smell for a month, just as he no longer noticed the stares and scowls of the people. It was the flooding that had done it, he decided. Such a very strange thing to do; drive the poorest and weakest people out of their homes for the sake of one day of pointless waste and killing. He reminded himself that something like that had happened to the other one, in another place, but it wasn't quite the same. *The city doesn't like me*, he thought, *it's as simple as that.*

The great lord, the tall, broad-shouldered young man who owned the weapons factory, had offered him a job. Well, then. One good thing to be said about this place, it positively bristled with opportunities. Back home, outside of harvest and haymaking, a man could spend a month going from door to door before he found work, assuming he didn't die of shame first.

Back home; no such place. He tumbled the coins back into the cloth and screwed it up tight. He still wasn't entirely sure what thirty-five trachy *meant*. A man with a hammer and two feet of copper wire could make himself a sackful of the things, and nobody ever looked closely at them. Yes, but in the time it'd take, you could earn yourself a sackful of the real thing; and it'd still only buy you a loaf of bread and a beer.

He stood up. Nobody much about at this time of day. He walked towards the fountain, to drink and wash his face. He hadn't gone ten yards when something hit him between the shoulder-blades, and he fell forward.

Not something, someone. There was a man, no, two men. At first he assumed they'd seen him go down and had come to help. Then one of them kicked him in the ribs. Luckily he wasn't very good at it, and nothing broke. The other one had got hold of his right hand and was trying to prise it open. Suddenly it dawned on Raffen that they were thieves, trying to steal his fifty-five stupid trachy.

He opened his right hand wide. The thief snatched the scrap of cloth; he and his comrade-in-arms backed away. They looked terrified, Raffen realised, but he couldn't help that. He gave them long measure, then sprang to his feet and took a long stride left, so that the left-hand man effectively shielded him from anything the right-hand man might choose to do. A fist swished through empty air a good six inches from his face as he stamped on the left-hand man's knee. Then, as the man went down, he leaned over him, easily avoided an attempt to deflect his arm, stuck his thumb in the right-hand man's throat (the hollow above where the collar-bones meet) clamped his fingers on the nape of his neck and closed his hand as hard as he could. He felt something squash and give way, so he took two short steps backwards, putting him in good position as the first thief started to get up. He kicked him very hard on the point of the chin, rocking his head back and snapping his neck.

Idiots, he thought.

He looked at them properly for the first time. One of them, the one who'd grabbed the coins, was a boy, fifteen or sixteen, short and skinny. The other was sixty-five to seventy, bald, tall; the skin had been loose around his neck, in flaps. The boy had dropped the money. He moved off to one side, just in case the boy was only shamming dead, and picked it up. No, not shamming. Presumably they'd seen him looking at the coins just now. In which case, surely, they'd have known he only had copper money, trash. Idiots.

I'm not a thief, he remembered someone saying. There are depths to which one does not stoop, no matter what. Back in the place the other one called home, you could make your peace with the family of someone you'd killed with a certain weight of silver (and you paid promptly and without haggling, regardless of whether you or the dead man was to blame) but thieves were slaughtered out of hand, immediately and with the minimum of fuss. It occurred to him to wonder if they did things differently here.

Just in case they did, he walked quickly away, down an alley, right at one intersection, left at another. He had no idea where he was, but he had a knack of finding his way again in these mazes; he guessed it came from living in the woods. He slowed down and turned himself into an aimless night-time stroller; plenty of those, in a place where you had to pay someone money in order to lie down and sleep.

All a question of value, he told himself. Nine ounces of silver is worth a farm worker, unmarried, under the age of twenty-one. A palmful of copper foil scraps is worth one day's labour. Fifty-five copper foil scraps is worth dying for. Thieves are worthless. The use of eighteen inches of a wooden shelf in a tavern outbuilding for one night is worth the same as half a day's unskilled labour in the arms factory or three quarts of really bad wine. Civilisation is worth the lives of a quarter of a million men, the homes of immigrant workers are worth fifty-two trachy a day but nothing as against one day's worth of public spectacle. Seventy-six loaves of bread equal one cart horse, three days of a working man's life are equivalent to a pair of shoes, three pairs of shoes make up a carpenter's plane. Who decided all this, for crying out loud?

He'd heard someone say that if you didn't have anywhere to sleep, there was a window round the back of the Golden Spire temple that didn't close properly. The Golden Spire was in Oldgate, which was three-quarters of the way up the steep hill—easy to find your way around the city if you simply pretended the buildings weren't there and thought of it as open country. He formed a mental picture and started to walk.

For once, something he'd overheard turned out to be perfectly true. He opened the window, climbed through and groped around in the dark until he found something that felt like a table, with a cloth over it. He lay down on the table, pulled the cloth over him up to his chin, and went straight to sleep.

The daylight woke him, flooding through an impossibly tall window made up of hundreds of little panes of coloured glass; he was lying in a pool of colour, his hands stained red, green and yellow, even a tiny splash of blue. He'd never been inside a temple before so he didn't know what any of it meant, but every square inch of the cloth he'd been lying under was stiff with embroidery, gold and silver wire. He squirmed out from under it, before anyone caught him, and looked round anxiously. Nobody home. There were other, smaller tables grouped all round the one he'd been sleeping on, and they were covered in great big jugs, plates and bowls, gold and silver. Probably a good idea to get out of there quickly, before someone mistook him for a thief. He gazed round, but had no idea which way he'd come in by; there were doors everywhere in this enormous space, but (as far as he knew) only one defective window to get out through.

It wasn't a good situation to be in. He tried half a dozen doors at random. Two of them led into small, narrow rooms with desks and stools and ledgers and inkwells. One of them was crammed with racks of the most extraordinary clothes. One of them was a latrine, and not a very good one. The other two were store-rooms, lined with shelves crowded with even more silver and gold tableware. None of them had any windows at all.

He was in the second treasury room when he heard voices, somewhere in the vast main hall. He froze. This wasn't a good place to be found in. Voices, however, implied that someone had come in from outside, which in turn implied an open door leading to the real world. Very carefully he opened the door two fingers' breadth and peered through the crack.

Five men. Immediately and instinctively he assessed them for their tactical value; four of them were old, fat or both, but the fifth looked big and strong. Then he looked again. The big, strong man was the owner of the arms factory, who'd offered him a job a few hours earlier. One of the other four was the man he'd been talking to.

He winced. Simply rushing past them, knocking them down if necessary, was no longer an option. The factory owner had recognised him at the reception, and therefore might well recognise him again, as the man who'd assaulted him while escaping from the temple he'd been discovered burgling. That meant he should stay put, but he didn't like that idea at all; in here, with all this ridiculous gold and silver. He considered it, as best he could in the faint gleam of light that crept in through the thin slice between door and frame. Nothing to hide under, or behind. If they took it into their heads to come in here, he'd just have to bash them, run and take his chances. He knelt down, his eye to the door, and tried to breathe as quietly as possible.

AIMERIC'S HEAD WAS hurting. That was hardly fair; he'd made a point of not drinking at the reception. By contrast, the archdeacon, who'd displayed no such restraint, was being loud, cheerful and energetic. A morning person, evidently. Aimeric tried very hard to forgive him for that.

"Thank you for coming along at this appallingly early hour," the archdeacon was saying. "I thought it'd be wise for us to get together before anyone's up and about to see us."

"We're not minuting this, then," asked the City Prefect.

"Good heavens, no. And perhaps it'd be as well if we don't mention this meeting to those of our colleagues who aren't here. This is a rather delicate matter."

"I see," growled Commissioner Astigern. "You're up to something."

"But in a good cause." From inside his coat the archdeacon produced a short brass tube, so thick that his fingers didn't quite meet round it. "As I said in my somewhat cryptic message, we've been handed a problem that's also an opportunity, courtesy of the Mezentine charge d'affaires."

"Ah, right," said the Prefect. "That idiotic prophesy."

The archdeacon smiled at him. "Scripture says, blessed are those that have not seen and yet have believed. This is more a case of those who *have* seen and yet have believed, if you get my drift."

"Have you read it?" demanded the Commissioner.

"No," the archdeacon replied, "and that's why I've asked my friend and colleague suffragan Edgelath to join us." The short, gloomy man gave them all a worried smile. "He's kindly agreed to translate for us."

The Prefect lifted his head. "Translate what?"

"Ah." The archdeacon tapped one end of the tube. At the other end, the stub of a thick roll of parchment peeped out of the brass. The archdeacon tweezered it out with his fingernails, laid it down on the Middle Station altar and smoothed out eight inches or so at the top of the roll. The Prefect leaned across to look at it, then turned to the archdeacon and scowled. "It's in bloody Mezentine," he said.

"Precisely. It's a Mezentine translation of the original. I've shown it to another colleague of mine, and he confirms that the type of parchment, the style of the handwriting and the types of ink and paint used are consistent with it being Mezentine, probably two and a half to three hundred years old. Isn't that right, Edgelath?" The worried man gave a worried nod. "In particular, I'd invite you to look at this capital here. The inside curve is picked out in Mezentine blue. As I'm sure you know, that's made by grinding up a semi-precious stone only found on the volcanic island of Scona, a Mezentine protectorate. Ever since its use was discovered six hundred years ago, the Mezentines have had an absolute monopoly of Mezentine blue; its export is forbidden on pain of death, so any document whose illuminations contain it must almost certainly have been written in Mezentia."

"Agreed," said the Prefect. "The question is, when?"

The worried man cleared his throat. "If you'd care to look at the gilding of this marginal decoration." They craned their necks to see. "The Mezentines apply gold leaf in an oil base containing sal draconis. It's an excellent fixative, but it does take a very long time to stabilise, anything between fifteen and sixty years. Until it's stable, it remains very slightly tacky. The recognised test is to sprinkle a little very fine oilstone dust." He had a little silver bottle in his hand; he drew out the cork stopper and twitched his hand over the parchment, then put his head down and blew. "You'll see that all the dust's gone. If the oil hadn't stabilised, a few grains would've stuck to it. Therefore, the manuscript is at least fifteen years old."

"Which means," the archdeacon went on, "it wasn't concocted in the last year or so to meet the demands of the current diplomatic situation. We all know the Mezentines like to play the long game, but even they can't plan that far ahead. If you think what the state of play was fifteen years ago—"

"Fine," the Prefect snapped. "It's an old piece of Mezentine paper. I've got a shelf full of them. What makes you think this one's the real deal and not just some parcel of nonsense some clown thought up so his grandson could sell it to a gullible emperor?"

"That," the archdeacon said with a certain degree of dignity, "is what we're here to find out. Edgelath, if you wouldn't mind."

This is all wrong, Aimeric thought; you wouldn't get away with it at the University (he'd originally thought, *where I come from*, but of course he wasn't a student any more, so made the mental substitution). I distinctly remember Orsella telling me, Mezentine blue's not a problem any more, and isn't there that stuff you can put over sal draconis that'll dry it out just fine in a week? Then he reminded himself that he'd just recommended Orsella to the archdeacon, who might not be quite as naive as he wanted to appear to be.

"I'll skip the introduction, if you don't mind," Edgelath was saying. "Briefly, it's a dedication by a scholar, Orseo Chrysodemus, to someone called Bonones, presumably his patron; he's pleased to present him with a true translation of the celebrated Imperial prophesies known as the Codex Synergius; then a long account of how the manuscript was obtained; a corrupt official at the Golden Spire—dear me—and something about smuggling it out of the country in the coffin of a deceased Mezentine diplomat. I have to say it all reads plausibly enough."

"What about the prophesy?" the Commissioner said.

"Ah yes. Now, before I came here this morning, I took the opportunity to cast an eye over the Fifth Orthodox Sylloge—that's a summary, carried out a hundred and twenty years ago, under Genseric II, of everything known at that time about the Codex. It's still our most reliable guide. Obviously it's restricted, but—"

"And?"

Edgelath nodded. "The Sylloge refers to five specific predictions that would appear to have come true in the two centuries prior to its compilation; the Battle of Enneacrunos, two well-documented earthquakes, the First Permian war and the assassination of Florian VI. We only have what purports to be original text of about five verses concerning the Permian war. As far as I can tell,—let's see, here," (he stabbed a spot on the parchment with his fingertip) "those verses are translated here word for word. It's conceivable that whoever wrote this manuscript had access to the Epitome, or the sources on which the Epitome draws, and which are of course now lost. However, since all materials relating to the Codex have been restricted for well over—"

"That won't wash," the Prefect said. "If this thing's genuine, it's based on a copy that got stolen from Golden Spire. Therefore, Imperial security isn't watertight. Therefore, this thing could equally well be a fake."

Edgelath smiled. "Perfectly true."

"So?"

"Yes," the archdeacon snapped, "but is it *likely*? Think about it, for crying out loud. You're suggesting that fifty years ago some Mezentine decided, purely on spec, to fake the Codex, knowing it'd be a couple of generations before it could pass as genuine and be worth money to anybody. So he went to all the trouble of bribing someone in the Inner Studium to give him a genuine quote from the Sylloge—"

"More probably," Edgelath went on, "a copy of the Sylloge itself. The correlations between this manuscript and the Sylloge are very extensive."

"Well," the archdeacon said, "there you go. Think how much it'd cost in bribes to make an illegal copy of a restricted text and get it out of the country. Ask yourself; who the hell would bother? If you had access to those sort of resources, there's dozens of better things to fake, and you wouldn't have to wait fifty years before you could collect."

The Prefect shrugged. "Be that as it may."

"Objection noted," the archdeacon said impatiently. "Go on, Edgelath. What else does it say?"

The worried man gave him a sad little smile. "I think the gentleman who gave you this wished to draw your attention to this passage here," he said, pointing. "You'll see these lines here, drawn in the margin with a soapstone pencil. Quite recent, I'd say within the last month. The smudging here, look—"

"Yes, fine. Go on."

"Very well." He frowned, as if he was about to dive off a high place into a deep pool. "The chapter is headed, 'Concerning the ascendency of the six six-fingered men.'"

Suddenly, he had everybody's undivided attention. There was a long pause. Then the Prefect said, "*Six* six-fingered—?"

"That's what it says. There will come six men with six fingers on their—*olethrie*, that's an awkward word to translate; something between wonderful and terrible, with connotations of unnaturalness and abomination—their *olethrie* hands. They will all wear the lorus and divitision. The first six-fingered man—" He paused for a long time. "I'm sorry, this is a bit obscure, I think the text may be corrupt at this point. I think we may be dealing with a third or even fourth generation copy of the original translation, in which case the original may be several centuries older than this manuscript—"

The Commissioner was keeping his temper, but only just. "What about the first six-fingered man?"

"I *think*," Edgelath said, "it says that the first six-fingered man will put down the red pig—"

"I think we can guess who that was," the archdeacon said.

"It goes on, he will elevate the son of a pimp and a whore, who will break the back of the dragon and harness it and plough the red earth between the last olive tree and the sea. But the plough will break open the *something* spring—I'm sorry, the text is quite obviously corrupt here—and the whole land will be flooded."

Dead silence. Then the archdeacon said, "The Great King's family crest is a dragon, that's plain enough. Am I right in thinking, olives don't grow east of the Olbos?"

Suddenly, the Prefect grinned. "Calojan's going to be so angry when he reads this."

"Not strictly accurate." The archdeacon was grinning too. "His father drew dirty books, he wasn't a pimp as such. As far as his mother's concerned—"

"Excuse me," Aimeric put in. "There was a word you left out. The something spring."

"Ah yes." Edgelath was pressing his fingers to the sides of his nose. "The word is *oionoisin*. Literally, it means dirty, muddy, soiled with earth, that sort of thing. It's also used as a poetic synonym for anything to do with farming, agriculture in general; by association, it can refer to peasants, slaves, the lower classes generally. There's also another meaning, smoky or sooty, without the pejorative connotations. If this text is as old as I think it is, it could also mean hard-working, aspiring, ambitious, though that usage was already fairly archaic by about AUC 1270. It's a feature of Mezentine poetry of this time, of course, to use words so that all their different meanings are present at the same time, so to speak."

"It could mean anything you want it to, in fact," muttered the Prefect.

"In a sense—"

"Wonderful. Thank you so much, professor."

"Please, Hunfort," said the archdeacon. "He's doing his best."

Edgelath smirked just a little. "The term *red pig* is interesting," he said. "I believe that in his native dialect, Hodda means wild boar."

"If they're all wearing the lorus and divitision," the Commissioner said, "that rules out Sechimer's father. He had six fingers, but he was never crowned."

"They reckon it runs in the family," the Prefect said. "In which case—"

"Quite," said the archdeacon. "Go on, Edgelath."

They're taking it seriously, Aimeric thought; but it's a fake, obviously, it has to be. You can't predict the future. He looked at the archdeacon, trying to figure out what sort of a game he was playing. As he understood it, the idea had been to substitute a fake of their own. He'd already written the letter to his friend at the University, sending for Orsella. When she got here, she'd explain to them how you got round the Mezentine blue and sal draconis problems. So, why let them make fools of themselves? Unless, of course, the archdeacon himself actually believed—

"The second six-fingered man," Edgelath went on, "will be shut up in a little golden cage. He will drive a cart drawn by four white dogs, and only his daughter will be able to calm him. In his time, the flood-waters will rise until they wash the blood from the clouds, and there will be a day with no sun or moon. He will—oh, for heaven's sake, *sphoe theoin*, I do apologise, I really should have thought to bring a dictionary. I'll look it up as soon as I get back to the library."

"It's all right," growled the archdeacon. "Skip that bit. What's after that?"

"He will meet his end," Edgelath went on nervously, "now, this is quite ambivalent. It could either be *at* Iachello, a place, or *at the hands of* Iachello, a person, or possibly *because of* Iachello. I'm sorry, I can't be more certain than that without more context."

"If it's a place it'll be in the Gazetteer," said the Prefect. "We can look it up."

"Unless it's a town or a castle that hasn't been built yet," the Commissioner objected. "Doesn't ring any bells with me, that's for sure."

"It could also be a common noun," Edgelath said sadly. "A loan-word, possibly. It's not Mezentine, which is why I assumed it was a name. But it could be a thing, a *iachel*. I'm sorry," he added, "I'm not being much help here."

"You're doing just fine," the archdeacon said grimly. "Moving on—"

"There's a worker at the factory called Atkel," Aimeric suddenly remembered. "One of the north-westerners. Could it be something like that?"

"It's possible, philologically speaking," Edgelath replied. "The initial I in Middle Imperial is a remnant of the lost letter Digamma, which was common to most of the family of languages from which Imperial derives. In north-western, it'd have been a *w* sound. It fell into general disuse across the whole group about nine hundred years ago, as far as we can tell. So an Imperial of, say, seven hundred years ago seeking to transcribe Watkel might well come up with Iatkel. The shift from the *k* to the *ch* sound, however, is marginally more problematic—"

"Can we please get on?" the Prefect said dangerously.

"I'm sorry. Where was I? Ah yes. The third six-fingered man will be pure gold. He will love the people and be loved by everybody except one, and it would have been better if he had never been born. The fourth six-fingered man will be the most beautiful and the ugliest; he will drown himself and the city and in himself; when he is ugliest he will be most beautiful; he will hold back the red and blue flood but he will not turn the tide. His son will have five fingers. The fifth six-fingered man will be copper washed with gold. He will live in the desert and eat peas, and his children will be afraid of him, because of his ugliness. When he is buried, the copper will be eaten away, and he will be the most beautiful of them all. He will plant an olive tree where olive trees should not grow. Its fruit will be so heavy that it breaks the branch, which will fall on him and kill him, and the empire will be stolen and hidden in the heel of a boot. The sixth six-fingered man will be copper washed with silver. He will eat poison in the desert and grow strong. He will sleep during the day and work hard at night. The empire will fall through a hole in a good man's pocket, and the sixth six-fingered man will pick it up and bring it home; it will be swallowed by a fish, and he will catch the fish and find the empire in its stomach. He will be the best of all bad men, and by his goodness and loving kindness he will do the most harm. He will live too long, and not long enough. After him, pigs will dig up the roots of Florian's tree, and sheep and goats will graze in the Perfect Square, but the walls he will build will not fall for three hundred years. After him, Florian will return, wearing a blue woollen shirt, and he will live in the forest and eat toadstools." Edgelath paused, rather breathless, and looked up. "There's a lot more. Would you like me to go on?"

"I think that's quite enough," the Prefect said. "Vorsiger, you didn't pay good money for this garbage, did you?"

"Certainly not," the archdeacon replied. "It was a gift, from the Mezentine Scriveners' Guild. And I'd be careful before I dismissed it as garbage, if I was you."

"It's meaningless," the Prefect said. "Goats and fish and olive trees. Are you seriously suggesting we should base *policy* on this drivel?"

"I'm not suggesting anything of the sort," the archdeacon said. "I thought it'd be interesting to hear what it had to say, that's all. Also, you have to admit, it's uncannily accurate about Sechimer and Calojan."

"The son of a pimp and a whore," the Commissioner said. "Quite. I think what Hunforth is trying to say is, we can't *use* this. And even if it's a true prophesy, most of it's to do with stuff that'll happen long after we're all dead and gone. Also, if it *is* a true prophesy, what'll happen will happen and there isn't a damn thing we can do about it."

"Arguably," interrupted Edgelath. "Although the ancients believed that it was possible, within the inevitable ambiguities of a prediction, so to engineer events that one possible interpretation could be made to replace another. To take the classic example; *if you cross the river, a great empire will be destroyed*. If you interpret that as a warning, you can revise your strategy, not make the mistake you were about to make, and thereby arrange it so that the empire destroyed is the enemy's rather than your own. The prophesy still comes true, but in a different way."

There was a short silence. Then the archdeacon said, "The proposal, as you all know, is to commission a fake version of this manuscript that says what we want it to say, and use it to stabilise our position until such time as Sechimer is well enough to take over. That's all. Obviously there's a certain element of risk, but I believe it's acceptable. The worst that can happen is that people treat the whole thing as a joke, and I suggest we plant the fake manuscript in such a way that we can plausibly deny any involvement. Probably the best thing would be to arrange a lapse in security and let the City rumour mill do its job. As for this—" He pointed at the roll of parchment. "Well, as far as our immediate concerns go, *if* it's true, mostly it only tells us what we know already, and beyond that it's too vague to be much concrete help, as the prefect has so kindly pointed out. It may be true or it may be sheer nonsense, but it's not purporting to tell us when to lower interest rates or sign a trade agreement with the Vesani. My view is that it's an interesting curiosity which will provide a fruitful field of endeavour for the few select scholars we allow to see it. For myself, I don't think I'll be losing much sleep over the muddy spring, or whatever Edgelath finally decides it's supposed to mean, and I recommend that we all take a similarly robust view."

The Prefect was frowning. "I'm inclined to think that Florian the Fifth had his head screwed on right. I say burn the wretched thing, before it falls into the hands of idiots."

The Commissioner smiled at him. "Arguably," he said, "that has already happened. No, it'd be vandalism to destroy it; and besides, we've all heard what it has to say, so the harm's already done, unless Hunforth believes we should all go home and slash our wrists. Personally, I think it's fascinating. But I'll go along with Vorsiger. Put it away somewhere safe, and get a good fake made."

The archdeacon smiled and turned to Aimeric. "You've been very quiet," he said. "What do you think?"

Aimeric shrugged. "The fake was my idea," he said. "So, yes, let's do that. As far as this is concerned—" He paused and squinted at the manuscript. Just squiggly lines on parchment to him. "I don't see that it's particularly important. I don't think we should get rid of it. I mean, it's old and unique and presumably quite valuable. But, like Vorsiger said, it's no *use* for anything."

"Agreed, then," the archdeacon said, and clapped his hands. "Edgelath, the council has great pleasure in presenting this manuscript to the Studium, on condition that access be restricted on the usual terms. Aimeric, this master forger of yours. How soon can he get here?"

"She, actually. About a week, if we get a move on."

"A lady forger," the archdeacon said, "how very Vesani. Splendid, see to it, there's a good fellow. Meanwhile, I'll see if I can put together a rough draft of what we want the fake prophesy to say; Edgelath, I'll need you to help me with the words, to make sure it sounds thoroughly authentic. Also, I'd be grateful if you could work closely with our forgeress when she gets here, make sure she gets the right paper and ink and so forth. I'm sure there must be plenty of useless old charters and things in the library that she can scrape down. Well, gentlemen, unless there's any other business—"

WHEN HE WAS sure they'd gone, Raffen slowly stood up and stretched his legs, which were horribly cramped from crouching. Atkel, he thought. Well.

He'd heard a key turn in a lock, so presumably he was still shut in. It was, however, a fairly safe assumption that he was now alone in the building, though how long that would remain the case he couldn't say. So; no time to lose.

Rather more systematically than the last time, he started opening doors. The first six he tried had no windows at all. The next two had windows, but they were firmly shuttered and bolted, the bolts secured by massive, crude antique padlocks, so rusted that they'd probably never open again. Three more without windows; all store-rooms for gold and silver plate. He'd heard that the Studium had voluntarily handed over its reserves of accumulated wealth to be cut up and minted into coin; maybe not quite all of it. The next room was another windowless store, this one so densely crammed with swords, shields, spears and helmets that he had trouble getting the door to close again. The next one—

Somebody hit him. His head swam, his knees started to fold and he nearly threw up. He wasn't sure where the blow had landed, too dizzy. He saw a blurred shape in front of him, one fuzzy arm drawn back. Without any real idea of what he was doing, he aimed himself at the shape and lunged forward. He crashed into something, and then he was on the floor;

he was doing something, but he wasn't sure what. Hands were clamped on his wrists, trying to pull them apart. He realised he'd got his own hands around a man's throat and was causing him considerable distress. He nearly let go, then remembered that this was probably the man who'd hit him; if he let go now, it might not be safe. The man was making a horrible rasping, bubbling noise. He couldn't make up his mind what to do. Then he noticed that the man's eyes were bulging alarmingly, as if they were about to pop out of his head; that scared him, and he let go and shuffled backwards on his bottom towards the door.

The man wasn't moving; he was trying to breathe in, but finding it very difficult. He was making a noise like a cross-cut saw in seasoned wood. Raffen stayed where he was, trying to decide whether he should help him or finish him off. Slowly, the noise grew less harsh and the man started to breathe more normally. Well, Raffen thought, he shouldn't have hit me, should he?

On the floor, he saw three broad gold dishes, but this room wasn't a store; it was empty apart from half a dozen wooden buckets and a stack of brooms. It also had a window, with a thin filigree of silver light between frame and sash. He tried to get up; his legs ached horribly, but he made it.

He edged across to the man, stood over him and said, "Are you all right?"

"No."

"What are you doing here?"

Actually, the dishes answered that question. He nudged one with his toe. It clattered as it scraped across the floor. "Here," he said, reaching out a hand. "Let me help you up. I was just leaving."

The man gave him a foul look, grabbed his hand and hauled himself upright; he looked down at the plates, but Raffen put his foot on the nearest one (I'm not a thief, someone said once). The man hesitated, but then his legs started to give way. Raffen grabbed him and they both swayed together for a moment, until Raffen got his balance back and pulled them both up straight again. "You'd better go," he said.

The man looked at him, feeling behind him with his hands for the window. Raffen reached past him and lifted it. The man twisted from the waist, stuck his upper half through the window, then sort of fell backwards. Raffen counted to ten, to let him get clear, then scrambled through the window, letting it slam shut behind him. Nobody in the alley, which was lucky. Is everyone in this city a thief, he wondered. It must be a stressful place to live.

Aimeric de Peguilhan, he remembered, had offered him a job. He shrugged, looked back at the window just in case, and started to walk.

Aimeric de Peguilhan to Orsella Cantacusena, greetings.

Well, here I am, back in the old country again. Sorry not to have written earlier. Actually, things have been rather strange for me since I saw you last. I'll tell you all about it when I see you.

Which, I very sincerely hope, will be soon. There's a job, right up your street. You can do it standing on your head, it pays really good money, and best of all, it's legal. Well, sort of.

Too good to be true, I hear you say. I guess that depends. All the above is perfectly true, but you'd have to come here, to the City—all expenses paid, of course, and you'll travel in the Imperial diplomatic coach; fastest ride anywhere, finest coaches money can buy, stay at Imperial post houses, you'll love it. You do the job, you get paid, that's it. And get this; materials provided free of charge, to your specification, by the library of the Lesser Studium.

Minor snag; you'll need to leave now, as in right away, as in yes, you've got time to finish your breakfast, but no, you haven't got time to wash up. Just grab your shoes and your hat and something to read on the coach, and go.

Honestly, it's all for real, guaranteed by me. Incidentally, I now work for the government. In fact, I'm one-thirteenth of the government; so, if I promise something, you can take it to the bank. And if that doesn't make you come out of sheer raw curiosity, I don't know what will.

See you soon. Do please come. It'll be fun.

"Well?" she said, as he closed the door quietly and sat down. "Did you get it?"

"No," Teudel replied. He poured himself some water and drank it painfully.

"What do you mean, no?"

"I mean I didn't get it. I got in there just fine through the window, like you showed me, and you're right, the place is stuffed to bursting. Never seen so much fine metal in my life."

"So?"

"So," Teudel said wearily, "some bastard caught me." A tapping sound startled him. He realised it was a drip of rain, from a leak in the roof. "A guard or something. He half killed me. I only just managed to get away."

"You clown."

Not the most sensitive of men, Teudel; but there was something in the way she said it that told him that their love, once so flamboyantly incandescent, had just died. "Not my fault," he said instinctively. "I was really quiet. Besides, I'm not a thief. I'm an artist."

"You'll have to go back."

Teudel massaged his neck. "Absolutely no chance," he said. "Breaking and entering is a totally different discipline, and I take a pretty Mezentine view of professional demarcation. Thieves don't strike coins, I don't rob buildings. You can go if you like. Not me."

For a moment he was sure she was going to hit him. He'd never been hit by a woman before, and wasn't quite sure what you're supposed to do. But she made an effort, reset her voice and said, "Sorry, but you've got to. We promised them, one thousand solidi, in ten days. If we don't give them what they want, they're going to be very angry."

He'd always been fascinated by the female use of pronouns. *We* promised them. If *we* don't give them what they want. He'd never met them, didn't even know their names. Not that he wanted to. "You go," he repeated. "Wear your waif-and-stray outfit. If you get caught, you can be a poor homeless soldier's widow seeking sanctuary in the Temple."

"People know me," she said bitterly.

True; once seen, she was terribly hard to forget. Ah well, he thought. But I still have the use of my hands. "I'll go back, then. Don't wait up."

"Sweetheart."

It was still raining. He pulled his coat up round his face and bundled out into the drip from the eaves, hurried across the street and round the corner, and stood for a while under the shelter of a butcher's awning. Farewell, he muttered under his breath, to his twenty-seven beautiful solidi (too beautiful, that was the problem), not to mention the quite superb set of dies he'd sweated blood making—his finest work to date, no question about it. Presumably she'd use them to buy off the wrath of the syndicate; a bloody good deal, from their point of view. Farewell also to his one true love, but what the hell. Plenty more sharks in the sea.

He felt in his pocket and identified, by feel and long practice, one solidus and twenty-nine trachy. He grinned. Careless of him; he was sure he'd given her all the money, like she'd told him to, but here nevertheless was one gold coin. Never mind.

It doesn't do to stand too long in one place in the Tanneries, even in the driving rain. He shuffled down the street, keeping in close to the buildings, wishing he hadn't lost his hat back at the Golden Spire. The question was; where next? All in all, he'd had enough of the City. Make that the

Empire as a whole. For one thing, it was just too poor; you need a prosperous society with a vibrant economy for passing off false coin, plenty of places where it's no big deal to walk in somewhere off the street and pay for something rich and rare with a fistful of solidi. It just wasn't like that any more, what with the war and the austerity and all that; if you showed up somewhere with money, people were inclined to wonder where you'd got it from. The hell with all that.

So. He turned down Broadgate, then left into Goosefair. The Vesani Republic; fitted all the requirements, except their medium of exchange was silver, not gold. He wasn't sure he could be bothered with cutting dies for those huge silver cartwheels, all that scrollwork and salad, and banging out enough of the smaller denominations would be too much like hard work. Forging solidi in the Republic was out of the question; the moneychangers there had the loathsome habit of touchstoning one coin in five, because of the unfortunate prevalence of false coin due to the activities of a few dishonest men. They used gold in Mezentia, but nothing on earth would induce him to go there. The Sashan empire no longer existed, which was a nuisance. Scona? Perimadeia? Suddenly the world had got very small.

Still, he couldn't stay here, he realised that now. He'd have left as soon as he escaped from the ship, if it hadn't been for running into Her again. Well out of that. The Vesani Republic it'd have to be, he decided. And why not? After all, through some official oversight he wasn't a wanted criminal in the Republic, so that'd be one less thing to worry about. Also, he had friends there. Well, a friend. He thought of her and smiled. Sometimes, one is all you need.

WHEN A GREAT Prince of the Aram Cosseilhatz dies in battle, or afterwards of wounds sustained in combat, the clan assembles beside the nearest river; the men on one bank, the women and children on the other. On the men's side, elaborate funeral games are staged. The events consist of the foot race, the long and high jump, throwing the hunting spear, wrestling on foot and on horseback, foot and mounted archery, fencing with sword, palache, sabre and halberd, throwing the weight, lifting the anvil, the catching game and, as a grand finale, the all-comers horse race. Prizes are awarded out of the dead man's share of plunder from his most recent campaign, ranging from armour and weapons for the running and jumping to horses, gold and silver plate and cattle for the major events. The games take up the whole of the first day, and the evening is spent in total silence. On the second day, prisoners of war are executed, one for each year of the dead man's life, and his most valuable personal possessions are ritually killed and thrown into the river. Then the men build a dam across the river. In the exposed riverbed they dig a pit fifteen feet deep. In this pit they lay the coffin— traditionally gold lined with silver lined with lead—and fill the rest of the space with treasures contributed by each family of the clan. Then the top of the pit is roofed over with sheet lead and heavy stone slabs. The dam is then removed, so that the river resumes its course.

Once this ceremony has been performed, the dead man's name is considered to be consecrated, and should not be spoken again for a hundred years; instead, he is referred to by a series of conventional periphrases; the old man, the other man, or simply *he* or *him*, said with a specific intonation. This rule is not inflexible or enforced with penalties, but a breach is regarded as boorish and reprehensible unless there's a very good reason; even then, it's considered polite for the offender to apologise personally to the dead man's heir at the earliest opportunity.

"Why?" Chauzida asked his grandmother.

She thought for a moment before answering. "Mostly to spare your feelings," she said. "So you won't be reminded of him."

"But I wouldn't mind that," Chauzida replied. "He was a good man, wasn't he?"

"Very good. He was a good prince and a good man."

"So why wouldn't I want to remember him?"

She smiled. "Remembering him's one thing. It's something you do inside. Being reminded of him's different. It might make you sad."

Chauzida considered that. "But when they say *the other one* I know exactly who they're talking about, so it doesn't work, does it?"

"No," his grandmother replied. "It doesn't, does it?"

"But that's—"

"Yes," she said gravely. "And so are a lot of other things that people have to do. But they've still got to do them, all the same."

"Oh." Chauzida frowned. "Can't I change all that, now I'm the Great Prince?"

"No."

He knew that tone of voice, so he took the issue no further. It didn't affect him anyway, since he'd never called or spoken of his father by his name; it had been *dad* or *father* instead. He was sad that they'd had to bury the beautiful white folding bed, but his grandmother explained that the other one would need it to sleep on, in his pit under the river, so he decided he didn't mind too much. Then he did as he'd been told and put the whole matter out of his mind.

Being the Great Prince didn't change very much, he discovered. He still had to do what people told him, and he couldn't order them about. There were occasions when he had to sit on the uncomfortable golden saddle; sitting perfectly still for a very long time, while people talked about things he didn't understand. It was boring, and he hated being bored, so he decided to learn about all that stuff, so he could follow the discussions. His grandmother was a woman and not allowed to know that sort of thing—he knew perfectly well that she did, more so than most of the men, but it was a sort of a secret—so he went to see his uncle Joiauz.

He found him mending harness by the end wagon. "Uncle."

Joiauz was concentrating, trying to thread a needle. Concentrating made him grumpy. "What?"

"Can you explain the stuff they talk about at council meetings?"

Joiauz pulled that funny face of his. "Has it got to be now?"

He knew that Uncle had trouble seeing small things these days. "Shall I thread the needle for you?"

"What? Oh, yes, right. That'd be a great help, actually. For some reason I can't get the stupid thing to go through."

So Chauzida took the needle, threaded it and handed it back. Uncle looked at him, a bit oddly. "So," he said. "You want to know about politics."

"Is that what it's called?"

"That's one word for it. Or you can say affairs of state, or clan business, or strategy and tactics. Really it's all the same thing."

"I see," Chauzida said. "Go on, then."

Joiauz thought for a moment. "I guess we'd better start with you," he said. "Now that the old man's gone, you're what's known as the Great Prince of the Aram Cosseilhatz. That's the name of our nation. There are five nations; the Cosseilhatz, the Chantat, the no Vei, the Senhor and the Rosinholet. Just to be confusing, you talk about the first four as the Aram Cosseilhatz, the Aram Chantat, the Aram no Vei and the Aram Senhor, but the Rosinholet are just the Rosinholet. No Aram." He paused and grinned. "Got that?"

"Yes. Go on."

Joiauz nodded. "Now then," he said. "Each nation is split up into about two dozen clans. A clan is like a big family; actually, it's hundreds of families all distantly related to each other a long way back. Each clan has a leader; he's usually the oldest and cleverest man in the clan, though it doesn't always work out quite like that. Anyway, when they have the meetings where you have to sit still on the golden saddle, all those old men are clan leaders. They meet together to figure out what the nation ought to do, when there's a problem. And sometimes," he added, "when there isn't."

"Sorry. I don't—"

"Forget it," Joiauz said quickly, and he knew his uncle had just made a joke, the sort he wasn't supposed to understand. "Anyhow, that's what the meetings are for. You've got to be there because you're the Great Prince, even though you're too young to do or say anything. When you're fifteen—"

"That's in two years."

"Quite right," Joiauz said solemnly. "When you're fifteen, you'll be old enough, and then you'll have to understand what's going on, because you'll be making the decisions. You'll listen carefully to what the old men say, but you'll have to decide. Often—make that usually—they won't agree about what's the right thing to do. They're all wise, clever men, but it's your decision that matters."

"Oh," Chauzida said.

"Yes. Until then, there's what we call a regent. Actually, that's me, because I'm the old man's brother. It's my job to do the deciding. I'm supposed to make the decisions you'd be making, if you were old enough."

"I don't understand."

"Me neither. Sorry, joke." Joiuaz pulled his thinking face. "What it means is, I'm not supposed to do what I think is the right thing. I've got to pretend I'm you, only older. It's complicated," he added, "and in practice, it's all about doing the thing that'll upset the fewest people while still getting done the things that need doing." He paused. "That bit's quite important," he said. "Do you want me to say it again?"

"No thanks, I think I've got it."

"Then explain it to me."

Chauzida took a moment to find the right words. "All the old men at the meeting are important people," he said, "so we don't want to upset them. But some things have got to be done, for everybody's good. What we've got to do is choose the right thing *and* make everyone feel they're still important and clever, even if we don't do what they said." He smiled. "How's that?"

"Not bad." Joiauz had stopped trying to sew. He hated sewing anyway, so that was all right. "Just bear that in mind and you'll do all right. Anyway, that's all about you."

"I see," Chauzida said thoughtfully. "So, what sort of thing do they talk about?"

Joiauz was absent-mindedly rubbing his left hand with his right. Chauzida knew that he had a terrible itch in that hand, because it had been shot through with an arrow at the end of the battle, when Joiauz and the guards went back in to rescue dad, rescue the other one, when he got knocked down and trampled on. There was a big white scar, and a red patch all around it where he was always rubbing. "Now this bit's really important," Joiauz said, "so I want you to pay special attention. There are five important things. There's the war, the nations, the journey, the weather and the clans. Repeat what I just said."

"The war," Chauzida said slowly. "The nations, the journey, the weather and—sorry, what was the last one again?"

"The clans," Joiauz said. "Right, here's what they mean. The war—well, that speaks for itself, doesn't it? It's *the* war because officially we're always at war with somebody, though we might not be actually fighting at this precise moment. Right now, the war's with the Aram no Vei."

"Oh. I thought the enemy were called Sashan. Wasn't it them who killed—?"

"It's *the* Sashan," Joiauz said, "and that war's over, at least as far as we're concerned. I believe the Imperial general's still sitting under the walls of some city somewhere, starving the poor devils out, but we've been paid and we're out of it. The Sashan Empire doesn't really exist any more, anyway. So," he went on, drawing in a breath, "as soon as one war's over, we move on to the next one. If there isn't a real next war, then officially we're at war with the no Vei." He hesitated and grinned. "Do you understand *officially?*"

"I think so," Chauzida said. "It's where something isn't really true, but we've all got to act like it is."

Joiauz seemed to think that was funny, though he didn't laugh. "You've got the idea. Anyway, when the clan elders meet, the war's always the first thing they talk about. If nothing much is happening, they move on to the next thing."

"The nations," Chauzida said.

"Very good, the nations. What that means is, what the other nations are up to—the Chantat and the no Vei and the Rosinholet, that lot. We have people watching what they're doing all the time. They report—send messages—to the elders, and they decide if the news is important and what needs to be done about it. Then they move on to the next thing."

"The journey," Chauzida said. "What does that mean?"

"Ah. The idea is," Joiauz said, "that we're always on the move. Officially. The journey means, where are we going, are we early or late, are there any problems, like snow or flooded rivers or enemies getting in the way; where we're going to camp next, will there be enough grass for the horses and the livestock or will we have to get hay and fodder from somewhere; all that. Very important stuff, when we're on the move. If we're not, like now, they pass on to—"

"The weather. Is that just what it sounds like?"

Joiauz nodded. "Pretty much. Years ago, we believed that we could control the weather by doing ceremonies, making sacrifices, saying special prayers and so on. It gradually sort of dawned on us that none of that stuff actually worked, so we don't bother with it so much now, except on big occasions when people still expect it. But we still make our best guesses at what the weather's going to be doing, because it's so important for the journey."

"I can see that," Chauzida said. "In that case, why don't you talk about the weather before you do the journey? Surely it makes a big difference to what you decide to do."

Joiauz frowned. "You know," he said, "you could just possibly be right. Don't say that out loud in a meeting, though, you'll give them a heart attack. Rule number one; you don't mess around with the way things have always been done."

"Really?"

Joiauz smiled. "Officially. Obviously we do change things, but we try and do it so nobody notices. That way, people don't get upset."

"What does the clans mean?"

Joiauz paused for a moment. "Everything else, really. It means anything happening here, among ourselves, that needs to be sorted out or talked about. People's private quarrels, if they get out of hand and look like they're going to affect the rest of us. Or people who may be going through a rough patch and need a little help. Or trade—you know what that means?"

"Of course I do."

"Of course you do. Well, if we need something, we talk about who we might be able to get it from and what we can give them in exchange, and which of us has got it or can get it or can make it, and what we're going to give *them*. I'll give you an example. Suppose we need hay for the horses, because we've reached a place where the grazing's not as good as we thought it'd be. We send a few men out to look around. They come back and tell us that there's some people living in a village over that mountain over there, and they've got hay to spare, and in return they'd be prepared to take two dozen deerskins, twelve dozen arrows and fifty sheeps' milk cheeses. The elders talk about it, and one of them says, So and so in our clan's got that many spare skins; someone else says, I know who's got more cheese than he needs; someone else says, we've got a damn good fletcher in our lot. Then we've got to decide what we're going to give the skins man for his skins and the cheese man for his cheese and the fletcher for making all those arrows. Now, because the hay's going to benefit everybody, it's only fair that everyone chips in to reward the skins man and the cheese man and the fletcher. The elders decide how they're going to go about collecting a bit of something from everyone and handing it over to the three men who're providing what we need. It gets a bit complicated, because sometimes, if say the cheese man doesn't actually need anything right now, we have to promise to give him something he needs later on, when he needs it. That's called *merit*, and obviously people think it's a very good thing to have, so quite often they're happy just piling up merit and not actually taking anything. It means everybody else respects them and goes around thinking what splendid people they are, and of course if it ever happens that they suddenly decide they need fifty sheep or five suits of Mezentine horse armour, they go to their clan leader and he's got to get it for them, soon as possible." He frowned. "Actually, it's not a perfect system, it can cause a lot of trouble. But it's what we do, and I reckon there's worse ways, at that."

Chauzida nodded slowly. "And that's all the clans, is it?"

"That's right. As often as not, that's most of what gets talked about; so we leave it till last, so we can take our time over it without having to rush through and get on to other things."

Chauzida looked down at his hands. He had a scab forming where he'd cut himself sharpening a bit of stick with the Sashan knife the other one had given him. It itched, and he thought about the scar on Joiauz' hand, which must itch so much more. "When I'm fifteen," he said, "will I have to decide about all that stuff?"

Joiauz looked straight at him. "Yes."

"I don't think I'll be able to. It's so complicated."

"You've got two years to learn," Joiauz said. "But yes, it's complicated, and very, very difficult sometimes. The elders are old and wise, they know all the facts, and all the ways we've dealt with problems in the past, so you should listen carefully to what they say. But you've got to remember, they're all there on behalf of their clans; they want what's best for their own people, and that may not always be the same as what's best for the nation as a whole. Or they may have very strong views on what's right and wrong, and sometimes they don't all agree about that kind of thing. Or sometimes," he added, with a sad sort of grin, "they're all just plain wrong, or you can see an idea that's even better than what they're suggesting. You've got to be able to tell them, we're going to do what *he* says and not what *you* say."

"Without upsetting anybody."

"Without upsetting anybody, that's right. And, what's more, you've got to make your mind up quickly; you can't say, all of you go away and come back in three days' time when I've had a chance to think it over, because that's not how we do things. You'll upset everyone if you do that. So no, it's not easy. Wish I could say it was, but it isn't."

Chauzida was still looking at his hands. "Have I got to be the Prince?"

"Oh yes. Believe me."

Chauzida looked up. "Will you help me? Promise you'll help me."

"Of course I will." For some reason, Joiauz was looking away. "That's what I'm here for. What I thought we'd do is, after each meeting, you and I can sit together like this and talk about what was said and the decisions that were made. I'll try and explain it all for you, and you can tell me what you'd have done if it'd been up to you. How does that sound?"

"That'd be great," Chauzida said with feeling. "If you wouldn't mind."

"Oh, I think I can make the time."

That reminded Chauzida of a question. "If you're the—what was that word?"

Joiauz smiled. "Regent," he said.

"Thanks. If you're the regent, and you've got all these important decisions to make, why do you have to milk goats and do setting-up and mend harness and everything? Wouldn't it be better if you spent all your time thinking about the problems and stuff, instead of doing things anybody could do?"

Joiauz frowned for a moment. "You can be forgiven for asking that," he said, "because that's how they do it in other places; the empire and the republics and the Sashan, they all think like that. But we don't. We say that if a prince can't do all the ruling in his spare time, then either he's not a very good prince, so we should get rid of him and choose someone different, or else there's too much ruling going on, in which case the prince is getting above himself and needs taking down a peg or two. Either way, it's not a good idea, so don't do it." He hesitated, then added, "Officially."

"Oh."

"Unofficially," Joiauz went on, "I milk some of my goats and do a bit of setting-up, and when I've finished making a pig's ear of these reins I'll probably hand them over to Garsio, who'll make a much better job of them than I could in about a quarter of the time. But officially, I'm the same as everyone else, so I do the same work, and being regent's just extra. Got that?"

"I think so. It doesn't seem fair."

Joiauz laughed. "The old man always seemed to manage," he said. "Actually, he liked working with the stock and fixing a busted wheel and all that sort of thing, he said it took his mind off things. He always had more energy than me, of course. I was the lazy brother, though of course it didn't matter, since he was the eldest. Better that way, I'd be less likely to interfere. No, don't worry about that, it's not important. Let's go and see if your aunt Guariz has baked some of those cheese-and-honey cakes your Gran doesn't like you eating too many of."

Orsella Cantacusena to Aimeric de Peguilhan, greetings.

You what? You want me to leave the Vesani Republic, epicentre of the civilised world, heart and brain of the human race, scintillating in its cultural and intellectual diversity and depth, and drag myself along appalling roads, in a coach driven by kettlehats, at this time of year, in order to imprison myself in a shithole like the City, where you're seriously suggesting I participate in dubious and probably illegal activities? Really?

Oh, all right then. Provided the money's adequate—you were so endearingly coy about precise figures—and I'm not committing myself to anything remotely longterm or permanent, I don't see why not. Actually, to be absolutely frank with you, it'd suit my plans quite well to get out of town for a little while. Everything is fine and I'm not in any kind of trouble or anything. It's just that certain people are making certain demands, mostly but not exclusively of a financial nature, so it'd be no bad thing for me to be somewhere else for a while and earn a large sum of money. I'll miss the music festival, of course, and the boat races, and the Phylarchus revival at the Comedy, but what the hell, there's always next year.

What the hell are you up to, Aimeric? And what was that throwaway line about working for the government supposed to mean? I think I can safely say I know you quite well. The thought of you working for the Imperial (or any) government is downright bizarre. The thought of you working at all is bad enough. I can only assume that such a monstrous reversal of the natural order of things must be a portent foretokening the end of the world, and—assuming the money is right—I simply can't wait to get down there and see it for myself.

So, just as soon as I get a letter from you with actual numbers in it, I'll be on my way, with just the bare necessities of life tied up in a big silk handkerchief. Write soon, before I die of curiosity.

HE APPEARED OUT of nowhere, presenting himself to the sentries at the main gate of the camp and demanding to speak to someone in authority. Anyone else would have spent the next six hours in the guardhouse before being allowed five minutes of the duty officer's precious time. Instead, he was escorted to the general's tent by a sergeant and two guardsmen.

"Allow me to introduce myself," he said to the back of the general's neck. "I am prince Hunza, rightful heir to the throne of the Great King of the Sashan."

General Calojan, who by this time had been awake for thirty-six hours straight, slowly turned round in his chair and looked at him. "Of course you are," he said. "Tell me, what's it like? I've often wondered."

"What's what like?" he said.

"Being dead," Calojan replied. "Because I was there when they cut your head off in the marketplace at Dura Escatoy, eight—sorry, nine years ago. Or had you forgotten about that?"

He frowned. "Obviously, that wasn't me."

"Obviously." Calojan lifted himself a little by pressing hard on the arms of the chair. "Equally obviously, you aren't Hunza, because Hunza's dead. Like I said, I saw him die. I was in the front row, standing next to the deputy secretary for military justice. It took the headsman three goes, and I got splashed with blood."

"That wasn't me. That was an impostor."

"That would explain it," Calojan said wearily. "Only, I met Hunza a year or so earlier, before he had his spot of trouble and had to leave Court in a hurry. He was four inches taller than you, his nose was shorter and he had one proper chin instead of several silly little ones. Be reasonable," he added with a faint smile. "You don't look anything like him."

"I don't know who you met, but I'm Hunza, and I can prove it."

Calojan closed his eyes. "And even if you were Hunza," he said, "which you aren't, you'd have to be out of your tiny mind to come within a hundred miles of the Imperial army, given that Hunza is—sorry, was—seventh or eighth in line to the throne and therefore would pose a threat to the empire and would be arrested on sight and either blinded or executed.

Luckily for you, you're not him. Otherwise you'd be in so much trouble you wouldn't believe it."

"I'm here," he said, "to negotiate peace terms. I'm the only one left with the authority to do so. Therefore it's my duty. I'm not particularly interested in your threats."

"Fine," Calojan said. "Sergeant, take this man and stick him in the Birdcage for an hour or so. Then throw him out and see to it he bounces. Try and make him understand that if I hear so much as a whisper about prince Hunza having risen from the grave and come back to lead his people, I'll cut off his head and stick it on a pole. That'll be all."

"Ten years ago," he said, raising his voice a little, "I was in prison in the cells under the Palace, as a result of lies spread about me by my brothers. I believe an actor was hired to impersonate me during that time, to avoid a popular uprising by my supporters, which would inevitably have resulted had news of my betrayal been made public. I assume the man you saw was the actor. I, however, am the real prince Hunza, and I claim full diplomatic status."

Calojan looked at him for a moment, then shook his head. "Sergeant," he said, "if I have to tell you again you'll be very unhappy."

The Birdcage, also known as the Lobster Pot, is a bell-shaped steel cage suspended twelve feet off the ground from a siege catapult frame. Its size and shape mean that a normal-sized man can neither sit down or stand upright. It was introduced as a form of military punishment by general Calojan, to replace the lash, the bastinado and various other methods traditional in some of the regional units. After an hour inside, Hunza couldn't stand unsupported, so they carried him to the gate and left him there. He must have gone away during the night. The sentries didn't see him go.

THE *CHARITY & COMPASSION* is a military inn on the New West Road, thirty-six miles west of Limes Regni. It's the seventh post house from the City, first overnight stop for the Imperial mail between the City and the Vesani frontier. Built in the reign of Geisimer II, it exhibits all the typical features of the period; round arches, symmetrical floor plan, fluted pillars, decorative arcading and four short, squat watchtowers at the cardinal points. Of interest are the mosaic floors in what is now the fodder store and the small iconostasis of the Invincible Sun Restored still just visible halfway up the south wall of the main dining room. The helmet and sword displayed on the wall of the back taproom are reputed to have been taken from the body of Orselius Ducas after the battle of Suessone; the sword would, however, appear to be a fairly typical Vesani type XIIa, which would suggest a date some eighty years later. The inn is otherwise unremarkable, and is rarely visited by civilians, except when the Corbin bridge is closed and the regular commercial stage is forced to divert by way of Boc Soheil.

She saw him in the courtyard. He was sitting on a barrel examining the sole of his shoe. She crept up quietly behind him and said, "Teudel?"

He jumped up, slithered on the wet cobblestones and had to sit down again in a hurry. Then he craned his neck and stared at her. "Orsella," he said. "What the hell are you doing here?"

She smiled at him. "You first."

"On my way to the Republic," he replied. "Stupid coach got diverted because some stupid bridge has fallen down. You?"

"Going the other way," she said, with a slight frown. "I'm headed for the City. Got a job there."

"Oh, hard luck," Teudel said sympathetically. "Only temporary, I hope."

"Me too," Orsella replied. "Let's go inside and you can buy me a drink."

At this point in his career, Teudel had just enough money left to pay for one meal a day for the rest of the journey and a bed for one night when he got there; that was including the emergency half-scudo hidden in the toe of his shoe. "Good idea," he said. "So, tell me all about it. What kind of a job?"

She didn't answer until they were seated at a table in the corner, facing each other with a bottle of surprisingly adequate Mesoge white between them. "I honestly don't know," she said. "Did you ever know a man called Aimeric?"

Teudel grinned. "You mean Aimeric de Peguilhan. He was at the University, wasn't he, before he came home. No, I never met him while he was in the Republic. Sure as hell wouldn't get to meet him now. Why?"

She had that look; like she was quietly, carefully reading his mind. "He wrote to me saying he'd got a job for me. Is it true he's working for the government?"

"You could say that. He's on the regency council. They're running the empire while the emperor's sick."

"Is that right?" No smile, at least not on the surface. "How come?"

Teudel was doing mental arithmetic. She'd been in her early twenties when he'd known her first, about six years older than him, so now she had to be, what, thirty-two, thirty-three? You wouldn't think it. "His father ran a big armour factory," he said.

"I know. Aimeric always did have plenty of money."

"Which went bust," Teudel went on, watching her face for a reaction. Nothing seen. "So Aimeric had to come home and sort it out. Which he did. Apparently, in some complicated way to do with supplies and materiel, he helped a lot with winning the war. So now he's very important and respectable."

"Aimeric de Peguilhan? Good heavens."

Teudel made himself smile. "You knew him quite well, then."

"Yes," she said; a sort of bitten-off sound. "Quite well. There was a period of about three months when cash flow got to be a real problem, so I had to supplement my income with other lines of work. Not exactly fun, but it could've been worse."

Teudel wasn't happy about that, but tried not to let it show. "Is that the sort of job—?"

"I hope not," she replied sharply, "because if so, I've had a wasted journey. Honestly, I'd rather scrub floors. No, I'm assuming he needs a quality manuscript in a hurry. Anyway, that's enough about me. What about you?"

"Ah." Teudel took a long drink. "Ups and downs, you might say."

"More ups than downs?"

"More downs than ups. I had legal difficulties."

"You poor darling."

"Quite. I suppose you heard about the grand victory celebrations?"

She nodded. "A bit," she said. "Parades and poetry recitals, and didn't they flood the Haymarket and stage a mock sea-battle?"

"Westponds, actually. But yes to the sea-battle. I was in it."

"You?"

He nodded. "The ships were manned by criminals on Death Row. Luckily, mine sank and I got away. Otherwise—"

"You were on—?"

"Mphm. Not a happy time. Which is why I'm off to the Republic before anyone realises I'm still alive. First thing I was going to do when I got there," he added, after a very slight pause, "was go and see you. Pity about that."

"Yes," she said. "But anyway, what are you planning to do? The same?"

He nodded. "Think of me bashing out thalers and meissergroschen in some cellar somewhere. I never did like working in silver. Horrible chewy stuff."

She narrowed her eyes slightly. "Not much of a living in it these days," she said. "Hadn't you heard? They just cut the thaler to seventy-two parts fine."

Teudel rolled his eyes. "Wonderful," he said. "When we do it, it's forgery. If the government does it, it's quantitative easing. The most you can get away with is sixty-three parts fine, any more than that and the copper shows through almost immediately. How's a man supposed to make a living on those margins?"

"Can't you do silver plating on copper?"

He pulled a face. "Fourree, we call that, and it's a mug's game. Also, the wash you've got to use is really foul stuff, rots your lungs. Not to mention being a wicked waste of my abilities. I wish you hadn't told me that, you've made me really depressed."

She studied him thoughtfully, as though she was thinking of buying him, but not at the asking price. "Did it ever occur to you," she said, "that you're in the wrong line of business?"

"Yes. When the judge looked down his nose at me and pronounced sentence. And," he added sadly, "just now, when you said about the bloody Vesani devaluing yet again. But it's what I do."

"And you do it magnificently," she said. "It's just a shame you don't get the credit you deserve. That said, have you ever thought about a change of direction? Same sector, more or less, but a different specialisation."

"Sorry, I don't follow."

"I was thinking about my side of the business," she said. "Manuscripts. It's mostly property deeds, wills, contracts, some letters. No, listen. I think you'd do well. You've clearly got an artistic streak, you're patient and careful, and you're used to dealing with—well, that sort of people. There's a lot of money in it, and always plenty of work about; I've been turning commissions away, I simply don't have the time. And it's safer, by and large. Much harder to detect; also, you're always working to order, half up front and half on delivery. You do need to know a lot of detailed technical stuff about types of parchment and ink, all the different techniques for aging and patinating, but that's all right. I can teach you."

With the last sentence she'd got his interest. "Would you? Why?"

She shrugged. "Would you believe, because we're friends? Also," she added quickly, "like I just said, I'm having to turn work down, and that's thoroughly bad business. Once a customer goes somewhere else, he doesn't always come back. You'd be surprised how many regulars I've got."

He gave her a puzzled look. "You want an *apprentice?*"

"That's not quite how I'd have put it," she said. "Actually, what I was thinking was, here's poor Teudel, going through a rough patch through no fault of his own, I wonder if I could help. I suggested you might care to work with me to start with because that'd be a good way for you to get into the trade. If you'd rather not—"

"No, really," he said quickly. "It's very kind of you, and yes, I'd be very interested. Except, you're going to the City, and I've just come from there, and there's absolutely no way in hell I can go back, for the reasons stated. So, for the time being at least—"

He tailed off. She had that look on her face. "Your problem might not be insurmountable," she said.

"Oh, I rather think it is."

"Not necessarily." She smiled. "It all depends on how much importance Aimeric de Peguilhan places on this job he wants me to do, and how much influence he's really got. I'm prepared to bet that if I tell him I can't possibly manage without my trusted assistant, who unfortunately can't be in the empire because technically he's a wanted man—"

"Technically?"

She smiled. "It sounds better like that. I can give it a try, if you like." She looked away for a moment. "And if it works and you come and work with me—well, it's not a dawn-to-dusk job, like farm work or plastering, you'll have some free time. What you care to get up to in your free time is your concern, provided I'm not implicated and you do really good work this time and don't get caught—"

Teudel nodded slowly. "There'd be a percentage, of course."

"If you chose to show your gratitude, it'd be ungracious to refuse."

Teudel made a show of thinking about it. He'd loved Orsella from the first moment he'd seen her, and trusted her about as far as he could throw Florian's Column. It was possible—plausible—that kickbacks from a small-scale gold forgery enterprise might be enough to motivate her; or her motives might just as easily be personal. He never had figured out where he stood with her in that regard, mostly because the state of play seemed to change on practically a daily basis. Alternatively, she could be playing a long, hard game in which he'd be an expendable pawn, though he was fairly sure their meeting here had been purely accidental. No idea which, then. He looked up at her out of the corner of his eye and decided it'd be interesting finding out. "All right, then," he said. "Yes, thank you. If you can swing it, I'd be delighted."

"Splendid." She gave him a beautiful, beautiful smile. "Right, then," she said. "You couldn't possibly hang on here for a few days, while I talk to Aimeric? It'd make it easier to find you."

He shook his head. "Sorry," he said. "Wrong side of the border."

"Oh, yes, I see what you mean. All right, how about if you wait at the *Perfect Union*, on the Lonazep road? That's on the Vesani side. Do you know it?"

"Been there once, I think. But there's another problem."

"What?"

He pulled a sad face. "I think they'd probably want me to pay for my room," he said. "Which I would be in no position to do, unfortunately."

"You're broke."

"Yes."

"Idiot." She smiled again. "Why didn't you say? All right, here's twenty scudi." She opened the hand she'd been resting on the table. Apparently the coins had been nested in her palm all the time. "And you might consider getting yourself something decent to wear," she added. "I didn't like to mention it, but you look like a scarecrow."

For some reason he hesitated, just for a moment or so. Then he reached out his hand across the table towards her, palm upwards. The four tiny gold coins dropped, from her hand to his. They were slightly warm.

"This is very good of you, you know," he decided to say.

"I'm a very good person," she replied. "Now then, do you suppose they serve food in this rathole? I'm famished."

Much later, when she was asleep, he felt for the coins she'd given him; quietly, so the scraping of the metal on the wood of the bedside table wouldn't wake her up. It was dark, of course, but he didn't need light to examine currency. He found that three of the coins were genuine; the fourth was a fake but a good one, probably done in Mezentia rather than abroad. Slight abrasions and a certain uncharacteristic coarseness in the lines of the dividing cross on the reverse suggested to him that they'd been made from decommissioned official dies, recut and deepened to remove the hacksaw-marks. They reckoned a quarter of the small gold in circulation in Mezentia these days was false, so yes, entirely plausible. He leaned back and tried to go to sleep, but instead lay in the dark, staring up at where he knew the ceiling to be.

JUST BEFORE DAWN on the third day after the start of the autumn solar cycle, the three hundred and fortieth anniversary of the signing of the Peace of Bohec, twelve days after his thirty-seventh birthday, the emperor Sechimer sat bolt upright in his bed, opened his eyes and demanded to know where he was.

The doctor on duty was a Vesani by the name of Zanipolo Bringas. His speciality was setting complex fractures, but he'd completed five tours with the 67th as senior staff surgeon and was generally considered a safe pair of hands. He put down the book he'd been reading and looked up. "Your Majesty?" he said.

Sechimer stared at him. "Where is this?" he said. "And who the hell are you?"

Bringas had been one of the doctors in attendance on the emperor ever since he was brought home, and immediately recognised the significance of these words. Previously, when addressed as Your Majesty, the emperor had appeared confused, sometimes looking over his shoulder to see who else was in the room. This time, he'd accepted the title without question. It was also the first time he'd shown any interest in his surroundings, or displayed any sort of temper.

"We're in the palace infirmary, Your Majesty," he said. "My name is Bringas, I'm a doctor."

Sechimer kicked aside the bedclothes, swung his legs over the side of the bed and stood up. "What am I doing in the infirmary? There's nothing wrong with me, is there?"

To which the straight answer was, no, apparently not. "You've been very ill," Bringas said gently. "However, I'm pleased to be able to tell you that you've made a good recovery, and—"

Sechimer's eyes were wide open. He stood beside his bed, stark naked, looking round for his clothes. "The battle," he said. "Damn it, I can't be in the palace. Five minutes ago I was in the battle. What—?"

Priorities, Bringas decided. "We won," he said. "The battle was won, the war is over. Please sit down and I'll try and explain."

Sechimer hesitated, then perched reluctantly on the edge of the bed. "We won."

"Conclusively."

"Thank God." The words exploded out of Sechimer's mouth like lava from a volcano. Then, "What happened to me? Last thing I remember, they were counter-attacking, I was standing in my stirrups trying to see—"

"You were hit by an arrow," Bringas said. "The wound was serious, but you've healed well and we think there's been no lasting damage. You were very lucky."

Sechimer drew in a deep breath. "I'll say," he said. "What about Calojan, is he all right? Did we take heavy losses?" He frowned. "What did you just say? The war is—"

"Over." Bringas nodded again. "I think you'd better hear the rest from your advisers rather than me, but I can set your mind at rest, the war really is over, and we won. Now, I need to do a few tests, and then I can discharge you." He pulled a stern face. "The sooner you lie down and keep still, the sooner I can start and you can get out of here. All right?"

"What? Oh, yes, sorry." Sechimer lay down, arms by his sides, staring straight up at the ceiling. "How long have I been out of it?" he said. "It must be at least three days, if I'm back here."

"Quiet, please," Bringas said briskly. "Now, I want you to look at my hand. How many fingers am I holding up?"

When he'd done all the tests he could think of, and several he'd made up on the spot, Bringas said, "Please wait there just a moment," left the room, closed the door behind him and fled. He ran to the bedroom of his superior, the Sashan doctor whose name none of them had yet learned to pronounce. He threw open the door and yelled, "He's better."

The doctor rolled over onto his side and opened one eye. "What?"

"The emperor is awake and sitting up. He knows who he is. I've done all the tests, and as far as I can see he's completely normal. I suggest you—"

The Sashan was suddenly out of bed and pulling on his slippers. "Go and tell the duty officer," he said. "Now."

So Bringas stepped back out of the way to let the Sashan scramble past him, then went down the corridor and up a flight of stairs to the operations room. The duty officer was a pale, thin young Imperial captain called Iachimer. He'd lost three fingers from his left hand at the Field of Red and Blue Flowers, and had been reassigned to administrative duties.

"He's what?" Iachimer said.

"He's fine," Bringas panted. "He's back to normal, and he wants to talk to someone."

"My God." Iachimer lifted his feet off the desk, knocking over an inkstand. He ignored the pool of ink gradually flooding the desktop. "Such as who?"

"I don't know, do I? I'm just a doctor."

"What? Yes, of course. Right, I'd better—" He stopped, his mouth wide open, frozen stiff.

"Maybe," Bringas said kindly, "you might want to start with a messenger to the archdeacon and the chancellor. Then you'd probably better get down there and see the emperor."

Iachimer looked terrified. "Me?"

"Well, somebody ought to. He's lying there on his own staring at the ceiling. I sent the Sashan down there, but I don't suppose he's the best person for His Majesty to talk to about what happened after the battle."

"My God," Iachimer repeated. "Right, yes, thank you." He grabbed his helmet, put it on, realised he didn't really need to wear it, stuck it under his arm and sprinted out of the room. When he'd gone, Bringas walked slowly out of the office and down the stairs, across to the quadrangle arch and out across the grass to the refectory. It was a bit early—the sun was just rising—but he needed a drink.

"HE WAS LIVID," the archdeacon said wearily, "absolutely furious. I reckon I'm lucky to have got out of there in one piece."

Aimeric looked anxious. "He doesn't want to see me, does he?"

"He didn't ask for you," the archdeacon said. "When I mentioned your name, he said *who the hell's that*, or something of the kind."

"Did you tell him I was against the idea?"

"No," the archdeacon said irritably, "because you weren't, or at least you didn't say anything out loud. I seem to remember you looked a bit anxious, but you always look anxious in council meetings. Anyway, as far as I can tell it's Maering and me he blames. If I were you I'd keep a low profile and stay out of the way for a while. I wish I could do the same, but obviously I can't." He paused, then slumped back in his chair. "I'm pretty sure he's not going to do anything about anything until Calojan gets back. That's all he keeps asking; where's Calojan, I need to see Calojan right now. I don't think he's prepared to trust anyone else."

Aimeric poured himself a large dose of the archdeacon's strong wine but didn't drink it. "How long before he gets home?"

"It's a five-day journey for the Mail. Knowing Calojan, he'll find a way to do it in four. So nine days, maybe ten. Till then, I imagine everything will stay pretty well frozen. We aren't in charge any more, I think His Majesty made that abundantly clear, but he's refusing to do any business at all until Calojan gets home, so—"

Aimeric frowned. "Are we sure he's better? I mean, that all sounds a bit funny to me."

The archdeacon smiled. "Aimeric," he said, "I do believe I can see the way your mind is working. If he's still ill, we can have him locked up by the doctors and carry on running things as before. Arguably he's acting irrationally, therefore he's still ill." Aimeric opened his mouth, but the archdeacon went on, "I won't say the thought hadn't tiptoed across my mind, but you can forget it. We'd never get away with it, for one thing. Also, and you may choose not to believe me but I promise you I'm quite sincere, I don't want to rule the empire, I want Sechimer to be well and take his old job back again, I want things to go back to how they used to be so that maybe I can finally get some sleep. And yes, I believe he's completely recovered, in body and mind. He wants Calojan here because he doesn't trust us, like I just said. That's not irrational behaviour, it's common sense. If I was in his shoes, I'd be thinking exactly the same way."

Aimeric wasn't so sure. "Yes, but flying off the handle like that about a comparatively trivial…"

The archdeacon shook his head. "Not to him." He sighed, to express resignation at the prospect of having to make a lengthy explanation. "I don't think you quite grasp how Sechimer's mind works. In a way, he's much luckier than me. He's a man of faith. He believes in the Invincible Sun, in the Precepts, in absolutes of right and wrong. So, here's how he sees it. Before the battle—I'm guessing, but I think I'm on fairly solid ground here—before the battle, he gets down on his knees and prays; dear God, I know it'll take a miracle, but please let me win, and if I do I promise I'll be good and lead a righteous life ever after. What happens? He wins, but gets struck down by an arrow. He comes round three months later, to find that his self-appointed proxies have celebrated the victory the Invincible Sun gave him in answer to his prayer by oppressing the weak and throwing innocent women and children out on the streets, simply in order to mount a display that's the very epitome of vainglorious pomp and blasphemous pride. Of course he's furious. He's scared stiff."

Aimeric stared at him. "That's really what he's thinking?"

"I'm quietly confident, yes." The archdeacon nodded gently. "I've had better opportunities than most to observe the thought processes of true believers, and that's exactly the way I'd expect one to react."

"You knew that," Aimeric said, "and you didn't stop them flooding the Westponds."

The archdeacon shrugged. "I thought Sechimer was going to die," he said. "I'm delighted to be able to say I was wrong. Now I'm afraid it looks rather as if our fates are in the hands of general Calojan." He smiled. "Ah well."

Aimeric got up to leave; then a horrible thought struck him. "The project," he said. It was a stupid word for it, but the only one that sprang to mind.

"What project?"

"The manuscript. Codex Synergicus."

"Oh, that. Postponed indefinitely, I think, don't you? After all, we don't need it now, do we?"

Aimeric felt as though he'd just been slammed against a wall. "But the forger will be here tomorrow."

"Then you'd better send him back home again, hadn't you? Give him some money—it'll have to come out of your own pocket, I'm afraid, as of now we have no funds at our disposal—and get him on the first coach out of town."

"I can't. I made promises."

The archdeacon looked at him. "I can't help that," he said. "Aimeric, maybe you don't quite understand. The regency is over, dissolved, finished. Rightly or wrongly, the emperor is furiously angry with us. Whether we retire quietly into private life or end up with a very good view of the Square depends on whether Calojan—" he almost spat the name "—is prepared to stick his neck out for us. The integrity of your solemn undertakings to prominent Vesani criminals is the last thing on my mind at the moment, trust me."

A very good view—? From the top of the Belltower arch, where the heads of traitors were displayed on meathooks. Aimeric suddenly felt very cold. "All right," he said. "I'll see to it."

"I think you should. I don't imagine it'd incline Sechimer to trust us if he found out we were intent on forging prophesies about him. And he'd only have our word as to what we intended them to say. In fact, I'd be inclined to send a messenger to turn this friend of yours back before he reaches the City."

She, Aimeric thought, not he. But the archdeacon was right. A shame, a great shame, but never mind. "I'll see to it right away," he said.

"Good boy. And now I think you ought to leave. The less we're seen together, the less likely it is that Sechimer will think we're up to something behind his back."

AIMERIC THOUGHT CAREFULLY about what the archdeacon had said. It was good advice, and he couldn't fault the archdeacon on his logic.

So he went to see his one friend in the military, a captain whose brother he'd given a job to. Captain Ortheric kept him waiting for an hour, then sent a clerk to say he could spare five minutes.

"Where's Calojan?" Aimeric asked.

Ortheric scowled at him from behind his desk. "I can't possibly tell you that."

Aimeric sighed and sat down. He hadn't been invited to. "Are you a betting man, Ortheric?"

"No, not really. Why?"

"I think you are," Aimeric said pleasantly. "I think you're gambling that I'm going to be disgraced along with the rest of the regency council, so you need to show everyone we aren't really friends. I think you may have miscalculated the odds."

"It's not like that," Ortheric said awkwardly. "But I can't go around giving away military secrets to civilians. If I tell you where Calojan is, you'll know the current location of the Fifth Army. That's information likely to be of use to an enemy."

"What enemy? They're all dead. Besides, I'm not just a member of the council, I'm also a contractor engaged in supplying vital military equipment. I need to speak to the general personally about important technical issues."

Ortheric was calmer now, and colder. "Fine," he said. "Go through channels."

Aimeric stood up. "You've placed your bet, then."

Ortheric hesitated, then said, "Yes. Sorry."

"No problem." Aimeric gave him a pleasant smile. "If you lose your bet, I'll try not to hold this against you. Good luck."

He left the office and the building, turned the corner, stopped and leant against a wall, breathing hard. On the one hand, he really hadn't expected the news of his disfavour to have travelled so fast. On the other hand, on Ortheric's desk had been a letter bearing Calojan's personal seal; routine orders about procuring oats and barley for the supply train carthorses, but at the top (as is usual with military correspondence) was the date and place. Aimeric had the useful knack of being able to read upside down. Two days ago, Calojan had been at the *Sublime Grace* at Vattenford. What Aimeric now needed most of all was a good map and a ruler.

He took Hosculd with him. He found it hard to explain why. He didn't want to tell Hosculd it was for luck, and no plausible lie sprang readily to mind.

In the event, Hosculd proved useful. "He'll be at Blockhouse 17," he said, as Aimeric squinted helplessly at the map. "Coming from that direction, you can be sure of it."

"There's no such—"

"Not marked," Hosculd explained. "Restricted. They only show it on command-level military maps. Of course, half the carters in the City know where it is. And so do I."

Fair enough. Hosculd had delivered military supplies often enough, before his promotion. "Can we get there in time?"

"If you don't mind riding. A chaise on those roads; forget it."

Hosculd was an accomplished horseman, a legacy from his boyhood on a farm in the Old Country. Aimeric followed, clinging on tight to a handful of mane and keeping his eyes fixed on the tail of Hosculd's horse. Hour after hour of terror, misery and pain; they slept four hours in a ditch and started off again in pitch darkness. Just after noon, Hosculd stopped, stood up in his stirrups and pointed. "There it is," he called out. "Blockhouse 17."

Aimeric could just make out a squareish grey blob through the mist. "Are you sure about that?"

"Nothing else it could be, out here."

Valid point. They'd been crossing the high moor instead of following the military road. Nothing lived up there, not even midges. "Right," Aimeric said, trying to sound brisk; it came out as a sort of plaintive wail. "Let's go and see the general."

HE'D HAVE LIKED a minute or so to catch his breath and scrape mud off his legs, but apparently Calojan could see him immediately. He followed the soldier up three flights of corkscrew stairs, the steps worn concave in the middle by six hundred years of issue boots. Calojan was sitting on his own at a table in the exact centre of a big square room, otherwise completely empty. The unshuttered window framed a wide-angle view of the moor like the most boring landscape mural in the world.

Calojan looked up. He was unshaven, in mud-splattered boots. "Hello," he said. "What the hell are you doing here?"

"I wanted to talk to you."

"I'd sort of gathered. What about?"

There was only one chair, and the table looked too frail to perch on. There was a map spread out on it; Calojan had been drawing lines on it with an ebony ruler and red, green and black inks. "I know," Calojan said, with a feeble grin. "I'm supposed to get back to the City as soon as possible, no stopping for any reason whatsoever. It simply doesn't work like that, of course. If I don't do this paperwork, myself in person, not a deputy, horses will starve and soldiers will have to camp out in the open for days, not knowing where they're supposed to be. So officially I'm wandering lost in the fog. Could happen to anyone."

Aimeric composed a smile. "Of course you are."

"Of course I am. So, what can I do for you?"

Aimeric hesitated, then said, "Did the emperor happen to mention—?"

"Oh yes." Calojan nodded firmly. "A great big long letter in his own handwriting—did you know he can't spell worth a damn? Hard to keep a straight face reading it, sometimes. You're in trouble." He pushed his chair back a little. "Is that why you're here?"

"Indirectly."

"Indirectly," Calojan repeated. "Well, I'd sort of guessed you're a brave man, Aimeric. I hadn't realised quite how brave."

"Me? I'm a coward. I dodged the draft."

Calojan shook his head. "Any man who's in as much trouble as you are and only wants to talk about that *indirectly* is brave enough to qualify for the Great King's personal guard. I assumed you want me to get you off the hook with Sechimer."

"That'd be nice," Aimeric said. "But there was something else."

"Good God." Calojan shrugged. "Go on."

Aimeric shifted his weight from his left foot to his right. He felt colossally stupid, talking like this standing up. "Before the emperor recovered," he said, "I suggested a plan of action to archdeacon Vorsiger. It involved hiring a professional forger from the Vesani Republic to fake a copy of the Codex Synergicus. I don't know if you heard, but the Mezentines—"

Calojan nodded. "Sounds interesting," he said. "Wouldn't mind a look at it myself."

"Anyway," Aimeric went on, "we thought it'd be a nice idea to make up a few prophecies, the sort of thing people would want to come true— victory, peace, universal prosperity, the emperor will reign for sixty years and it'll be a new Age of Gold, that sort of thing. Lots of people will know by now that a true copy of the Codex has arrived from Mezentia, so it's rather a good opportunity. That was my idea, at any rate."

Calojan shrugged. "Not bad," he said, "though perhaps you're over-estimating the gullibility of the average Imperial citizen. Not an unduly superstitious lot, I've always found."

"There would also be a number of prophesies predicting recent events in considerable detail. These prophesies have obviously come true. The manuscript has an unimpeachable provenance and has been certified genuine by all the relevant experts. That's science, not superstition."

"Fine." Calojan smiled. "Yes, I'd vote for that, I guess, so long as you make it look like the thing's been unofficially leaked." He looked at Aimeric closely. "So?"

"So, because the council's out of favour, the project's on hold. But the forger will be arriving very soon, she may already be in the City. If I turn round and tell her, sorry, the deal's off, that'll be that, she won't come back again. And she's the only forger capable of doing a really convincing job. The opportunity would be lost for ever."

Calojan's face hadn't changed when he heard Aimeric's choice of pronoun. "And you think that's a big deal," he said.

"I do, yes."

"Of more immediate concern to you than saving your own neck."

Aimeric took a deep breath. "Well, you see," he said, "I was kind of assuming you'd put in a good word for me in any event, without me having to ask."

"Did you now."

Aimeric smiled. "Because when you needed tanged dogwood arrows and they wouldn't let you have them, I got you what you wanted. And, next time you need something really badly, you know I'll get it for you. So, I'm useful to you. Also, unlike pretty well everybody else at the court apart from the emperor himself, you're a man of honour and principle. You scared me to death and made a fool out of me when you were tricking the enemy into thinking you'd been recalled. Therefore, you'd stick your neck out for me because you're grateful."

"Is that right?"

"Yes."

Calojan pushed his chair back further still, stretched his legs out and put his hands behind his head. "Aimeric," he said, "let me tell you something I've learned over the years about luck. Luck is like a bow. You stretch it so far, it'll shoot straight and fast and hit the mark. Stretch it just a little bit further, it'll break, the top limb will bash you on the head and the lower limb will hit you in the balls so hard your eyes'll water. Would you like us to start this conversation again from the beginning?"

"No, thanks."

"Fine." He sat up straight and edged his chair close to the table. "All right, here's what I'll do. I'll tell Sechimer that in my opinion, what the regency council did was wrong; they shouldn't have flooded the slums and driven out all those poor people, it was inhumane and arrogant, and anybody who knows Sechimer would also know he'd never do such a thing. But, I'll go on, what's done is done and the people who did it happen to be the wisest and most trustworthy men in the Imperial service—which isn't saying much, of course, but there you are. At this particularly delicate moment, with the economy in a mess and everything really fragile after the hammering we've taken in the war, it'd be highly injudicious for His Majesty to deprive himself of the advice of his best men at a time when he most needs them, all because they did one bad, stupid thing. I might even draw his attention to the Sashan way of doing things, one mistake and you're dead, and ask him to reflect on whether that approach served the Great King well." He paused for breath, then went on; "That's what I'd have said anyway, even if you hadn't come to see me."

"Thank you," Aimeric said.

"It happens to be what I think," Calojan said. "Now, assuming Sechimer listens to me, you and your fellow idiots on the council will all be back in post in a day or two, and therefore in a position to carry out any projects, any *worthwhile* projects, you'd already set in motion. What you do in the meantime is up to you, and if it's even remotely illegal, you never told me about it. Clear?"

It was a moment before Aimeric could speak. "Clear," he said.

"Splendid." He was frowning; he relaxed just a little. "Sticking my neck out is what I do," he said. "Really, it's the only thing I'm good at. So far, it's served me and the empire well. By the same token, a man falling off a very tall building can say when he reaches the halfway point that so far, he's come to no harm and he's thoroughly enjoying the ride. I don't know what you're up to, Aimeric, but I won't ask, because I don't want to prompt you to lie to me, it'd be bad for our working relationship. Just promise me it won't hurt the emperor. Well?"

"I promise."

"You do know, don't you, what'll happen to you if you mess me around?"

"I can guess."

"No," Calojan said gently, "You've led a sheltered life, so I don't suppose you can. But that's fine, I'm sure you've got the message. Another snippet of homely folk wisdom from my inexhaustible supply; it may be chilly outside, but setting fire to your coat is a bloody stupid way to keep warm. Do think long and hard before you stick your neck out too far." He yawned and rubbed his eyes. "I've got to go," he said. "I can't stay lost on the moors forever, much as I'd like to. I'd offer you a lift back to Town, but I don't want to be seen with you right now."

As well as a hundred and eighty trachy a day, the job at the de Peguilhan factory provided accommodation (a bunk in a long shed where two dozen other workers lived) and a meal each evening. It was cleaner and quieter than Westponds, but Raffen wasn't sure he liked the people he was working with. They were all refugees from Mondhem; shorter and stockier than the City people, and miserable most of the time. They didn't seem to like people from outside the empire—offcomers was one of the words they used; the others were presumably meant to be insulting, but Raffen didn't know enough Imperial slang to catch the nuances. He'd had to fight twice, putting five highly skilled men out of action for several weeks. But the supervisor was a Permian who didn't like Imperials, so he kept his job, just about, and there was no more of that sort of trouble.

The work itself was hard but not too disagreeable. When he'd reported to the deputy chief supervisor on his first morning, he'd been asked what he could do. Fortuitously, while he'd been waiting to be seen, he'd witnessed a furious argument between a man and one of the other supervisors, which ended with the supervisor calling for someone to escort the quarrelsome man off the site. He'd gathered that the quarrelsome man was a striker's mate on the trip, whatever that meant.

"Well," he had said, therefore, "a bit of everything, really. But last place I was at, I was a striker's mate on the trip."

He'd said the right thing; the deputy chief stared at him, then laughed. "That's all right," he said. "Where did you say you were at?"

"United Forge," Raffen replied, hoping there wasn't such a firm. "It was just a small outfit, in Mondhem."

"Never heard of it," the deputy chief said. "Still, I was never in Mondhem. Can't have been that small if it had a trip."

"We did specialist work," Raffen replied. "Government stuff."

Better still. It turned out that a trip was a trip hammer, a huge rectangular block of solid iron mounted on a swinging arm operated by a cam off a flywheel driven by an overshot water wheel. The striker's mate's job was to position a piece of cherry-red-hot steel on the anvil while the block pounded it into the required shape. You held the steel in long tongs, and there were various tools that slotted into a square hole on the back of the anvil—swedges, fullers, dies—that formed the metal into specific shapes, such as round or square rods, rectangular bars and so on. Mostly, though, the trip was used to beat rough bars of newly smelted iron into thin flat sheets, for making plate armour. He'd stood and watched for a few minutes, on the pretext of seeing how they did things differently from what he'd been used to at United Forge, until he got the general idea. Actually, it wasn't so bad. You had to concentrate on what you were doing, but otherwise it was pretty straightforward—

"You're a good worker," the deputy chief said, when he came off his first shift. "I'm surprised."

"Oh," Raffen said. His throat was bone dry. The rest of him was soaking wet with sweat. "Why's that?"

"Well," said the deputy chief, "You don't look like a forge hand. I'd have said you'd never been in a hot-work shop in your life before."

"What makes you say that?"

The deputy chief smiled. "Your arms," he said, "backs of your hands. No burn marks." He rolled up his own sleeve; his hand and arm were pitted with dozens of small pink spots and weals. "I said to myself, he's never been in no forge. Still, the big boss man sent you here, so I had to give you a shout."

"Ah." Raffen smiled. "Where I come from, we wear big leather gloves, cuffs right down to here. Keeps the clinker off."

"In Mondhem?"

"Back home," Raffen replied, "up north. I brought my gloves down south with me, but I lost them when we left Mondhem. Feels strange working without them, but I expect I'll get used to it."

He'd done so well in his first week on the sheet-iron trip that they'd moved him to doing profiles—fiddly, delicate work, making thin rods and bars with splayed or scrolled ends. He found he was very good at it, which was just as well, since he was still very unpopular with the other men. Then one day there was an accident. The striker, who controlled the operation of the machine, got his arm caught in the linkages. He'd been careless for a split second, turning his head to listen to someone shouting something at him; a moment later there was a messy red pulp where his right arm had been, and an hour after that he was dead. The trouble was, there were no other strikers experienced enough to run the profiling trip; it meant promotion and more money, but nobody wanted to do it, because of the danger. A profiles striker, the deputy chief explained when Raffen asked, had to have a really light touch; he ought to be able to crack the shell of a boiled egg without squashing it. Raffen could see his point. The striker's mate on profiling had to get in very close to the work sometimes. He'd always trusted the old striker implicitly, because he had to, but to begin with he'd been painfully aware that a false move on the striker's part would cost him a hand or an arm.

"I was a striker back in Mondhem for a while," he said. "Of course, it was a smaller trip we had back there, only three tons. But we did a lot of small work."

The deputy chief gave him an odd look. "I've been asking some of the other Mondhem lads," he said. "None of them ever heard of United Forge. That was where you said you were, right?"

"Like I said, we did government stuff," Raffen replied. "Restricted, a lot of it. We sort of kept ourselves to ourselves."

So they powered up the profiling trip, and Raffen stood for a moment or so figuring out the controls. The big lever was a clutch, which connected or disconnected the hammer from the drive train. The foot plate governed the speed of the swinging arm, which in turn controlled the force of the blow; you stood on it hard for a full strike, or nudged it gently for a little tap. Nothing to it, really.

They heated up a bar and laid it on the anvil, and he played around for a while, getting the feel of the machine. By the time the bar had cooled to dark red he reckoned he'd got the hang of it. So, apparently, did the deputy chief. "You're quite right," he said, "you're a striker. All right, you carry on." He gave Raffen another of those odd looks and added, "Just be a bit bloody careful, will you? That's my men's hands and arms under that bloody block."

So he concentrated; for four days he worked with a cricked neck and a constant headache, and then it wasn't so bad. The striker's mate who worked with him was an old man, from the City rather than Mondhem; he had a house of his own at the bottom of Sharrowgate, a wife and four children, all grown up and gone. He had thin wrists and huge hands, and he was very good indeed at his job. For the first five days or so they hardly spoke to each other; the old man was fairly deaf after a lifetime on the trip, though he always carefully stuffed his ears with fresh bog-cotton at the start of each shift, and it was hard enough to make yourself heard at the best of times. On the sixth day, when they were resting between morning and afternoon shifts (there was always a pause about noon, to give the firemen a chance to pull out the fused clinker from the fire, damp down and relay) the old man sat down next to him and said, "I'm Geuta. Who're you?"

"Raffen." The old man shook his head, then turned so his left ear was facing. "Raffen," he repeated, a little louder.

"Offcomer."

Raffen nodded. "That's right."

"Quick learner," Geuta said, "I'll say that for you. Why'd you make out you were a striker, when you never done it before?"

Raffen was quiet for a moment or two. Geuta didn't seem in a hurry for an answer. He thought about it for a while, then said, "I reckoned I could do the job, and it's better money. How did you know?"

"Been working with strikers forty year. You're right handed, but you use your left foot. But when you started, you used your right foot."

"Ah." Raffen nodded. "Yes, I found I've got more control that way. Don't know why, but I do."

"It's because you need your right foot, your master foot, to keep your balance. Balance is the most important thing, see. If you're off balance, you haven't got the fine touch."

"That figures," Raffen said.

"You got good balance. I used to have, but when I got deaf I lost it, so I had to quit to striking and do this job instead. You want to take care of your ears, boy, or you won't be a striker very long."

"Thanks."

Geuta fished in his pocket and took out a big, flat biscuit, wrapped in clean cloth. He broke it neatly down the middle and gave Raffen one half. It was the first time anyone had shared anything with him. The biscuit was rock hard and tasted of compressed dust. "My old lady bakes 'em," Geuta said. "Keeps you on your feet, afternoon shift."

"Thank you."

"So," Geuta said, "what do you do really? Where you come from?"

"Stockman," Raffen said. "But that was a long time ago."

"Farm boy, huh?"

"We worked for a man called Sighvat." Now where had that name come from? "He had a big spread and a lot of livestock, so he had a dozen stockmen. But times got bad, so I had to go. So I came down here, to Mondhem."

"You were never in Mondhem," Geuta said. "I asked the lads. No offcomers in Mondhem."

Raffen grinned. "I thought it'd sound better," he said. "I guessed the deputy chief would know if I said I'd been working here, he'd have asked me where I was before, and I don't know any of the places in the City."

"You're new to forge work," Geuta said. "But you learned bloody quick. You're all right. Better than most I worked with. Careful."

"I try to be."

"That's good. How long you been in the City?"

Raffen shrugged. "A few months."

"And before that you were a farm hand?"

"That's right."

"You must be pretty smart, then, if you can learn so fast."

Raffen laughed. "Not really," he said. "On the farm you have to pick things up quickly, or figure them out for yourself. There's always too much to do and no time to do it in."

"They all like you back where you come from, then?"

"Pretty much. I was nobody special." He smiled. "I like it here. It's a sight better than some places I've been."

Two days later there was a new striker's mate. He was from Mondhem, perfectly competent. At midday, Raffen asked him, "Where's Geuta?"

"Who?"

"The man who had your job."

"Oh, him." The new man looked surprised. "Hadn't you heard?"

Geuta had been murdered. They found his body a hundred yards from his home. His skull had been crushed from behind and his pocket had been emptied. The murderers, everyone said, were almost certainly offcomers, the northerners who'd been turned out of Westponds and sent home. The few that had stayed in the City had all turned to crime; must have done, since there were no jobs for them now, so how were they feeding themselves? You want to watch out, the new man concluded; everyone knows you worked with him, so maybe you knew where he lived, or followed him home.

Raffen shook his head. "I'm not a thief," he said.

"Didn't say you were. But that's what people are saying. Thought you ought to know."

When the afternoon shift ended, Raffen didn't go back to the bunkhouse. Instead, he went out through the foundry gate, found a quiet alley, opened the cloth bag he kept his money in and tried to guess how much there was. You couldn't count all those tiny saucer-shaped scraps of copper foil, so you made your best estimate based on weight. Well over two thousand trachy; probably nearer three.

He had no idea where to go; but that hadn't hindered him in the forest, so he made his best guess and headed east, towards the Perfect Square. When he got to the good neighbourhoods, where they lit the streets at night with oil-lamps on high posts, he went in to a tavern and asked directions. They looked doubtfully at him—what would someone like you be wanting a money-changer for?—but told him; out of here, first right, second left, go on fifty yards, sign of the Golden Locust, you can't miss it.

The man at the Golden Locust was young, well-dressed and smiling as he talked to an elderly customer. On the table he sat behind were twenty or so long, narrow wooden boxes, all full of gold coins. Three very strange-looking men stood motionless behind him; they wore beautiful silk clothes under gilded chain-mail, and held drawn swords. Raffen guessed they were either genuine Aram Cosseilhatz or locals dressed up to look like them.

The smiling man was in no hurry; but neither was Raffen, who leaned against the doorpost and waited patiently. Eventually the elderly man picked up a cloth bag—heavy, by the way it dragged his hand down when he first lifted it—and left the shop; Raffen politely stood aside to let him pass. Apparently he was invisible, but he didn't mind that.

"Yes?" said the smiling man, who'd stopped smiling.

"I want to change some money."

"What've you got?"

"Trachy," Raffen replied. "I'd like to change them for gold."

The man looked at him. "The exchange rate," he said, "is twenty-six thousand seven hundred trachy to the solidus. How many have you got?"

Raffen frowned. "About three thousand."

"Sorry, can't help you," the man said briskly. "Thanks for calling in."

Raffen stayed where he was. "Isn't there anything smaller than a solidus?"

"No." The man's lips twitched at the edges. "There's your one-solidus, your five and your ten. That's current Imperial, at seven eight five fine. Also there's your one, two and five solidi obsolete Imperial heavy, at nine two five fine, obviously they're worth more because there's more gold in them. There's foreign stuff, of course, like your Vesani tremissis, twenty to the solidus, your Mezentine scudi, six to the solidus, your Sashan mancus, they're not legal tender now, goes without saying, but as bullion two of them'll buy you three solidi, your Perimadeian angel, three to the solidus, your Scherian angel, five to the solidus, and those stonking great big Scherian cartwheel jobs, which we don't handle. All out of your price-range, I'm afraid. Sorry."

"I see," Raffen said. "So what can I do with—?"

"Spend it," the man said with a shrug. "Get yourself a good meal and a girl and lots and lots of beer, that's what copper money's for. Strictly for the poor folks. I only deal in hard currency here. Goodbye."

The brightly-coloured guards hadn't moved, but they appeared to have noticed him. "Thank you," Raffen said, and left.

It was good advice, but he didn't feel like taking it. Instead, he found a small covered portico, out of the way and deserted apart from a couple of old men, sound asleep and snoring under frayed grain sacks. He rolled up his coat for a pillow and closed his eyes. When he woke up in the morning, the old men had gone, and so had his money and his shoes.

General Calojan at his side, the emperor did public penance for the flooding of Westponds. Starting at Florian's Column, he walked to the Golden Spire, barefoot and dressed in a novice monk's habit, stopping every ten yards to bow towards the spire and repeat the Shorter Contrition. He was met on the temple steps by the members of the regency council, dressed in white and linked together by a chain stapled to the slaves' collars they wore round their necks. There, in front of an estimated fifty thousand people, Sechimer formally forgave them; the chains were struck off, the rivets cut and the collars removed. Archdeacon Vorsiger then conducted them inside the temple, where he celebrated the Conditional Office. When it was over, Sechimer returned to the palace in a plain military chaise, escorted by Calojan and forty mounted guardsmen. The council went out the back way, each making his own way quietly home.

"Well?" she said.

Aimeric sank down in a chair and threw a heavy metal band on the floor. "Bloody thing didn't half chafe my neck," he said. "You'd have thought they could've put in a little bit of discreet padding."

Orsella picked it up. "Silver," she said. "About nine two five fine."

"Shinier," Aimeric said, with a grin. "Got to be shiny so everyone in the crowd could see it."

"But you get to keep it."

Aimeric shrugged. "The point wasn't specifically addressed," he said. "Anyway, it's over and done with and we're officially forgiven. Now maybe we can get on with business."

She perched on the arm of the chair and kissed him. She took her time over it. If a thing's worth doing, it's worth doing properly.

"And now I'd like to see this manuscript," she said.

He breathed in deeply. "We can't," he said. "It's in the Old Library at the Studium. You need a letter from a don or a priest."

"I don't think so," she said sweetly. "You're a member of the council, one of the most important men in the empire. Well, aren't you?"

"Yes, but—" He paused and frowned. "Good point," he said. "Let's go now."

In the event there was no trouble at all. The senior clerk recognised Aimeric from the victory celebrations and sent a novice running to fetch the key. "We won't be long," Aimeric told him. "If you could just show us where it's kept, we won't keep you."

It wasn't as simple as that, not by a long way. From the porter's lodge they walked across the Great Yard to the Inner Court, enclosed by crenelated walls that a dozen men could have held against an army. Once through the massive bronze gates of the Court, they made their way through the Deacon's Garden, with its unique collection of flowering trees and shrubs from every corner of the empire, until they reached the

Solar, popularly known as the Eye of God; a ten-storey circular tower surmounted by a copper dome. The Old Library occupied the whole of the top floor. You got up there by way of a tiny corkscrew stair—there were bells you rang, to warn people not to come down when you were coming up, because there was no way two human beings could pass on those stairs—which brought you to a tiny landing, basically just a narrow step a bird could perch on if it was careful, facing a massive iron door. There were two keys to this door; the senior clerk had one, the emperor had the other. It made a sound like a child screaming as it turned in the lock.

The Library was built by Florian III, with the proceeds of his campaign against the Iasyges—look for them on a map and you won't find them; Florian was extremely thorough, and the entire wealth of that once mighty nation just about paid for the building work and the fixtures and fittings, though not the books. The interior of the dome was covered in gilded mosaic depicting the Ascent of the Invincible Sun, the Three Passions and the Day of Reckoning. Opinions differ as to their artistic merit; most of the work is late Mannerist, which is an acquired taste, but extensive restoration was carried out after the fire in Genseric IV's time, and the restorer was Garalio the Elder, at the height of his middle period; it's a shame, some people say, that the fire damage wasn't considerably more extensive. The twelve great bay windows still have most of their original Mezentine stained glass, so that, depending on when you visit, the room is flooded with different subtle and otherworldly blends of coloured light. For serious reading of difficult manuscripts, the visitor is advised to take his book onto the upper gallery and make use of the clear golden light that pours in through the four inner skylights; the Scherian crystal glass has some sort of magnifying effect that nobody now understands, giving rise to what is reckoned to be the best reading light in the world.

"This way," said the senior clerk.

On the side opposite the door there was a sort of golden box built against the wall, about fifteen feet square. Aimeric didn't see the door until the clerk unlocked it and held it open for them. When they were inside—pitch dark—he closed it and locked it behind them, then fumbled with a tinderbox and lit a small oil lamp. "The restricted area," he explained. "Sorry about this."

Actually it wasn't too bad; the gilding on the walls reflected and amplified the light of the lamp so well that it was almost as bright as daylight. It helped that the ceiling was one enormous mirror—

"That's so that the attendant clerk can make sure you're not copying out stuff," Orsella said cheerfully. "I've heard all about this place, but it's wonderful to actually be here."

As far as the clerk was concerned she didn't exist. "Now then," he said. "You wanted to see the Codex Synergicus."

"That's right."

The clerk nodded, then stooped and pulled out a box from under a table. It cost him a great deal of effort; the box was iron, with four blued-steel Mezentine padlocks. There was a different key for each one. He opened the lid and lowered it gently until it rested against the gilded floor.

"Thanks ever so much," Orsella said. "If you wouldn't mind waiting outside, we'll let you know when we're finished."

The clerk looked as though she'd just stabbed the emperor. Aimeric took a deep breath and said, "It's all right. We won't be long. We'll knock on the door and you can let us out."

The clerk looked at him for a very long time, then unlocked the door and went out. They heard the key turn. "Was that necessary?" Aimeric said.

"Oh, I think so." Orsella was on her knees beside the box, peering at the manuscript. "It probably wouldn't be a good idea if he overheard us. You see, it's a fake."

Aimeric stared at her. "What?"

She turned her head and smiled at him. "A forgery. No bloody good. Well," she added, "let me qualify that statement a little. You told me it's supposed to be over three hundred years old."

"That's right."

She shook her head. "More like three months," she said. "Look here, at this illuminated capital."

"The blue one?"

"The blue one. Mezentine colours are always standard. There's guild specifications for how you mix them, they've got to be just right or they throw you out of the guild and you starve. Now, as I'm sure you know, the Mezentines mix their oils with stuff that doesn't completely dry for ages and ages. You can fake that, with stuff you make by grinding up a special kind of rock salt; it dries the oils out in no time flat. But it also does funny things to the colour blue. Makes it slightly deeper. Now, that effect wears off relatively quickly—about six months—and once it's worn off you can't tell the difference. But this blue letter here's that slightly darker shade. Therefore, this lot was written two to six months ago, no later than that. Sorry."

Aimeric's head was spinning. "So the whole thing's just junk."

Her smile grew warmer. "Not necessarily," she said. "Think about it. Even if it was the genuine article, it's still only a copy of a translation. For all we know, this is just a slightly more recent copy of that copy. Could be the Mezentines didn't want to give us the original, so they had a copy made and thought it'd be good enough to fool you. Which it was," she added pleasantly, "until I showed up. Perfectly reasonable risk for them to have taken, given that there's only one of me in the whole wide world."

He tried to think. "You're sure about this? It's not just the funny light in here or something."

"Absolutely sure," she replied. "I know all about the use of sal draconis for faking Mezentine blue. I discovered it, for crying out loud."

"Ah."

"And, as everybody knows, I never leave the Vesani Republic. So, there you are. The manuscript's a fake. That's not to say by any means that the content isn't perfectly authentic."

He looked at her helplessly. "So what does that mean?"

"It means this may be a true copy of the now-lost Codex or it may not. Furthermore, the prophesies contained in the Codex may or may not be trustworthy indications of what will happen in the future." She grinned. "You pays your money and you takes your choice."

"Thank you so fucking much."

"You're welcome. Meanwhile—" She'd taken the manuscript out of the box and was unrolling it slowly and carefully, "let's have a closer look at this baby. Even if it's an outright phoney, it can still tell us what the Mezentines want us to believe. That's valuable diplomatic intelligence, surely."

Aimeric scowled. "I have this mental picture of a bunch of Mezentine guild masters in a room somewhere killing themselves laughing at all the aggravation they're causing us. I think we should forget about the whole thing right now."

"Oh, you. You're no fun. The whole point is, only you and I know this is a—let's say, a recent copy. Only the council knows what it says. Your original scheme is still as brilliant as ever. And when I've done my fake of this fake—which'll be ten times better, I can promise you that—the people of the empire will end up with the prophesies they need so they can feel really good about the future, and we'll all live happily ever after. I don't know," she added sadly. "So many people these days have a morbid obsession with the truth. Nine times out of ten no good comes of it."

He looked at her, lost in a curious mixture of anger and admiration. "Fine," he said. "We'll do that. Now, if you've seen enough—"

"Whoa there, hold on." She was scrolling through the manuscript; she had the knack of being able to read very quickly. "This is fascinating stuff. How much of it did they translate for you?"

"Hang on," he said. "You can read ancient Mezentine?"

"Of course," she said, as though it was a silly question. "Now, this is interesting. If this really is a complete fabrication, their linguists are much better at it than their forgers. Stylistically, grammatically and syntactically, this reads very much like the genuine article."

Aimeric was getting impatient. He didn't like being inside the golden box, he didn't want to keep the chief clerk hanging about for too long in case he got suspicious, and he needed a pee. "Like you said, it doesn't really matter, does it? After all—"

"The Mezentines," she went on, as though he hadn't spoken, "are notoriously bad at pastiching the earlier forms of their own language. I guess it's because it's changed relatively little for so long; they just can't detect the subtle nuances. If you want my professional opinion, on the balance of probabilities I'd say this text was written at least four hundred years ago. Like, whoever wrote this knew the proper use of the pluperfect subjunctive. Modern Mezentines always get it wrong."

It was impossible that she could ever get on his nerves. But—"You don't, of course."

"Of course. I took the trouble to learn it. The Mezentines think they know it already. So," she said crisply, looking up for a moment, "that would tend to support my theory that this is a modern copy of an ancient original. It may not be the actual Codex Synergicus, but if it's hooky, at least it's *old* hooky. You want to read some of this, by the way. It's fascinating."

"I can't—"

"Just as well you've got me, then, isn't it? Listen to this. 'On the same day, two kings will walk barefoot in the Perfect Square. One king with his dog will strike the chains off the necks of his enemies. He will move a river and find his grave, and those who move rivers will dig it for him. One king will come from under the water. The river will flood and he will walk barefoot until he meets with the second six-fingered man, and he will always be what he claims to be. This will be true; I have already seen it.' Now that's just plain weird."

"Well, yes," Aimeric said. "But it doesn't mean anything. It's drivel."

"Really? A king will walk barefoot in the Perfect Square? He will strike the chains off the necks of his enemies? Come on, Aimeric, you were *there*. It's talking about *today*."

He stared at her. "Give me strength," he whimpered. "Orsella, you don't seriously mean you believe in this dogshit? You just told me, it's a fake."

She nodded, slowly and angrily. "Sure," she said. "It's a fake, written about three months ago. And it's come true today."

"Oh come on. It could mean anything."

"One king with his dog. You know what Calojan means in Permian? That's where his family comes from. Calojan means 'good dog.' Coincidence?"

"Fine. So who's the other barefoot king, then? There's supposed to have been two, but I only saw one. Well?"

"I don't know, do I? I'm just saying—"

"Let's see, now," Aimeric went on. "There's the king of Asirhoene; not here today. There's the king of Naissus. There's the Great King, I suppose, he was there, or at least his head was; I'm not sure that counts are barefoot, though. The Aram Cosseilhatz have princes who are really kings, but they didn't even send a representative. There's some character called the Red King down south somewhere on the other side of the desert. Can you think of any others? Not that many kings about these days. Therefore, it didn't come true. Therefore—"

"Oh, forget it," Orsella said angrily. "It's not worth arguing over. I just thought it was interesting, that's all. I didn't think you'd take it personally."

Suddenly, Aimeric grinned. "Does Calojan really mean good dog?"

"Well, more beautiful than good, but yes."

"You know Permian."

"All seven dialects."

He smiled at her. "You're wonderful, do you know that? I can't wait to tell Vorsiger. It'll make his day."

She was rolling up the manuscript. "If you like," she said, "and for the right price, I could do you a perfect hitherto-undiscovered lost masterpiece by Calojan's dad. With full-page illustrations, in twelve colours including Mezentine blue. You could give it to him for his birthday."

THEY MET IN Semplan's tent, in the middle of the night. There were six of them, a tight fit. Semplan had borrowed two folding stools from his nephew—beautiful things, Imperial, rosewood carved with vines and strange-looking flowers nobody could put a name to. Semplan himself chose to sit on the floor.

"Well now," he said, as Joiauz came in and sat down. "Without your shadow for once."

Joiauz pulled a sad face. "He's learning so quickly," he replied. "And the questions he asks. It's enough to scare you to death."

Viatges laughed. "Must get that from his mother's side," he said.

"I imagine you're right," Joiauz said. "The old man was brave as a lion but not exactly a thinker, and I'd far rather be fishing. Still, it's a relief to be able to talk without having those terrible big eyes on the back of my neck all the time. I love him to bits, but he wears me out."

Autet poured himself a drink and passed the jug on. "Right," he said. "Are we doing this properly, or are we just here to tell hunting stories?"

"Properly," Joiauz replied, after a moment's consideration. "I know it's not binding if he's not here, but we're supposed to be making policy."

"Whatever you like," Semplan said, as the jug reached him. He peered into it and shrugged. "All right, then, the war."

"Quite," Joiauz said. "Which is, of course, over. I can confirm that Calojan's paid us in full, on the nail, no quibbling."

"Gold coins?"

"Yes," said Joiauz. "I take it you're all happy to leave the choice of a burial site to me, same as usual."

Everyone nodded. Semplan said, "This isn't me talking, it's a couple of my neighbours. Don't you think you should tell someone else where you've buried the stuff, just in case something happens to you? It'd be an awful shame if we can't find it again."

Joiauz nodded. "The same thought did cross my mind," he said. "In the past, as you know, we've always restricted the location of buried treasure to one man, the Great Prince. I'd like to suggest that this case is different. First, I'm not actually the prince, I'm just a regent. Second, we've never had to hide anything like this much stuff before. The biggest deposit I know about was back in DePartetz's time, when they cached six hundred pounds of gold coin in the Westfalls—which, incidentally, was never recovered. We're talking about well over ten times that. I'm not particularly comfortable with the thought of nearly seven tons of gold sitting in a hole in the ground that only I know about. Question is, who should I share that knowledge with?"

He paused and waited for a moment. Silence. Then Autet said, "Don't look at me."

"Exactly," Joiauz said. "I take it the same goes for all of you. Quite. Now, you six are the only ones I'd trust with the location, so that rules out the rest of the council. Anybody below council level is obviously out of the question."

"Fine," Viatges said. "So we do it the usual way."

"Yes," Joiauz said. "Or there's one other choice. How about Chauzida?"

"He's a kid," Semplan objected.

"A very bright kid," Joiauz replied. "And he's the Great Prince. Properly speaking, it's all his stuff anyway. So, he won't steal it, and the other great danger, someone getting hold of him and forcing the location out of him, is hardly a serious problem given who he is. What do you think?"

Short pause for thought; then Autet said, "We'll do that, then. Good idea."

Joiauz grinned. "That's a weight off my mind. Seven tons, to be precise. Anyhow, back to the war."

"The no Vei," Luzir said.

"The bloody no Vei." Autet scowled. "Can any of you tell me what the hell they think they're playing at? I've heard the reports. It was some of my people got hit in the last lot. This isn't just your normal playful cattle raiding, or young idiots showing off to impress the girls. It's deliberate and nasty, and they're up to something."

"Agreed," said Luzir. "What, though?"

"Good question," Semplan muttered. "If you look at the facts— grassland deliberately burned, wells poisoned, bridges broken down, all that—you'd have to say they're trying to push us out of the whole of Northfold. Maybe I wasn't paying attention when my father explained the rules, but that's not right. Northfold's common ground, always has been."

Joiauz shook his head. "I think things have got a bit more complicated lately," he said. "Sorry, properly speaking this should wait till we do the nations, but I think we should consider it now." He paused for objections, then continued; "While I was with Calojan, he told me some of the stuff he'd been hearing from his own spies out north-east. As you know, the Imperials have got a bloody impressive spy network, even that far out. I'm ashamed to say, they hear an awful lot more about things beyond the mountains than we do."

"Well, they can afford it," Autet said defensively.

"Quite right," Joiauz said. "No reproach intended. Anyway, Calojan's men reckon they've heard rumours from reliable sources that the Shan Tan and the Jin are moving westwards—drought or an earthquake or something; in any event, it's not just raiding, they're looking for a new home. That means the Goida are getting squeezed, and there's only one direction they can go. Up till now they've never dared cross the mountains, but you just don't know how desperate they are. Now, if the no Vei and the Chantat have been hearing the same thing, it begins to make a certain degree of sense. If they lose all their ground in the foothills to the Goida, they're going to be in big trouble. So, they're looking at the Northfold, and we're in the way."

"Why us?" Semplan asked.

"We're weak," Joiauz said. "Leaderless, for one thing. We've lost good men fighting the emperor's war. Likewise, we've used up a lot of resources over there, depleted our hay and fodder and munitions and got nothing but gold coins in return. If the choice is between us and the Rosinholet, who would you choose to pick a fight with?"

"All right," said Semplan. "We've got a problem. What do we do?"

Joiauz thought before answering. "I say we move," he said. "We're too weak for a real slogging match with the no Vei. The no Vei and the Chantat combined, forget it. If they want the Northfold, let them have it. We'll have to find somewhere else, that's all."

"Oh, sure," Luzir said angrily. "We'll just say our prayers, and tomorrow morning we'll find a brand new valley nobody's ever noticed before. Simple as that."

"Actually," Joiauz said gently, "that's not so far from what I had in mind."

Everyone was silent for a while. Then Semplan said, "I don't think I like where this is going."

"The Essa," Joiauz said firmly. "Yes, it's Imperial territory. Yes, the last time we tried to go there, we got the shit kicked out of us by the Imperial heavy infantry. But guess what. That was a hundred and twenty years ago, things were very different. There's nearly twice as many of us now. And the empire is weak."

They looked at him. "Tell the Sashan that," Luzir said.

Joiauz smiled. "Can't," he said, "there's none left. And who killed them all? We did. Not the empire, because the Imperials lost so many men fighting the Sashan before Calojan came along that they couldn't make up three full battalions without enlisting old men and boys. The empire may look stronger than it's ever been, but the truth is, they're on their knees. They're desperately short of manpower, and a large part of their national wealth is sitting in big pottery jars on the carts out there, waiting for me and the boy to bury it. Forget the military strength of the empire; the military strength of the empire is *us*."

"And Calojan," Autet said quietly. "Do you really want to start a fight with him?"

Joiauz shook his head vigorously. "Not if I can possibly avoid it," he said. "Believe me, I've met him, I've spent hours in his company. I watched him take apart the Sashan, and I still couldn't tell you exactly how he did it. He scares the life out of me, and that's the truth."

"Well, then," said Semplan.

Joiauz took a deep breath. "I think we're at cross purposes," he said. "I said we should move across the Essa. I didn't say we should take it by force. I say we should ask Sechimer to give it to us."

Another dead silence. Autet broke it. "Are you out of your mind?"

"I don't think so," Joiauz said quietly. "I've just come through there, on my way home. The place is practically deserted. The emperor before Sechimer, the red-head, he forcibly enlisted tens of thousands of men from the farms and villages, and those poor buggers never came home. The people that're left simply can't work the land any more. They're moving out in droves, heading for the cities or the lowlands. It won't be long before all that lot is just moorland. It's no earthly good to Sechimer like that. But what would be useful to him—more to the point, what'd be useful to Calojan, would be a large, friendly nation living there who'd be no trouble, stand ready to fight his wars for him, and keep the door firmly shut against the really ugly bastards who may start pouring over the mountain passes any day now. See? It's good for them, and it's good for us. Right now, we're being eaten alive by the no Vei. So, we give them what they want, and we go where they'd never dare bother us again. They don't know the state the empire's in. All they know is, the emperor just wiped the Sashan off the face of the earth. Catch them picking a fight with someone who could do that."

Autet smiled at him. "I can see why you didn't want the boy to hear all that," he said.

"Quite." Joiauz grinned. "It's at least three distinct counts of treason against the Ancestors, and he's been taking an unhealthy interest in the law recently. Anyway, what do you think? Honestly, I don't see we've got much of a choice, and if we do nothing, we're screwed. Come on, Partetz, you've been very quiet. What do you reckon?"

The old man was sitting at the back, almost outside the circle of light cast by the charcoal brazier. "I'd be inclined to agree with you," he said, "if it wasn't for one thing. We can't just give up the Northfold. It's not ours to give away. It belongs to the Cosseilhatz, not us."

"If we don't," Joiauz said gently, "it'll be taken from us."

Partetz shrugged. "That's different," he said. "That wouldn't be our fault. Just giving in would be. Come on, Joiauz, you're an intelligent man, like your father was before you. You understand what I'm saying."

"What I understand is that if we try and hold on to it, a lot of our people will get killed and the outcome will be the same. No, I take that back. The outcome won't be the same, because if we lose too many men defending the Northfold, we won't have the strength to bargain with the emperor, and we won't get the Essa valleys. Then what?"

Partetz shook his head. "I'm not getting at you," he said. "You're a brave, clever man trying to do the right thing. But you simply can't do this. It's not an option."

"Chauzida—"

"Couldn't do it either, even if he was old enough. I'm very sorry, but there it is."

There was a very long silence. Then Autet said, "What about the emperor? He owes us. He could help us, against the no Vei."

Joiauz scowled at him. "You haven't been listening."

"He could lend us Calojan," Viatges said. "He could beat the no Vei. Then we'd give the emperor back his gold, to say thank you. That'd solve his problem, and he'd have solved ours."

"Actually, that's not a bad idea," Semplan said. "Joiauz? Could Calojan beat the no Vei?"

"It's possible," Joiauz said. "I honestly don't know. If any one man could, it'd be him."

"Well," Luzir said sharply, "now we've got two options. A moment ago, we only had one. I call that progress. You talk to Calojan, Joiauz, he'd have to listen to you. See what he says."

"I can tell you that," Joiauz replied. "He'll say, he's just finished one war, he doesn't want to go straight into another one, certainly not against an enemy he doesn't know, in a strange country, in a fight that's nothing to do with him and his people."

"That's exactly what we did, though," Semplan pointed out. "Fair's fair. We've got merit against him. If he wants to be our friend, he's got to help us."

"I think he'd say the gold coins cover all of that," Joiauz said. "That's how the Imperials see things. They're a bit hazy about concepts like merit."

"You're the regent," Partetz said. "You have to decide. But I think I can safely say, the meeting's against your idea, and we'd like you to try the other way."

Joiauz held up his hands. "I'll try," he said. "I'll do my best, I promise you. Just don't hold your breath, is all I'm saying. But I'm warning you, even if we do it your way and it works, you're just postponing the evil day. If the Goida are coming, we'll face this problem all over again."

"If they're coming," Semplan said gently. "One dragon at a time, isn't that what they say nowadays? Eat what's on your plate and worry about pudding later."

Joiauz sighed. "All right," he said. "Trouble with you is, you won't take yes for an answer. Look, all of you, not a word about this where the boy might hear, all right? I'd really rather leave him out of it, until we're quite sure what we're going to do."

On the other side of the tent flap, Chauzida backed away slowly until he was outside the light from the watch fire. Poor uncle, he thought; he's right, and they won't let him do what he wants, and I can't help because I'm not supposed to know. He yawned. He was tired out and he had a busy day tomorrow. He crept back the way he'd come, nearly got seen by the night stockman but just about made it, and was fast asleep in bed by the time Joiauz came home.

RAFFEN WALKED NORTH from the City for two days before he found a pair of boots. They were lying in a ditch. There was a man in them, but he was dead. Raffen considered him for a while. His face was buried in nettles but he had small hands and thick grey hair. His coat was northern homespun, and someone had tried valiantly to keep it going as long as possible. The boots were City-made, presumably from one of the five big companies who operated in the Tanneries. They were slightly too big, so he padded them out with grass. He wondered if he was now a thief, but he couldn't come to a definite conclusion. Before he moved on he tore strips from the dead man's shirt and wound them tight around his feet. Two days of barefoot walking had made rather a mess of them, but the binding helped considerably. He had to take out some of the grass to compensate.

It wasn't stealing, he told himself as he continued along the road, because soldiers in wars take boots and clothes and weapons from the bodies of their dead enemies, and that's perfectly acceptable. The logic was flawed, he knew perfectly well, because the dead man wasn't his enemy and he hadn't killed him. Presumably somewhere the dead man had heirs, to whom the boots belonged, though it would be impractical to try and trace them; by the time you did that, assuming it was possible at all, the boots would've rotted through and be no use to anyone. His grandmother had told him when he was a boy that if he ever found himself in a position where he was uncertain about the proper course to pursue, all he needed to ask himself was, What would Bolverk the Dragonslayer do? Well, that was easy; he'd take the boots, and quite likely they'd turn out to be magic boots that made you fly through the air or walk unseen past your enemies. That still didn't make it right, though. He'd crossed the line. He was now a thief.

The countryside to the north of the outskirts of the City was flat; good black soil, large hedgeless fields of cabbages, beet, the dried-up helm of peas and beans. This was where they grew vegetables for nearly a million people, and the road was basically two deep ruts gouged out by the wheels of heavy carts. He walked on the raised platform between the ruts; it was smooth and level, having been planed down by axles and cart-beds for a thousand years. Halfway through the morning of the third day, he came to the first village out from the City—during the Sashan war, the City had been besieged five times, and all the nearby villages had been burnt down. It wasn't much. There were a dozen large houses, maybe three times as many cottages, a flint-built shrine with a thin, high tower; a baker's shop, an inn and a forge.

The blacksmith was making gate hinges. Raffen waited until the iron was back in the fire and walked in. The smith looked at him; coat, then boots, then face. "What do you want?" he asked.

"I'm looking for work."

"Get lost."

"I was a striker in the arms factory."

The smith grinned. "See any trip hammers here? No. Go away."

"I can do hand work. I had my own forge, back in the old country."

"Piss off."

"Your hinge is burning."

White sparks were jumping out of the fire. "Shit," said the smith, dragging a white-hot fused lump out of the coals. "Now look what you made me do. Get out of here before I smash your face in."

So he tried the bakery. The baker was more polite—sorry, but we can't use your sort here—and suggested he might try the quarry, where they had so much trouble keeping their men that they'd probably hire anyone. Raffen thanked him politely and walked on.

The quarry foreman was actually pleased to see him. Yes, we can use you. We had three of the buggers die on us last week, and we've got thirty-six tons to deliver by month's end. They gave him a pick, and a bit of rag to tie over his face. Mind your eyes with the flying chips, they said, though they didn't specify what you were meant to do to avoid them.

It wasn't so bad. He stood in one place for a long time, which was good for his feet. After four days, the foreman promoted him to facing work, a lot of which you could do sitting down. You're good at this, they said, and Raffen explained that he'd done a lot of it in the old country; there was a good stone pit on our farm, he said, we sold a lot of stone to the neighbours.

On the fifth day, when they stopped for the midday meal (three meals a day in the quarry; good wheat bread and some sort of appropriately hard cheese) the foreman came and stood over him, looked at him curiously for a while, and then told him he had visitors.

"Me?" Raffen looked up. "Don't think so."

"You. On your feet."

So he scrambled up, put the rest of the bread carefully in his pocket, and followed the foreman to the rickety old shed behind the bunkhouse, where the foreman had his chequer-board and did the tallies. Inside were three men, a woman and one chair. The visitors were all standing. The men wore fine coats of red and blue broadcloth; the woman was dressed in a red gown with a fur collar. He thought for a moment that he recognised her. For some reason, they bowed as he walked in.

"That's him," the woman said. Then she looked straight at him and smiled. She said hello, and then a name.

"I'm sorry," he replied. "My name is Raffen."

"It's all right," said one of the men, tall with short white hair. "We're not Sighvat's people, we mean you no harm. Quite the reverse."

They were—no, not frightened of him, but something quite close to that. The woman was nervous but trying not to show it. "It's me," she said. "Sitry. Your cousin."

Which was a strange coincidence, because the other one had a cousin called Sitry, and it's not a common name these days; a bit old-fashioned. The other one hadn't seen her for twenty years, and she'd been a child then, no more than twelve years old. She'd married a man in Hammerfirth.

"We've had a devil of a job finding you," said the youngest man; about forty, short but very strong, with a big red beard. "It was sheer fluke we came this way, and then the blacksmith described you exactly."

"I'm sorry," Raffen said again. "Who are you looking for?"

The older man said that name again. Raffen shook his head. "He's dead, isn't he? Lord Sighvat killed him."

The woman gave him such a sad look. "No he didn't," she said.

"Yes he did." He hadn't meant to raise his voice; no call for that. "Lord Sighvat had him thrown down a well. He's dead."

The third man, who hadn't spoken yet, shook his head. "We looked in the well," he said. "We sent men down on ropes, and then we dug through from the other side. There was no body down there. We figured out how you escaped. Amazing."

"We've had the Companions scouring the whole country," the younger man said. "They found the men who told you about getting work in the City. We've been there and talked to the people in that dreadful camp."

"You made quite a name for yourself," the older man said. "You're quite a hero."

That made no sense. "I didn't do anything," Raffen said. "And then someone robbed me and took my shoes."

"He doesn't know," the third man said. "He can't have heard."

The woman looked at him again. He quite liked her. She was calm, and reasonably pretty. Kind eyes. "King Halfdan is dead," she said.

"I'm sorry to hear that," he replied automatically. "What's that got to do with me?"

"So are his sons," the elder man went on, "and his brothers, and most of the family. There's been a civil war while you've been away. Which means—" He stopped. Whatever it was, he didn't seem to want to say it.

"You're related to the royal family," the woman said.

He laughed, then paused to choose his words. "The man you mentioned just now," he said, "was sort of an off-relation. But very distant."

"In direct line to the throne," said the third man.

"Fourteenth in line," Raffen said without thinking.

"Yes," said the older man. "The other thirteen are all dead." He lowered his head. "Which means that you—"

"Don't be so bloody stupid," Raffen said. His hands were shaking, and he wanted to run away. "The man you mentioned is dead, Sighvat killed him. I don't know him. I never even met him."

"It's him all right," the woman said. "I'd know him anywhere."

"You're lying." Why was he shouting? "It's not true."

She was smiling. "He came to stay at our house when I was twelve," she said. "I had a crush on him, because he was so handsome. I climbed an apple-tree and I fell out, and he caught me. The hobnails on my shoe gave him a deep gash on the side of his head." She came forward and gently parted his hair with her fingers. They felt like fire. "There," she said. "Here's the scar."

He looked at her, then the other three. His legs were going. "Would it be all right if I sat down?" he said.

The younger man actually brought the chair to him. He sat down. His head was swimming. The woman knelt down beside him and took his hand. He let her. "It's all right," she said. "We know what you've been through, it must have been terrible. You've put it all out of your mind, I can understand that. But you've got to come home now. You're needed."

He turned his head and looked at her. "She was your sister," he said.

She nodded.

"I'm so sorry," he said. "It was all my fault."

"No," the third man said sharply. "It was Sighvat's fault, and you'll be pleased to hear he's still alive and we've got him safe. You can deal with him as soon as we get home."

He turned and looked at him. "Torcetil. From Laxriver."

The man nodded. "And this is Einar Lefson," he said, nodding toward the red-bearded man, "and this is Prince Cari Godmondson."

"We have met," the older man said, "a good many years ago. I knew your father quite well."

The woman, Sitry, was still holding his hand. He gently pulled it free. "What do you want me to do?" he said.

"Come home," Cari said. "The civil war's more or less burnt itself out, but things are in a terrible state. Nothing like it's ever happened before. It got quite vicious just before the end."

Raffen looked up at him. "Who won?"

"Torsten Halfdanson," Einar replied. "But he died of his wounds three days after the battle. He was the last of them. The whole thing was for nothing, just a complete waste. People are so shocked, they simply don't know what to do. We're all that's left of the old Court. Cari was about to be strung up, I was on the run, hiding in barns. Torcetil stayed at Court and tried to keep things going, he's the only one anybody would listen to, but there's basically nothing left. That's why you've got to come home. We need to see that the bodies get buried, find food for the people whose farms were burnt down. There's hundreds of families living in the forest because they're too scared to come out. We can't deal with that, we need the king. Otherwise, I just don't know what'll happen."

Raffen sat up a little straighter in the chair. "That name you mentioned just now," he said. "I don't want to hear it ever again, is that clear?"

There was a brief, awkward silence. Then Cari said, "I believe it's quite in order for the king to choose a new name on his accession; one of the lucky ones, Torcel, Egil, Erald, Hrafnkel—"

"Hrafnkel," Raffen said. "Raffen for short."

"Which would make you Hrafnkel the Eighth. Good choice." Cari smiled. "Hrafnkel the Fourth reunited the kingdom after the Second Permian War. Hrafnkel the Sixth instituted the common land reforms. It's always the even numbers that work out best, so you should be just fine."

"I DON'T KNOW how to do this," Calojan said.

The enemy were drawn up on the other side of the valley; a basic formation, centre and two wings. The centre looked like armoured infantry, there were horsemen on the left and what looked like archers on the right. They had appeared so quickly that nobody had had a chance to get close enough to take a good look. Calojan's best scouts had gone out at dawn to make the usual observations. It was now midday and they hadn't come back. The report had said *unidentified savages from the north-east, origin unknown.*

"You're just saying that," Apsimar said cheerfully.

"I don't just say anything," Calojan replied. "This one's beyond me. I have no idea who they are or what they can do, and my mind's a complete blank. If you'd like to take command, be my guest. You'd be doing me a favour."

Apsimar looked even more magnificent than usual today. His armour was closely modelled on the suit worn by Fortitude in Ozaches' *Battle for the Soul of Man*, except that the pauldrons were the right way round and the ventral plates were articulated, which made it possible for him to breathe. The colours and the gilding were, however, an exact copy. "Oh come on," he said. "They're savages. After what you did to the Sashan—"

"Would you mind shifting a bit to the left?" Calojan said sweetly. "You're blocking my view."

He walked forward half a dozen paces and shaded his eyes. He wouldn't admit it to anyone, but he couldn't make out fine detail at long range like he used to. He could feel Apsimar's eyes on the back of his head.

"Are you serious?" Apsimar said. "About taking command? Because if you are—"

"Do me a favour," Calojan said. "Nip back and get them to find captain Bessas. Quick as you can."

"Of course."

It was easier to concentrate without the heir to the throne breathing down his neck. He rubbed his eyes. It didn't help. Somewhere between seven and nine thousand of the enemy, depending on whether the long grey blur in the far distance was a substantial mobile reserve or a hedge. If they've killed all my best scouts, he told himself, I shall be seriously annoyed.

Bessas came lumbering up, struggling to do up the side-straps of his breastplate. The idea was, you got a friend to do them up for you. Inevitably, Bessas had to manage on his own.

"There you are," Calojan said. "Right, you see that grey blur over there, between the enemy centre and the skyline."

"You mean the cavalry."

God, Calojan thought. But Bessas had the best eyesight in the army. "You're sure that's what they are."

"Quite sure. Four squadrons, about five hundred men each."

A 2,000-strong cavalry reserve. It just gets better and better. "Just as I thought," he said. "Right, Bessas, I'd like you to stick around, I need your eyes. Watch those cavalry like a hawk; the moment they move so much as an inch, you tell me." He frowned, then said, "Oh, and one other thing."

"Sir?"

"If anything happens to me in the battle," Calojan said, "and I don't make it, I want you to find prince Apsimar, go straight to him and kill him. You got that?"

Bessas looked at him, half-grinning. "You're not serious."

"Of course I'm serious," Calojan replied. "If that clown takes command of this army, you'll all be dead in half an hour. Do it, understood? Direct order."

"They're moving."

Sure enough, the grey blur had shifted. On his own, he wouldn't have noticed. "Where? Which way?"

"To our right, about fifty yards. Still going."

Calojan nodded. "Tell me when they stop."

Two thousand cavalry. Heavy or light? Even Bessas couldn't see that clearly. He was fairly sure the two squadrons on the left wing were heavy-armoured. You wouldn't stick your dragoons out on the wing and keep your light brigade in reserve—not unless you were Calojan at Trinaxa, and that was a special case. But perhaps these savages would; maybe their entire strategy was based around it, and in an hour or so their reasons for doing so would become painfully obvious. No more pathetic epitaph for a general than *Why didn't I think of that?* He tried to focus his mind. In this situation, he asked himself, what would general Calojan do? Answer; he'd send his Aram Cosseilhatz round in a big loop and round the buggers up like sheep. If he had any Aram Cosseilhatz. But I haven't.

Screw Calojan. Half his victories were sheer luck, anyway; and the other half were the Cosseilhatz, combined with painstaking attention to detail and really first-class intelligence about the enemy's strength and leadership. Deprive him of his pet horse-archers and confront him with opponents about whom he knows nothing at all, you'll soon find out just how smart he really is. And we're outnumbered, and they've got water for their horses and we haven't, and they've got that great big wood at their backs while we're stuck out in the open like an archery target. Of course, Calojan would never have allowed himself to get in this position in the first place.

"They've stopped," Bessas said. Calojan strained his eyes, then closed them, to impress the new position on his mind. "Stay there," he said, "I'll be back in a minute."

It's an unwritten law of arms that the men should never see their commander-in-chief taking a pee; it would be liable to lower him in their estimation, which would be disastrous for morale. On a bare hillside, with the army drawn up in long ranks behind him, that was a problem. He had to walk back through the front line until he found a supply cart, and the last hundred yards were decidedly uncomfortable. Would Bessas really do it, he wondered, if it came to it? On the one hand a direct order; on the other hand, the thought of having to explain to the authorities exactly why he'd stabbed the emperor's nephew to death in cold blood in the middle of a battle. On the balance of probabilities, he reckoned the direct order would win out in the end, but it'd be a close-run thing. The best course of action, therefore, would not to let himself get killed. Right then, agreed. We'll do that.

With the pressure off his bladder he was able to think a little straighter. Somewhere in his vast mental library there had to be a precept suitable for this occasion. *When the enemy is strong, play to his strength.* Yes, love to. How, exactly? Or what about *do what they expect; it'll confuse them to death?* But he had no reason to assume they'd ever heard of him, so the Calojan mystique, which had destroyed the Great King of the Sashan, was probably going to be useless today. *If you can't win, don't fight.* He pulled up his trousers and adjusted his armour. You'll think of something, he told himself.

Walking back through the lines, he saw two soldiers fighting. One was considerably bigger than the other, but he was hindered by the sack of flour he had clamped tight under his right arm, with his hand encircling it like a girl's waist at a dance; all he could do was fend off the other man's attacks, delivered with half a broken tent pole. When they saw him they froze, looking terrified, but the big man didn't let go of the flour sack. Both of them, he noticed, were wearing Sashan boots, and a big rip in the smaller man's far-too-big Sashan mailshirt was clumsily darned with wire.

Calojan fixed his eyes on the smaller man. "Soldier," he said. "You're out of uniform."

"Sir."

"When this lot's over, report to the quartermaster for new boots and armour. Tell him I sent you."

They stared at him as though he was the Invincible Sun made flesh, then the bigger man carefully put down the flour. "Dismissed," Calojan said, and they both bolted like rabbits.

Fine, he thought, as he quickened his pace, another story to add to the Calojan legend. Trouble was, the army was falling apart, to the point where even stories like that wouldn't be able to hold it together. Ten years' constant action had made the Imperial infantry hard as nails, what was left of it, but the men had no boots and hadn't been paid for over a year; two thirds of them were conscripts, with farms going to ruin. They'd had to empty the City jails to make up the Seventeenth to full strength. It wasn't supposed to be this way. *It doesn't matter*, the Chancellor had told him, *there's no-one left to fight.*

"There you are," Apsimar yapped at him, as he took his place again. "I've sent men to find you. They're on the move."

Bessas was looking at the back of Apsimar's head, like a butcher at a cattle market. If I do get killed today, Calojan thought; no, forget about that. Not today, I've got too much work to do. "Are those cavalry still at the back?" he asked, and Bessas nodded. He looked down into the valley and thought; if I were you, what would you most want me to do right now?

He didn't look round. There would be a messenger there waiting, like an arrow on the bowstring. "Tell the Twenty-third to get out of there *now*," he said.

Apsimar was looking at him. He pretended not to have noticed. He felt a hand on his shoulder.

"You can't do that. They'll have their backs to those cavalry on the left there."

Without looking round he said, "Thank you so much, Apsimar. Now then, tell the Seventeenth to pull back, quartering right."

"That's crazy. You can't do that. You're opening a hole they can drive a wedge into."

"We'll see. Oh, and I want the Ninth to close up to the right. Not much, just twenty yards."

Another eager young man swung into the saddle and thundered away, his horse's hooves kicking up divots. There would be a long line of them, just behind his right shoulder.

"At the very least," Apsimar yammered in his ear, "bring the dragoons in tight to cover the withdrawal. Otherwise, we might as well—"

"Bessas." He spat the name out like catarrh. Bessas nodded, recognising the tone of voice; then he swung round and punched Apsimar in the mouth. There was an uneasy moment—Apsimar was six feet eight and massive as an ox. Then he sort of folded at the knees, waist and neck, and dropped to the ground as though his clothes had nobody inside them. "Thank you," Calojan said. "Now then, as soon as their cavalry begins to move, I want the Ninth to go hard left and the Twenty-third to go inside out. Got that?"

So it was that when the enemy cavalry swooped down on the disordered and vulnerable Imperial centre, they were met with a dense shower of arrows from the five companies of archers embedded in the middle of the suddenly-shifting phalanx; reeling away, they collided with an infantry brigade that seemed to appear out of nowhere and stopped them dead, as though they'd run into a brick wall. Seeing his prize lancers trapped and on the point of being encircled, the enemy general had no option but to commit his main infantry. It was a sensible, businesslike move, and in the short time left to him the general simply couldn't understand where the Imperial cavalry came from or how they'd managed to get there. He yelled for his own cavalry reserve, only to find that they weren't available; Imperial auxiliary cavalry had materialised on their right flank, ripped a hole in them and darted away, so that they'd followed instinctively, like a dog chasing a cat, straight into a point-blank volley from six companies of archers. The general looked round for something, anything, to plug the gap with, and realised with a sort of dreamy amazement that he suddenly had nothing left; all his men were fighting, being savaged in flank and rear, or herded like sheep, or shot up by massed archers, and his superior numbers had melted away, and he was now outnumbered and about ten minutes from being completely surrounded, and there was absolutely nothing he could do, and how the hell had that happened? He had just about enough time to draw his short, sharp knife and, his eyes fixed on the rapidly approaching Imperial heavy lancers, slice the blade into the arteries of his wrist. Then his army sort of slumped all around him, the way a burning house subsides a little just before the roof falls in, and the Imperials closed up their ever-tightening circle, until they met in the middle and there was nothing left for them to do.

"I'M JUST SO sorry I doubted you," Apsimar said later; it was hard not to laugh, he sounded so funny talking with a lower lip three times its normal size. "I should've known you had it all figured out. You might have let me in on it, though."

The soldiers were gathering the enemy dead and loading them on flat-bed carts. It was a loathsome job, reserved for defaulters and men the sergeants didn't like, though there was a hard core of regulars who volunteered because it meant they got first pickings. From the disappointed slump of their shoulders, Calojan guessed that the enemy weren't much given to jewellery and personal adornment. High-ranking Sashan officers wore gold earrings to indicate status; it was quicker and more efficient to slice off the lobe. Whoever these people were, they were too poor to merit more than the occasional nudge with the toe of a boot. Marvellous, Calojan thought. We managed to find an enemy even more threadbare than ourselves.

"Actually," he said, "you were quite right. We were this close to disaster. I didn't have the faintest idea what to do, so I repeated the last battle against the Sashan." He stooped and picked something out of the grass; a gold filigree brooch in the shape of two dogs pulling down a stag. Three ounces of fine yellow gold, seven solidi but probably worth more to a collector. Some people, he decided, have more luck than they deserve. He slipped it into his pocket without showing it to anyone. "It would've been a stupid risk even if we'd had the Cosseilhatz; without them, relying on Imperials, it was practically suicidal. If they'd been a minute late, if a messenger's horse had put its foot down a rabbit-hole, it'd be them looting us right now." He shrugged. "But we got away with it, and please God we'll never see these people again, so what the hell."

Apsimar gave him a puzzled look. "Come off it," he said. "General Calojan making it up as he went along? I find that hard to believe."

"Of course you do," Calojan replied. "I'm like the leper in the story."

"What story?"

Calojan sighed. He wasn't in the mood; but Apsimar was the heir apparent, and he was being frightfully decent about the punch in the mouth. "Once upon a time," Calojan said, "there was a leper. He was horribly disfigured, and people who saw his face ran away screaming. So he made himself a mask, out of shoe leather. Before he got sick he'd been a sculptor, so the mask he made was sublimely handsome. Wherever he went, people used to come out of their houses just to look at him. He took up his old trade, and soon he was getting commissions from the best families. When people asked him why the mask, he politely changed the subject, so they assumed it was a clever way of advertising. One day a priest came to see him; they had an old statue in their temple, but they'd had a fire and the stone had cracked. It wasn't a particularly good statue, not by anybody famous, and they were a poor parish, so they couldn't pay much. The leper said that was all right, he'd do it for free. He made a new head for the statue, and it turned out to be his finest work. People came from all over the City to worship at the temple. Soon that district of Town became quite fashionable; the poor people moved out and they pulled down the slums and rebuilt, with wide streets and a fine square. The temple got a new façade and endowments for forty monks. Shortly after that, the leper woke up and found the mask had fallen off while he was asleep. Horrified, he scrambled to a mirror to put it back on, only to find that he wasn't a leper any more; furthermore, his face had grown back and somehow been moulded by the mask, so that now he was just as handsome as the thing he'd created. I'm assuming he went on to live happily ever after, but the story doesn't say so specifically."

There was a puzzled silence; then Apsimar said, "That's a nice story."

"Yes," Calojan replied. "I sort of grew up with it. I liked it so much, my dad painted it for me when I was nine years old; a triptych, on limewood." He smiled. "I think it was the best thing he ever did, but we had to sell it when dad was in prison one time."

"That's sad," Apsimar said. "Actually, I'm a great admirer of your father's work. I believe he's seriously undervalued as an artist."

The casualty figures were not good; they'd killed nine thousand savages and taken four thousand able-bodied prisoners, but they'd lost nearly six hundred Imperial infantry and two hundred irrepleaceable cavalrymen. Apsimar suggested asking the prisoners if they wanted to enlist. "After all," he said, "they fought pretty well, and it wasn't their fault they were up against *you*." Calojan changed the subject rather than insult a prince of the blood; later, though, when he interviewed a dozen high-ranking prisoners, he broached the subject as tactfully as he could.

"Yes," said the spokesman, without hesitation. He was tall and ridiculously broad across the shoulders; he had a small head that reminded Calojan, for some reason, of an apple. He wore his hair long, in braids, but was going thin on top. "We would be honoured to serve in the Great King's army. You must know that we are landless men, outcasts in our own country. We came here only because at home we were starving. We have so little, and you are so rich. We would serve you very well."

Calojan frowned. "The Great King," he repeated.

"We have heard so much about him," the spokesman replied eagerly. "His great power, his noble bearing, his generosity to those who serve him well. We will fight to the death to defend his people against the Empire."

Calojan counted to five under his breath, then said, "We're the Empire."

"You?"

"That's right. We wiped out the Sashan a few months ago. The Great King is dead."

The spokesman looked at him warily. "It would be an even greater honour," he said, "to serve the illustrious emperor. We have heard such wonderful things about him. In our country, we think he must be like a god."

Calojan sighed. "I'll tell him you said that," he said. "He's called Sechimer, by the way."

"Sechimer." The spokesman repeated it carefully. "We will serve him well."

They came, it turned out, from the far north-east, where they'd been pushed out of their ancestral homeland by a race of wandering horsemen called the Goida. They'd moved to the foothills of some mountains Calojan had never heard of, but the land was poor there, not nearly good enough to support the whole nation. There had been a brief, nasty civil war, and these men were the losing side. It wasn't the best recommendation—fought two, lost two—but they were good fighters; they'd probably have smashed the Imperials if they hadn't had the bad luck to come up against a lunatic prepared to back his own cleverness against certain death. A thousand trachy a month sounded like unimaginable wealth to them; later, Calojan found out that they didn't use money back home, and a thousand of anything had to be much, much better than nothing at all. The spokesman's name was Ohtar; it meant "little cat", for what that was worth. Calojan appointed him commander-in-chief of his unit, and sent to the City for a suit of shiny armour.

"Aimeric doesn't like you very much," she said.

Teudel grinned and wriggled onto his back. "Hardly surprising," he said. "I'm sleeping with the girl he loves, who foisted me onto him even though I'm a convicted criminal. You keep telling him I'm essential for the grand plan but he's yet to see any real evidence of it. That too is hardly surprising, since all I've done since I've been here is—"

Orsella put her finger on his lower lip. "Learn," she said. "And you're coming on really well. Didn't I say you'd be a natural?"

Teudel lifted his right hand and held it out. "I'm not sure I want to be," he said. "Look at it, will you? It's so cramped and sore I can barely make a fist. I used to be able to do fine detail with that hand."

"Better yours than mine," she replied with a sweet smile. "It'll heal, you'll see."

Teudel wasn't so sure about that. He'd spent a week rubbing down old parchment with brick dust, to scour the writing off five hundred year old property deeds and household accounts. It had occurred to him that parchment was just a form of skin, and so was his hand. What scoured one was inevitably bound to scour the other. The worst part of it was probably the flakes of old ink, which lodged in the cracks in his skin and stung mercilessly. He dreaded to think what horrible noxious substances were in ancient ink. "A whole week, and all I've done is two sheets. How many are you going to need?"

She shrugged. "A dozen."

"My God."

"It's easier once you've got the hang of it."

"I'm not sure I want to."

"That's fine, then. You can go back to forging coins and they'll catch you and stick your head up on a pole. Assuming," she added pleasantly, "they can find a pole strong enough to bear the weight of something that big. Do try not to be so ungrateful, Teu. When I rescued you, you were one step away from sleeping in hedgerows."

He sighed. "I'm sorry," he said. "I just feel a bit useless, that's all. Also, my hands hurt."

"Poor darling. Let mummy lick them better."

Some time later, Orsella said, "I think it's high time Sechimer got married. Don't you?"

Teudel was just drifting off to sleep. "I suppose so. None of my business, of course."

"He's the emperor. It's his duty to ensure the succession. What the empire needs most right now is stability, or it'll never get a chance to rebuild on a solid foundation. The economy—"

"Orsella. What are you going on about?"

"Sechimer has to marry," she said, propping herself up on one elbow. "The only question is, who?"

Teudel wrenched his head round to look at her. "Now just a minute," he said. "You're not suggesting—"

She smiled at him. "Not me, silly. Not that I wouldn't make a perfectly divine empress, but I suspect it'd be more trouble than it's worth to arrange. So we'll have to make do with second best."

Teudel could feel one of those headaches coming on. "Orsella," he said. "faking coins and old manuscripts is one thing. I really don't think we can forge a queen."

She smiled at him, and for a moment he'd have agreed to anything. "Oh, I don't know," she said.

He stood in front of the blackened ruin of the barn and looked towards where he knew the well must be, hidden under a waist-high growth of nettles. He wanted to ask if anyone had thought to bury the bodies; but asking would constitute a level of involvement for which he wasn't quite sure he was ready. There's that story, where the prince is abducted by the Queen of the Dead, and she lays out a banquet, all his favourite things to eat and drink, and he's so hungry and thirsty; but one mouthful of anything would mean he'd never be able to go back. Lately a little voice in his head had kept urging him, *never accept*. He wasn't sure if it was particularly good advice, but he'd been following it anyway.

"I want all this cleared away," he said. "Level it off flat and plant trees or something. We'll build the new hall over there, where the pear orchard—"

He tailed off. His father had felled the pear orchard twenty-seven years ago.

"Over there," Cari said. "Right, we'll do that. It's a good location, as a matter of fact. Good communications with all four districts."

"That's why I chose it," Raffen replied. He'd chosen it simply because he didn't think it was fair to build his new house on someone else's land. "Tell Sighvat I'll pay for it. You'll need a jury of seven neighbours to decide a fair price. That's how it's always been done around here."

Cari knew that, of course. "Are you absolutely sure about Sighvat?" he said. "In your shoes—"

Raffen laughed. "Private joke," he explained. "And yes, I have no quarrel with Sighvat. I want everybody to know that. Nothing bad is going to happen to him, is that clear?"

The seven neighbours weren't told who the purchaser was, in case it clouded their judgement. In the event, Raffen insisted on paying four marks more than the price they decided on. Anything less, he said, would be a slight on his late father's husbandry.

It took a hundred and twenty men six days to build the house; forty-one cartloads of lumber, nine cartloads each of clay and cow-dung just to lay the floor, another six of each to make daub for the walls; an acre of turf for the roof. Eighty men in heavy boots jumped up and down for a day to get the floor compacted and level. They brought the royal roof-boards seventy miles over the hills, packed in a ton of straw so the carvings wouldn't get chipped or split. Regrettably, the wall-hangings from the old king's hall had been looted during the fighting, and nobody had owned up to having them; Cari, Torcetil and Sitry lent him their own hangings while new ones were being woven. The carpenters made him tables and benches, and Eyvind of Gulsness sent him a chair; it was Mezentine, some very heavy black wood, carved in the shape of a hand—you sat on the palm, and the curled fingers made up a back and arms. Eyvind said it was hundreds of years old and had belonged to his great-grandfather, who brought it back from Permia. It was rather more comfortable than it looked. They told him the hall was the biggest house ever built in the whole of the country. It was about half as long and a third as wide as the de Peguilhan factory shed. The hangings were too short, but they plugged up most of the draughts with handfuls of coarse felt.

Standing inside it for the first time, Raffen looked up and studied the roof. "There's no chimney," he said.

"No what?"

He realised he'd used the Imperial word without thinking. "It's like a sort of square hollow brick column," he said. "The smoke goes up through it, so you don't have that thick blue fug eighteen inches over the top of your head."

They looked at him as if he was mad. Eventually, Sitry said, "That's silly. Every time it rains, you'd get a great big puddle on the floor."

Fair point. He tried to remember how they'd built them in the City, but he hadn't paid enough attention. "Not to worry," he said. "It'll be fine."

You could seat four hundred in the hall, and there was a private room at the back, just for him. He wasn't sure how he felt about that. Except for his time in the forest, he'd never slept on his own before; it seemed unfriendly, somehow. In the old house, the other one and his wife had had a curtain they could pull across, but they rarely bothered with it.

"Talking of which," Sitry said briskly, "you'll need to get married again. The sooner you produce an heir, the quicker things'll settle down."

He looked at her. "Fine," he said. "You're not married, are you?"

"Me? You know I'm not. What's that got to do with anything?"

After a brief discussion, they decided to combine the wedding with the coronation; it would save people having to make two journeys, and cut down on the expense. Then she looked sideways at him and said, "Are you sure?"

"I think so. How about you?"

"Well." She hesitated. "My sister never had any complaints, so I guess not. But shouldn't you think about it some more? It's a big step."

He smiled at her. "I'm counting on picking it up as I go along. I'm quite good at that."

CARI AND THE new Court agreed that it was a sensible thing to do; it'd save making new alliances, which might offend disappointed candidates, and since Sitry was theoretically now sixth in line to succeed if anything happened to the king, it forestalled the risk of someone else marrying her to support a claim of his own. Dynastically speaking—

"Yes," Raffen said, "thank you, I take it we're all agreed." He looked down the table at them. They were watching him as though he was a falling tree; would he land on them, or simply crash in a tangled mess of broken branches? "Let's move on."

Gulbrand of Brendale (his third cousin; heard of him, never met him before; tall man with long grey hair and a button nose) stood up and said, "We'd like to ask you a bit about the City and the empire. So many of our people have been going there lately. Are they doing well?"

Raffen nodded to him to sit down. "Well," he said, "it's an extraordinary place. Imagine a triangle jutting out into the sea. On the land side, they've got walls a hundred and fifty feet high and wide enough that two carts can pass comfortably on the top walkway. There are square towers at intervals along the wall, so close together that a sentry can throw an apple underarm to his friend on the next tower along. On each tower there's a machine that can hurl a rock so big that it takes two men to lift it; I saw them doing target practice with these things, and they can shoot over two hundred yards, and they've got white posts set out in the plain below to mark the various distances. The sea walls aren't quite so tall and thick, but they've got just as many towers and machines. You couldn't get in close with a ship, you'd be sunk. So long as they control the sea, they can't be starved out, and there are wells and great big cisterns, so they'll never run short of water. They say that the City's been there for more than a thousand years, it's been attacked seventy-three times and never been taken by storm."

He watched them as he spoke. I was right, he decided; the thought had crossed their minds. "What about the people?" Eyvind asked. "Are they all as rich as people say?"

"Yes, by and large," Raffen replied. "Of course, if you went up to someone in the street and asked him, are you rich or poor, he'd groan and pull a face and say how desperately poor he is, what with the war and the taxes and foreigners coming in and taking all the jobs. But at least three-quarters of the families have a house all to themselves; three rooms, a table and three or four chairs, a couple of beds, pewter cups and plates. They eat bread twice a day, porridge and soup and vegetables in the evening—not much meat, but a lot of fish, which is so cheap the rich won't touch it. Everybody's got two coats and two pairs of shoes, most of the women and some of the men wear jewellery, even if it's only bronze. The majority of the men can read and write, a lot of the women too. I should say that most of the people in the City live better than you chieftains do, even the ones who say they're so poor. And if anyone's starving hungry, they can stand outside one of the temples on the day when they go to prayers, and the priests hand out bread and dried beans, though it's surprising how few people turn up to take any. They're too proud, apparently. If you take the priests' food, it means you're nobody and your neighbours look down on you. If you walk down the street and look in through the windows of the houses, you'll see brass lamps and wicker baskets for keeping the charcoal in, and nearly every house has got a little painting hanging on the wall, the Ascent of the Invincible Sun or something like that, in a brass frame. The houses all have strong doors with locks on, because the whole City is full of thieves. Oh, and they make their roofs with baked clay tiles, not turf or thatch."

"You're joking," someone said.

"It's the law," Raffen replied. "They're terrified of fire, which is understandable, since all the houses are packed in so close together. Every ten years or so there's the most horrific fire and half the City burns down, and then they rebuild it."

"What do they all do for a living?" asked Gunlaug of Scarpness. "Where do they grow their crops and keep their livestock?"

"They don't," Raffen said with a smile. "I guess you could say they're all craftsmen, except that they don't have workshops of their own. Nearly everyone works for someone else, in great big sheds and buildings bigger than this hall. They get paid in copper money, and they buy food in the markets—the women go there nearly every day. Nobody keeps cows or sheep, there's a few chickens and in some streets they get together and raise a couple of pigs; nobody grows anything, except for the very rich, who have tiny little orchards behind their houses. There's no room, you see. It's a huge place and there are some enormous buildings, but mostly everything's very, very small."

"They hold a market every day?" Sitry said.

"There's at least a dozen big paved yards," Raffen told her, "one in each main district. Hundreds of stalls in each one. Not just food, either. Clothes, tools, furniture, crockery, anything you like. No weapons, but pretty much everything else."

"That's ridiculous," Einar said. "What do they need all those *things* for?"

Raffen laughed. "If you'd been there, you wouldn't need to ask. Owning things is how they keep score. We do it by our reputations, what people think of us; honour and shame, if you want to put it like that. In the City, you are what you own. I guess that's why they need so many laws, and why they aren't allowed to have weapons."

Einar said, "They what?"

"Strictly forbidden," Raffen said, "though it doesn't quite work. The rich have fine swords hanging on the wall and the very poor all carry knives, and practically every day there's a murder somewhere."

"Hang on," Cari said. "I thought they had the best army in the world. How did they beat the Sashan if they're unarmed?"

"There are full-time soldiers," Raffen said, "and in an emergency they round up people from the countryside and arm them. But the soldiers who won the war for them were mercenaries, foreigners. Horse people, from far away in the east." He smiled. "The City people don't fight."

"That's insane," Gunlaug said. "You mean to say that if an enemy came right up to the walls, all the men in the City would stay at home and not do anything?"

Raffen nodded. "It's happened scores of times in the past," he said, "and yes, they stay indoors and leave defending the walls to the paid men and the foreigners. Don't look so surprised," he added, as Gunlaug made a despairing gesture, "that's how their minds work. They believe in specialists, you see. Every man can do just the one thing; you're a forge-hand or a foundryman or a woodworker in a factory, or you're a porter or a clerk for a merchant, or you work on a market stall, or you're a bricklayer or a stonemason or a weaver. That's all you do. More than that, you only do one very small part of a job. You roll out thin iron bars in a great big mill in a half-acre shed, and someone else cuts the bars into short lengths, and someone else bends them into chain-links, and someone else joins the links together and welds them shut. Like I said, everything in the City is very big and very, very small. So, when it comes to fighting, they have specialist fighters. The stonemasons don't fight and the soldiers don't cut stone into blocks. I think," he went on, "that's why our people find it so hard to understand it there. You see, in the City, it's absolutely essential to know who you are, and what your place is. We don't, of course. We're farmers mostly, but any one of us can do a bit of carpentry or a bit of smithing, or build a wall or put up a house, or make a pair of shoes. Of course, the things they make are truly wonderful, much better than anything we can do; or else they can make you ten thousand of something, all of them practically identical, and dirt cheap, of course, compared to what it'd cost you here." He smiled. "I have to say, I didn't do too badly, mostly because while I was there I was sort of nobody, in my own head, which meant I could be anyone I liked. If they said, we need a foundryman, I was a foundryman. But most of our people feel so *cramped*, if you know what I mean. It's like you've got the full use of all your limbs, but you're only allowed to move one finger. Also, the

City people don't like us. They think we're savages, and they're afraid of us because we're happy living in sheds and getting paid far less than they are for doing the same job. And we don't fit together like they do."

"What does that mean?" Gulbrand said.

Raffen thought for a moment. "Suppose you took a pottery bowl and you smashed it," he said. "Then you pick up the bits and fit them together. You get some wire and a drill—well, you all know how to mend a broken pot, don't you?"

"Yes," Cari said. "I won't pretend I'm very good at it. Don't have the patience."

"Well," Raffen said, "people in the City are like the bits of pot. Put together, they make up something that's useful and holds water. On their own, without all the others to fit in with, they're useless; junk, only fit for the trash. Of course, put that many people together and you get a very big pot, a cauldron. We're not like that. Pull us apart and you've got a handful of individuals, like grains in an ear of corn. Plant each seed, it'll grown on its own and in a few months you've got twelve new stalks. The City people wouldn't survive on their own, they wouldn't know how. One link on its own can't be a chain. I don't suppose one man in a thousand in the City knows how to mend a pot. The thousandth man does nothing but mend pots, all day every day. He's very good at it, very quick, he's got a box of special tools just for pot-mending; he'll do a much better job than you or me. But stand him in front of a plough or give him two dozen sheep to look after, he'd just stare at you, what am I supposed to do with this? That's where the paradox comes from. They're very big and very, very small, very strong and very, very weak, very grand and so unimportant they hardly exist. The rich and powerful are huge, like gods, and the ordinary people are tiny, they don't matter a damn to anyone. That's why they thought it was all right to divert a river and flood thousands of people out of their homes, just for one day's fun and games. When you're so big and your neighbours are so small, it's pretty easy to lose sight of them."

There was a long silence. Then Gulbrand leaned forward across the table. "All right," he said. "Suppose someone took it into his head to break the big pot, to get at what's inside. From what you're saying, he'd have to hit it pretty hard, but when it broke, there'd be nothing left at all, just waste."

Raffen looked at him for a long time. "Now why," he said, "would any-one want to do a thing like that?"

"I just said," Gulbrand replied. "To get what's inside."

"That'd be stealing. We're not thieves."

Cari filled his cup from the jug and passed it on. "If you follow that line of argument," he said, "we're all living on stolen land. Our great-great-great-*great*-grandfathers took this whole side, from here to Laxness, off the people who lived here before them. The whole of Sutherdale—"

"That's different."

"Is it?" Cari smiled. "Or is it just a long time ago?"

"They had to come here," Eyvind said. "They were pushed out of their homes in the east by the horse people."

"That's like saying, I only stole your sheep because I was hungry. You might let the thief go, if you believe him and you feel sorry for him, but he's still a thief."

"Besides," Raffen said, "I don't think taking their land was what Gulbrand's got in mind. I mean, the City's huge for a city, but it's still only, what, six hundred acres. That's seven farms. No, I'm guessing Gulbrand's interested in all the stuff, the things. And that would be stealing."

Gulbrand shrugged. "You may care to reflect on the fact that only a century and a half ago, the imperial border was the Eigen. Now it's a hundred and five miles closer to where we're sitting now. We may not be thieves; they definitely are. There's an argument to be made for breaking them before they smash us."

Sitry laughed. "Oh come on," she said. "What do we have that the Emperor could conceivably want?"

There was a ripple of laughter; then Raffen said suddenly, "Manpower."

Eyvind said, "Excuse me?"

"People," Raffen said. "That's one thing the empire hasn't got enough of right now. This war of theirs against the Sashan; by rights, they really shouldn't have won it. They only came out on top because they've got this genius general. But before he came along they were losing. Scores of big cities got captured or burnt, tens of thousands, maybe hundreds of thousands of people were killed, driven off their land, marched off in chains by the Sashan to the other end of the world. A whole lot more were forcibly drafted, someone stuck a spear and a shield in their hands and told them they were soldiers, before Calojan came along, and the Sashan slaughtered them like catching salmon in a weir. There's vast stretches of what was once good farmland lying empty, right in the heart of the empire, because the people who used to live there are dead or gone away. I really don't think you need to worry about the emperor wanting our cold, damp bits of hillside. For a while there he wanted us, to work in the factories while his people were away at the war, but not any more. I honestly don't think we have anything to fear from Sechimer and his people, not for a very long time indeed. So, if you're looking for an excuse for bashing down his door and burgling his house, I don't think self-defence is going to cover it."

NOT SO LONG ago, the daily Elevations were held in the Red Chamber of the palace. When he became emperor, Sechimer moved Elevations to the Silver Court. The Red Chamber, he said, was a beautiful thing, one of the wonders of the world; but the glorious Eparchus stained-glass windows didn't really give enough light to read by, except at midday, and it cost two solidi an hour in candles to light the place adequately. The Silver Court, on the other hand, was basically one enormous mirror; one candle, reflected in the silver-sheathed walls and ceiling, lit the whole enormous room as bright as daylight, making it a sublime fusion of breathtaking display and wholesome economy. Now, according to Orders of the Day, Elevations were to be held in the chapter-house of the Chapel Royal—

"Why?" Aimeric asked.

The archdeacon hesitated, then lowered his voice. "Don't tell a soul," he said, "but they're stripping off all the silver and melting it down. When they've finished, there's going to be a mysterious fire, which will wreck the Silver Chamber and the Old Processional. It'll be mourned as a national disaster, and Sechimer will make a passionate speech about rebuilding it, as good as it used to be or better; it'll make him ever so popular with the middle classes, and the silver will pay the interest on what we owe the Vesani bankers. I gather the Chancellor's struck a very satisfactory deal with a Mezentine consortium for the statues in the Processional, and of course nobody ever goes to Mezentia, so no-one will ever know they're there."

Aimeric stared at him, until the archdeacon told him to stop making an exhibition of himself. "It's that bad?" Aimeric said.

"Oh yes," the archdeacon replied with feeling. "Fortunately, Sechimer doesn't know."

"You mean you're deliberately going to burn down half the palace, and the emperor doesn't know—"

"He'd never agree," the archdeacon said. "So obviously we can't tell him, can we? But a fire in the old wing is horribly plausible, there's bound to be one sooner or later. I gather the Amber Hall is going to be next, as soon as we can find a buyer."

"That's appalling," Aimeric said. "You can't just—"

"What we can't just do," the archdeacon said sharply, "is allow the empire to go bankrupt while we're sitting on millions of solidi in precious metals and works of art. Naturally we can't be seen to be selling off the family silver. So, this is a sensible way of dealing with the problem." The archdeacon looked up and down the portico to see if anyone was watching them, then sat down and pulled Aimeric down next to him by the sleeve. "Also," he said, "we can use this, if we're clever."

"Use it?"

The archdeacon nodded. "You know how superstitious Sechimer's getting, ever since his illness. Well, I need you to tell your pet forger to include a reference to the Great Fire in her prophesy."

"The Great—you mean the fire you're conspiring to start."

"Indeed," the archdeacon said with a frown. "The fire will have been foretold centuries ago. I'm not one for mysticism, but I recommend to you the imagery of the phoenix. There will be a great fire, something about silver so it's obvious what it's referring to, and then a lot of stuff about a marvellous golden palace rising out of the ashes. That way, the poor man will be left thinking a seriously destructive fire in his house is somehow a good thing. We do want him to be happy, after all."

"I see," Aimeric said. "Anything else you want put in there?"

"Oh, ever so many things," the archdeacon said gravely, "but we must be sensible. The prophesy is supposed to span a thousand years. It would be presumptuous to suppose that we're living in the most exciting and meaningful half-decade in a whole millennium. While we're on the subject," the archdeacon went on, "where exactly are we on that? Naturally I don't want to know too much about it, but a general idea of progress—"

"The parchment is nearly ready," Aimeric said. "We're just starting work on the text itself. So, if there is anything you want putting in there, now would be a good time."

"Dear me, we are moving quickly, aren't we?" The archdeacon gave him a look with a definite hint of disapproval in it, which Aimeric thought was a little harsh. "I'll put together some notes for you as soon as I've had a chance to speak to the others."

"I meant to ask you about that," Aimeric said. "Why does it have to go through you? No disrespect," he added, quickly and too late. "But why can't I talk to them myself? It'd save time, and—"

The archdeacon smiled. "They don't like you," he said. "Partly because they see you as too close to Calojan, partly because you are, when all is said and done, in trade; partly, I have to say, because you're young, brash, gauche and—as far as they're concerned—innately dishonest. I, on the other hand," he went on, widening his smile into a beam, "think you're a splendid young fellow, highly capable, blessed with an originality of mind that is necessarily denied to the rest of us and, within certain tightly defined parameters, reasonably trustworthy."

"Thank you so much."

"Don't mention it. I believe you're even more scared of Calojan than the rest of us. Also, as an outsider and a parvenu, you've got much more to lose than we have. Finally, I'm confident of being able to control you, and that's what really matters in any relationship, don't you think?"

Aimeric breathed in slowly. "What makes you say that?"

"Oh, I know things about you which would finish you off in two minutes," the archdeacon said cheerfully. "I know you're sponsoring, not to mention sleeping with, a woman who has a long list of criminal convictions in the Vesani Republic, for offences that make her involvement in this project wildly problematic, to say the least; who also has close contacts with known enemies of the empire—"

"That's not true."

"Another thing I like about you," the archdeacon said, "is that despite your treacherous and cynical nature, you have an underlying streak of the most absurd naivety. I imagine you think the relationship between your Orsella and her assistant Teudel is strictly business."

"It is."

"Dear boy. Anyway, Teudel is a wanted fugitive, believed to have died in the galleys in the mock sea-battle. He is—well, all three of you are at liberty still because I have personally interceded with the Prefect, on a wholly informal basis. The warrants for Teudel and Orsella have been filed and sworn and are on record at the Prefecture. Literally one word from me, and they'll be carried out with the full vigour of the law. If that were to happen, you would have to go to Calojan to save yourself; assuming you were able to reach him, he would then have to decide whether you were worth the risk. I don't imagine our national hero would relish being associated in the public mind with Orsella and Teudel, do you?"

Aimeric's legs were cold to above the knee and his chest felt painfully tight. "Fine," he said, "I'll make her get rid of Teudel. Will that satisfy you?"

"No need." The archdeacon made a gesture, appeasing and patronising, like a big man begging his tiny son not to hit him with his wooden sword. "From what I gather about your Orsella, I'm sure her patronage of the man Teudel is based on something far stronger than mere intimate friendship. I don't know what she wants him for, but if it helps the project, God speed them both. I simply wanted you to understand that my warm personal regard for you is reinforced by certain safeguards. If it makes you feel any better, I take similar precautions with all my dearest and closest friends. It's so much easier to trust someone implicitly if you've got your knife pressed to his throat."

Aimeric breathed out through his nose. "That's all right, then."

"Indeed. My poor brother had a cat once," the archdeacon went on, rising slowly to his feet. "It ignored most people, but sometimes it would jump on someone's lap and bite him deeply, right down to the bone. It's all right, my brother used to say, it means she likes you. It never bit me, of course. If it had, I'd have had it quietly poisoned. Good heavens," he added, "we'd better get a move on, or we'll be late for Elevations."

ELEVATIONS IN THE chapter house proved to be a great success, and the archdeacon was widely congratulated for his inspired suggestion. Although the space was rather smaller than the assembled court was used to, the superb acoustics and the uncluttered lines of sight meant that officials who'd been attending the ceremony for years said afterwards that it was the first time they'd ever been able to see and hear clearly and therefore understand what it was all supposed to be about. The emperor himself was visibly pleased, and wrote the archdeacon a personal note; for the first time since his accession, he said, he'd been able to properly appreciate the true spiritual significance of the ritual; assuming it wouldn't cause too much inconvenience, he'd like to hold the ceremony there every day until further notice. Several people commented on the absence of general Calojan, even though he was known to be in the City. No explanation had been given, almost as if Calojan felt he didn't need to explain. Sechimer himself made no comment, though it was rumoured that he was somewhat displeased.

After the service and the brief formal council meeting that followed it, Aimeric left the palace and walked down the Mile as far as the Bronze Gate, where he turned left into Sweetwater and then right into the tight cluster of narrow streets that surrounded the Treasury building like small rivers in a delta. He stopped outside a tall, windowless four-storey brick building, originally built as a warehouse before the river silted up and the Treasury district was renovated and made fashionable. He took a key from his pocket and let himself in.

"This is a pleasant surprise," Orsella said, looking up from her work. She had a large sheet of milk-white vellum on the desk, and an inkwell and at least two dozen pens. He looked over her shoulder; the vellum was three-quarters covered with the Mezentine letter A.

"I can do all the other twenty-six letters," she said, "but I'm having the most dreadful trouble with A. I've tried everything, and it just doesn't look right."

Aimeric peered down. The letters all looked identical. The top joint of the middle finger of her left hand was red and creased by the pen. "I didn't know you were left-handed," he said.

"I'm not. Well, sort of ambidextrous. But a surprising number of Mezentine scribes around this time wrote with their left; you can tell, if you know what to look for. It's the sort of thing a Mezentine scholar would notice and find convincing."

Aimeric raised his eyebrows. "Good for you," he said.

She grinned at him. "Anyway," she said, "what are you doing here? I thought you had Elevations and then meetings all morning."

"I'm ill," Aimeric replied. "Anyway, it was nothing important. How's it going?"

She laid the pen carefully on the desk, the nib projecting over the edge. "Well," she said, "the parchment's all done and we've got all the ingredients we need for the ink, so if only I can teach myself to write one stupid letter, we're ready to go. All we really need," she added pleasantly, "is for someone to tell us what to write."

Aimeric nodded. "Is Teudel about?"

"I'm not sure. Teudel!" She waited five seconds or so. "He must've gone out for something. Oh, I know. I sent him to get some of that special pumice, you remember, I told you about it."

"Isn't it a bit of a risk," Aimeric said, "him walking about the streets in broad daylight? Someone could recognise him."

Her face didn't change. "Not really," she said. "The place is down in the Tanneries. Teudel's practically invisible anywhere south of Sheep Street."

He looked at her, but she somehow deflected him, like a mirror placed at an angle. "You could have told me."

"I spoke to your friend the archdeacon," she said. "He told me he was making all the arrangements. I assumed he'd fill you in."

"He did. Just now."

"It must have slipped his mind. Before you ask," she went on—her voice strengthened without the slightest hint of harshness—"I wouldn't be able to do any of this without him. He's the only man I'd trust to sand down old parchment just right."

Aimeric nodded. "You've known him some time, then."

"I worked with him once or twice. To be honest, usually I don't need that level of expertise. This job, however, nothing but the best. That's right, isn't it?"

"Of course." Aimeric looked at her again, but she was better fortified than Perimadeia.

"That's fine, then. What did you want to see him about?"

He hadn't prepared an answer to that. "To be honest, just curiosity, really. I've never met a dead man before."

She gave him a puzzled, faintly amused look. "I beg your pardon?"

"He died, didn't he? In the sea-battle. It says so, in the official record, which is infallible and can't be called into question. And if he's dead, he can't be walking round the streets buying pumice. There might be a man who looks remarkably like him, but it can't be him, because he's dead." He turned away slightly. He didn't really want to see how she reacted to that. "Just see to it he understands that, all right?"

"Leave it to me," she replied solemnly. "And I'm reluctantly forced to the conclusion that the man who's been passing himself off as the late Teudel must be an impostor. But he's very good at scraping down parchment, so I won't fire him just yet. Is that acceptable?"

She was doing that not-quite-a-smile that made a mockery of all his defences, but maybe the time he'd spent with Calojan had had some effect; he avoided it neatly by looking past her. "Now then," he said. "The text." He reached in his pocket and took out a sheet of parchment, folded small and thick. "Also," he went on, "we need you to predict a fire in the Silver Court. It'll be completely destroyed, but from the ashes, phoenix-like, a golden shrine will arise that will do something or other that Sechimer will like. Is that all right?"

"Not a phoenix," she said. "No phoenixes in Imperial literature until the late Mannerists. First reference is in Sarsimer's *Ode to Light*. Dead giveaway."

"It's a prophesy," Aimeric said. "The prophet peered into the future and saw phoenixes."

"No."

"Fine." He scowled. "The archdeacon will not be happy. He specifically wanted a phoenix."

"He can have a fire-dragon instead," she said helpfully. "They do basically the same stuff and they're immaculately period."

"All right, then. Just translate it as phoenix in the fair copy for the Court. They won't know the difference, and I won't get moaned at."

"Funny man." He'd got it wrong again. "Now please go away and stop getting under my feet. And if you want to make any changes or put anything else in, you'll have to let me know by this time tomorrow at the very latest. Once I start actually writing the thing, I won't be able to stop. I'll have twelve hours, maybe fourteen if I'm very lucky and the weather turns cold, and then the base medium starts to dry and basically you've got to stop, or else you can spoil the whole thing. Come back in three days and you can have a look."

When she'd heard his footsteps on the stairs and the street door closing, she went into the back room and said, "Well?"

Teudel was cutting gold leaf into thin strips with a tiny pair of shears. "Well what?"

"You heard what he said."

"Of course I did. You intended me to."

She beamed at him. "Anyway," she said, "he's no trouble to anyone. How are you doing?"

"You don't need me," he said, dropping the shears on the table. "Not for this, anyway. I shudder to think what it is you really need me for. I've done forty-six little strips and I've got thirty-seven still to go."

"Splendid. Keep at it."

"Orsella," he said, trying to grab her wrist; he was very fast, but she was faster. "Just out of interest. What do you need me for?"

"Menial tasks that even a child could do," she replied. "But I need *you* to do them. All right?"

He looked at her, but couldn't see anything he could understand. For a split second he was reminded of the thing he feared most in all the world. It was called the Divine Clemency of the Emperor, and it was a punishment reserved for extreme forms of treason; forging coins counted as treason, but Divine Clemency was usually reserved for the gang bosses rather than the lowly strikers and die-cutters. Instead of killing you, they cut out your tongue, gouged out your eyes and slit your nose open lengthways. Then you were sent to a confessional, which was a sort of prison monastery, usually on a small island in the middle of the sea. The lay brothers looked after you—there were no cramped dungeons or rats, but every day they woke you up an hour before dawn and led you in a long shuffling procession to the chapel, where you stood or knelt according to the gentle pressure of a hand on your shoulders and heard the sequence of offices sung by a choir. There were two meals a day, bread and vegetables mashed into a sort of porridge, and at night you were led back to a sort of stone box where you were kept when not in use. Sooner or later you died; but the diet was healthy, the place was kept spotlessly clean and there was virtually no chance of meeting with an accident, so people tended to live for a very long time. He thought: I hear her voice, but I can't see her, I can't make her hear me and there's absolutely nothing I can do; the music, on the other hand, is particularly soothing, once you get the taste for it.

It was just another archery contest, second from last event in the funeral games of a man Chauzida hadn't known; he was rich but not important, and the mourners seemed suspiciously cheerful. Apparently his wife had died some time ago and his only son had been killed in the war. They'd put up a white falcon as the archery prize. It stood, hooded and jessed, on a post hammered into the ground to mark the fifty yard line. The targets were Sashan boiled-leather breastplates, with rings painted on them for scoring. Your arrowhead had to go through and come out the other side, to stop people from cheating by using light practice bows or flight arrows.

Joiauz was having a bad day. He was expected to win, because he was the regent, but he'd woken up with a headache, and he was pulling his shots. The first two had been outers, the third was all right, but the fourth barely clipped the target and went soaring off into the long grass. Chauzida could see he was trying too hard. Each bad shot made him tense up and hold too long on the loose. The bowstring should, of course, slip from the fingers like a perfectly ripe apple dropping from a tree. That wasn't happening for Joiauz today, but Chauzida decided against telling him what he was doing wrong. People claimed to lay a lot of store by the truth, but there were times when they really didn't want to hear it.

"Quick." Joiauz was deliberately not looking at him. "Get your knife out. No, don't be obvious about it, we don't want anyone to see."

Chauzida had learned a lot about not being seen over the years. He caught the top of the handle in his palm, between the base of his fingers and the mound of his thumb, and eased it forward out of the sheath so that the whole knife was hidden behind his palm and wrist. "Now what?"

"Just run the edge across my string," Joiauz muttered. "Just enough to fray it, that's all."

The string was twenty plies of very fine linen. He manipulated the knife so that the edge was outwards. "Drop the bow," he said.

"What?"

"Drop it on the ground."

Joiauz let it fall; Chauzida knelt down to pick it up. He grazed the string about a quarter of the way through, in the middle. It was very delicate work. "Here you are," he said, handing the bow back.

"Thanks." Joiauz took it in his left hand, nocked an arrow, drew and loosed. It was a fine shot; a little low and right, but cleanly inside the central ring. Chauzida handed him another arrow. Joiauz nocked it and drew, and the string broke. The bow sprang forwards out of his hand and cartwheeled twice over the grass before dropping on its side. "Shit," Joiauz said loudly, rubbing his wrist.

A man called Dreitz, who was winning with four middles and an inner, gave him a sour look, but Joiauz quickly gathered up his bow and remaining arrows, and left the line. "Thanks," he said, as they walked away. "Neatly done."

"Why did you—?"

"If I'm out of the match I can't lose," Joiauz said. "Losing to Dreitz would be mildly humiliating. But a broken string is just bad luck."

Chauzida had already guessed that much. He eased his knife back into its sheath. "So Dreitz will get the falcon," he said.

"So what?"

"I wanted it," Chauzida said. "It's white, we haven't got a white one."

"They're very rare," Joiauz said. "They come from Permia. They don't fly any better than the ordinary ones."

"Can I have a go in the contest?" Chauzida asked. "I'm quite a good shot, and it's an easy target."

Tactless. Joiauz frowned. "Your bow wouldn't go through the leather," he said.

"They could change the rules."

Joiauz thought about it for a moment. "I don't think so," he said. "It'd be fine if you win, but if you lose it'll look bad. Sorry."

"All right." He waited a moment, then said, "I'd quite like to stay and watch the rest of the match."

Joiauz shrugged. "Go ahead."

Chauzida waited till Joiauz had gone, then ran back to his tent and got his bow and quiver. Then he went back to the line and stood near the judges until they had to notice him. "Excuse me," he said. "I know I can't take part *officially*, because my bow's not strong enough, but can I shoot just for practice? I'd like to see what sort of a score I could get."

The judges looked worried. They wanted to discuss the problem but didn't feel they could with the Great Chief standing there looking up at them. "I think that would be in order," the oldest judge said.

Chauzida thanked them politely, then walked to the place in the line where Joiauz had been standing. When the end was over, the stewards pulled the arrows out of the target and set it up again. Dreitz had scored eight middles and two inners.

Chauzida strung his bow against the calf of his leg, took a good stance and addressed the target. The bow had been specially made for him; it was very light and easy to hold at full draw, but with a surprisingly good cast. He had a dozen arrows shafted in a special sort of dense reed, so well matched that there was only one barley-grain of weight between them. The others were all using war-bows; no matter how strong you were, they tended to snatch the string out of your fingers, so you had to loose the moment your thumb brushed the corner of your mouth. The rings painted on the breastplate were a bit bigger than those on the straw bosses he practiced with. I can do this, he thought, so long as I pretend it doesn't matter.

His first shot was very good indeed, which was worrying; if the first one was bang in the middle, he usually tended to pull the next one, or the one after that. He could feel the worry tugging at him, but all he could do was try and ignore it. The second shot was in, just cutting the line. He took three deep breaths, in slow and out slow, and the third arrow pitched so close to the second that it made it quiver. That was dangerous. He badly wanted to do exactly the same again, because so far he'd got away with it, but he was right on the edge of the ring. He forced himself to raise his aim just a little, and the fourth shot pitched high and left, just inside the circle. He shot the fifth without thinking. It followed the fourth but pitched just outside the line; an inner, not a middle.

He drew a deep breath, counted to four and let it go. He was still in the game, but he couldn't afford to drop another one. Suddenly he realised that he was doing a very stupid thing, just for a stupid white hawk, and Joiauz had expressly told him not to. The game wasn't a game any more; it was politics and honour and war, and the outcome would walk alongside him for the rest of his life. Unfortunately, he'd got himself into it now. He'd made four good shots, but it's not the hits that matter, it's the misses. He wished he could do the trick with fraying the bowstring, but unfortunately that option had been taken from him.

He told himself; you've made this really difficult for yourself, but it's still not *difficult*. You can drop in five out of five, you've done it before, you're perfectly capable. But that, he knew, wasn't the way to think about it, he was implicitly threatening himself with failure, and that really didn't help. Instead, he told himself; the sixth arrow is already in the middle, I shot it and it went in just nice. Now let's step back and see how I did that.

He drew, and saw the tip of the arrowhead, and looked over it at the aiming mark. There was nothing else in the world except that mark, he was standing in the desert under a bare blue sky and he was completely alone. The shot had already hit the target, so all he had to do was let go of the string; neatly, of course, but that's no big deal. So he let go, and the arrow flew, and it pitched just to the left of his first shot, where he knew it would. He put two more just under it. The ninth shot went in just fine, but at a slight angle, so that the shaft masked most of the open part of the middle ring. It happened that way sometimes; it was bad luck and nobody's fault. His left arm felt paralysed, and he had to make himself breathe in. It was as though he'd walked into a clearing in the woods and found himself eye to eye with a boar, nesting in a tangle of briars; it had seen him, and if he moved at all, it would charge and tear him open.

He negotiated with himself. He'd already scored eight middles, which was enough to equal Dreitz, if he could only drop the tenth shot somewhere in the inner. A draw would be all right, not a victory but not a defeat, he could probably get away with that and come out of this mess without lasting damage. But, he knew, if he shot for anything less than dead centre this time, he'd pull it or flog it and be lucky to scrape a three. He tried to see the tenth shot already in the target, but he couldn't, because the ninth shaft was in the way. He was standing in front of the gates of the City, and the great bronze gates were shut.

Diplomacy, he realised, wasn't going to help him here. In fact, there was no help for him anywhere, not from any living man, not from any tool or artefact, not even magic. He was about to do something that mattered more than anything he'd ever done, completely alone, as if in the desert. There was no artifice, no self-deception, and the target was now very, very small. He suddenly realised that he was drawing the bow and that it was too late to stop the draw. The knuckle of his thumb pressed down into the corner of his mouth; it felt cold and dangerous. The bowstring told him it was time to let go, as if he was seeing someone he loved for the last time. The resistance in his fingers faded and the string pushed past them.

He tried not to look.

It was in; middle right, cleanly inside the line. He felt no pleasure. He had the feeling of having just made a bargain with an enemy, which he would later come to regret. Then someone slapped him on the back—one of the Councilmen, a familiar face with a name that temporarily escaped him; well done, the man was saying, clearly not understanding the full implications of the moment. He tried to look pleased.

No, Dreitz insisted, of course he should have the falcon. He'd shot the better score, it was only right and proper. But he couldn't get out of his mind the wounded look Dreitz had given him, and the backward glance at the lightweight bow and the matched flight arrows, as if to say *what harm did I ever do you?* To which, of course, he had no answer; Dreitz had simply been the other man, the opponent, the enemy, as innocent and irrelevant as the target he'd just shot ten arrows into.

"What you've done is," Joiauz said later, "you've invented yourself. You're now the king who, as a boy, outshot the grown men. We know all about him, people will know what to expect from now on. I'm not entirely sure that's who you ought to want to be, but it's done now. I don't know what Dreitz did to deserve a public humiliation. That said, I never liked him much anyway."

I only wanted the falcon, Chauzida didn't say. "I'm sorry," he said.

"Sorry," Joiauz repeated, as if the word was in a different language. "No, don't be sorry. The man you've just invented isn't *sorry* when he does things like that. He takes huge risks when there's absolutely no need, and if he wins it's marvellous and the people love him, and if he loses and a whole army gets slaughtered—"

"Yes?"

"He's soon gone and quickly forgotten," Joiauz said harshly. "That's the sort of man he is; no half measures, no cautious hedging of bets, no way back from the edge of the cliff. If you can keep on hitting middles, they'll be singing songs about you five hundred years after you're dead. If not—" He shrugged. "You must've thought it was worth the gamble or you wouldn't have done it."

"I don't want the hawk," Chauzida said. "Would you like it?"

Joiauz shook his head. "It's just as well you don't want it," he said, "because you can't keep it. You'll have to give it to someone. The problem is deciding who to give it to. It'll be a supremely noble gift, so it's an extremely delicate decision. If it's all the same to you, I think you should leave it to me."

"Yes, please," Chauzida said gratefully.

That made Joiauz smile. "Cheer up," he said. "We've accomplished a great deal on what looked like it'd be a perfectly ordinary day. Just, next time—"

"Ask you first?"

Joiauz thought about that. "No," he said, "because I won't like it, the next time you do something I've told you not to." For some reason he looked sad and almost angry for a moment, but it passed quickly. "Next time," he said, "just make bloody sure you hit the middle. All right?"

It only remained to be seen whether the balustrade would bear his weight. He considered it carefully. It was original, therefore (since this was the east wing, added by Florian IV as part of his somewhat overambitious expansion of the palace) over six hundred years old. On the other hand, it was stone, and stone doesn't get brittle with age. That said, it was a purely ornamental feature, not designed with load-bearing in mind. He knelt down and looked carefully; the top rail wasn't intregral with the pillars, so there had to be some sort of join. He couldn't see mortar, or evidence of pinning, so presumably all that held it in place was a tight fit between a tenon and a hole. But, he told himself, I'll only be standing on it for a fraction of a second, so if it does give way—He tried to visualise the process, the way he imagined troop movements in the heat of battle. He decided it might well give way, but not instantaneously. By the time it collapsed, he'd be in mid air, on his way across the gap. That left the issue of what would happen to the debris. He took a firm hold on the window-frame and leaned out until he was looking straight down. At least ninety feet of sheer drop; if the broken balustrade fell, and someone happened to be passing underneath at the time, the result couldn't help but be fatal. Yes, but the courtyard below was a restricted area, and the guards didn't patrol along that line, therefore the risk of someone being down there was acceptably small. I'm dithering, he realised, that's not like me at all. True, but I so very rarely have the luxury of time to dither in—

Calojan checked to make sure that the flaps of his bag were securely buckled down, then took a deep breath and sprang up onto the balustrade. It wobbled just a little under his foot as he applied force to it; then he was sailing through the air; then he felt a greater than anticipated jarring sensation in his left ankle as he touched down on the flat roof of the Great Hall. He let his legs fold, and ended up squatting, his back to the gap he'd just jumped over, while he caught his breath.

Idiot, he thought. Still, he was here now, safe, apparently undetected. Might as well carry on, having come this far.

The Great Hall was fifty-seven yards long. At the south end, it was a relatively simple matter to drop down onto the balcony of the royal belvedere; from there, he was able to trot down the stairs to ground level in a civilised manner. His right ankle was protesting a little—he was lucky to have got away with such a trivial level of injury—and he had a feeling he'd pulled something in his neck hopping down onto the balcony.

At first light, on a day when there's no ceremony in the parade yard, the southern end of the old palace was practically deserted. All approaches from outside were covered by the watchtowers on the curtain wall; anybody approaching the towers from behind had to have come from inside the palace and would therefore not be deemed a threat. Calojan grinned. For the first time in a long time he was alone and out and about, and nobody knew where he was.

The view he'd chosen was from the raised semicircular platform at the top end of the parade yard, where the musicians usually stood when the emperor reviewed the Guards. From there, he could see out over the box hedges of the rose garden to the half-mile gravelled walk through the Inner Park. There was still a touch of morning mist, so he couldn't make out the Mardonius Gates at the far end; but he knew what they looked like, and could add them from memory. He set up the lightweight folding easel he'd had made in Mondhem, laid the thin limewood board in the groove of the shelf and took a stick of thin willow charcoal from the box.

"General." He closed his eyes. "There you are. I've been looking for you everywhere."

He laid the charcoal down carefully, so it wouldn't roll off the easel and shatter. "Apsimar," he said. "You're up early."

"My uncle sent for you," Apsimar said. "Nearly an hour ago."

Unlikely, Calojan decided. An hour ago, he was still in his room, carefully rubbing down the limewood board with pumice dust. Even Apsimar would've tried his bedroom first. "Fine," he said. "I'm on my way. Where is he?"

"North tower. Must rush. Be seeing you."

Oh, Calojan thought. Sechimer had been spending far too much time up there lately. He disappeared up there for hours on end, and was always quiet and moody when he eventually came down. He collapsed the legs of the easel and packed it away in its canvas case.

It was dark in the tower room. Sechimer had closed the shutters; the only light came from a single taper, and its reflection in the gold halo of the Invincible Sun in the icon on the wall. He didn't look up when Calojan came in. "Where were you?" he said.

"Outside, in the grounds. I'm sorry I kept you waiting."

Sechimer shifted his weight a little; he was kneeling in front of the icon. Beside him on the floor was the divitision—silver-embroidered cloth of gold, massive, heavy as a cavalryman's mailshirt; folded neatly on top of it was the lorus, laid out as if for kit inspection. Sechimer was wearing a hemp grain sack, slit for the neck and arms. Even in the dim light,

Calojan could see where the coarse fibres had chafed his neck and shoulders raw red. You wouldn't notice it, of course, under the great robes of state, whose monstrous weight would grind the sackcloth into the skin, like sandpaper. Calojan took a deep breath. "Exactly what do you think you're doing?" he said.

Sechimer straightened his back, rested his hands on his knees. "Atoning for my sins," he said. "Only I have a feeling it isn't working like it should. I asked the Master of the Studium, and he said this was the approved method. Maybe I'm not doing it right."

"What sins?"

"Oh, well, let's see," Sechimer said wearily. "Rebellion, oath-breaking, regicide—"

"Sorry," Calojan said. "You'll have to do better than that. Not regicide so much as pesticide."

"All right, then. I was responsible for an act of the most unforgivable arrogance, to celebrate a victory which wasn't mine but His. Will that do?"

"I was under the impression I won that battle," Calojan said mildly. "Yes, all right, flooding the Westponds was a pretty crass thing to do, but it wasn't your fault. You didn't actually do it. At the time you were completely off your head and out of it. Furthermore," he added, "and you'll have to forgive me if I've missed the finer points, but if He was upset with you for that, surely you'd know about it by now. There'd be plague, or earthquakes, or enemies at the gates."

"That would seem to suggest," Sechimer said quietly, "that my penances have proved acceptable. For now, at any rate. I don't *feel* forgiven, though. Quite the reverse."

"You could try not wearing that horrible thing, for a start. That's enough to make anyone depressed."

Sechimer laughed, and stood up with a quick, fluid movement. In the golden light, his skin was the colour of honey. "Also," he said, "the war would appear not to be quite as over as we thought. Read this."

He handed Calojan a short brass tube, slightly thicker than a thumb. Inside was a single sheet of reed paper. "Oh," Calojan said. "Him."

"You've heard of him."

"Met him," Calojan said. "He turned up in camp, claiming to be the heir apparent of the Sashan. Bullshit. The real Hunza was executed years ago. I know, I was there. This Hunza's just some chancer."

Sechimer had carefully shifted the lorus to one side and was unfolding the divitision. Calojan took it from him and helped him into it. The weight hurt his elbows. "Well," Sechimer said, "he may just be an impostor but it seems he's got an army. Sorry, but—"

"Of course," Calojan said. "I'll leave in the morning."

"Thank you."

"In return." He paused. Sechimer was looking straight at him, as though this moment was somehow very important. "In return," he said, "if we win, I want you to accept it as a sign of divine favour and stop getting your underwear from the corn chandlers'. Agreed?"

Sechimer smiled. "No," he said.

"Up to you." Calojan got as far as the door, then said, "Really, you've got nothing to feel guilty about. And anyone who tells you otherwise is up to something."

"We'll see." Sechimer had his back to him; he was kneeling down, eyes fixed on the icon. "I'm sorry to make you go off soldiering again," he said. "For a nation finally at peace, we do seem to have had a lot of war lately."

"Oh, we've finished dinner, this is just the cheese and dried figs. Perfectly normal."

"If you say so. I wouldn't know. I was in the Navy."

"Exactly," Calojan replied. "Never done an honest day's work in your life."

He heard Sechimer laughing as he closed the door, but the gloom and the gold light stayed with him until he was outside in the sun.

THE MESSENGER, JOIAUZ explained, was a Carchedonian, from the province of the empire closest to Mezentia. It was very hot down there, and the people had lived in those parts so long that the sun had turned their skins brown. It was rude to stare.

"So if I went and lived there for a long time—"

Joiauz grinned and shook his head. "It doesn't work like that," he said. "People don't change that much just because they live somewhere else. You always stay what you are to begin with. That's life."

Chauzida made that slight movement with his head; not forward to signify agreement or backwards for dissent, just a slight motion that took official notice and declined to comment. "What does he want?"

Joiauz sighed and put down the whetstone. He enjoyed sharpening things; it relaxed him. Chauzida could understand why. A man in his position must take pleasure from being able to improve something, immediately and perceptibly and without having to shout. "The emperor wants us for another war," he said. "Not a very big one, apparently."

Joiauz' voice was getting softer as he spoke, which usually meant he was undecided about something. "Apparently?"

"Not quite sure what to make of it," Joiauz replied. "The messenger wanted me to believe it's just a minor mopping-up operation, no big deal, everyone home in time for dinner. On the other hand, he wants seven thousand men. That's a lot for clearing up loose ends."

"You think he was lying."

"I think he was lied to," Joiauz replied. "What I mean is, he was given his instructions, told what to say, and whoever gave him those instructions wasn't telling the whole story. Still," he added, "general Calojan's still in charge, so presumably it'll be all right. It's the Sashan again."

"I thought they were all dead."

Joiauz smiled. "I think they're like rabbits," he said. "You think you've got the last one, and suddenly there's forty-six eating the spring grass. Bear in mind, it was a vast empire and a lot of people lived there. Calojan wiped out several armies, but even he can't exterminate an entire nation in a handful of battles."

"So we're going," Chauzida said.

"Yes," Joiauz replied, and now he sounded sad; more so than Chauzida could ever remember. "I think we have to."

"Why?"

Joiauz shrugged. "They pay well, and we need to stay on good terms with them. If the empire's overthrown and the Sashan come back, they're likely to make a lot of trouble for us. Also, we're obligated. It's a matter of honour." Rather late, Joiauz had recognised something in the tone of the original question. "Of course, it's up to you. You have to decide. But your council will advise you strongly to agree."

Something prompted Chauzida to say, "But I don't have to."

Was Uncle shocked, or just surprised? "No," he said, "but there'd have to be a very good reason, which for the moment I can't think of. Maybe you'd care to explain it to me."

It's so difficult for him, Chauzida thought; he's not quite my father and not quite my servant. One minute he's telling me to polish my boots and tidy my tent, the next he has to ask my permission to go to war. He felt an enormous surge of affection, which he struggled to put aside. "I just wanted to know why we've got to go," he said. "Because surely, if we don't *have* to, it's better if we don't."

"Peace is better than war." Joiauz was trying not to smile. "Now there's a novel point of view for a Great Prince."

"Is it?"

"The Cosseilhatz nation is permanently at war," Joiauz said. "Officially. You know that. It's why all meetings always start with the war. We fight like fish swim."

"That's how it's always been."

Joiauz frowned. "Yes, I know it's not a particularly satisfying argument. Hard to overcome, though. I guess—" He paused for a moment. "I guess every day in our lives is pretty much like another, and everything stays more or less the same, except in war. In war, you can suddenly become a great hero, or capture a cartload of gold. Or you can get killed, or have an arm or a leg chopped off. It's the only way things can change. So, we embrace war." He laughed. "You know, this is probably the first time I've thought about it, deliberately, I mean. So many important things are just there, like the sky, and you don't think about them till you have to explain them to someone else."

"It's not like that for me," Chauzida said. "It's like I'm having to think about everything, all the time."

"Quite," Joiauz said gravely. "So, what do you think about this?"

Chauzida looked at him. "Is it really up to me? I can actually decide."

"Yes."

(Which struck Chauzida as very strange, but he was in no position to argue.) "You were telling me the other day," he said, "about the other Aram nations, and the Goida, and how things are going to get much worse fairly soon. Was all that true?"

"Of course it was."

"And you also said how nice it would be if we could all move inside the empire, into those places where people don't live any more, and where we'd be safe."

"Well, yes. But I don't see the emperor ever agreeing to that."

"How'd it be if we said, we'll come and fight your war for you, but we don't want any more gold and silver, we want to be allowed to come and live in the empty bits of your empire. If we explained it like you explained it to me, I don't see how he could say no."

"I do," Joiauz said.

And Chauzida did too, though he wasn't quite sure how. But he *knew*, which was enough. "In that case," he said, "I've made my decision. We'll go to the war if we can have land inside the empire, but not otherwise."

Joiauz' eyes were wide and he was very still. "That's a very big decision," he said. "Explain it."

Chauzida nodded gladly. "The emperor will say no," he said. "Calojan will go and fight the enemy without us. I imagine he'll win, but he'll really wish we'd been there, and he'll talk to the emperor, and the emperor's *got* to do what he says, because he wins all the battles. Then, next time we ask, the emperor will say yes." He paused. It hadn't sounded as authoritative out loud as it had inside his head. "What do you think?"

"You really want me to tell you?"

Oh, Chauzida thought. "Yes."

"I think that's what we'll do," Joiauz said. "It's something I'd never dare do, on my own. But if you order me to, I've got no choice, have I?"

"Uncle—"

Joiauz shook his head. "Something my father used to tell me," he said. "When all else fails and you're alone and unarmed and they're coming to get you, hide behind a child. He said it always worked for him."

"That's not very—"

"Sometimes," Joiauz said, "sometimes it is."

THREE KETTLEHATS CAME to the factory in the middle of the day. One of them (gilded pauldrons; lieutenant of the Personal Guard) asked to see Hosculd. They found him in the exchequer room, in the middle of a calculation so complicated that it needed three boxes of counters. He asked if they could wait just two minutes while he finished. No, they said.

The deputy supervisor decided they'd better tell Aimeric, so they sent a boy who eventually ran him down in the cold room of the bath-house of the New Metropolitan temple, where he was discussing long-term fiscal policy with the Chancellor and the assistant governor of the Treasury. He made his excuses and left at once, and was at the factory when Hosculd came back, shortly before sunset.

"Well," Hosculd said, "they put me in this huge circular room with the most amazing painted ceiling. There was one chair in the exact centre of the room, and I sat down on it, and they went away, and about three hours later they came back and took me to see Calojan."

Aimeric nodded but didn't speak.

"He gave me a drink and asked me how things were going at the factory, the Type Seven helmets—he knows about the problem with the rivets, I have no idea how, but he didn't seem unduly upset about it."

"That was it?"

Hosculd frowned. "He asked me about the dead stock—you know, all the stuff we've been stuck with over the years and haven't been able to find a buyer for. Wanted to know how much we'd take for it, as a job lot."

"He asked you that."

Hosculd shrugged. "Well, I told him I couldn't say offhand, I'd have to look in the books. Then he started talking about—well, me, basically. Where I was from, when I left home, how long I'd been away, my family, stuff like that."

Aimeric frowned. "Why?"

"No idea. I just answered his questions. He didn't say much, so I just kept talking to fill in the spaces, so to speak. And he just sat there and nodded, and from time to time he'd ask another question."

"Such as?"

"Oh, how many people lived in our village, are there many villages or just a few, was my family poor or well off, did we have chieftains and elders, that sort of thing. I'm sure I told him far more than he wanted to know, but he let me babble on. Then he nodded, said thank you, you can go home now. Then he rang a little bell, and two kettlehats came and brought me straight back here. And that's all, really."

"He had you arrested for a chat."

"Something like that."

Aimeric thought for a long time. "How much dead stock have we got?"

Hosculd grinned. "No idea. At least two warehouses, out in the suburbs. I don't suppose anyone's been in them since before your father died."

"I want an inventory and current valuation," Aimeric said. "By the morning."

Hosculd didn't whimper, but he clearly wanted to. "Understood."

"And he just asked you questions, about the old country."

Hosculd nodded. "If I hadn't known who I was talking to, I'd have said he was perfectly charming. Only," he added grimly, "perfectly charming people don't have you arrested."

"Oh, I don't know."

That night, instead of going to Orsella, he went home to his father's house, repurchased from the receiver and refurnished with as much of the old furniture as he'd been able to trace and buy back. It was now an authentic forgery of the original. He hadn't been back for a while (he couldn't remember exactly how long) but even so he hadn't been expecting—

"What," he said, "is that?"

His mother gave him a grim smile. "Your sister brought it home," she said. "Talk to her about it."

Not that he'd have objected to it if it had been somewhere else. He quite admired late Reactionist sculpture, in an impersonal, dispassionate sort of a way. In a cloister garden, it'd have been fine. A large cloister garden, or a public park.

"Gesel," he said, trying to sound calm and reasonable, "it can't stay there."

"Why not?" His sister looked through him, as if he was a window on a rainy day. "Besides, it's got nothing to do with you. You don't live here any more."

"Yes I do."

"Funny," she said. "I don't remember seeing you much in the last six months. Well, ever since you came back from university."

Between them, the Invincible Sun towered like the tallest tree in the forest; the tree that was there before the forest grew up, and its wide spread of branches block out the light, so that nothing can survive under them. How they'd managed to get it through the door without knocking its head off, he had no idea. "It's too big," he said.

"It's a masterpiece of religious art," she said calmly. "Having it here makes me feel at peace."

"Gesel, it takes up the whole bloody room."

She turned and started to walk away. He followed her, stopped abruptly, just in time to save himself from bashing his head against the Sun's outstretched left arm. "Gesel, listen. I have no problem at all with you finding solace in religion."

"Thank you so much."

"Can't it go in the garden? It'd look much better outside. Statues like that are meant to be seen in natural light."

"I want it in here," Gesel said. "With me. I can sit under it and feel safe."

"For crying out loud." He stopped. He'd raised his voice, and that somehow meant she'd won. "Fine," he said. "We'll build a house next door and live in that, and you two can stay here and be cosy together."

"You can if you like," she said. "You can do whatever you want, it's no concern of mine."

"Gesel." She turned her head and was looking at him as though he was something she'd brought in on the sole of her shoe. "What's the matter?"

"Oh, nothing."

It was the sort of oh, nothing that means, *where do I start?* He stifled a big sigh. At the very least, this was going to take a very long time, and he was tired. "Gesel," he said. "This religion thing. Is it—?"

"Religion isn't a *thing*," she snapped. "Please do try not to be offensive."

"If I've done something wrong—"

"You? Do something wrong? Perish the thought."

He felt as though his heart would burst with rage, but somehow he couldn't quite bring himself to rant and yell while standing under the armpit of the Invincible Sun. "Fine," he said. "It's up to you. Tell me what's the matter, I'll apologise and do something about it. Or if you prefer, I'll just go. You choose."

"Just go away, Aimeric. You're not my brother any more. Go away and leave us in peace."

He looked at her and reflected that some battles aren't worth winning. "I'll be in my room," he said. "Come and talk to me if you want to. If not—" He couldn't think of an if-not, so he left the room (he had to squeeze sideways) and went upstairs. His room was empty, just walls and floorboards. He sat on the floor with his back to the wall and waited, but nobody came. After a while, he heard Gesel's voice, muffled and filtered by the intervening architecture. She was singing the Office of Intercession, praying for his soul, loudly and off-key. That was as much as he could take. He left the room, slamming the door behind him, and went to see his mother.

"What?" she said, without looking round. She was brushing her hair. It was a sort of dirty grey and, released from captivity, came down to her waist.

"Gesel's praying for me."

"That's nice of her."

"It's the service for the dead." Aimeric sat down on the dressing-table stool. "What's got in to her?"

"That's rich, coming from you." She put down the brush—ivory, with an embossed silver back; he hadn't seen it before—and scowled at him. "What's got in to you, Aimeric? What do you think you're playing at?"

He raised both eyebrows. "Me? Gosh, let's see. Running the family business, governing the empire. It helps pass the time. What was I supposed to be doing?"

"Don't be clever with me. Where have you been? We haven't seen you for months. Where are you living?"

"Mother, for pity's sake." He looked up at her. "I've got a couple of rooms in Town. It's more convenient for work, and government business. Meanwhile, your daughter, my sister, is turning into a religious maniac. Aren't you a bit concerned about that?"

"That Vesani woman you're living with—"

"She's an art historian." Which was true. "I met her while I was away. I expect we'll get married at some point, but right now I'm just too busy. Mother, there's a temple-sized statue of God in our living room. That's not normal."

"She's upset. She doesn't like what's been happening. She thinks you're getting yourself in the most terrible trouble. And so do I."

"Don't be silly," he said gently. "The business is doing really well, the commander-in-chief is my personal friend, I'm a member of the Council and I've met a girl I really like. That's all. I promise you."

She studied him for a while. "Aimeric," she said, "you've always been a disappointment to me, but I wasn't ever ashamed of you, not till recently. If you must insist on destroying yourself, do please try and keep your sister and me out of it, if that's at all possible. Please don't come back here again, it unsettles Gesel and you can see what sort of a state she's in. Now if you wouldn't mind, I'd like you to go home now. I expect your friend will be wondering where you've got to."

He had nothing to say to that, so he walked out. He went to Orsella's, but she yelled at him for opening the door and letting the wrong sort of dust in while the size was still wet. It was dark, and coming on to rain. He walked to the factory, but the gates were shut and padlocked. He realised that he had no home, something he'd clearly neglected to notice while his mind was on other things. On the other hand, he had thirty-seven solidi in his pocket, and that was just walking-around money. So he turned left down Hallgate and went to the Theatre. The performance was about a quarter of the way through, but it was a Hieronymus comedy, so he hadn't missed anything. After the show, he sent his compliments, deep admiration and five solidi backstage to the actress who'd played the Queen of the Gods, and the rest of the evening didn't turn out too badly after all.

THE DAY STARTED early in the offcomers' camp in North Foregate. An hour before dawn, the women set off with every bucket, pail, jug and bottle they could find and walked the three miles to the Drovers' well. The night carts had to be out of the City by sunrise, and the day traffic wasn't allowed in until an hour after. During that hour, by tacit agreement of the Northgate sub-prefect, the women from the camp were allowed to draw water from the well. This was, of course, against the law, but the sub-prefect had done six tours of duty in the provinces and knew better than to try and enforce regulations against people who had nothing left to lose. Shortly after the women left the camp, the food carts from the Golden Spire and the Metropolitan arrived and unloaded, accompanied by five platoons of kettlehats. The charity officers in change of distribution had calculated the amounts necessary by reference to the tables in the fifth appendix to

Stratocrates' *Natural Science*, which was written in North Scheria seven hundred years ago. It was possible that something had got lost in translation—some scholars believe that Stratocrates copied his data from an earlier Mezentine source, drawing on Perimadeian texts from the fourth century AUC; the camp spokesmen maintained that a pound and a half of flour per head per day wasn't enough to live on: the priests, being educated men, knew better. Each day, when the sacks had been unloaded, the offcomers' spokesmen repeated their formal protest, to be conveyed to the temple commissioners; each day, a junior official delivered the commissioners' reply to the previous day's protest, to the effect that the provisions delivered were charity rather than any kind of entitlement, and the recipients therefore had no say in the quantity or quality of the merciful relief provided. Furthermore, he pointed out, the supplies represented the grace of the Invincible Sun, delegated through the appropriate channels operated by the proper officials, and raising questions or objections therefore constituted blasphemy, which He could not be expected to tolerate indefinitely.

Calojan arrived not long after the women came back from the well. By that time, the men had done their work for the day and were mostly sitting on the ground outside their tents, playing pickstones or simply staring at the ground. Calojan looked round for someone to talk to, but nobody seemed prepared to acknowledge that he existed; the men simply walked away and the women stared at him and shook their heads, while the children ran off and hid. Eventually, a worried-looking man with a bald head appeared out of a tent. He had a baby in his arms. "Did you want something?" he asked.

"My name is general Calojan. I want to talk to whoever's in charge."

The man grinned at him. "That'd be me."

That statement struck Calojan as absurd, but he was in no position to argue. "Is there somewhere we can talk?"

The man frowned, as though he'd been asked to do complex mental arithmetic. "In the tent," he said, and Calojan followed him.

The tent was about forty grain-sacks, discarded after long use, slit open at the sides and stitched together and hung off laundry poles and vine props stolen from the nearby farms. Inside was blue with smoke from a small peat fire, over which a broken-and-wired-together pot hung off three sticks. There were three children and a woman sitting in there, apparently not bothered by the smoke. They stared at Calojan but neither moved nor spoke.

"Take a seat," the man said, squatting on the floor and settling the baby against his chest. "What can I do for you?"

Calojan sat down and tucked his legs in close. "You're the leader of these people."

"Me? Not really." The man shrugged. "I go and argue with the priests each morning when they bring the flour; me and a couple of others, but I do the talking. I guess that's all the leading that goes on around here. My name's Asburn, for what it's worth."

Calojan took a cloth bundle from his pocket, untied the corners and emptied it on the ground. "That's ten gold solidi," he said. "That's just for talking to me. Now, are you the leader of these people?"

Asburn stared at the coins, then handed the baby to the woman. "Yes, that'd be me."

"Splendid. I need soldiers. Your people have no work and nothing to eat except the Temple charity, which can be withdrawn at any time. Can your lot fight?"

Asburn smiled at him. "Are you serious?"

"Can they fight?"

"Back home," Asburn said, "by the time a boy's twelve years old, he's expected to be able to throw a spear twenty yards and shoot an arrow into a rolling wheel at fifty yards. It's a father's responsibility to teach his son the spear and the short axe, which are the weapons every man's required to own by customary law. Freeholders' sons usually take part in their first spear-games when they turn seventeen—that's things like throwing the javelin or carrying off the ring on your spearpoint, all on horseback, and then there's the general melee and exercises like that. When you get five or more of our people together in one place for more than half an hour, chances are they'll have an archery contest. As far as proper fighting's concerned, we try and keep it to a minimum, but we don't always succeed. Every thirty years or so there tends to be a war somewhere; you don't have to join in, but it helps keep the peace, if you follow me."

Calojan nodded. "I'm offering two solidi a man, real gold money; also, I'll feed the women and children while you're away and pay five solidi compensation for every man killed. Weapons and armour supplied, horses for those who can ride them, but you've got to give them back afterwards." He paused. "Do you need time to think about it?"

"No."

THREE DAYS LATER, the new army paraded on the open heath beside the camp. There were just over five thousand of them, kitted out in forty years'

worth of unsaleable stock from the de Peguilhan warehouses, and Apsimar leaned close to Calojan and said softly, "Why are we doing this?"

They did actually look quite like soldiers. They were standing still in long lines, shields and spears at rest. The lines were straight and there was no talking in the ranks. Calojan lowered his voice. "Why is it," he said, "that neither you nor your uncle ever bother to listen to me? No matter, I'll say it again. We have *no army*. There are *no soldiers*. The Cosseilhatz refused to come unless your uncle gave them some land; he, in his infinite wisdom, refused. So, I'm taking what I can get. It was this or press-ganging dock workers."

Apsimar gave him a troubled look. "You aren't seriously suggesting we give imperial territory to savages."

Calojan sighed. "I'm not suggesting anything," he said. "All that side of things is most definitely none of my business, I just do the war. As of this morning, what with time-expired discharges and desertions, we have four thousand regular infantry and nine hundred heavy cavalry; basically, they're the ones with no homes to go to. Reliable reports put Hunza's army at four thousand cavalry and eleven thousand foot. There is effectively *nothing at all* standing between Hunza and the City except these men here. Do you understand, or would you like me to write it down for you?"

"Calojan, be reasonable," Apsimar said. "You don't know anything about these people. You have no idea whether they'll fight or not, or if they can obey orders, or—"

"Apsimar," Calojan said. "Be quiet."

"I'm sorry, but I think you're taking a rather cavalier attitude to—"

"*Quiet.*"

For the next two hours, Calojan took them through some fairly rudimentary drill. Afterwards he summoned Asburn. "You lied to me," he said.

"What?"

Calojan grinned. "You told me these men haven't ever done any formal military training. Obviously they have."

Asburn shook his head. "We just listen carefully and do what we're told," he said.

"Is that right." Calojan narrowed his eyes, as though he was trying to read something almost too far away to be legible. "Are there a lot of you, where you come from?"

"Where we—?"

"Beyond the north-western frontier of the empire."

Asburn smiled. "Yes," he said. "Hundreds of thousands, probably. We breed like rabbits. Why?"

"Just interested, that's all."

Sechimer arrived to review the troops. He looked at them for a long time without saying anything, then turned to Calojan and said, "Where did all these men come from?"

"They were here all the time," Calojan replied. "In the City, and then stuck out here, doing nothing. Like the forty trachy you find in the lining of your coat. I think they'll do."

"What makes you say that?"

Calojan shrugged. "I've been among soldiers most of my life." He called over a junior officer and told him to stand the men down. "I think they've demonstrated that they can keep still," he said. "Let's see what they do next."

The officer bawled out the command, and the ranks quietly relaxed, like a bow drawn and then not loosed. The men planted their spears and sat down on the ground, cross-legged, pulling their mailshirts over their knees. There was a low hum of conversation, like a distant swarm of bees. "I think they know how to be patient," Sechimer said. "That's important."

"I think they'll do," Calojan repeated. "I had a long talk with Aimeric de Peguilhan's foreman. He's one of them, but he's been here so long you can talk to him like he's one of us."

Sechimer laughed. "I could say the same thing about you."

"Quite. From time to time I do tend to forget I'm a foreigner. It's kind of you to remind me."

"There are no nations and races inside the empire," Sechimer said. "There's just the emperor and his people."

"Good old Florian. I sometimes wonder if he meant it the way it sounds."

Sechimer shrugged. "Don't ask me," he said. "I only know the quotations, I've never read the actual speech. But I'm happy to take that line at face value."

"Quite so." Calojan nodded. "But you won't let the Cosseilhatz settle in the empty valleys."

"That's different."

"Of course it is. And this lot?"

Sechimer frowned. "They work hard, they don't make trouble, they keep themselves to themselves. Also, we treated them abominably, so we ought to do something for them." Suddenly he laughed. "Three hundred years ago, I'd be thinking; I like these people, they'd be a useful addition to the imperial family; let's conquer them. Now—" He clicked his tongue. "I think it's like the old question, can a man ever really be just friends with a woman? Can we be friends with people like this without subconsciously wanting to absorb them; what do you think?"

Calojan looked at the long lines of armed men. The last time he'd seen them, they'd reminded him of the old stories about the living dead. "They look like they're going on an outing," he said. "A hunting party, or a festival or something. Not afraid, not seething with righteous fervour, just moderately happy and content, waiting to find out what happens. I've seen soldiers like this, but not for a long time."

"That's not an answer to my question."

"I think the empire's like a disease," Calojan replied. "I think it's contagious; either you catch it or you find a medicine to fight it off, you can't just live next to it and choose not to join in. Think about it. These people came here. We didn't ask them to, they just came; a few to begin with, and then, when they discovered there was work here, and they saw all the wealth and sophistication, they came in hundreds, like flies. For a while we let them come, and then we tried to shoo them away."

"Now there's a question," Sechimer said. "Is the fly the fault of the apple?"

Calojan rolled his eyes. "I'll leave that one to you. But, if you like the analogy, you might care to consider that flies tend to gather thickest on fruit when it's starting to rot."

"Charming." Sechimer frowned. Then he said, "Those helmets with the raised rib across the crown. Weren't they recalled because of metallurgical flaws?"

"They were cheap."

"Ah."

"Also," Calojan said, "they were available. When I told young Aimeric I'd take the lot sight unseen, his jaw dropped so much he nearly swallowed himself."

"I can imagine," Sechimer said. He arched his back and wriggled his shoulders; standing in one place too long in full ceremonial armour. "Please don't be too hard on Apsimar. I know he can be annoying, but he's the only heir apparent we've got. I'd hate for him not to like you, for his sake."

"If he's the only heir you've got, get another one."

Sechimer was silent for a long time. Then he said, "Funny you should say that."

"Really?"

"You know this prophesy everyone's talking about."

"Oh, that." Calojan frowned. "That Mezentine thing."

"They're deciphering it right now. Apparently it's all rather obscure and the language is difficult. But I was talking to archdeacon Vorsiger, and he says there's at least one bit that looks like it could be about me. The six-fingered man."

Calojan looked straight ahead. "Go on."

"He says the six-fingered man will marry the spear-maker's daughter, and their son will rule the world, from the grey apple tree to the white."

"Good heavens," Calojan said. "Does that actually mean anything?"

"Aimeric de Peguilhan's father supplied the army with over a million spears, three times as many as any other contractor. According to the archdeacon, there are apple trees in the far north that bear a sort of greyish fruit, while right out beyond the Claw Mountains they grow apples that are nearly pure white." He paused. "Aimeric's got a sister, hasn't he?"

"I believe so."

"Apparently," Sechimer said, in a strangely detached voice, "the spear-maker's daughter will save the six-fingered man from the deep water." He drew in a deep breath and let it go. "I don't think I can ignore that."

"Can't you? I could. Sechimer, it's *garbage*. You can't seriously be considering marrying a woman you've never met—De Peguilhan's sister, for crying out loud—just because of the ramblings of a dead madman, unreliably translated from the Mezentine. It's so bizarre it makes me wonder if I'm dreaming."

"Talking of dreams," Sechimer said softly, "I've been having the same one over and over again, ever since I woke up after the battle."

"Oh, not dreams, please."

"I'm at the bottom of a deep wellshaft," Sechimer said, "the walls are brick and covered in green moss, and there's water coming up from under my feet and pouring in from overhead. I'm just about to drown, and a hand reaches down and I stretch out for it."

"And?"

"And then I wake up."

Calojan sighed. "Too much Permian pickled cabbage just before going to bed, that's what that's all about." He frowned. A staff officer was hovering with a brass message-tube in his hand, clearly not prepared to interrupt an audience with the emperor. "At the very least," he said, "promise me you won't do anything drastic till I get back. Promise?"

"Define drastic."

"Don't do *anything*. How's that?"

Sechimer shrugged. "Fine," he said. "That's assuming you do come back. If you're pinning all our hopes on this lot, that's hardly a foregone conclusion."

All our hopes, Calojan thought; all our hopes are pinned on me, and one of these days the pin will pierce my heart and I'll die. "They'll be just fine," he said. "You'll see."

While Calojan read his despatches they brought up the imperial chaise; limewood under gilded plaster, wheel-spokes thin as straws, but a hundred and twenty years ago it had borne the weight of Huneric II, the fattest man ever to strain the joints of Florian's throne. Two milk-white horses drew it, and the coachman was the eldest son of the Minister of Supply. Sechimer had said once; everything I own these days is second-hand. His shoulders slumped as the chaise moved off; he doesn't have to try when he's alone, Calojan realised, so he doesn't bother.

It was just starting to spit with rain. Calojan pulled the fur hood of his cloak over his head, hesitated for a moment, then strolled slowly down the slope to the front rank. The man on the far end looked up at him and started to get to his feet. Calojan shook his head. "As you were."

"What?"

Calojan frowned. "That's army talk," he said, "for don't bother to get up. What's your name?"

The man was quite young, tall and thin, with a long neck and a bushy black beard. His hair was thinning on top, but there remained a thick clump about the size of a man's hand right at the front. "Ascetil," the man replied. "Who are you?"

"Apsimar."

"Pleased to meet you."

If we were in a bar, Calojan thought, he'd be offering to buy me a drink. "So," he said, "how long have you been in the City?"

Ascetil thought before answering. "Thirteen months."

"Like it here?"

"It was good when we were living in Westponds," Ascetil replied. "The camp's not so bad, but it's boring not having anything to do."

"Better than home?"

Another pause for thought. "Yes. Warmer. And all the *stuff* they've got here, it's amazing."

"What about being a soldier?" Calojan asked. "Do you like the idea?"

"Are you joking?" Ascetil suddenly smiled, and his face became beautiful. "Never could've been one back home. Couldn't afford the gear, and who wants to be one of the poor sods hanging round the edges throwing stones? This'll be something to tell my grandsons about."

"You do realise," Calojan said, "people get killed in war. You might not make it."

"Ah well." Ascetil scratched his ear. "Some people reckon that if you die in battle you go to Warfather's house, and you drink beer all day long and eat and fight, and it's just like being a chieftain, even if you're someone like me. Or if that's not true, it's all over and you're out of it, like being let off work early. Can't say I'm bothered either way. Also, the emperor says if I get killed he'll give my mother five gold coins." He grinned. "There's seven of us back home, on nine acres. Five gold coins, they could buy the valley."

Calojan nodded. "You'll make it," he said. "I gather the general's quite smart."

"Genius, so they say. Never lost a battle."

"Not that you hear about, anyway. So," Calojan went on, "you reckon soldiering might be for you, in the long term?"

"Why not?" Ascetil shrugged. "Better than home, better than sitting round in the camp. And all this stuff they give you, it's incredible. Good boots, good shirt, really good padded coat. And all this *armour*, it's fantastic. Chieftains back home don't have anything like this good, and here they've given it to all of us. They must be so rich."

Calojan frowned. The scale *clibanion* Ascetil was wearing was basically a way of using up offcuts of steel plate, or recycling battlefield pick-up breastplates and greaves too badly damaged to be repaired. The Armoury Board had rejected that particular batch on grounds of slovenly workmanship. "I believe you're supposed to give it back when the war's over."

Ascetil grinned. "I don't think so," he said. "No, it's great, I can't wait to see the looks on their faces when I get home. Not that I'm in any hurry. They reckon that after the battle, you can go round the dead bodies and help yourself to as much as you can carry, and then a man from the government comes and pays you money for it." He looked up hopefully. "Is that true?"

"That's quite right," Calojan said. "It's called the bounty system. They've done it for years."

"Amazing. Gold money, or that copper rubbish?"

Calojan laughed. "Gold money. They don't try that copper trick on with the army."

"If that doesn't beat cock-fighting." Ascetil beamed at him. "Someone told me, they have real problems getting men for the emperor's army. I can't understand that. You'd think they'd be queuing up."

Seven of them, on nine acres. Calojan tried to remember when he'd last been hungry; not just for a few hours, but days on end. On campaign, when the supply line had been cut. Not the same thing at all. Of course, nobody went hungry among the Cosseilhatz. You could eat as much as you could cram down yourself, so long as you liked cheese.

THE QUICKEST WAY to reach Hunza's army was through Brocia, following the Great Military Road as far as Shastel Rosc, then cutting across country. Calojan had a clear mental image of Shastel, from when his family had lived there when he was seven, but when they got there they found ruins; indeterminate shapes under rich green mountains of brambles and nettles, the occasional outcrop of brick or broken masonry. It was like a heavy fall of green snow, masking a familiar landscape. He tried to superimpose his memories on what he saw, but the two pictures simply wouldn't fit together. It was two days since they'd seen anyone at all.

Asburn, the first Northerner he'd spoken to, was still nominally in charge of his countrymen; at least, he passed on Calojan's orders, and they were obeyed with a certain bewildered compliance. When not shuttling backwards and forwards he rode at Calojan's side, looking about him with a permanent puzzled frown.

"Where did all the people go?" he asked.

"The town," Calojan told him. "Then, as the Sashan picked off the towns one by one, they headed for the City. I guess about half of them made it."

Asburn digested that for a while. Then he said, "But there's peace now. Why don't they go home?"

The fields on either side of the road were shoulder-high weeds, just starting to brown off and die. Massive seed-pods were yellowing paper-thin. Before the war, the farmers in these parts had looked after their land well; it would stay fertile for another three or four generations of weed, and then it would be completely drained. "I guess they prefer city life," Calojan said.

"If it was me," Asburn said, "I'd top off this rubbish and run pigs on it, then plough three times and it'd be right as rain. Corn one year, grazing the next. It's so warm down here, I bet you'd get grass as fat as butter."

Few things bored Calojan more acutely than agriculture, but he didn't have to pay attention if he didn't want to. He let the tide of excited chatter wash round him, and tried to think of something clever he could do against Hunza. But nothing came; it was like trying to compose music when you haven't got the faintest spark of a tune in your head. I'll think of something when the time comes, he promised himself; I always do.

THERE WAS NOTHING to talk about, but they talked anyway. Hunza rode up on a white horse, escorted by seven enormous men in gold armour. Calojan wore his old felt hat and took Apsimar, on the grounds that it might just possibly be a trap.

"Hello, Hunza," he said. "Still dead?"

Hunza didn't reply; he held out his hand and one of the massive guards handed him something brown and flat. It looked painfully like an artist's portfolio. Hunza leaned forward over his horse's neck to give it to him.

"Let me guess," Calojan said.

"From the Great King's personal library," Hunza said. "Charcoal sketches for *The Frog And The Crane*. I've always thought it was your father's best work."

"Thank you so much," Calojan said. "Well, I suppose while we're here, we should go through the motions. How about you surrender and your men can go free?"

Hunza looked at him for about four seconds. "You will withdraw your forces to the far side of the river Sotopis," he said. "You will surrender the keys of the six fortified towns between here and Shastel Rosc. You will disband your mercenary army. You will pay war reparations of seventeen million solidi."

"No," Calojan said.

Hunza gathered his reins. "In that case, we have nothing to say to each other."

"Agreed." Calojan smiled. "It's all right for you, though. When we cut off your head and stick it on a pole, you won't feel a thing, since you've already been dead for five years. That must be such a comfort."

One of the guards wore a puzzled look. It'd be all across the camp by morning, at which time Hunza would call on them all to make the supreme sacrifice for his sake. And they'd all be thinking, *but if he's not really who he says he is*—"I'm sorry," Calojan said. "It's just work, nothing personal. Good luck."

Later, comparing the map with what he could see from the top of the only hill for miles around, he told himself, *not looking good*. Tomorrow's battlefield was flat and open; ideal cavalry country, and Hunza had nine thousand cavalry. His main infantry formation would line up in front of a long, wide stand of pine trees. He had three thousand archers. He'd have to be crazy to make the first move, so the imperials would have to come to him, advancing untried infantry a long way over open ground to attack at odds of two to one. If the Cosseilhatz were there, it'd be different, but they weren't. Come on, he told himself, think of something. But nothing came.

AT FIRST LIGHT, Apsimar came to his tent, in full gilded Classical armour, his plumed helmet cradled under his arm so that the feathers sort of gushed up into his armpit. He drew back the door-flap and said, "Come on, it's time we were—oh."

Calojan grinned up at him. "It's all right," he said, "it's my mother. I don't know who the man is." He pushed the sketches back into the folder, closed and buckled the flap. "Right then, we'd better make a move."

Apsimar scowled at him. "You haven't put your armour on."

"Can't be bothered," Calojan said. "If the fighting gets that close, whoever kills me will be doing me a favour." He reached for his hat, hesitated. It had belonged to his father, and he really didn't want to lose it. Instead, he took the felt arming cap he wore when it rained. "Ready," he said. "Let's go and get it over with."

He set off at a brisk pace, so that Apsimar ended up trotting at his heels like a lazy dog. As he passed through the camp there was a joyful cheer from the regulars—it'd have been heartening if only there'd been a few more of them—but the Northerners stared. I know what they're asking themselves, Calojan thought; who's the tramp walking in front of the general? To which the answer was, that's Calojan, the man who's just about to think of something, any minute now.

They were approaching the edge of the camp, beyond which lay the battlefield, and then the enemy. Apsimar skipped a few steps to close the distance between them. "Was that really your mother?" he said.

Calojan nodded. "It's funny," he said. "I mostly remember her as a tense, fierce woman, always worried about money. But to the Great King of the Sashan, apparently, she was a remote and mysterious object of desire."

"Ah. Why's it called the Frog and the Crane?"

Calojan looked at him. "No idea," he said. They'd reached the edge of the camp, and Calojan stopped. There was now nothing but open space and grass between them and the enemy, just over a mile away. It was like standing on the shore, looking at the ocean.

"I've got a favour to ask," Apsimar said behind him. "I'll quite understand if you say no."

Calojan had other things on his mind. "What?"

"Would it be all right if I led the attack? I wouldn't make decisions or give orders or anything. I'd just like to know what it feels like."

"I can tell you that," Calojan replied distractedly. "It's horrible and terrifying. Why in God's name would you want to put yourself through that?"

"Well." Apsimar hesitated. "Well," he went on, "it could well be that I'll be emperor one day, and my uncle always makes a point of fighting right up at the front. I feel it's something I ought to do."

And look what happened—Calojan didn't say that. He tried to think of a tactful way of saying, *No, I can't let you, you're too stupid and useless to be put in harm's way*; but he couldn't think, his mind was too busy scrabbling at a closed door—*I'll think of something, I always do.* "Fine," he said. "You do that, the men'll appreciate it, especially the offcomers. I think they have heroes in their culture. You look like a hero. It'll make them happy."

Apsimar was suddenly, happily silent; God, Calojan thought, he's taken that as a compliment. "Just take care of yourself," he added. "Look pretty and keep out of the way, all right?"

"I'll be fine," Apsimar said. "I've been training four hours a day with the toughest drill sergeants in the Guards. I can handle myself."

"Of course you can." And he was thinking; with just five hundred Cosseilhatz, I could hook their right wing as it swings round to enfilade our left; time it just right, I could roll them up like a carpet, and they'd never expect it because that's where they're strongest. Just five hundred. "Go and see Asburn, tell him you'll be leading and get him to put twelve good men with you. He'll be thrilled to bits, he thinks you're in charge."

They brought him his horse. The wretched thing was in a mood. It got like that from time to time, mostly when it hadn't had enough exercise; it stamped its feet, backed up, tossed its head, pulling him sharply forward by the reins. He tried soothing words, but knew he was wasting his time. It was going to be one of those days. He watched the men form up, according to the order of battle he'd finally decided on in the early hours of the morning, not because he'd thought of something but simply so that he could go to bed and try and sleep. It was pathetically simple; offcomers in the centre, regulars in two blocks to cover the ends of their line, archers on the wings; cavalry, what little there was of it, held back as a last-chance mobile reserve. He'd drawn it out on a piece of paper, then looked at it and written *4/10, must try harder* at the bottom. It was what Apsimar would've come up with if he'd been in command. Time to think of something was starting to run out.

He realised, with a terrible jolt in the pit of his stomach, that he hadn't yet found a vantage point from which to watch and control the battle; he hadn't done it yet because there wasn't one. The small hill where they'd pitched camp was the only high ground in sight, and the enemy were a mile away. For the hundredth time he considered calling the whole thing off; pulling out, going away, starting again from scratch somewhere else. For the hundredth time, he reminded himself that that was impossible; he was at the very end of his supply chain and there simply wasn't enough food, the reasons for which he intended to discuss forcefully with Supply as and when he got back to the City. The mistake had already been made and was past fixing. It had to be here and now—in which case, the only place he'd be able to see from would be right up close, far closer to the actual fighting than he'd been for about ten years. He realised that he was sweating and shivering, and his knees were freezing cold. Ah, he thought, I'm a coward, that's interesting. Hell of a time to find out, but useful to know nevertheless.

Well, he thought, I may be a coward but the horse isn't. He gave it a harder kick than strictly necessary, and it jolted forward, with a buck and a half-hearted rear. Heroes' horses do that sort of thing. Maybe it's because heroes kick them too hard, because they're terrified.

He was halfway across the plain towards the enemy before he remembered he hadn't got his armour on.

Hunza, according to the reliable sources, positioned himself in the exact centre of his front line. He arrived in a silver-plated chariot, complete with purple canopy and scythed wheels, that had belonged to Casharo the Great, conqueror of the Known East; he was flanked by nine hundred veterans of the old Invincible Guard, who'd travelled from all four corners of the former Sashan empire to be at his side. The centre of his formation was Sashan regular heavy infantry—the Ninth Army, which hadn't seen action in the last stages of the war and was practically at full strength; they'd been on garrison duty in Agpatana, nine hundred miles away, when the Great King was overthrown. On the wings were twenty squadrons of Matapaean dragoons. The reserve was five thousand Zeugite heavy infantry; time-discharged twenty-year men recalled to the colours from their smallholdings in the Mesoge. It was only scraps and leftovers of the might of the Sashan, but Hunza had twenty-six thousand men—fifteen hundred tons of steel armour—against Calojan's twelve, and the imperials had seen fit to attack.

The imperial line advanced, with a cloud of staff officers buzzing around the ranks like flies, trying to keep the front straight and level. The trouble was, the offcomers walked faster than the regulars—later, Calojan figured out it was simply because they were taller, so had longer legs—and they didn't seem inclined to listen to the riders who kept telling them to slow down. By the time they were within a long bowshot of the enemy, they were seventy yards clear of the regulars, puffing along in their wake.

A Sashan captain who was with Hunza at this point later recalled that all his senior advisers told him to send the dragoons out to hook and outflank this advance unit, but Hunza refused; he knew Calojan, he said, and clearly this was a deadly trap, into which he was not disposed to fall. The dragoons, therefore, stayed exactly where they were as the five thousand men of the imperial advance guard crashed into Hunza's centre.

I CAN'T SEE. Calojan realised he was shouting it out loud, but the noise was so great he couldn't hear himself. It was like being suddenly struck blind. In front of him, on the far side of the backs of his infantry reserve, one hell of a battle was going on. He could hear it, but that was all. Everything was going wrong, and he had no idea what to do.

This is hopeless, he told himself. He gave the horse a brutal kick and yanked its head over, swerving round the side of the reserves and out into the open, where he could see—

He'd forgotten. It had been a long time. It all looks so different from a long way away.

The offcomers were tearing a hole in Hunza's front line. Confronted with a rock-steady hedge of spearpoints, the front rank had dropped their shields, ducked under the spears, grabbed the shafts and pushed them apart, wide enough for two or three from the second rank to wedge themselves into the gap. The Sashan, gripping shield and spear as though they were frozen to their hands, had no way to defend themselves or get out of the way; the offcomers pulled their helmets off with one hand and crushed their skulls with the other. They were fighting like animals, the way Calojan had seen deer and pigs and dogs fight each other, a scrambling, violent mess which bore no resemblance to the drill manuals or the skill-at-arms displays. The Sashan, as far as he could tell, weren't even trying to fight back. They were shocked, terrified, as if the enemy were werewolves or trolls, unnatural and inhuman. The attack was eating into the formation like acid on metal, and deep inside there shone a gleam of flickering gold;

Apsimar, in his ridiculous armour, cutting a path straight at a shining silver chariot gridlocked in the dead centre of the line.

This is insane, Calojan thought. He stood up in his stirrups, thinking, what about the dragoons, for crying out loud? They should be pouring in on the flanks by now but he could see no sign of them. He tried to think, though he'd never felt more stupid in his life. They're not moving, because they haven't had orders; orders can't reach them, because Hunza's in that ludicrous shiny chariot, and my savages are in the way. He looked round for a rider—there were always at least a dozen riders with him when he was running a battle, close enough that they could hear him dictate orders without having to lean forward; no, not this time, he'd left them behind. He panicked, as though he'd unexpectedly lost his voice; then he kicked the horse forward, right up close to the horrible, wet, red fighting, until he saw what he was looking for; a man in reject-stock lamellar armour, picking himself up off the ground.

"You," he shouted.

The man looked at him. He must've been knocked out and only just come round. There was blood running down his face, but scalp wounds bleed like hell. Calojan reined in the horse and slid off it. "You," he repeated. "Can you ride?"

"Who the hell are you?"

"I'm Calojan." He grabbed the man's hand and pressed the reins into it, closing the fingers around them. "Ride to the regular infantry division on the left, give them this message. Quarter wheel towards the dragoons and fucking stay there. Those exact words. Then you ride over to the other division on the right, tell them the exact same thing. You got that?"

The man wiped blood out of his eyes. "You're the general?"

"Yes."

"But I thought—" He pointed vaguely in the direction of the centre. "In the gold armour. We were following—"

"Not him," Calojan shouted; for some reason, he felt mortally offended. "Me. Now move."

The man dragged himself onto the horse with a handful of mane, gave it a ferocious kick. His feet weren't in the stirrups; probably he'd never used them, since they'd be made of iron and therefore too expensive. Calojan watched him out of sight, then remembered where he was; ten yards from the fighting and completely unarmed.

Fortunately, a sword wasn't hard to come by, though he had to prise it out of the previous owner's hand, finger by finger; Sashan, some sort of officer, his head split open like a log, dust on his open eyes. He'd forgotten about all that, and for a moment he stood staring at the weapon he was holding, wondering what on earth he was supposed to do with it. Answer; as little as possible. Now he could really do with a horse, but there wasn't one anywhere.

Something was happening. It took him ten seconds, a very long time in context, to figure it out. The Sashan line was starting to crumple, but there wasn't anywhere for it to crumple into; the back six ranks couldn't see what was happening at the front, probably had no idea that the front five ranks had ceased to exist, and were standing their ground; the middle five was trying to push through them, walking backwards because there was no room to turn; nobody could ask or answer, because you couldn't hear yourself think over the blacksmithing noises. Now, if his messenger had got through and been taken seriously by the divisional commanders, he had two regular divisions facing off against the dragoons on the Sashan wings; if they called his bluff and charged, that would be the end of the matter, but they wouldn't, because they weren't getting orders from Hunza and they'd be too scared of invincible, infinitely cunning General Calojan to use their initiative and attack anyway. Meanwhile, the offcomer division was continuing to consume the Sashan centre like fire burning a bundle of dry sticks.

Luck, he thought bitterly; it was practically obscene. Still, it was doing a better job than he was capable of, in the circumstances. As for his part in all this—the only way they could lose now would be if invincible Calojan the Miracle-Worker contrived to get himself killed, in which case the regulars would simply drop their weapons and run. His duty, therefore, was to get the hell out of it, as quickly and discreetly as possible.

Running was out of the question, so he turned and walked briskly, away from the fighting, towards the camp. He felt ridiculous, but he couldn't help that. Behind his back, men were dying, for or because of him. He tried to think about something else.

THAT EVENING, HE walked back again, this time to view the bodies. The offcomers, who took that sort of thing rather seriously, had laid out their dead in rows, each man lying under his shield, feet crossed (he wanted to ask about that, but decided another time would do just as well); at the end of each row was a huge pile of manufactured goods, the proceeds of enthusiastic scavenging. Calojan didn't have the heart to tell them that half of the stuff—worn-out boots, bloodsoaked trousers—wouldn't repay the cost of carting it to the City. The rest of it, mostly armour and weapons, would make a little money on a saturated market. It would probably constitute unimaginable wealth to the offcomers.

The fifteen thousand dead Sashan, by contrast, were piled up in long, low heaps, slumped where they'd been pitched off the tailgates of carts, like road-makers' chippings. All the bodies were naked except the one he'd been brought to see. He looked down, then knelt and made a show of examining it closely, though there was no need. He'd seen from ten yards away that the corpse in the shiny silver-plated scale armour wasn't Hunza, who had presumably exchanged outfits with a gullible subordinate, then made his way quietly off the field, like someone else he could mention. Of course, it was worth bearing in mind that Hunza wasn't Hunza, just someone pretending to be him; now, presumably, pretending not to be the man he'd pretended he was.

He stood up. "That's him," he said. "I'd know him anywhere. Strip the body and burn it with the others."

The other body he'd come to see was lying on its own, on a stretcher made from broken spears and one of Hunza's more flamboyant banners. Apsimar had died from one of about twelve deep, slicing cuts, most likely from a Sashan cavalryman's sabre. Someone had been to a lot of trouble to try and squash his arm and shoulder back onto the torso, but it wouldn't line up right. His face had a diagonal red-and-black line across it, as though someone had crossed him out. Apparently he'd got within five yards of Hunza (or the fake Hunza, more likely) before his frenzied attempt to end the battle with one glorious stroke had run out of energy and luck. Forty-seven men, nearly a third of the offcomer dead, had been killed retrieving his body. Next to him, the offcomers had made a heap of the finest weapons taken from the dead; they'd snapped the bows, crushed and smashed the shields, heated the swords to soften them and twisted them into semi-circles. The idea was that the killed weapons would accompany the dead man to some place where slaughtered heroes go. The offcomers had repeatedly insisted that they didn't expect to be paid for these weapons; they were a present, to their fallen lord.

It rained in the night, so that next morning there was no dry wood available for burning the Sashan bodies. The regulars objected that the picks and shovels were with the reserve supply train, which hadn't arrived yet. They could wait for the wagons, of course, but there was no way of knowing how long they'd take to arrive, and the quartermaster wanted it put on the record that they only had food for another two days. The northern savages, they added, had their own picks and shovels, not military issue but perfectly serviceable. The offcomers explained politely that they didn't bury their enemies, it was disrespectful to their own dead. The Chief Augur helpfully reminded him that leaving the bodies of the enemy to rot on the battlefield was anathema and would incur divine wrath; Calojan might be inclined to take a relaxed view of such issues, but he ventured to suggest that the emperor would not. So Calojan went back to the offcomers and offered to pay them five hundred solidi if they'd lend their privately-owned digging tools to the regulars. That, apparently, was entirely acceptable. Then the regulars objected that because of the heavy overnight rain the ground was too wet for excavating the usual deep-cut mass graves; the sides of the trenches might fall in, which posed an unacceptable risk to the men doing the digging. By this point, Calojan's head was hurting so much he could hardly see straight; then he remembered that in the wagons containing Hunza's personal belongings were twelve forty-gallon casks of rose-scented sacramental oil, of the sort that Sashan noblemen used as a cologne after bathing. A quick test confirmed that it was extremely inflammable, even when sprinkled on something wet.

The smell—roses, and something rather like burnt pork fat—followed them on a south-westerly breeze almost as far as Chastel Rosc. A cloth dipped in water and tied over the nose and mouth helped a bit, but it was a week before any of them managed to get it out of their hair.

ALTHOUGH THE FESTIVITIES themselves were of almost unparalleled ingenuity and splendour, the prevailing mood among the crowds who watched Sechimer walk the half mile from the Newgate to the Golden Spire was confusion. They were there, so they'd been told, to celebrate two things; the deliverance of the empire from the Sashan threat, and the marriage of the emperor to Gesel de Peguilhan. Fine; but hadn't the Sashan already been wiped off the face of the earth six months or so ago; and why was their tall, handsome young emperor, now the undisputed master of the entire world, marrying a mousy, horse-faced little commoner two years older than himself, who nobody had ever heard of before?

Good questions, both of them; and the Council dealt with them by having the fountains in the Perfect Square run with wine instead of water from noon until dusk, and handing out fifty million trachy from huge hampers on the Temple steps. This response proved to be popular but not satisfactory. Why, people persisted in asking, had the bride and groom gone to their wedding on foot, in sackcloth, to the accompaniment of monks singing the Intercession for the Dead? Why wasn't Calojan at the wedding? And, given that they'd just been told that the purchase tax, the wine tax, the property tax and salt duty were all about to go up because of financial stringency, who exactly was paying for all this, and what with?

"Actually," the archdeacon said, as he piled smoked-fish rolls on his plate at the reception, "that's a *very* good question. Officially, it's coming out of the vast treasure captured after the battle. The truth is, we got barely enough out of it to cover the cost of the campaign, particularly since Calojan was so very generous to these new savages of his."

Aimeric had tried one of the fish rolls; too salty. "So who did pay for it?"

"We did," the archdeacon replied grimly. "Mostly the Golden Spire, though the New and the White Star promised to cover a third, though we've yet to see the colour of their money. No, the last of the offertory plate had to go, and the clerestory screens, and all four of the Mezentine officiary chalices. We're now in the unhappy position of genuinely being as poor as we've been telling people we are for the last ten years. The only bright side to it is that we don't have to pay for feeding all those wretched savages at that ghastly camp any more. They're on the army payroll now, heaven help them. If you ask me, the savages and the paymasters' office are ideally matched, the utterly insatiable versus the sublimely unsatisfactory. Still, you never know."

Aimeric nodded. "So why the funeral service? And where's Calojan?"

"The Intercession was for that fool Apsimar." The archdeacon sniffed a fish roll and put it back on the far side of his plate. "And Calojan's not here because he can't face being forgiven by Sechimer for getting his last living relative killed. You can see his point. I mean, I have no objection to religion," the archdeacon went on, "in moderation, but lately Sechimer's become little short of insufferable. The sackcloth is a case in point."

"Actually," Aimeric mumbled, "I think that was Gesel's idea."

The archdeacon nodded. "A marriage made in heaven, so to speak. I confess, I'd pay good money to see the expressions on their faces on their wedding night. That's a scene that calls for Calojan's father, at the very height of his powers. Still, it's all for the best, now that Apsimar's gone. A clear-cut succession is the single most important thing in politics. Without it, you simply don't stand a chance." He paused, and gave Aimeric a look he didn't understand. "For which," he added drily, "I assume we have you to thank."

"Me?" Aimeric was mildly stunned. "I assumed it was your idea. I was going to ask you, what the hell were you playing at?"

"Oh." For the first time since he'd known him, the archdeacon was completely lost for words. "No, it most certainly wasn't me, I can assure you of that. In which case—"

"It's simple," Teudel said, twitching the coverlet so that it covered his toes. "Sechimer rules the world, his wife controls Sechimer, Aimeric controls his sister, you control Aimeric. Therefore, you rule the world. Happy now?"

Orsella pulled a doubtful face. "You're overlooking the fact," she said, "that Gesel can't stand the sight of Aimeric. He told me so himself."

"Temporary brother-and-sister quarrel," Teudel replied airily. "You wouldn't know, being an only child. Trust me, mortal dudgeon is the normal default state. Doesn't mean she won't do exactly what he tells her to, provided he can pull the right strings."

Orsella nodded. "You left out a step," she said. "I rule the world, and you control me."

Teudel laughed. "Never in a million years. The Invincible Sun, on a good day, maybe. Me, never. I'm just working for your greater glory. It's what worshippers do."

"You don't strike me as the worshipping sort, Teudel. Even so," she went on, twisting a few strands of his hair round her fingers, until he yelped, "getting poor dear Aimeric's toe in the palace door isn't a bad idea. And it's about time he earned his keep." She sighed, and nestled closer. "I'll miss you."

"Why? I'm not going anywhere." He paused, and lifted his head off the pillow. "Am I?"

"Dreadfully sorry. If I'm going to be controlling Aimeric, that's got to be pretty much a full-time job. Can't have you around the place, he wouldn't like it. I suggest you revert to your original plan and head for the Vesani Republic. With your share of the forgery money, you can set yourself up quite snugly. Buy yourself a nice little shop or something. I should think you'd do quite well, you've got the right instincts."

A three-second pause. "You are joking, aren't you?"

"It's been tremendous fun, Teudel, and obviously this gig won't last for ever. You will wait for me, won't you?"

"Like hell."

She wrinkled her nose. "That's not very romantic."

"I mean," Teudel said, "I'm not going."

"Sweetheart." She ran a fingernail lightly down his cheek. "Don't be tiresome. You're so much better off than you were six months ago, and all because of me."

A much longer silence. Then; "Tell me," Teudel said. "What exactly did you need me for?"

"What a peculiar question."

"Humour me."

"Well." She smiled at him. "You did lots of boring, tedious work scraping parchment and grinding colours and so on. You wrote the text, which I simply couldn't have managed, I'm hopeless when I try and write anything."

"And?"

"You made Aimeric jealous, which kept him firmly in the game. And you kept me company. I'd have been ever so lonely without you."

Teudel shook his head. "You could've hired four professional colourmen for what you paid me," he said. "And I just came up with the ideas; you translated them into flawless Old Mezentine verse. Making Aimeric jealous hardly calls for a highly-paid specialist, and the same goes for keeping you company." He drew back slightly, until her hand couldn't reach his face unless she moved. "What did you need me for, Orsella?"

"The reasons stated," she replied blandly. "Oh, and your splendid criminal record, of course. If it had all gone horribly wrong and we all got found out for fraud, I'd simply have pleaded ignorance and put all the blame on you. As a convicted criminal under sentence of death—"

He wriggled away from her, until he could go no further without falling off the bed. "You really expect me to believe," he said, "that you translated all the stuff about the spear-maker's daughter, and you didn't know what it was about, and you weren't sufficiently curious to ask?"

"I thought it was just drivel," she said. "Padding, to fill in the gaps between the bits we'd discussed. Terribly good drivel, of course."

"I don't believe you."

"You can believe what you like."

He was perfectly still and quiet for a while. Then he said, "All right, let's see what we've got. Without the spear-maker's daughter and your hand firmly on Aimeric's leash, what'd be in it for you? A nice fee for artistic services rendered, but otherwise nothing to show for it except the satisfaction of a job well done."

She sighed. "Don't be all bitter and unpleasant, Teudel. It's been so much fun, and now it's time to move on."

"Whereas," he continued, "as things stand, thanks to an entirely unexpected stroke of good luck, you've just been handed the empire on a plate."

"Which is why," she said sweetly, "you've got to go. You do see that, don't you?"

For a moment it occurred to him to wonder roughly how long he'd have left to live if he punched her in the mouth—now, quickly, as hard as he could, before he had time to think better of it; hours, he decided, rather than days, and besides, as he closed his hand to make the fist he discovered that it was the last thing he wanted to do; physically impossible to make himself do it, like flying. So, like a dog chasing a bird, or a man falling from a rooftop, he was left furious, wretched, helpless, choiceless. He was stranded on an island watching his ship sail away.

"Suit yourself," he said. "About the money."

"Oh, you don't need to worry about that," she said. "As soon as I get paid, I'll send your share on to you. Probably best not to send coins; I'll do you a bill of exchange on the Carloman brothers in Boc Bohec."

So; there wasn't going to be any money, either. On the other hand, to be strictly fair, she hadn't had him murdered, or at least not yet. "How much are we talking about, exactly?" he asked. "In very round numbers."

The figure she quoted was about half what he'd been expecting; not that it mattered, since he'd never see a trachy of it anyway. Even so. "That'll be fine," he said. "You couldn't let me have a few solidi for the road, could you? I'm not particularly keen on walking to Boc Bohec."

She explained that she was a bit short right now, what with having to pay for materials up front and other unavoidable expenses. "I can let you have four tremisses," she said, "but that's about it. Anyway, gold wouldn't be much use to you on the road. Nobody'd be able to give you change."

He left an hour late, carrying everything he owned in his pockets. A small man followed him. He went to Longwall Street; the woman there was surprised to see him, but let him come in. Yes, he could have the cellar, if he wanted, and was he in any trouble? That, he told her, was a bit of a grey area, but it was all right, he'd only be staying for a week or so. She looked disappointed, which pleased him enormously.

EVERYONE WAS TALKING about the prophesy, rumours of which were now streaming out, like blood from under the slaughterhouse door. It was because of the prophesy that the emperor had married the plain girl; she would cleanse him of all his sins (what sins? Presumably some they hadn't heard about) and their progeny would usher in the Age of Gold. That was only the start of it. The drowned man would tip the scales; there was a lot of debate about that one. The she-wolf's whelp would curl up at the feet of the prince of the twilight and save him from the crows; splendid stuff. Two dragons would fight over the lion's carcass, but the wren would have its heart. The chosen one would nearly die of joy, but he would conquer joy and stand before the gates of the King of Worms. Because of the beautiful stranger, the streets would run with blood; he would lift the Crown of Teeth, but place it on the head of another. And, best of all, if the great enemy of all mankind crossed the river Essa, it would be destroyed; only its head would remain, to be carried back to the City. That one led to a run on maps; quite soon they were sold out at the cartographer's in Chapelgate, and new stock was having to be drawn, with the Essa helpfully highlighted in Mezentine blue.

Aimeric eventually gave up on trying to get Gesel to see him and wrote her a letter instead. He got a reply by return—

...*All your fault. I have no idea what you think you're playing at, but I regard your conduct as unforgivable.*

That said, and bearing in mind that I never wanted a husband in the first place, so far I find that Sechimer and I are surprisingly well suited (no thanks whatsoever to you). He is a deeply spiritual man, with a deep-rooted and utterly sincere faith, something I could never expect you to understand. He has proved to me that he is genuinely concerned about the welfare, moral as well as physical, of the people of the empire, regarding himself as their servant rather than their master. On that basis I have reluctantly agreed to share his bed until the succession is assured...

...Our mother is properly looked after, I have sent for her to join me here in the palace, where she will have her own suite of rooms and access to the chapel royal for morning and evening worship. The house in Lattenyard will therefore be sold, and I shall give the proceeds of sale to the Golden Spire, for poor relief. I shall arrange for any possessions of yours still on the premises to be put in store, at your expense.

Please don't write to me again. I am extremely busy with charitable work, and have no time for frivolous correspondence.

The good news was that Orsella had finally sent the odious Teudel packing. She'd caught him out in some unspecified act of petty dishonesty, he'd made a dreadful scene, and she'd shown him the door. He was now safely on his way to the Vesani Republic; no great loss, since now that the prophesy was finished she had absolutely no use for him any more. Furthermore, with the job done and out of the way she had plenty of time on her hands; it'd be much more convenient for both of them, therefore, if Aimeric found a nice place for them to live; she was sick to death of the poky little garret on Cornmarket, and there was a rather lovely place in Tiltyards on the market for a very reasonable price; it had a cloistered garden with a fountain, and a genuine minstrel's gallery in the main hall. Maybe they could go and look at it together, quite soon.

AN EMBASSY ARRIVED from Raffen, king of Selbst. After a brief flurry of activity in the map room of the palace, Selbst was identified as the place where the offcomers came from, and Sechimer and Calojan received the ambassadors in the Old Throne Room. There were three of them; an old man with a shaven head, a thin middle-aged woman and a boy. They were wearing fur coats—the only clothes they'd brought with them—and were suffering terribly in the heat. Sechimer, trussed up like a chicken in chlamys, lorus and divitision, could sympathise; he sent for iced water, which the ambassadors politely declined. There was an awkward silence. Then Calojan said, "Well, what can we do for you?"

The old man wiped a pint of sweat out of his eyes, opened his mouth, thought better of it and stared at the floor. The woman cleared her throat. "Our king would be interested to hear how our countrymen living in your kingdom are getting on," she said. "Last time we heard about them, they were living in some sort of camp, out in a field somewhere."

The word *kingdom* had made two of the attendant clerks wince visibly. Sechimer was about to answer, but Calojan spoke first. "They've been making themselves useful," he said. "Extremely useful, in fact. I recruited them into the imperial army, and they recently did a good job for me. I'm happy to tell you the camp's closed down, they've moved into the old barracks in Eastwood, where they've settled in nicely, and they're quite happy and delighted to stay on."

The old man nodded. "King Raffen will be relieved to hear that," he said.

"In fact," Calojan went on, "you've saved me a job, because I was just about to send someone to see you. Basically, I'd like to know if there's any more at home like the ones we've got here already. If so, send them this way and you'll be doing us a favour. As many as you like," he added, "within reason."

The woman peered at him, as if trying to decide if he was human, animal or divine. "You'd like to recruit more of our people for your army?"

"Absolutely," Calojan said. "We're offering good money for the right men, and there's death-in-service benefits which I think you'll find interesting. Which reminds me," he added. "Something you can help me with.

I have just over five hundred pieces of gold sitting in my exchequer office which belongs to the families of some of your people who didn't make it in the battle I mentioned just now. Three pieces of gold a head, payable to the next of kin. We know the names, but there's the matter of actually getting the money out to the families. If you could help us with that, we'd be most grateful."

A strange look passed over the faces of the ambassadors. "Three pieces of gold," the old man said.

"That's right. We pay that to the family if one if your lot dies on active service. We feel it's the least we can do. Also, of course, the family also gets the dead man's back pay, and any share of plunder he may have been entitled to."

"We'd be delighted to help in any way we can," the woman said quickly. "If it would help you, we'd be prepared to take the money back with us and make sure it's sent on."

"Would you?" Calojan beamed at her. "Thank you so much. I'm sorry to dwell on death and casualties and so forth; I'm probably making it sound much worse than it really is. Fact is, the battle in question was a bit of a miracle, really. As regards your people we lost around a hundred and fifty, out of five thousand. The enemy lost fifteen thousand men." He grinned. "Not wanting to boast, but we're quite good at fighting wars. Your people would be in good hands."

The old man was staring. The boy cleared his throat and said, "Excuse me, but if you're so good at warfare, what do you need us for?"

Sechimer twitched visibly. Calojan said, "I'm sorry, I don't quite see what point you're trying to make."

The boy was about fifteen, tall and broad for his age but somewhat baby-faced. He cleared his throat again before he answered. "It seems to me," he said, "that someone in your position would need a large number of extra soldiers either because he's lost a lot of his own men and needs to make his numbers back up, or else because he's planning some big operation, like invading another country. Excuse me for putting it like this, but if it's the first one, you're weak, and if it's the second, you're dangerous. Either way, maybe our king should be a bit careful about getting too closely involved with you."

Calojan looked as though he was about to reply, but he didn't speak. Sechimer said, "We've been engaged in a long and very bitter war with our oldest and strongest enemy, the Sashan. I took over the throne because the previous emperor had been managing the war very badly. During that time, we lost a great many men. However, that war has now been won.

The battle your countrymen fought in was the last stage of it, and we were completely successful."

"I see," the boy said. "So now there's nobody left for you to fight. In that case, why do you need a big new army?"

Calojan laughed. "We had allies," he said. "They helped us a lot in the war. But now they've got troubles of their own, so they've gone home. We'd like your people to replace them. It's true," he went on, "there's no-one left to fight *right now*. But next year, or in ten years' time, who knows? Meanwhile, your people can earn good money. And with any luck, just by having a big new army, we'll convince anyone who might want to pick a fight with us that it wouldn't be a good idea."

The boy nodded. "Thank you," he said. "I think I understand now."

Another slightly awkward pause; then the woman said, "This is Breniolf, one of our leading chieftains. He came of age two months ago."

"It was a good question," Sechimer said. "I hope we've answered it clearly enough."

"Perfectly clearly, thank you," the woman said. "We'll go back to our king and let him know what you've said." She smiled; the effect was rather disconcerting, and made her look ten years younger. "Thank you for seeing us. I hope we didn't break too many diplomatic protocols. This is the first time we've been ambassadors, you see."

"You did it very well," Calojan said. He waited for a moment, then added, "Was there anything else? Only—"

The old man was struggling with himself; one part of him must have won, because he coughed loudly and said, "May I ask something?"

Calojan looked at Sechimer, who said, "By all means."

The old man looked at Sechimer for three seconds. Then he said, "Since it's so very hot, why are you wearing that great big embroidered scarf? It must be very uncomfortable."

Calojan made a sort of strangled noise and turned sharply away. "Well," Sechimer said, "it's called the lorus, it's very old, and all my predecessors have worn it, right back to Florian's time. I guess it's to show people I'm the emperor."

"Ah." The old man looked relieved. "We have something quite like that in our country. It's a very old helmet, which the king wears. It's made of hardened oxhide, and it's decorated with teeth pulled from the jaws of the king's enemies after their heads have been cut off. At the last count," he added, "there were six hundred and twenty-four."

Sechimer greeted that with a sort of glazed smile. Calojan said, "That's rather neat, and it's always helpful to have a way of keeping the score. But what if the king had an enemy who was so old that all his teeth had fallen out? You wouldn't be able to count him, surely."

"Oh, that's all right." The woman looked straight at him. "Our king's enemies don't live that long."

THE END OF the world began with a goat; to be precise, a nanny goat and two kids. They belonged to Rutetz, a junior elder of the Blue Flower Cosseilhatz. The Blue Flower tended to leave shearing rather later than the other Families, claiming that their bloodline was thoroughbred northern stock and shed its wool in early summer rather than late spring. Accordingly, they delayed shearing until they reached the summer lowland pastures, and used shearing pens built on the north bank of the Rociander, a tributary of the Essa which marks the nominal boundary between the western Cosseilhatz marches and the imperial protectorate of Crebriand. At the beginning of summer, the Rociander is usually in mild spate, because of the spring rains in the mountains. That year, however, the rain had come early and been followed by a long dry spell; as a result, the ford at Crowsnest was passable two months earlier than usual.

Rutetz came last in the shearing lottery, which meant he had to wait until everyone else had finished with the pens before he could drive his flocks down off the foothills. To make matters worse, several large herds of deer, forced down into the valley by the dry weather and poor grazing, had eaten off much of the fat spring grass, which Rutetz had been relying on to bulk out his flock before the long drove south-east to the main summer pastures; having to leave them on the close-cropped foothills while he waited his turn at the pens meant that they were losing condition rather than gaining it, and hunger was tempting the more adventurous animals to stray.

Amportat, his eldest son, suggested compensating for their losses by taking a few days off and shooting as many of the deer as they could; this would give them salt meat in hand and hides which could later be traded for hay when they reached the autumn layover, which would help put some fat back on the animals before winter. It was a plausible enough suggestion, though Rutetz reckoned it had more to do with Amportat's newly-acquired ninety-pounder bow than a hard-headed appraisal of the season's prospects; he compromised and sent Amportat and two of the men to hunt deer while the rest of the household waited for the shearing pens to become free. As a result, he was three men short when his neighbours finished their shearing earlier than anticipated and he was finally able to drive his flock down to the river.

Even so, he would probably have been able to cope if the goats hadn't been hungry, because of the depredations of the deer and the enforced delay. As it was, he had all sorts of trouble keeping the wretched creatures from wandering off or breaking out. The cold, dry spell made the fleeces heavier than usual; an excellent thing in itself, but it meant that the goats took longer to shear, which in turn meant that the flock spent rather longer than he'd have liked cooped up in the pens, with no grazing. Six weeks of continuous use had left their mark on the pens; the idea was that the households using them patched them up after they'd finished, but it never seemed to work like that, and by the time Rutetz' turn came round they were in a rather sorry state, with broken rails hastily bound up with string and patched with half-sprung hurdles. The only pairs of hands Rutetz could spare from shearing to keep the goats in the pen were his younger son Partetz and his three sisters. They did their best, but it was like trying to hold water in a sieve; as soon as a goat broke out and trotted off in search of grass, three of them had to go and chase after it before it got too far, leaving one (usually Razos, the youngest girl) to keep the others from following the fugitive and mend the breach in the defences.

In the circumstances it was hardly surprising that disaster eventually struck. Partetz and his two elder sisters were off chasing a billy-goat with a remarkable turn of speed up the lower slopes of the mountain. Razos, eleven years old and profoundly unhappy with her role in the proceedings, was trying to tie together the two ends of a broken rail. She ran out of twine; she'd asked the others to bring her some more from the wagons, but they'd been busy and hadn't got around to it. So she went to fetch it herself, and while she was away, a nanny-goat and two kids eased their way through the half-mended breach and set off for the river-bank, where the grass was greenest. By the time Razos got back, they had a hundred yard start. She dumped the ball of twine and chased after them, but all she achieved was to spook them and make them run faster. By the time she ran out of breath, the goats had reached the ford and were halfway across the river.

There was no sign of Partetz or her sisters. All she could think of to do was run to the shearing trap and tell her father. Predictably, Rutetz wasn't amused. He said some rather unkind things about his family in general and his daughters in particular, then set off with two of the men and their wives to see if they could somehow catch up with the goats and turn them round before they went too far into forbidden imperial territory. On the way, he happened to encounter a man called Glaia, the senior stockman for one of the other households. Glaia had been sent to cut withies for hurdle-making, but quickly realised the seriousness of the situation and offered to help, which offer was gratefully accepted.

It was Glaia who pointed out that if they swam the river rather than running to the ford, they could get ahead of the errant goats and stand some chance of turning them round, instead of merely driving them deeper inland. The idea worked. By cutting across some sloping ground and coming up on the goats over the brow of a small hill, they were able to execute a flawless ambush and send them running back towards the river. It didn't particularly matter which precise direction they took; once they reached the river, they'd have no option but to follow the bank until they came to the ford, and if Glaia and two others ran around in a wide loop and came up on the far side of the ford, they'd be able to turn the goats back if they tried to carry on downstream. They'd be left with nowhere to go except back across the ford, and that'd be the worst bit done.

It couldn't have gone better. The goats, moving fast, reached the river-bank about a quarter of a mile upstream of the ford, which gave Glaia and his detachment plenty of time to get in position, while Rutetz drove the goats down along the bank. At just the right moment, Glaia jumped up out of the long grass waving his arms; the goats darted back across the ford, as if that was what they'd wanted to do all along.

Once they were back on the Cosseilhatz side of the river, Rutetz detailed a woman called Chanzos to hold the ford in case the stupid creatures tried to double back, then deployed his troops in a classic encircling manoeuvre. Regrettably, it was too successful. The goats, seeing they were completely surrounded, darted back the way they'd just come. Chanzos, confronted with a charging nanny-goat, swerved to block it; the two kids darted past her; she swung back to try and stop them, and the nanny slipped past her on the other side. By the time she realised what had happened, all three goats were back across the ford and deep inside the empire, running very fast.

Rutetz was all for going back to the wagon for his bow and shooting the miserable creatures, but Glaia, who'd learned true patience from thirty years' incessant warfare with livestock, just grinned and said they'd just have to start over, was all; they'd managed it once, so they could do it again, and this time, he'd guard the ford and stop them getting through a second time. So, after a few minutes to catch their breath, the pursuers set off on the heading they'd last seen the goats following.

It took them a while to catch up. Rutetz was all for giving up and going back, arguing that the goats were younger and fitter than any of them and would be uncatchable in open country. Glaia pointed out that they'd just been running; as soon as they felt they were safe, they'd stop to catch their breath and graze. All that was needed was to come up on them steadily and quietly, so as not to spook them again. With luck, most of the mischief and pent-up energy from being stuck in a pen for two days would have been run out of them by now. Provided everyone stayed calm, it ought to be possible to walk them peacefully back to the ford.

After an hour's walk, they caught sight of the goats grazing on the brow of a hill, about a third of a mile away. To avoid being seen, they dropped down out of sight and skirted the hill, then plodded up the scarp face to bring themselves out on the far side. They looked down. There, sure enough, were the goats. Between them and where they stood, however, Auzida could make out four horsemen, riding fast in single file, apparently straight at the goats.

"That's good," he said. "They're going to round them up for us."

Glaia scowled. "I don't think so," he said.

He was quite right. The horsemen broke into a gallop. The goats lifted their heads, saw them, and fled. The horsemen closed in; they had bows, and started shooting. They weren't very good shots, at least not by Cosseilhatz standards, but their horses were fast enough to get them in so close that they could barely miss.

Furiously angry, Rutetz broke into a run; Glaia hesitated for quite some time, then followed him, with the others at his heels. Rutetz was yelling as he ran. The horsemen heard him and looked round to see who was yelling at them.

"You bloody fools," Rutetz shouted. "What's the matter with you? Can't you tell tame goats from wild?"

Probably not; unshorn, to southern imperials, the difference wouldn't be immediately apparent. That thought occurred to Rutetz while he was still shouting; also, he noticed that the men were soldiers.

Their leader, the youngest of them, and the best dressed, looked at him and said, "Who the hell are you?" He spoke in Imperial, which Rutetz could understand; he'd been shouting in Aram, which presumably the soldier could not. Chances were, however, that an officer in the imperial forces would recognise Aram for what it was, even if he couldn't understand it.

"The goats you just shot," Rutetz said. "They're mine."

Another man, older, said, "This is imperial territory. You shouldn't be here."

It occurred to Rutetz that there might be more at stake here than straightforward property rights. "I was chasing the goats," he said. "They got across the river."

The officer seemed troubled by that. "Unlikely," he said. "River's in spate this time of year. Ford's closed till midsummer."

Rutetz opened his mouth to explain, but realised that anything he said wasn't likely to be believed. At that moment, the older man turned his head, saw something that made him start, and pointed. All of them, Rutetz included, followed the line he was indicating; Glaia and the rest of the pursuers, suddenly emerging out of the long grass.

Rutetz could see how bad it looked. He knew Glaia had approached slowly and quietly simply because he was a stockman and always moved that way. The patrol captain, however, wasn't to know that. Nor was he to know that Glaia had an axe in his hand simply because it was the axe he'd brought to cut withies with, it had fallen out of his belt a moment or so before, he'd picked it up but hadn't yet put it back. All the captain saw was a Cosseilhatz on the wrong side of the Rociander, creeping up on him with an axe in his hand while his attention was being distracted by some man babbling at him about goats. He yelled, "Shoot him!", and two of the troopers immediately drew and loosed. One of them shot high and missed. The other hit Glaia square in the middle of his forehead.

Later, Rutetz freely admitted that what happened next was all his fault. He wasn't even sure what actually happened, or how. Presumably he must have stooped, picked up the fallen axe and either swung it or, more likely, thrown it at the nearest archer. When that man dropped from the saddle, he must have grabbed his bow and an arrow from his quiver and shot the officer. He remembered shooting the other two troopers, because they turned and fled; he could distinctly recall thinking that he daren't let them get away, in case they came back with a squadron and slaughtered the entire Blue Flower. Later, of course, he saw the flaws in that line of reasoning; but not before he'd picked off both of the departing troopers, one at forty yards, the other at nearly seventy—not bad shooting, he said ruefully, with a bow he wasn't used to, and piss-poor imperial arrows.

About two seconds after he'd killed the last of the troopers, he realised what a terrible mistake he'd made. Panic set in. Without stopping to see if Glaia was miraculously still alive, or sparing a thought for the other four, who'd stood rock-still throughout, he turned and ran as fast as he could back to the ford. It was only once he'd crossed the river that he realised he was still holding the soldier's bow. He threw it in the river; it was sheer bad luck that, before the Blue Flower hastily broke camp and headed up the mountain, a boy from another household who hadn't heard what had happened chanced to find it, trapped in some reeds, and took it back to his wagon.

It was further bad luck that that particular wagon was the first one stopped and searched by the imperial punitive expedition, immediately launched by the frontier garrison commander once the troopers' bodies were discovered, in company with one dead Cosseilhatz and an axe of unmistakable Aram design. The troopers, on finding the bow, decided straight away that it constituted conclusive evidence, and started lashing out with their sabres at everyone they could reach. They'd killed a dozen or so, mostly women, by the time the men realised what was going on and dashed back to their wagons for their bows. This time, four imperial troopers managed to get away, though one of them died of his wounds shortly after he got back to camp. Their account of the engagement may have been influenced by their retrospective doubts about the legality of slaughtering the women without first referring the matter to their commanding officer; as they told it, they'd stopped and searched a wagon, found the incriminating bow, and been shot to pieces by a pre-arranged ambush.

The garrison commander was a regular, but had somehow avoided seeing any significant action during the war; he'd heard ever so many stories about the Cosseilhatz but never served with them or seen them fight. It took him about three seconds to form his own interpretation of the evidence; however, he decided that things had gone too far for a summary reaction, and sent an urgent report to the governor, with a request for instructions and substantial reinforcements.

Rutetz, meanwhile, was taken by the Blue Flower elders to explain himself to the Family council, who immediately despatched him to Joiauz. He told the story more or less straight. Describing the interview later, he said that Joiauz sort of froze for a while, his face completely blank, then thanked him politely and asked if he wouldn't mind waiting around for a bit in case the Council had any questions. Two men he didn't know then led him to a tent, where he was given white wheat bread and half a jug of exceptionally good wine, together with the strong impression that trying to leave the tent would be the last thing he ever did.

"Right," Joiauz said, in a rather high voice. "Let's start with the war, shall we?"

The others looked at him. Then one of them said, "Is it that bad?"

"Oh, I think so," Joiauz replied furiously. "After all, it looks like we've already had a battle. Where there's battles, there's a war, right?"

"Let's just slow down a little," murmured Semplan of the Four Birds. "There's been a *misunderstanding*. No, let me finish. Our man *inadvertently* trespasses. Their man *mistakenly* kills our man's stockman. Our man *unthinkingly* fights back. Their cavalry raid—"

"Slaughters twelve women before they get what they deserve," Autet of the South-East interrupted angrily. "Are you saying we should just forget about that?"

"I'm saying," Semplan replied calmly, "that there's facts, and there's ways of looking at those facts. Some ways lead to more people getting killed. It's not what actually happened that matters, it's what happens next."

Luzir of the Long Arrow made a sort of hissing noise. "I don't agree with the principle," he said. "But I don't think it's going to help anyone if we stagger into a war with the empire. We've got enough on our plate with the no Vei, for crying out loud, and the Chantat, and the Goida are right behind them. If the empire wants to fight us, they'll just have to wait their turn."

Autet sighed. "Agreed," he said, "we don't want a war. But—"

"Don't we, though?"

They all turned and stared at him. Joiauz, however, was smiling. It wasn't a happy smile. "What did you just say?" Semplan asked.

Joiauz leaned forward, his elbows on his knees, his face in his hands. "Do we want a war?" he said. "I think we do. The right war, of course."

"Joiauz, you're making no sense," Luzir said. "Do you really want to pick a fight with general Calojan? You, of all people?"

"I've been thinking about him," Joiauz said. "I've been thinking about him a lot. And I spoke to a man who was at the battle, the recent one, where they beat the Sashan without us. And I think I know why Calojan always wins."

There was a silence that seemed longer that it actually was. Then Semplan said, "Go on."

"Calojan," Joiauz said, "always wins because—" He stopped, and drew a deep breath. "He wins because he understands that the old nations have had their day—the Sashan, and the empire too. He's figured out that their people just don't want to fight any more, or else they can't—don't know how to, or there just aren't enough of them. Think about that, will you? I've spent twenty years learning about the empire; not deliberately, but you can't help picking things up as you go along. Five hundred years ago, a thousand years ago, all the countries in the empire were doing well, they were crowded with people; every bit of land was ploughed and manured and harrowed and planted, the countryside was crowded out with small farmers, there were too many people and not enough land. So the imperials raised big armies and went out and conquered half the world, and the Sashan conquered the other half; and then what happened? The best soldiers turned into great noblemen, with huge estates worked by hired men and slaves. That made them rich, and they wanted to get richer, to compete with each other, because how rich you are is their only way of keeping score. So what happened? The great nobles and their great estates started buying out the small farms, or simply taking them over, fencing off the shared land. The empire and the Sashan started fighting each other almost all the time, so they needed more and more soldiers; that meant more farmers getting called up to fight, which meant they weren't home to work their land, so it got neglected and the great nobles came in and got hold of it—security for loans that could never be paid back, that sort of thing. Then the nobles started rearing huge herds of livestock, so they could sell meat and hides and wool for money; they grassed over the ploughed land, and that meant two or three stockmen were all that were needed where ten years before there'd been twenty families on the same ground. People who couldn't make a living in the country any more went to the cities, to make things in factories to sell for even more money. Meanwhile, with all the endless wars against the Sashan, thousands of men got killed every year. That's how it happened. It wasn't planned, and I'm not even sure any of them have noticed, except possibly Calojan himself. But the fact is, the empire's like an old dried-up walnut. It's hard on the outside, but inside there's a little shrivelled thing and a lot of empty space. I think Calojan knows this. What he's done that's so clever is, he's gone out, outside the empire, and brought in people like us to do his fighting for him. He knows that we're still prepared to fight, and there's a lot of us. He turns us loose on the Sashan, who are just as weak and brittle as the empire, and we slaughter them. He knows we'll win, because the Sashan are basically just like the empire, another walnut shell. Then, when we won't fight any more, he finds these northerners; and guess what, he wins again. You want to know what Calojan's secret weapon is? We are. We're it. Which is why," he said quietly, "we can beat him. If we want to."

"Agreed," Luzir said, after a long silence. "But do we want to?"

Joiauz nodded vigorously. "Yes," he said, "I think we do. I think we want to move our people away from here, across the Essa, into Crebriand and then west, as far as we want to go. The no Vei and the Rosinholet and the Chantat want our land; I say let them have it. They need to move on, because they've got the Goida breathing down their necks. The Goida are on the move because way out east somewhere there's someone even bigger and nastier than they are, pushing up against them. If we all stay still, I can tell you what'll happen. Us, the no Vei, the Chantat, all the Aram will wear ourselves out fighting each other, and then the Goida will come and slaughter what's left, and we'll all be dead. So, let's not fight. Let's not have a war; at least, not the war we don't want, against people we can't beat. If we've got to fight, let's fight someone we know is weaker than us, and take what we need, and maybe the Cosseilhatz will still be around in a hundred years' time. Really, I believe it's as simple as that. What do you think?"

Nobody spoke or even moved for a very long time. Then Semplan said, "It's not up to us, though. Is it?"

Joiauz nodded wearily. "That's right," he said. "It's up to Chauzida, and he's just a kid. But you all know I'm right, don't you? It's not like we've got a choice. The Goida are coming, tomorrow or the next day, or the day after that. If it wasn't for Calojan, I don't think any of us would hesitate."

Autet shivered. "They say he's never lost a battle."

"That's the other thing." Joiauz lifted his head; his eyes were glittering, as though he had a fever. "I think there's a good chance Calojan won't fight. Well, why should he? He knows us. He knows taking us on would be completely different from fighting the Sashan. For him to fight us would be like the head declaring war on the hands; and it's the hands that hold the weapons. I think he'd refuse, and then the emperor wouldn't have any choice. He'd have to let us take as much land as we want—and there's plenty of room for us, that's the thing. We could live inside the empire and be their dogs, if that's how it has to be. We could live in their house and chase away the wolves from their door, it'd be a good thing for all of us. Calojan will tell Sechimer that, and Sechimer will have to listen. He's not a fool. He'll have to."

Luzir nodded. "And if he doesn't?"

"We take what we want anyway," Joiauz replied. "But I don't see it coming to that. It's like we're challenging Calojan to a fight, and we've got his sword. Without us, he can't fight. Simple as that."

"What about these new people he's got?" Autet said. "These northerners?"

Joiuaz' face relaxed into a broad grin. "There's only five thousand of them," he said. "And they're footsoldiers. Since when have the Aram been scared of anyone who hasn't even got a horse?"

"All right." Semplan looked round, as if hoping someone would contradict him, then went on, "We need to tell the boy."

"We need him to make the right choice," Autet added. "Joiauz, you'll have to talk to him first."

Joiauz nodded. "He's a very smart kid," he said. "I believe I can make him understand. He'll listen to me. It's not like he's got anyone else to talk to."

263

CHAUZIDA STARED DOWN at the terrible thing he'd just done, and groaned out loud.

There it lay, in nine pieces, on the floor of the tent. It was just his rotten luck that it should have fallen, not on the soft rug which might have cushioned its fall, but on the projecting claw-shaped foot of the stupid folding table, which shattered it instantly and beyond all hope of repair. He gazed at it, hating it, desperate with guilt. His father had brought it back from the war, his most valued trophy, a genuine Mezentine porcelain wine cooler; look, he'd announced, what I've got. They'd gawped at it—it's a pot, big deal—and he'd explained; it's a very *old* pot, it's really rare, it's from a very long way away; then (as an afterthought) it's very beautiful; then, when nobody seemed particularly convinced, it's a very *valuable* old rare pot. It's worth six imperial gold coins, and Calojan gave it to me personally.

And now, Chauzida reflected, I've killed it. His father had explained about that. With very old, rare, valuable pots, if they get broken, they aren't valuable any more, even if you wire them back together. It's the not-being-broken-after-having-been-around-all-that-time that makes them desirable; that and the exquisite beauty, which barbarians like themselves would have to take on trust.

I'm going to be in so much trouble, Chauzida thought.

His first instinct was to gather up the fragments of pottery corpse and bury them somewhere, and fall back on the what-me? defence. But it had never worked in the past, not once; they could always tell he was lying just by looking him in the eyes, and the lie, apparently, just made it all so much worse. He cast about for other options. A sudden gust of wind. The dog did it. (But if the dog was in the tent, that would be his fault too; in fact, it would be an exacerbating factor rather than a defence.)

He tried to think. He asked himself; in my shoes, what would general Calojan do? Various strategies flashed across his mind like shooting stars; he could be discovered lying on the ground, apparently unconscious, a fainting fit, they'd be so worried about him they wouldn't care about a dumb old pot. Well, maybe not. He tried to picture himself standing upright and tall; I am your king and this was my pot, if I choose to break it—No. Hard to imagine anything that could make the situation worse, but that could well be it.

So, what *would* Calojan do? Answer; Calojan wouldn't have broken it in the first place. Calojan wouldn't have been practicing close-order hand-to-hand combat, with an imaginary axe against an imaginary opponent, and if he had he'd have looked where he was backhand-parrying an imaginary downward diagonal cut in fourth guard; and even if he'd not looked and broken the stupid pot, Calojan wouldn't be in more trouble than anyone ever in the history of the world, because Calojan was a *grown-up*—

"Chauzida, there you are. I've been looking for you."

He hadn't heard Joiauz come in. He froze. On the ground at his feet, the potsherds looked bigger than mountains. He had one second to come up with a plausible lie—

"I'm so sorry," he said; the words burst out of him. "It was an accident, really. I just sort of brushed against it, and—"

Joiauz caught sight of the potsherds. The corners of his mouth twitched. "That's that horrible pot."

"I just sort of touched it, and it fell. I'm really, really sorry."

Joiauz shrugged. "You know what," he said, "I never liked it much anyway. But the other one was always so mad keen on it, I never said anything."

It was as though he was standing on a stool with a rope round his neck, and instead of kicking the stool away they'd grinned and said, *Only kidding*. He looked up at Joiauz' face, and his heart went cold. "What is it?" he asked. "What's happened?"

"I need to talk to you," Joiauz said. "Tell you what. Let's walk down to the river, see if we can get a couple of ducks."

Chuazida hesitated for a moment, just in case it was a trick and Joiauz was about to start yelling about the pot. Then he dived into the long box in the corner of the tent and got out his bow. Joiauz didn't like hunting, he didn't have the patience. A voice in his head told him, *something is very wrong*, but he'd seen two dozen ducks down in the ox-bow that very morning. Whatever it was, it couldn't be that bad.

The ducks were still there. Inevitably they put them up as they shoved their way through the tall reeds; they exploded off the water and soared into the air but that was all right, they'd circle for a while and then come back. Very carefully, so as to keep movement to a bare minimum, Chauzida teased the seven blunt-head arrows out of the quiver and laid them down beside him, locating them by feel so he wouldn't have to look down when the time came. The air was perfectly still, and the only sound was the river.

"Chauzida." He wished his uncle would keep quiet. "There's going to be a war."

Well, he knew that. "Because of the soldiers attacking the Blue Flower."

"That's right."

Well. It was bad news, he assumed, but no reason to scare the ducks. Still, his uncle felt the need to talk about it, so he did his best. "Is there anything we can do to stop it?"

A pause. Chauzida craned his head sideways, to look up without presenting the high-flying ducks with a warning flash of white face. "Yes," Joiauz said. "We could negotiate, send an embassy, sort it out. The situation's pretty bad, but there's probably still time to fix it."

"That's good."

Joiauz shifted a little. Cramp, presumably. "It's entirely up to you, of course," Joiauz went on. "You have to make the decision."

"What's there to decide?"

Out of nowhere, a duck swooped down, opened its wings to brake, and dropped onto the water. Not daring to breathe, Chauzida groped for an arrow, nocked it, drew swiftly and smoothly, took a sight along the arrowshaft, drew back a little more until he felt the tip of his middle finger graze the corner of his mouth. At that moment, just as it should, the force behind the string became too much for his hooked fingers to resist. The string slipped free, and for an everlasting fraction of a second, he watched the arrow loop and twist in the air. Then there was a clearly audible smack; the duck thrashed on the water, flapped desperately two or three times—it was already dead, but its wings hadn't realised that yet—and sort of flopped sideways. A surge of joy filled him, but he remembered to look for the arrow, quickly sinking through the water, so he'd know where to dive for it later. "Shot," Chauzida muttered, and for a moment, the whole world was a bright blaze of glory. Then he remembered, and said, "Sorry, what were you saying?"

"You need to decide," Joiauz said. "Do we make peace, or do we go to war?"

Chauzida glanced up again. The ducks were still circling, tiny black footprints in blue snow. Maybe he'd missed something. "Why would we want to have a war?" he asked.

Joiauz explained. There was going to be a war, no question about it; the decision really was who they'd end up fighting. One enemy was strong, the other was weak. The future of the Cosseilhatz was at stake. It looked like a choice, but really it was something else; do the sensible thing, or make a bad mistake. You didn't have to be a genius to work that out.

"Well?" Joiauz said.

Chauzida was vividly aware of the feel of the bow handle in his hand. A few minutes ago, he'd been so purely happy. "It's not really up to me, is it?" he said. "I mean, it can't be. I'm just a kid."

Joiauz looked so unhappy. "No," he said. "It's got to be you. I can't decide for you, I can only advise. Otherwise it'd be all wrong."

"You decide. That's my decision. I—" What was the word? "I *authorise* you to choose for me. I can do that, can't I?"

"No." Joiauz sounded—not angry, or at least not angry with him. "Look, I'm sorry, but that's how it is. Some things you can cheat with, some things, you've got to do it absolutely straight or it comes out very bad indeed."

"But nobody would know."

"I'd know," Joiauz said, "and so would you." He sort of wriggled, as though he was itching. "Would you like me to explain it again? Maybe I didn't make it clear."

Chauzida shook his head. "You want us to start this war with the empire, don't you?"

"It's not—"

"No, please. *You* think that would be the best thing to do."

Joiauz hesitated, then nodded firmly. "Yes."

"I think you're far more likely to be right than me."

Joiauz breathed in deeply, then out again, slow. "You're saying you don't think we should do it."

"I—" Chauzida felt his hand tighten on the bow handle, as if he was trying to squeeze a resolution out of it. "It's really stupid, but no, I don't. I think Calojan and the empire have always been our friends, and this thing with the Blue Flower, we both know it was really just an accident, even though they behaved very badly over it. But they lost more men, we *won*, so it sort of evens out. It's definitely not something to fight a war over. It'd be an excuse. We'd be lying. And if it's not all right to lie about whose decision it is," he added quickly, "I don't think it can be right to lie about the reason for doing it. Can it?"

Joiauz was looking past him. "A while back I sent a message to Calojan, and the emperor," he said. "I asked, could we come and live in the empire, to protect them and be protected ourselves. They said no. So yes, you're right, I'm saying we should use this stupid thing as an excuse for doing what I originally wanted to do. And yes, that's a lie."

"And you said," Chauzida went on, "we shouldn't lie about important things."

"I did, didn't I?" Joiauz was kneading the palm of his left hand with the thumb of his right. He did that sometimes, but Chauzida was never sure what it meant. "So you've decided."

"I'm really sorry," Chauzida said. "And I'd far rather you did what you think is right. You know so much more about it than me."

"Yes," Joiauz replied. "I do. And I know I'm right. But it's not up to me."

Chauzida felt terrible. All his life, as long as he could remember, his uncle had been on his side. When he'd done bad things and his father and mother were angry with him, Joiauz had spoken up for him, made a joke of it to calm them down. He'd always treated him as a grown-up, told him the truth; it was probably because he didn't have any children of his own, or something like that. Now, for the first time, his uncle had asked him for something, and he'd refused. "I've changed my mind," he said. "I think we should do the war."

Joiauz grinned at him. "Liar."

"No, really." He tried desperately to find some words. "I've decided that my first decision was wrong, and doing what's best for our people is more important than not lying about why we do it. That's my decision and I'm *ordering* you to respect it. All right?"

Joiuaz shook his head. "You can't do that," he said. "And you shouldn't try, it's not fair on me." He stood up; there was a snapping sound, he'd stepped on one of Chauzida's arrows. He should have sworn loudly, then laughed; that was what his uncle Joiauz would've done, the man he'd known all his life. This man, whoever he was, looked down as though he'd just trodden in something. "Come on," he said. "We'd best get back. Your grandmother will be wondering where you are."

He almost wanted to smile. A moment ago, he'd been a king; now he was a child whose grandmother fretted when she didn't know where he was. "What about the duck?" he said.

"Forget the stupid duck."

Uncle Joiauz had taught him that the hunter always retrieves the dead game; it's part of the covenant, if you kill it, you don't let it go to waste. It was a point of honour. Presumably he was supposed to forget about the arrow, too. He trudged back in Joiauz' footsteps. It was one of the worst moments of his life.

A man he thought he recognised but couldn't put a name to was waiting by the tailgate of the blue-painted wagon. When he saw Joiauz he loped forward and said something to him in a low voice. Joiauz listened intently, nodded, thanked him and sent him on his way. Suddenly he looked tired; like that time when the wagons got stuck in the deep mud crossing one of the northern fords, and it had taken all of them three days and two nights to dig them out. "Now there's a thing," he said.

"Uncle?"

Joiauz hesitated for a moment, then reached out and put his arm round Chauzida's shoulder. "While we were sitting out there in the reeds talking about this important choice you've had to make, some stupid bugger's been and made it for us. Last night, completely unprovoked and without telling anyone, thirty young idiots from the Long Arrow carved up a convoy of imperial merchants on the Lonazep road. Killed the lot of them, seventeen unarmed men, six boys and four convoy guards." He opened his mouth and yawned widely, until Chauzida was afraid his mouth would split. "Well, then," he said. "Now what?"

THERE WERE TWENTY-FOUR captains called Bathanaric in the imperial regular infantry; it was a popular name. Seventeen of the twenty-four were from distinguished families. There was a Bathanaric de Cadenet, a Bathanaric de Birnamanz, and so on. Captain Bathanaric of the 27th Infantry wasn't one of them. His grandfather was the last of a long line of charcoal burners in the endless forests of the eastern Mesoge, who'd started tanning pig hides as a sideline. His son, Bathanaric's father, had worked long and hard building up the business; when the war broke out, he got a contract to supply oak-tanned oxhides to the military, for making shields. It made him moderately rich, although by the time the war ended no amount of washing and scouring could ever get the smell of brains out of his skin and hair. His son got his commission in an unfashionable infantry regiment, decimated in the war and restocked from conscripted factory workers and discharged criminals, two weeks before the Field of Red and Blue Flowers. Accordingly, he'd never seen action, though he'd heard about it endlessly from the other subalterns, some of whom were two or three years younger than him. Bathanaric wasn't a bad officer, but he wasn't a particularly good one, either. It was an accurate reflection of the regiment's reputation that, when Calojan was scraping the barrel to make up numbers against Hunza, the 27th was posted to garrison duty in a part of the frontier where no trouble was anticipated.

When the news reached him about the massacre of an imperial merchant convoy by a Cosseilhatz faction he'd never heard of, his first reaction was cold, horrified panic. It reminded him of the dream he kept having, where he'd agreed to lead the Ascension Day prayers in Temple; he'd be standing in front of the high altar, with everyone watching him, and suddenly he'd realise he didn't know any of the words.

His second reaction was to send a messenger to Division to ask for instructions. But Division was three days away (and that was assuming the fords were passable); three days there, three days back, six days at the earliest, and by then the whole frontier could be ablaze. He tried to imagine how he'd explain the delay at his court martial, but inspiration was singularly lacking.

His third reaction was to seek advice from his more experienced subordinates; but there weren't any. The 27th was nine-tenths new recruits;

even his colour-sergeant was new to field operations, ten years' indifferent service in the supply corps, promoted to the double green stripe simply because there wasn't anybody else. The standard-bearer had done two tours in the war, but then he'd been broken down from master sergeant for stealing and cowardice in the face of the enemy, so asking him for advice probably wasn't a good idea. It dawned on Bathanaric, slowly and horribly, that he was going to have to make the decisions himself.

Which was what the Book was for. *A Manual of Field Operations*, written three centuries ago by the emperor Genseric IV (the same emperor who'd lost most of Raetica and been disastrously defeated by the Aelians) occupied the place of honour on the wobbly-legged trestle table that constituted Bathanaric's office. Frantically, he searched the table of contents, but the closest thing he could find was *Punitive Expeditions against Jazygite Slave Traders, justifications for.* He read it anyway. It started off, *make a detailed assessment of the strategic and political situation* and then went on to talk about supply trains. The Jazygites had been wiped out two hundred years ago. Presumably the revisions to the manual were held up in committee somewhere.

He'd almost resolved to send to Division and risk the consequences when a rider arrived with news of the slaughter of an entire half-squadron of imperial regular cavalry by another Cosseilhatz sect, the Blue Flower, four days ago. Details were few and vague; there was something about the fighting having taken place on the wrong side of the river, but that was hard to believe. The Cosseilhatz were still supposed to be the empire's allies, even if they'd been too scared to join up against Hunza. Therefore it was unthinkable that imperial troops would've been trespassing on their land. It was possible that they'd been invited there, lured into a trap; but details of that sort didn't really matter very much. The simple fact was that the Cosseilhatz appeared to have turned from friends into enemies—

The implications hit Bathanaric like a hammer. No, he hadn't been in the war; but everyone who had told stories of Calojan's invincible barbarian auxiliaries, butchers of the Sashan; the speed of their attack, their elan, their astonishing marksmanship and skill at arms, their unswerving determination, their reckless savagery once battle was joined. Wonderful people, if somewhat unnerving, to have on your side. Not so good if they were the enemy.

He sent for his two junior subalterns, both of whom he despised. One of them, Dodila, was minor nobility, the third or fourth son of someone important's younger brother. He was a good-natured young man, but hopelessly stupid. The other one, Bessas, had ended up out here because nobody at division could stand the sight of him; he was arrogant, lazy and completely unreliable. He told them what had happened, then said, "Well? What do we do?"

Dodila gawped at him. Bessas leaned back in his chair (standard issue, folding; it creaked ominously) and said, "Nothing."

"Excuse me?"

"Let's just think about this calmly, shall we?" Bessas said. "The Cosseilhatz are Calojan's pet savages, right? So, one, they'd have us for breakfast, two, if we do anything to them, Calojan will have our heads, three, all we have is sketchy and unreliable reports and no orders. Therefore, we do nothing. You send a rider to Division, let them deal with it."

Bathanaric squinted at him, as if he was a badly-written page. "That's all?"

Bessas grinned insufferably. "Consider the alternative. You do something. What? You lead the men across the river, find some Cosseilhatz and attack them. Likeliest outcome, they cut us to pieces. That's not going to help matters. Second likeliest, we kill a bunch of old men and kids, then turn round and come home. That's improved matters how, exactly?"

Bathanaric pursed his lips. "It's a show of force."

"So is walking into a bar and hitting the biggest man you can find. All right, so you don't attack. Instead, you close the gates, recall all detached units, lay in provisions, stand ready for an assault. What happens? Almost certainly, nothing. You look like a fool, the savages see how scared we are of them. Small but material risk that such action would in itself be interpreted as a display of hostility, which means that if this isn't all just a storm in a bottle and there really is trouble brewing somewhere, you've just made things worse. Or you do nothing. Correction; you put out scouts, so that if the savages are on the warpath and come galloping up the valley, you can get the gates shut in good time, for all the very little good it'll do you, because if the Cosseilhatz actually do mean to do us harm, we're dead and there's nothing we can do about it." He smiled, and turned to Dodila. "That's what I think. How about you?"

"Me?" Dodila started nervously. "Oh, I agree."

"Splendid. So, what are our orders?"

Bathanaric shrugged. "Post scouts and do nothing, I suppose," he said. "Dodila, see to it, would you? And get me someone to ride to Division." He scowled at Bessas, then added, "I guess our first duty in a situation like this is not to make matters worse by over-reacting. All right, dismissed."

The Cosseilhatz attacked his outpost at dawn the next day. They must have stalked and killed the scouts, because the first Bathanaric knew about the assault was riders on the skyline, which he wouldn't have noticed if he hadn't had to get up early to visit the latrine. He stared for about five seconds, until he was sure of what he'd seen; then he ran up to the guard tower, yelling at the top of his voice.

At first, the guard sergeant assumed he was drunk, and just grinned. Bathanaric grabbed him by the neck-rim of his breastplate, dragged him to the gateway and pointed. By then, of course, the riders were a hundred yards closer. "Shut the gates," Bathanaric screamed in the sergeant's ear. "Now."

The yelling had brought men out of the barrack huts. Bathanaric gave the sergeant a shove; he scrambled away to the gatehouse. "The savages are coming," Bathanaric howled. "Everybody—" It took him a moment to remember the right form of words. "Stations for primary assault," he said gratefully. The men who'd come out were just looking at him. He realised, they didn't know what to do. The men took their orders from their sergeants, who took theirs from the junior officers. He could yell at them until he was blue in the face, but thanks to the chain of command they couldn't hear him.

Mercifully, Bessas appeared, with the colour-sergeant right behind him. Between them, the three of them were able to operate the relevant protocols and get men up on the ramparts just in time for the Cosseilhatz' horse archers to shoot them down.

As the bodies slumped, Bathanaric could do nothing but stare. He'd been trained to deal with living soldiers; somehow he'd never anticipated losses, the idea that his command had suddenly been reduced by a fifth. It was Bessas who made them get their heads down, and who got archers up to the arrow-slits, and artillery teams to the scorpions. Their return volley fell short, because by then the Cosseilhatz had looped back, as they always did; but at least something had been done.

Pulling himself together at that point was the hardest thing Bathanaric ever had to do. He managed it somehow, mostly by pretending he was a soldier, and knew what to do. He sent men to the walls to replace the dead, got the rest of his troops out of the barracks, armed and armoured, detached the archers from the spearmen, sent orderlies to pick up the wounded; it was all pointless, he knew, because in five minutes, or fifteen, the Cosseilhatz would come over his wall and everybody would be killed. In the meanwhile, however, he had a job to hide behind.

Dodila proved to be useless; he froze in terror as soon as he saw his first dead man, neglected to get his head down, and got himself shot through the neck. Two orderlies hauled him away to the surgeon, and Bathanaric dismissed him from his mind. Bessas, on the other hand, seemed to know what he was doing. He scrambled up the twelve block steps onto the rampart as soon as the volley had been loosed, crouched down to take a long, careful look, then came running back. "I'd say there's about six hundred," he said breathlessly, "though I can't see past the high ground, obviously. All mounted, I couldn't see carts or a siege train, so they don't look like they've got ladders or engines. If they're coming for us, it'll have to be through the gate."

Bathanaric just about managed to figure out what he was being told. The enemy didn't have ladders or siege towers, so for the time being the walls would keep them safe; but he should expect them to try and bash down the gate. "Or fire," he said. "They could burn us out."

"No," Bessas said patiently, "because we've got hide curtains and a cistern of water for putting out fire arrows. You should damp down all round the gatehouse, though, because that's all timber."

The standard bearer, standing behind Bessas' shoulder, looked at him; he nodded, and the standard bearer hurried away. "Anything else?"

Bessas grinned. "Last time I said do nothing, I was probably wrong," he said. "But no, I think we just wait and see what they do next. Anything else is just giving them targets to shoot at."

That sounded plausible. "Right," Bathanaric said. "Where should I go now?"

Bessas thought for a moment. "Best place for you is the guard tower," he said. "Keep low, see what they're up to. Make sure the colour sergeant knows where you are, and get a corporal to run messages. I'll be chivvying up the scorpion teams, and then I'll be getting arrows up from the store to the walls. All right?"

Bathanaric looked at him. He'd never loved anyone more in his life. "Look after yourself," he said.

"You too."

Bessas walked away; quickly but not running or scurrying. Bathanaric watched him go, then crossed the parade yard to the foot of the guard tower stairs. They'd moved the wounded, but the dead were still lying where they'd fallen, untidy bundles that looked disturbingly out of place. It was very quiet. He opened the guard house door, and the creak from the hinges startled him. Hard to believe that these were the last few minutes of his life, but probably best not to dwell on that.

From the parapet at the top of the tower, squatting on his heels and peeping over the sawn-log battlement, he could see the Cosseilhatz quite clearly. They were sitting motionless on perfectly still horses—one of them chose that moment to lift its tail and dump a steaming brown triangle, but its rider didn't seem interested; they'd formed up in a semicircle, in the centre of which stood four riders who were talking to each other. He could hear the voices but couldn't make out the words; they sounded quite calm, businesslike, just another day at work. He was no good at judging distances, so he couldn't say whether they were within bow-shot—presumably not, or they'd be further back. For some reason, their calmness infuriated him, making him feel as though he was some trivial chore to be got around to when they'd finished chatting, and he decided he wanted to hurt them, while he still had the time and the means to do so. At that moment the colour sergeant joined him, creeping along with exaggerated care just below the level of the battlement. Without taking his eyes off the four horsemen, he said, "See those four bastards down there, at the front? Sergeant?"

"Sir."

Well, why not? "Who's on number one scorpion?"

The sergeant thought for a moment, then reeled off some names. They didn't mean anything to him; he couldn't think why he'd asked. "Tell them," he said, "a solidus each if they can hit one of those buggers. Four tremissis if they get his horse."

As the sergeant withdrew, he thought; four men on a scorpion, have I actually got four solidi in the world? He couldn't remember. Still, the chances of him being called on to pay were remote. He waited; the horsemen stayed where they were, no hurry, probably talking about the weather. One of them was wearing a Sashan helmet; the others were in blue or green shirts and red trousers, probably their best clothes, for special occasions.

The characteristic noise of a scorpion being loosed is the steel slider bashing into the oak stop; it's a sort of dead thump. The projectile is a half-inch thick steel rod, four feet long. Accuracy varies, depending on age, maintenance and which contractor made it; the three at the outpost were old and not particularly well cared-for, so it was probably just luck. The bolt hit the helmeted rider in the thick of the thigh, passed straight through the saddle and the horse's flank, on into the rider's other thigh, where it stopped. The horse reared, but the rider was pinned to it and couldn't be thrown; his arms flew out wide and his head rocked back; the helmet was tied on under his chin. The horse bucked wildly, kicking the horse next to it. Then its legs folded and it dropped. There was a loud, sharp crack; a bone breaking. The rider was still alive, flailing at the ground with one arm. The horse lifted its head. The other three riders stared for a second or two, then fled.

What was all that about, Bathanaric wondered; it was a remarkable thing to have seen, but for the life of him he couldn't figure out what it meant, or whether it meant anything. The Cosseilhatz horsemen weren't still any more. They moved like the surface of simmering water, backing up or stepping forward a pace or two before turning in a tight circle; Bathanaric guessed the horses were about to spook, picking up from their riders. The colour sergeant was back; he was grinning, the fool. Bathanaric wondered if he'd had time to get a bet on.

"Well," the sergeant said, "we've taught them to keep their distance, anyhow."

Bathanaric didn't reply. He knew he'd done either a very clever or a profoundly stupid thing, and that luck had taken his intuitive, badly-thought-out idea and made a big deal out of it. The Cosseilhatz were slowly getting their horses back under control. The shot horse was trying to get up; its front legs were working, but its back end was dead.

"I want a white flag," he said. "Quickly."

A moment or so later, someone gave him a spear with a shirt tied to it by the cuffs. He held it up as far as he could get it to go, then counted to three and stood up slowly. They'd seen him. He took a deep breath and tried to think what to say.

He yelled; "Come and get your man. We won't shoot."

They were staring at him as though he wasn't right in the head. He yelled it again. The three survivors were having an animated discussion; then half a dozen riders from the rank behind them shot forward, swerved round them and trotted over to where the horse and rider were lying. They dismounted—the three leaders were shouting at them, presumably ordering them to come back right now—and tried to lift the horse, but it was too heavy. The man screamed with pain—something they'd done; it was ludicrous, a comedy turn. Now they were trying to pull the bolt out, but they only had two inches to try and get a grip on, and the bolt was three and a bit feet into solid meat. Bathanaric had to fight an overpowering urge to run down there and see if he could help; he never could abide watching fools do something badly.

More of the Cosseilhatz had joined the rescue party; enough of them, eventually, to get the horse upright—it was struggling, but didn't have the strength; now they were trying to pull the rider's legs apart so they'd lift off the ends of the bolt, but there was too much gash either side, and all they did was make him scream horribly. What they needed, Bathanaric could see, was a hacksaw, but he guessed they didn't have one. Someone had drawn a sword, his gestures suggested he was urgently recommending a double amputation, but fortunately he wasn't getting any support for his proposal.

Any minute now, Bathanaric guessed, the poor man will bleed to death and save them the bother. The hell with it. He ran down the stairs to the guard tower back room, where he'd seen a box of tools. He had to empty the whole thing out before he found a hacksaw. He'd only ever used one once, and made a hash of it.

"Open the gates," he said. He had to repeat it three times before they did as they were told. He took a deep breath, held out the hacksaw at arm's length, and ran towards the Cosseilhatz. He'd gone half way before he realised that, in all the hurry and panic, he'd forgotten to bring the white flag.

About four of them drew and aimed at him, but didn't loose. He walked straight at them, past them—he was terrified, but there was a man bleeding to death for want of a hacksaw, and until that had been sorted out, there simply wasn't *time*—

Somebody had just tried something, and it hadn't worked. The trapped rider was almost too exhausted to yell any more; his voice was hoarse and faint, and between screams he panted like a dog. Ridiculous, Bathanaric thought. He shouldered his way between two stunned-looking men, and a third stepped forward and put his hand on his chest, palm outstretched, to keep him back.

"I can help," Bathanaric said. "With this."

The man stared, at him, then the saw, then back at him. "What's that?"

"It cuts through steel."

There was a split second when he thought; no, it's not working, they're going to kill me right now. Then the man drew his hand away and stepped back to give him room.

There was so much blood; but he couldn't afford to think about that. He knelt down, his knee sinking into the wet red mud. Everything was red and gleaming, and the smell made him feel sick. He inserted his hand between the rider's thigh and the saddle until he could feel the steel bolt, but there wasn't enough room to get the hacksaw in there. Then he remembered; once, long ago, he'd been an officer in the army. "You," he said, to nobody in particular, "gently pull the leg away from the saddle and hold it there. Got that?"

He felt the hacksaw bite, and sawed, and sawed. His arm started to hurt, the tendon at the top of his forearm just in front of the elbow. His fingers wrapped round the saw handle started to go numb. Nothing seemed to be happening. He tried to think about something else, but there wasn't anything else; just the fear, the pain, the smell and the endless, endless saw-cut. Then, abruptly, the saw snagged and bound; he wrestled to get it free, and realised he was through, as the last thin strand of the bolt gave way and he fell forward. A hand on his shoulder pulled him back onto his knees. His back was agony.

"Now the other one," he said; and his hand hurt so much he could hardly get his fingers to close, it was like gripping a fistful of short nails. This isn't going to work, he thought, as he sawed and sawed, and came through, and it was over.

"Lift him off," he said.

At some point the horse had died and he hadn't noticed. They lifted it to free the trapped legs, and hoisted the rider up into the air, raised him free and put him down on the ground. Bathanaric tried to let go of the saw, but his fingers were locked on to it. I wonder if they'll kill me now, he thought, but in all honesty he didn't care.

"Will he be all right?" he heard himself say. Nobody answered. Four men manhandled the wounded rider up onto a horse and led it away; one of the men turned back and came up to him. "Who the hell are you?" he said.

"Me? I'm the garrison carpenter."

The man gave him a sad look. "In that case," he said, "don't let your captain see you walking around in his uniform." He flicked his head backwards, towards the outpost. "You in charge back there?"

Bathanaric nodded.

"You're a lunatic, is what you are," the Cosseilhatz said.

"I was just—" He didn't finish the sentence. The Cosseilhatz sighed, like someone who's just been told he can't go home until he's ploughed another half acre. "Here's what we'll do, " he said. "You go back and you get your men, and you go. Just go. All right?"

Bathanaric opened his mouth, then shut it again.

"My orders were," the Cosseilhatz went on, "to kill the lot of you. Start a war. Do something no amount of diplomacy could get around." He shrugged. "Well, tomorrow's another day."

"That man," Bathanaric said.

"My father."

There didn't seem to be anything left to say. Except—

"Why?" Bathanaric asked. "I thought we were allies."

The Cosseilhatz shook his head. "Do me a favour," he said. "You go to Calojan and you tell him, king Chauzida has taken all the land between the Essa and the Bathamo as payment for our service in the war. If Calojan wants his gold coins back, he can have them. This land is now rightfully ours, and if he tries to stop us, we'll kill the lot of you. Got that?"

Bathanaric nodded; then he said; "What was that name again?"

"Chauzida. Write it down when you've got a minute, so you don't forget it." He took a long step back, as though Bathanaric was contagious. "Now go away. Please," he added.

BATHANARIC DIDN'T FEEL lucky on the long walk to Reserve at Boc Leal. He felt as though he'd made the biggest mistake of his life; embarking on a four day march without food across mountains, shale and scrub, painfully aware that he'd abandoned his post without even a show of a fight, at times sadly convinced that they wouldn't make it and he'd be responsible for the death of seventy men, having achieved nothing, all because of his own personal cowardice. Bessas was completely insufferable every step of the way, not even pretending to respect his authority, taking every opportunity to pass snide comments which made the men angry and depressed; four times, Bathanaric rounded on him in fury, threatening him with court-martial, the stockade and death, but Bessas just grinned at him. By the time they limped up the long, steep climb from the river valley to Boc Leal, Bathanaric had silently vowed to resign his commission immediately, in the unlikely circumstance that he wasn't cashiered on the spot as soon as he told the duty officer what he'd done. For the last day of the march, he'd entertained himself by drafting the charge sheet in his head; cowardice in the face of the enemy, abandoning his position without orders, recklessly endangering his command, failure to display qualities of leadership, and about thirty counts of total lack of moral fibre. He could picture his father saying, *if only he'd died before he got to Boc Leal; at least we'd have been spared the shame.*

He was stunned, therefore, to discover that he and his men were heroes, and his abject surrender and flight were somehow a victory, and his half-witted impulse to run out into mortal danger waving a hacksaw was the most brilliant piece of tactical thinking since Longinus the Great—Bathanaric Number One, Calojan nowhere, on the military genius roll of honour. All this, he discovered later, was because six other frontier outposts, the entire imperial presence along the Essa, had been wiped out to the last man, so that there was now nothing except Reserve's six hundred auxiliary horse archers between the Aram Cosseilhatz and four major cities. Quite apart from augmenting the manpower of the Army of the East by over ten per cent, he'd achieved the miracle, in context, of not getting killed by the savages, a triumph that had eluded nearly a thousand braver, more dutiful soldiers. Mindful of his solemn vow, he nevertheless tried to resign his commission to anyone who'd listen, but nobody seemed able to hear him, and he gave up.

HE ARRIVED AT the camp just as the sun was rising—not a coincidence, they all reckoned later; whatever else this curious man might or might not be, he was someone with a gift for melodrama—and demanded an audience with King Chauzida. The two sixteen-year-olds lumbered with sentry duty that morning took one look at him, in his ragged purple gold-embroidered robes and one purple riding boot, and took him to their father, who'd just got back from dipping forty sheep. He was wet through, cold and looking forward very much to his breakfast, but he'd been in the war and recognised a high-ranking Sashan when he saw one. He realised at once that this was far too difficult for him to deal with, and sent his eldest daughter to fetch the elders. Then he sat down, took his boots off and offered the stranger a cup of tea.

"I don't want tea," the stranger said. "I demand to see the king."

That was rude, but maybe he didn't know any better. The sentries' father forgave him under his breath and got on with his breakfast, not offering to share. The elders showed up while he was still eating.

"My sons found him," he told them, with his mouth full. "He wants to see the king. Oh, and he's not thirsty."

The elders sat down, looked at the stranger in silence for about half a minute, then explained that they were the king's counsellors. The stranger identified himself as Hunza, rightful Great King of the Sashan. That, apparently, was all he was prepared to say to the likes of them.

The elders backed out of the tent and held a quick, frantic council meeting in the teeth of the biting east wind. Resolved that they should take the lunatic to Joiauz and let him deal with him. Accordingly, not long afterwards, the stranger sat face to face with Joiauz, with a small but efficient imperial military stove between them. "My name is Hunza," the stranger said. "You may have heard of me."

Joiauz nodded. "I heard there was a battle," he said. "Calojan slaughtered a last-ditch Sashan army, led by someone saying he was the new Great King. That was you?"

Hunza nodded.

"Ah well." Joiauz poured himself a cup of tea from the brass pot on top of the stove. "What do you want?" he said.

"My birthright," the stranger replied. "The throne of my ancestors. What else?"

Joiauz shrugged. "I was under the impression your great kingdom doesn't exist any more," he said. "But if you want to call yourself Great King, go ahead. No skin off my nose."

The stranger gave him a pained look. "I'm here to propose an alliance," he said. "Your people and the Sashan against the empire. We've been enemies in the past, but now, as I understand it, your people are at war with Sechimer. Our interests, therefore, coincide."

"Fair enough," Joiauz said. "So tell me, how many men have you got?"

"None," the stranger replied. "My army was shattered. Those that survived the battle were either hunted down and killed or dispersed back to their homes. That's not important. I have only to say the word and a hundred thousand Sashan veterans will flock to my banner."

Joiuaz grinned. "You've got a banner," he said. "Show me."

"Metaphorically speaking," the stranger said irritably. "Meanwhile, I'm in a unique position to advise you on the strengths and weaknesses of Calojan's army. I have reliable, up-to-date intelligence about its numbers, composition and deployment; in particular," he added, "Calojan's new auxiliaries, the northern barbarians. I imagine that would be of great interest to you at this time."

Joiauz thought for a moment. "Sure you wouldn't like a cup of tea?" The stranger didn't answer. "Actually," Joiauz went on, "yes, it would. Now, I have no idea if you're who you say you are, or whether you're just some chancer in a dead man's boots. Boot," he amended. "How's your left foot, by the way? If you've walked any distance barefoot in this weather—"

"I have frostbite," the stranger replied calmly. "I have lost a toe. That doesn't matter. And I assure you, I am King Hunza of the Sashan. My great-uncle—"

"Of course," Joiauz said quickly, slightly unnerved. "What I was going to say is, if you were at the battle and you got a good look at Calojan's new soldiers in action, I'd be very interested to hear about it. First, though, we really should get that foot seen to. If gangrene sets in, you won't be anybody for very long."

The stranger shrugged, graciously making a concession. "As you wish," he said. "Then I'll address your war council, and we can conclude the terms of our alliance."

"Stay there," Joiauz said. He got up, went outside and called over the first man he saw. "Do me a favour," he said. "Run and get Chanzos, tell her to bring her medicine bag. There's some idiot in here with frostbite, might be quite bad. And when you've done that," he added, "see if you can find Semplan and Luzir."

The man looked at him. "What did your last servant die of?"

"Please?"

The man shrugged and ran off. Joiauz went back inside the tent. The stranger was sitting bolt upright, but he'd passed out.

"Is HE REALLY the Great King?" Chauzida whispered.

The stranger was sleeping peacefully, in Joiauz' tent, in his bed. Chanzos had done whatever it was she did and declared that it wasn't as bad as all that; it was mostly just exhaustion and not eating, he wouldn't lose the foot, in a day or so he'd be fine, anybody stupid enough to go walking around this time of year without proper footwear didn't deserve to be that lucky. Joiauz thanked her until she went away, held a quick conference with Semplan and Luzir, then went in search of his nephew. He'd found him up by the ox pens, throwing sticks for the dogs.

"I don't know," Joiauz replied. "He says he is."

"You don't believe him."

"I can't be bothered to form an opinion, to tell you the truth. On balance I'm inclined to believe he thinks he's the Great King, but so what?"

Chauzida frowned. "So he's not important."

"That's different." Joiauz led him back outside. It was just starting to snow; the first soft, wet powdery flakes, the sort that don't really stand a chance. "I am inclined to believe he was in the battle, and I'd dearly love to know more about Calojan's new soldiers. On that basis, if he wants to be the king of an extinct nation, let him." Joiauz shivered, and pulled his collar round his cheeks. "Can I sleep in your tent tonight? I'd rather not share with his Celestial Highness."

"Of course you can," Chauzida replied. They walked on a little, and Chauzida said, "Is it all right now? About the war, I mean."

Joiauz laughed. "That remains to be seen," he said. "But if you mean about you deciding against, I suggest we forget about that. As it turned out, you didn't have to choose after all. So it's all hypothetical, really."

Chauzida wasn't sure he knew what that word meant, but he didn't like to ask. "Is it going all right? Are we winning?"

"So far," Joiauz said. "But right now, it's like we've just punched the other man and we're waiting for him to hit back. I guess we're about to discover if he's holding a horseshoe."

"Calojan's new soldiers."

"That's right. They made a real mess of the Sashan, by all accounts. On the other hand, if that really is Hunza in there, the Sashan were being led by an idiot."

Chauzida stopped. It was a moment before Joiauz realised and turned round. "What?"

"It just occurred to me," Chauzida said. "These northerners."

"What about them?"

"Calojan will have sent to their king asking for more of them."

"If he's smart, which he is."

Chauzida nodded. "Why don't we send to their king and ask him to join us, instead of the empire? Then, if he agrees, there won't have to be a war after all."

"Funny you should say that." Joiauz gave him a curiously distant look. "First, of course, we've got to find out where these people live. So far, all we've got to go on is, they live in the north, and that's a quarter of the world. Once we've narrowed it down a bit, I'll be doing exactly what you just said."

Later, when the stranger woke up, there was an audience. Chauzida wasn't sure who was granting it to whom; he was vaguely aware that he was the one standing up, while the stranger was lying on his back, but the circumstances were unusual. Hunza looked at him, frowned, then made some sort of mental adjustment whereby Chauzida was turned into an adult for the purposes of the conversation, rather like the floorspace of an embassy is deemed to be foreign soil. Hunza spoke briefly and succinctly about the mutual benefits of an alliance against the common enemy; Chauzida glanced at Joiauz, who nodded, then replied that he agreed. That, apparently, was that. When they were outside again, Chauzida asked Joiauz, "What happened?"

Joiauz smiled. "You concluded a thirty-year offensive and defensive alliance with the Sashan," he replied. "You and what's-his-face in there are now brothers in arms to the death against the empire. Don't worry about it," he added, "it's meaningless. But he wouldn't tell us about the new soldiers until we'd been through the performance."

Several hours later, Joiauz went back, alone. Much to his surprise, he found Hunza exceptionally useful and informative; he anticipated all Joiauz' prepared questions, and answered them clearly and comprehensively. The northerners came from a country called Selbst; their north-eastern border was only four days ride away, on the far side of the Middle Lie Forest. The imperial emissaries would take the forest road, but Joiauz could save a whole day if his embassy skirted the eastern edge and cut across the moors; that would bring them into Selbst a mere twenty miles from king Raffen's new castle, at a place called Sitricstead. As for the qualities of the northerners, they were simple and unsophisticated but tough, resourceful and fiercely confident in their own abilities; also, there were a lot of them, too many for the way they chose to live and farm; too many younger sons and brothers with no land of their own, in a society where a man without at least a little scrap of land of his own counted for nothing. None of them were starving, because the grass was good and abundant and the growing season was long, but most of them thought of themselves as poorer than they ought to be. Nearly all of them had weapons and had been trained from childhood to use them, after a fashion. Their military tactics were crude but effective, and they were particularly good spear-throwers and archers, though relatively few of them fought from horseback; for some reason, they saw fit to ride to the battlefield, dismount and fight on foot. As for their links to the empire, several thousand men had gone to the City to work during the war—these were the men Calojan had enlisted—but there was no long-standing diplomatic or cultural relationship, no friendship or loyalty. On the other hand, the empire had stolen a lead by paying Calojan's five thousand a very substantial amount of money, which the Aram Cosseilhatz couldn't hope to match. The northerners didn't use money as a medium of everyday exchange, but they used uncoined gold and silver to buy and sell land and pay compensation for men killed in blood-feuds; imperial gold would therefore be extremely welcome to the chieftains, who dealt in land and engaged in feuds and made decisions about foreign policy. When Joiauz, rather taken aback, asked how he knew all this, Hunza appeared to take offence; naturally he'd gathered the necessary intelligence before embarking on military action. The Sashan were masters of the art of espionage, and a number of their sleepers were still embedded in the imperial service, ready and willing to gather further information as and when Hunza, or his new allies, asked for it.

"So he *is* who he says he is," Chauzida said. "Or how would he know all the secrets from the spies?"

Joiauz shook his head wearily. "Also," he said, "he's not such an idiot as I first thought. I really don't know what to make of him, though an archery target springs to mind. Anyway, he's told us what we really needed to know. They're the Selbst, or their country's called that, and they live on the other side of the big woods. So, first thing in the morning—"

IN THE EVENT, what with one thing and another, Semplan and his three sons didn't leave the camp on their diplomatic mission until just before midday. Consequently, they were still out on the open moor, rather than down in the more sheltered valley, when the rain started. Not that it bothered them. They had goatskin capes and waxed leather hats, and the Aram Cosseilhatz pride themselves on not being made of salt, liable to dissolve at the first touch of water. It was sheer bad luck that Semplan's horse stumbled, threw him into a bog pool and bolted; by the time the boys had caught it and brought it back, Semplan was soaked to the skin. He dried himself off as best he could and put his dry clothes on, but they didn't stay dry for long. It was one of those rare late autumn downpours, when a month's worth of rain falls in an hour, and it lasted the rest of the day and well into the night. The delay because of the bolted horse meant that they were still out in the open at sunset, so they had to sit the night out with rainwater pooling in the creases of their sodden clothes. By noon the next day it was fairly obvious that Semplan had caught a chill. Garsio, his eldest son, said they ought to turn back, but Semplan wouldn't hear of it. The job he'd been given to do was important; if it wasn't, someone else would've been sent instead. Also, if he went creeping home just because of a few sniffles, the entire Cosseilhatz nation would laugh at him, and quite right too.

The rain stopped just before they reached the forest. Garsio insisted that as soon as they made the cover of the woods they should stop, light a fire and dry out properly. The fact that his father agreed put him on notice that something wasn't right; normally the old man would've rejected his suggestion on principle. It wasn't long before Garsio realised his father was genuinely ill, and that if something wasn't done, it could get very bad. Unfortunately, Garsio didn't have a clue what you did when someone was sweating and shaking like that. The brains and experience of the party was his father, and he wasn't making any sense.

Under these difficult circumstances, Garsio made the first decision of his life. He told his brothers to ride back to the camp, as quick as they possibly could, and fetch someone. He'd stay right there with Dad, keep the fire going, try and get him to eat something. He was fairly sure it was a bad decision, but his brothers couldn't think of anything better. They galloped away, leaving Garsio with his appalling responsibility.

There can, therefore, have been few happier men anywhere than Garsio when he looked up, at some point during the next morning, and saw five elegant horsemen in long red cloaks with grey fur hoods coming towards him along the forest road. The hooded cloaks meant imperial cavalry; the wheel-hub-sized gold brooch one of them was wearing meant general staff. Everybody knew the imperials were extraordinarily wise and learned in all the arts and sciences, especially medicine, even if they were lousy soldiers who couldn't fight their way out of a wet cloth bag.

Better still; the leader of the party, a man called Ruaric, had been in the war and knew all about fevers and what you do. As soon as he'd been made aware that the sick man was an important dignitary of the Aram Cosseilhatz, he couldn't have been nicer, or more efficient. These marvellous people carried basic medicines with them wherever they went. It wasn't long before Semplan was sitting up and taking notice—

"Hello, Semplan," Ruaric said. "Fancy meeting you out here in the middle of nowhere."

Semplan didn't groan, though he wanted to. "You're—"

"Ruaric. You remember me, don't you?"

Oh yes. Try as he might, Semplan would never forget the four days they'd spent together as prisoners of the Sashan, after a minor setback in the Nuvi valley campaign. They'd been well treated, housed quite comfortably in a dry shed with plenty of legroom, looked after rather than guarded by five Sashan troopers who'd shared their own food with them because the rations provided for the prisoners weren't up to their exacting standards of hospitality. What had made those four days into a horror that made Semplan wake up in the night sweating five years later was Ruaric. He was the most boring man in the history of the world, and he wouldn't stop talking.

For his part, Ruaric was clearly overjoyed at the opportunity to renew his acquaintance with his Cosseilhatz friend. He'd often thought, he said (several times), about the days they'd spent together, getting to know one another, cutting through all the superficial differences of race and culture and discovering that under all that they were really just the same (Semplan would never forgive him for that; not ever). It had been, Ruaric confessed, Semplan's calm, quiet stoicism and dry nomad wit that had helped him cope with the nightmare of captivity; how wonderful, therefore, that he should now have a chance to repay the debt he owed to his dear friend by saving his life.

It's not as bad as that, it's just a chill, Semplan had tried to tell him, but unfortunately his teeth were chattering too much. Luckily, at that stage in the fever, he kept passing out, which saved him a certain amount of torment. But the imperial medicines worked annoyingly well, and quite soon he was denied even that relief, while still being too weak to get up and run away.

"Sheer chance," Ruaric went on, "that we happened to be passing this way—lucky for you, of course, or you'd be dead by now, most likely. And just think. Of all the people you could've run into on this road, it turned out to be me."

Semplan grinned weakly. It was most incredibly lucky, and he was so grateful. But now the worst of it had passed, thanks to Ruaric's wonderful care, and it'd be sheer wickedness to waste any more of Ruaric's valuable time, when undoubtedly he had vital matters to attend to somewhere else—

"Not a bit of it," Ruaric replied happily. "All the time in the world, as it happens. Now if we'd met up a few days ago, it'd have been different. But we've done our job and we're on our way home, so there's absolutely no hurry, no hurry at all. I can stay with you till you're completely better."

Semplan started to say he was completely better now, but a coughing fit spoiled all that. Somehow, Ruaric interpreted the noises he made as an enquiry about what he'd been doing.

"We've been on an important diplomatic mission," he said proudly. "Real feather in my cap, and you wouldn't believe how I got it. You remember me telling you about my idiot younger brother, the one who was never going to amount to anything? Well, was I wrong. Our Bathanaric is suddenly the hero of the hour. He was officer commanding a little fort somewhere, and the enemy—" He stopped suddenly, remembering too late who the enemy had been. "Anyhow," he said, "he's safely back in the City now and everybody says he's a great hero, and just being his brother meant I got chosen to be the emperor's personal envoy to the King of Selbst. You won't have heard of them," Ruaric added with a smile, "they're savages, on the other side of this forest. I say savages, actually they're the most charming people, a bit odd in some respects but very genuine, very hospitable once you really get to know them. We got on terribly well."

"That's nice," Semplan croaked.

"It's how you talk to people that makes all the difference," Ruaric said, helping him to a sip of water. "I've always found that if you can look past the differences to the similarities, you can get on with practically anyone. And really, these Selbst aren't all that different from us; I mean, they eat and sleep, love their children, worry about the future, just like we do, even if they do live in sheds instead of stone houses. And they're not so red hot when it comes to washing, either, but you have to rise above that sort of thing, don't you?"

Semplan would cheerfully have risen above Ruaric, the better to crush his skull with a stone, but he was still too weak. "How right you are," he said. "So, I take it your mission was a success."

"Oh yes," Ruaric replied; then he hesitated, perhaps aware that the man he was talking to was nominally his enemy. "Yes, we're all the best of friends now, I'm pleased to say. It's always good to bring a bit more friendship into the world if you possibly can, especially in these difficult times, with all the misunderstandings we seem to be having at the moment. So," he added, looking away, "what brings you out here?"

"Trading expedition," Semplan said. "King Chauzida wants to see if we can trade furs and hides with the charcoal burners."

"Well, best of luck." Ruaric frowned, pursed his lips. He was nerving himself to say something difficult. "You know," he said, "it nearly broke my heart when I heard about the trouble there's been, between your people and us. I mean, it only seems like yesterday that we were brothers in arms, fighting side by side against the common enemy. And now, apparently, they're even talking about war, though I really don't see how it could possibly ever come to that." He hesitated again, then went on, "Semplan, we're old friends, we understand each other. Just how bad is it, really?"

Ruaric's four guards, who'd been listening to all of that, were looking at him with unreadable faces. "Oh, just a storm in a bottle," Semplan said. "Something and nothing, really. It's a shame it's got out of hand, but Prince Chauzida's doing everything he possibly can to sort it out. After all, he's not a fool. And he's got the best interests of his people at heart."

"Of course." Ruaric smiled. "It's like I was saying to King Raffen, only the other day. In war, nobody really wins except the crows. Which is why friendships like ours are so important, don't you think? I truly believe that as long as people like you and me can talk to each other, like we're doing now, there's no problem so bad that it can't be sorted out just by trying to understand the other man's point of view."

"Quite," Semplan said. "And this King Raffen. He's the sort of man you can talk to."

"Oh, most definitely. Odd chap, doesn't say much, but you can tell his heart's in the right place. We had a really long talk, and I think I can safely say that he understands us and we understand him. And that's what really counts, isn't it?"

Semplan was doing mental arithmetic; two days minimum to the Selbst royal hall, and they'd been stuck here, what, another two days, possibly three. It was like some horrible dream. Still, he could salvage something from the mess if only he could get the exact terms of the treaty, or agreement in principle, or whatever King Raffen had agreed to simply in order to get this impossible man to shut up. "I don't suppose you can tell me any details," he said, trying to sound sad. "I mean, if you tell me you're not allowed to, I'll quite understand. Only," he went on, as Ruaric drew breath to interrupt, "it occurs to me that if I were to tell our king that the empire's just forged an alliance with powerful new allies, it might be enough to give him the ammunition he needs to stop all this nonsense and put the war faction in their place."

Ruaric studied him for a moment, and he thought; I've overdone it, even Ruaric's not that stupid. But then Ruaric said, "You know what, that's not a bad idea. And it'll be common knowledge soon enough. I don't doubt. If you think it'd help keep the peace—"

"It can't hurt," Semplan said, wishing he could see his own face. "At times like this, I think it's up to men like you and me to take a few chances, with so much at stake. But of course, if you've got orders—"

Ruaric glanced over his shoulder, possibly the most sinister gesture Semplan had ever seen, then leant forward and whispered noisily in Semplan's ear, "I think what we've just agreed with King Raffen ought to be enough to put an end to any thoughts your people might have about starting a war with us. King Raffen has agreed to send us twenty thousand fighting men, to be despatched as soon as the agreement is formally ratified by Sechimer. We're paying through the nose for them, as it happens, but since it should mean that nobody's going to want to pick a fight with us for the foreseeable future, I honestly think it's a small price to pay for peace."

Semplan's mouth was suddenly dry. "Twenty thousand."

"To begin with," Ruaric said. "With an option on twenty thousand more, if needed. So there you are," he added happily. "The genius of general Calojan and forty thousand fearless barbarian warriors. Only a lunatic would want a war with odds like that against him."

Ten days to raise an army of twenty thousand men.

"It can be done," Sitry said, after the long silence that followed his announcement. "It'll be difficult, but we can do it."

The rest of the council stared at her. She ignored them. "You'll have to raise the levy, of course. That'll mean lighting the beacons, so there'll be panic to start with, but if we send messengers out to the villages to explain—"

Raffen shook his head. "The levy's only for when we're being invaded," he said. "And it's compulsory. I don't want anyone to join up for this unless they want to go."

"In that case," Einar said, "it's impossible. Simple as that."

Raffen smiled at him. "My grandmother used to say, there's no such word as *can't*. It always annoyed me, because it was obviously not true. But I think we can do it."

"That's all right, then," Cari said. "How, exactly?"

Raffen hadn't given it any thought at all. "Here's what we'll do," he said. Suddenly, everyone who lived or worked at the royal hall and could ride a horse was a duly accredited royal herald. Raffen and Sitry worked out the most efficient itineraries, so that the sixty or so riders could reach as many villages and large farms as possible in the shortest time, without backtracking. The plan relied on the riders being able to deputise at least two men at each port of call to carry the word to outlying settlements; but there'd be a bonus for messenger duty, so that shouldn't be a problem. "Of course," Raffen had said, "we'll only make it in time if the people we recruit can ride to the rendezvous, there isn't time for them to walk. So the first twenty thousand will have to be cavalry. It's just as well there's so many people with horses."

Which gave rise to another problem; if twenty thousand horses suddenly converged on the royal hall, what were they all going to eat? A quick inventory of the royal barns confirmed that there would be enough hay, just about; it was meant to feed the king's cattle all through the winter, but that was a difficulty that could be postponed.

"Just a thought," Eyvind said to him quietly, the day after the messengers had departed. "You promised the imperials twenty thousand infantry. They may not want that many horsemen."

"It'll be fine," Raffen said. "You'll see."

The first detachments began to arrive on the sixth day. The heralds had said; don't bring anything, clothes, weapons, stuff like that; when we get there, the emperor will give you clothes and weapons and armour fit for a king. What about boots, some of the more cautious had asked. Boots too, the heralds had been instructed to reply. Boots like you've heard of in song and story but never dreamed you'd ever be in the same house with, let alone own. By the ninth day, they were having to send men home. But don't worry, Raffen told them. As soon as the emperor sees he's getting the best fighting men in the world, there'll be jobs for everyone. Guaranteed.

("Is it true about the boots?" Einar asked him quietly, as they walked back from the meadow where the army was camped. "Or was that just—?"

By way of reply, Raffen pulled his trouser leg up five inches or so. "Bought these in the City," he said. "Off a second-hand stall in the junk market."

Einar glanced down, then up again. His eyes were practically shining, and his voice was suddenly hoarse. "Do you think you could get me a pair like that?"

"No problem." Raffen gave him an alarming grin. "Boots for everyone.")

There was just about enough food, but Raffen was relieved when the imperial delegation returned, bringing with them a huge roll of parchment. Unfurled, it was over seven feet long, nearly all covered in fine writing. Eyvind wanted to know where the emperor had got a sheep that big from. Cari said it had to be two skins joined together; Eyvind invited him to point out the seam, because he couldn't see one. They all crowded round, trying to feel a bump with their fingertips, until Raffen suggested taking it outside and holding it up to the light; whereupon a splice could just be made out.

"It's a lovely piece of work," Raffen said to the ambassadors. "What does it say?"

"Oh, just the usual terms and conditions," the chief ambassador replied. "It's the empire's standard offensive and defensive treaty. We've used it for over three hundred years, and nobody's complained so far."

Raffen peered at it. He'd picked up basic reading quite quickly while he was in the City, but the writing was very small and cramped. "Once it's signed, do we get to keep it?"

The ambassador smiled. "Sorry, no. The original will be kept in the imperial cartulary in the library of the Golden Spire temple—"

"I've been there," Raffen said. "Very impressive building. But I wouldn't keep anything valuable there if I were you."

The ambassador didn't know what to make of that, so he moved smoothly on. "You will, of course, receive a copy in due course."

"Just like this one?"

"More or less. A bit smaller, perhaps."

Raffen frowned. "I think we'd like one just like this," he said. "It'd look really good up on that wall there. Keep the draughts out, too."

The junior ambassador smiled. "We'll see what we can do."

"Splendid. All right, where do I sign?"

The junior ambassador produced a beautiful traveller's writing case from inside his coat. It was ivory, with a lid that folded down to give you a firm place to write on. There were two ink bottles, one gold and one silver, and two ivory pens with gold nibs, and a small flask of fine white sand for blotting, and a tiny file for touching up the nibs if they got blunt, and a stick of dark red wax, and the smallest oil lamp anyone had ever seen, for melting the wax. Raffen, who'd been practicing with a sharpened reed and soot shaken in rainwater, wrote RAFFEN IMP in remarkably good Classical capitals; he'd seen writing like that on wall-paintings in the imperial palace, he explained, and he'd based it on that. The ambassador congratulated him on his fine hand and knowledge of formal abbreviations, but pointed out that IMP was short for emperor; as a king, he should more properly have written RAFFEN R. Raffen offered to scrape it out with his knife and try again, but the ambassador said it was done now and not to worry. Raffen pulled a sad face when the junior ambassador started to pack away the writing case. The junior ambassador's smile froze on his face and he said, please keep it, as a gift. Sadly, the delegation couldn't stay for the feast and drinking contest; they had to get back to the City as quickly as possible. They'd send the copy of the treaty as soon as it was ready, and it was a pleasure to have done business with them all.

When they'd gone, Raffen asked if anyone knew anything about the people who lived to the north of Selbst. A man called Gulbrand, from the North Quarter, replied that he'd been to Sceaf when he was young, and it was pretty much like Selbst, except the grazing was poorer and the same went for the people. "But they're no trouble, really," Eyvind assured him. "We get a few cattle raids when times are hard up there, but we always pay them back in kind. We don't tend to bother them otherwise; they haven't got anything we want."

"And what's beyond Sceaf?" Raffen asked.

"I'm not sure," Gulbrand replied. "People do live up there, but nobody knows very much about them. There's stories, like half the year it's pitch dark, even in the daytime, and the other half the sun never sets. But that's just ridiculous."

"See if you can find out any more," Raffen said. "I'd be interested."

Later, when they were alone, Sitry asked him, "Why were you asking about Sceaf all of a sudden?"

"Was I? Oh yes." He was taking off his boots. After he'd eased them over his heels, he stood them up in the corner of the room, like a tiny parade of soldiers. "Just curious, that's all."

She picked up her comb. He always watched her comb her hair, just as he'd watched her sister. "I think it's because the sight of all those soldiers is making you think dangerous thoughts."

"Dangerous?"

She nodded. "I think living in the City, you may have caught imperial fever."

"Let me guess." He grinned. She saw him, in her mirror. "Symptoms are a burning desire to invade other countries."

"Something like that."

"You may be right, but I hope not. You can die of things like that. Maybe I'm more concerned about other people invading us."

"Mphm." She had to tug a little to pull through a tangle. "Well, it could be argued that sending all your soldiers to a foreign country might be seen as a temptation. But I don't think the Sceaf are like that."

"Aren't they?"

"Too busy fighting each other, from what I've heard. Which isn't much," she added. She pulled against another tangle, then clicked her tongue. "Damn," she said. "That's another tooth broken. Do you think I could have a new comb? This one's pretty much had it."

He didn't reply, and she remembered that the comb was one of a pair; their father had bought them when she and her sister were girls. "Sure," he said, turning his head away slightly. "You don't need to ask, you're the queen. Where do you get combs from?"

"Oh, there's a pedlar who comes round. Actually, I don't think I'll bother. This one'll do just fine."

"Suit yourself."

Something was wrong, she could feel it. She didn't think it was her fault, but she could probably make it worse if she said the wrong thing. Probably best to change the subject. "Do you think all the high-class imperials are as bad as that? The ambassador was so far up himself he was practically coming out of his own ear."

He smiled. "The ones I met varied," he said. "Some were like that, others were fairly straightforward. Of course, the circumstances were different."

"They're just not like us, though. You can't really imagine them *doing* anything. They're like the clothes you keep for best."

"They can do things when they want to, believe me."

He didn't often speak with such feeling. It was like being caught up in brambles; the more she tried to get free, the more she got snagged and caught up. Oh well, she thought. When all else fails, say what you're really thinking. "What's the matter? What's bothering you?"

"I haven't forgotten them, you know. I act like nothing happened, but—" He shook his head, as though the thoughts were flies. "I look at you, but I see her. I'm sorry. It's not like I do it on purpose."

"I know," she heard herself say. "It's all right. For what it's worth, I think you're a very wise man."

"Do you?" He sounded surprised, almost disappointed. "Sometimes I think I must still be in the forest, eating tree fungus. It's like that's the last thing I can remember, and everything after that feels like a dream.

You know; you believe it's real, but deep down you know it isn't." He was very still, making himself stay still, like you do when you're trying to catch the bull when it's spooked and burst out of the pen; you look it straight in the eye and you don't move, and gradually it calms down, but the slightest twitch will send it shying and frisking away, wilder and madder than ever. "I really do need to get a grip," he said. "Dwelling on the past isn't going to solve anything."

She couldn't bring herself to respond to that. Instead, she said, "When the army leaves, will you be going with them?"

He took so long to reply that she wondered if he'd heard her. "Yes," he said eventually. "I suppose I ought to. What do you think?"

"I think it's not up to me."

"You don't think I should go."

"That's not what I said."

"Fine. I'll go." He appeared to relax, as though he'd just achieved something substantial. "Shouldn't be away for long," he said, "it's not like I'll be leading them into battle or anything. I'll just lead them to where they need to be and leave them to it."

"That's fine," she said. She'd finished combing her hair; he'd been preoccupied, and missed it. "Are you coming to bed?"

"Not yet."

"Mind if I blow out the candle?"

"Go ahead."

The last she saw of him, before she blew, was a man sitting forward, elbows on knees, hands gripping wrists; he was staring at an empty space in the middle of the floor, as if he could see something there, and his eyes didn't blink. For some reason, she got the idea that he could see as well in the dark as the light, the way some animals do. When she woke up next morning, his side of the bed had been slept in, but he'd gone.

Calojan to Aimeric de Peguilhan.

I need forty thousand half-armours, munitions grade. Any old rubbish will do. Delivery in nine days, earlier would be nice. Confirm acceptance by return of this messenger.

He read it three times before he was forced to concede that it said what he'd thought it said. Forty thousand. *Forty thousand.*

The messenger was waiting, looking at him. He cleared his throat noisily. "That's fine," he said. "Tell him it won't be a problem."

Forty thousand half-armours. The key was, to keep calm. Making all that stuff in nine days was out of the questions, so he was going to have to think where forty thousand helmets and forty thousand cuirasses might be lying hidden, forgotten, unwanted, their owner just waiting for someone to come along and make him an offer. It didn't seem likely, somehow.

At that moment, she walked in, carrying a tray of tiny pots. "Are you still here?" she said. "I thought you were going out."

He turned and looked at her. "Any idea where I might buy forty thousand suits of armour?"

"New or second hand?"

"I'm not bothered. Look—"

She put the tray down and moved a stray curl off her forehead. "If you don't mind used stuff, you could always try the Ceuta brothers."

That didn't make any sense. "They're scrap metal dealers. I want—"

"Scrap metal." She smiled at him. "Seventy per cent of enemy equipment salvaged off the battlefield ends up as scrap. About half of that is fixable, but usually it's not worth the cost of fixing, bearing in mind that the market for bulk used arms and armour is pretty circumscribed, while everybody wants scrap. If you want a lot of gear in a hurry—I take it you're in a hurry."

"Oh yes."

She smiled. "Then the Ceuta boys are your best bet. You'll have to be a bit careful how you go about it. Trading in used arms legally will be a new and strange experience for them."

How did she know all these things? He decided he was never, ever going to ask. "Thanks," he said. "You just saved my life. And probably the empire."

"Another day, another miracle. You know where their yard is?"

"Yes. No," he amended. She gave him directions; then, knowing him too well, she drew him a little map.

THE CEUTA BROTHERS had three sheds, each about a hundred yards long, on the east bank of the river, just up from Westponds. When the Festival committee made the arena for the sea-battle, they'd dug a special drain to make sure the Ceuta sheds weren't flooded out. Since then, the brothers had acquired a patch of the reclaimed land and were building two more sheds, about half as long again. Aimeric's father had bought scrap plate armour from them—breastplates and backplates, mostly, pieces big enough to cut up into the small plates they used for scale and lamellar. There were four brothers, but nobody could remember ever having seen the eldest. It took quite a long time for Aimeric to persuade them that he was serious; once he'd made the breakthrough, however, they were wildly enthusiastic. Sure, they told him, we've got loads of good stuff, just right for you, new stock, just in; a quick scrub down and a few taps with a hammer, good as new.

They weren't exaggerating. They took Aimeric to the nearest of the three sheds. This is the Grade A, they told him; the other sheds are B and C, but it's all good stuff. It took Aimeric a while for his eyes to adjust to the gloom; then he realised what he was looking at.

While he was at the University, he'd strayed into a geography lecture. It wasn't on his timetable, but in the Republic they let girls attend some of the courses—they couldn't take a degree, naturally, but they could turn up and listen, so long as they didn't make nuisances of themselves. Geography was one of the specified courses; the others were mostly medical, and Aimeric didn't fancy watching a dead body being cut up. In the event he did indeed get a girl out of it, though she wasn't up to much and anyway, he couldn't seem to concentrate. Instead, his mind kept going back to something the lecturer had said. The great chalk cliffs at Phianassa, he'd asserted, weren't stone at all. Rather, they were the compressed remains of the shells and bones of millions and millions of little fish, who'd died some absurdly long time ago and drifted to the sea bed; their flesh had long since rotted away, but their bones survived, and the sheer weight of all that water—it weighs ten pounds a gallon—had slowly compacted the bones, like cheese in a press, until it could be mistaken for rock. Then something drastic had happened, an earthquake or a volcano, and the sea had been thrown back and the sea-bed had been pushed up clear of the water, and that's what the White Cliffs really were; enough tiny dead things to make a mountain.

It was, of course, absurd. Nobody believed it, except as a rather lame analogy (and he much preferred the one about dwarfs on the shoulders of giants, which was far more elegant and amounted to the same thing) but for some reason the image had stayed with him, maybe because when he was a boy he'd been taken to see the great ossiary on the Isle of the Dead, where the monks of the Studium dumped the bones of their long-dead predecessors, when the graveyard got too full. The ossiary was a great hill of bones, with peaks higher than a tall tree—they had cranes to winch the sacks of bones ashore, because the hills were too high to be safely climbed—and just suppose all that lot got crushed down into powder, the way they made mortar out of limestone, and stamped flat by some unimaginable weight. Just imagine.

The shed was a bit like that. He thought of the lecturer and his mussels and oysters—the flesh dissipates, the shell stays behind—because the shed was packed solid with the shells of dead men, their helmets, breastplates, greaves, cuisses, tassets, pauldrons, cops and sabatons, the flesh has faded away but the shape is preserved in an iron shell, and every one of them had died a violent death; each shell fragment preserved that moment of violence and defeat with perfect, vivid clarity. He stooped and picked up a helmet, and saw where the steel had been torn apart by a cut. The lips of the tear were open, like a mouth screaming; like the splash when a stone hits the water, and the surface is ripped open, flows upwards and outwards from the violent displacement; the fluid movement of the splash frozen in steel, as if the life bursting out through the wound had chilled it to ice. He thought of the insects he'd seen in knobs of amber, permanently trapped in the torment of the moment of death; here, the fly had rotted away, but the incuse of its body was remembered in the savage failure of steel, the exposed crystalline grain and the sharp, twisted edges. And Calojan, it occurred to him, had done all this; one solitary man who'd built a chalk mountain.

"That's nothing," said the youngest Ceuta, standing next to him. "Few taps with a hammer, maybe braze on a patch, it'll be fine. Just what you're looking for."

Aimeric threw the helmet back onto the heap. "How long has all this been here?"

"Oh, it's all new stock," another Ceuta said. "Pile it high, sell it quick, that's our motto. All good Sashan iron, they don't make any rubbish. And the stuff that's past repair, you can cut it up for patches for the better pieces. No waste, see."

"What you want," the third brother said, "is stuff off men who got killed by the Cosseilhatz. Arrow-wounds, see. Neat round holes. Close up the burrs from the inside with a two-pound ball pein, you don't even need a patch. Just right if you're in a hurry."

"Good for business, the Cosseilhatz," observed the youngest brother. "This new lot the general's got, they make a real old mess with their axes and all. We still get charged the same price, mind. But you can have your pick of the better stuff. No extra charge."

They discussed money, then shook on it. Aimeric said he'd send his workers over straight away, and left. He was glad to get out of the sheds. He walked home along the river, which was higher than usual. As part of the Westponds development they were reinforcing the embankments, to reduce the risk of flooding—a certain irony there, he thought, but logical. It wouldn't do for the river to get loose, now that it knew what it could achieve once it got over the embankment walls. What if the whole City were to flood, and all the people drown, and their bones were to sink to the bottom and squash down; what sort of stone would they make, and would it be suitable for building with?

"Well?" she asked him. "Any good?"

"Like all your suggestions, it was brilliant," he said. "Problem solved."

He spent the rest of the day hiring; casuals to sift the heaps, find the least damaged pieces, make the minimum repairs; carters and their carts, to shift it all; porters to load and unload. He went to the sheds early next morning to find they were already hard at work. Five carts passed him as he walked along the embankment, heaped up with the empty shapes of men—like other carts he'd seen once, when the plague broke out in the Vesani Republic, other shells, other scrap. For the first time it occurred to him that he might just possibly pull off this miracle and be in a position to give Calojan what he'd asked for. After an hour at the sheds, Hosculd politely told him to go away and stop getting under people's feet. He hitched a ride on one of his carts as far as Whitegates, then went to a concert at the Academy.

"ONE QUESTION," CALOJAN asked him. They were unloading at the barracks. Calojan had called out the entire City garrison to help. "Why do you think it's a good idea for my men to go into battle disguised as the Sashan?"

Aimeric shrugged. "Forty thousand half-armours, two days early, cheap," he said. "You didn't specify a particular pattern."

"You're selling me back my own plunder."

Aimeric shook his head. "You sold it to the scrap dealers," he said. "I bought it back and fixed it up. I know it sounds ridiculously simple, but you didn't think of it. I did."

"Oh, I'm not complaining." Calojan yawned. He looked like he hadn't slept for days. "For what it's worth, Sashan gear is top quality. It was what they put inside it that caused the problems. No, it'll keep the Selbst happy, and that's all I care about."

"The who?"

"That's what they're called," Calojan explained. "The northerners. You know, you hired a whole bunch of them to make my arrows."

"Oh, them." Aimeric tried not to sound shocked. "They're your new army."

"That's right. Which is why I'm not too concerned about the garbage you're selling me. They're great tinkerers, the Selbst, they love tarting things up and making them nice. You should see what a job they've done on the last load of rubbish I had off you. I bet you, in a couple of days they'll have this lot properly repaired and buffed up like mirrors." He yawned again, and rubbed his eyes with his fists. "I've been hearing things about you, Aimeric. Apparently, when you were at the University, you were an ardent pacifist. War is the greatest of all evils, and all that. There was this big student debate, and you—"

"Yes," Aimeric said.

"Ah. So, what happened?"

"Suddenly the money ran out."

"That's all?"

Aimeric scowled at him. "It was the end of the world," he said. "I guess I found the one cause I believed was worth fighting for."

Calojan laughed. "I envy you," he said. "I've been a soldier most of my life, but I never did see anything that could justify the things I do. I keep telling myself, once this war's over I'll retire to a monastery, spend the rest of my life painting icons. Trouble is, the war is never over. I don't suppose it ever will be, not in my lifetime."

Aimeric suddenly wanted, more than anything, to be somewhere else. "A wise man once said, when you're tired of killing, you're tired of life. Will you be wanting any more of this stuff? Only, if not, I can lay off my casual workers. Since you're paying them, I thought I'd ask."

"I wouldn't do that just yet," Calojan said.

CHAUZIDA INSISTED ON being there when the Aram Cosseilhatz crossed the Essa. Joiauz had tried to dissuade him; it might be dangerous, if the imperials tried to dispute the crossing, which was just the sort of thing Calojan might try. Chauzida listened respectfully while he made his speech, then just said, "Please?"

Joiauz had decided on the ford at Bohec Essa; the imperials would be watching it, but the country was wide and flat on both sides of the river, so they'd see an imperial force coming with time to react. The idea was to cross at dawn, but there were problems. Rain just before midnight turned a usually solid stretch of moorland into glue; forty carts got stuck before anyone realised what was happening, whereupon the rest of the column swung out to avoid them and stumbled into an equally sticky patch a hundred yards further over. All the shouting and confusion in the pitch dark spooked the Two Ravens' sheep, which bolted and ended up in the Naida, a narrow but fast-running tributary of the Essa. By the time Joiauz had sorted it all out, the sun was up, and it was a beautiful autumn day; no mist, even close to the river. You could see for miles.

Joiauz dealt with that by driving the flocks ahead of the army, to give the imperial scouts the impression that they'd come to graze the riverbank rather than invade. Sure enough, the scouts came down off the skyline and up to the river, to watch the show, whereupon Joiauz sent a hundred of his best riders across, about eight hundred yards below the ford, with instructions to loop in behind the scouts and cut them off. It nearly worked, but not quite; at the last minute, the scouts got through the skirmish line and away. By the time the column was across the ford, it was a safe bet that the imperial cavalry would arrive. The important thing, therefore, was to get enough men across the ford before then, so as to have overwhelming force on the empire side of the river. The Cosseilhatz, however, were rather more concerned with their sheep than tactical subtleties. Since Joiauz had insisted on bringing the flocks to the front, they had to be kept in order and conducted across the ford, which needed the skill and horsemanship of grown men rather than boys and women. Until they were sure the sheep were all right, the war was just going to have to wait.

A full division of imperial cavalry turned up around mid-morning, while the drove across the ford was still in full swing. When he saw them, Joiauz swam his horse across the river and organised such men as he had on the empire side into a coherent but inadequate screen. That, however, seemed to do the trick. Later he reckoned that the imperials must have decided that the drove was some sort of cunning stratagem, designed to lure them into a trap—too long in the company of general Calojan for their own good. In any event, the imperials formed up into six attack wedges, but stayed where they were. Six men and a white flag trotted nervously over, and stopped well outside maximum range. A young man in shining armour raised his voice and asked to speak to whoever was in charge.

Having nothing else to do at this point, Joiauz rode fifty yards in his direction and said, That'll be me. The shining one asked him if he was aware that his sheep were trespassing on the territory of the empire.

"No, you're wrong there," Joiauz replied. "The border's the Essa, isn't it?"

The shining one said, "This is the Essa."

"I don't think so," Joiauz replied. "This is the Naida. The Essa's five miles back the way you came from."

The imperial heralds went all thoughtful. They had, after all, crossed a river about five miles back (the Traimon, if Joiauz remembered his geography correctly). "Are you sure?" they asked.

"'Course I'm sure. This is our land, so if anyone's trespassing, it's you. Not that I want to press the point, if it's an honest mistake, but if I were you I'd leave, before something stupid happens and we start a war. All right?"

They were fumbling with a map, which the shining one contrived to tear and then drop. "This is the Essa," he called out. "The river back there was the Traimon."

"You're not from around here, are you?"

Out of the corner of his eye, Joiauz could see a large body of his own horsemen coming towards him. The shining one had dismounted and was looking down at the map, then up at the skyline. "No, listen," he said. "That lot directly behind you has got to be the White Mountains, which means this plain here is the Parapros—" he pronounced it wrong—"and this ford must be Bohec Essa. The Naida is seven miles or so over that way."

The reinforcements had closed in behind his skirmish line. He did some quick mental arithmetic. "Oh, right," he replied. "In that case—" He raised his right arm, then brought it down in a slicing gesture towards the heralds. "Charge!"

Deep down, he probably believed the imperials would run. They didn't. The heralds made it back to their line, which surged forward like floodwater. For obvious reasons, Joiauz had never faced a charge by imperial lancers before; Sashan lancers, scores of times, but the imperial heavy cavalry were in a different league. Just for a moment, his heart stopped and his hands and feet turned cold. Then he remembered, and nudged his horse into a canter, guiding it straight at the oncoming wave.

They know us, he thought, *they know what's going to happen.* But, when he gave the sign and the front of his formation broke like a green stick and peeled left, loosing their first volley at the apex of the wedge, it all started to work just as he'd planned it. The imperial wedge foundered as its point dissolved into a tangled thicket of fallen horses; the base swerved to avoid the mess and was met with the second and third volleys; then the Cosseilhatz swept up on either side, enfilading at will, melting the wedge like flames licking ice. The lancers pressed on, though there was nothing left to charge. The Cosseilhatz slid in behind them, shooting fast and close, always aiming at the horses. What was left of the wedge crumbled, and the Cosseilhatz buzzed them, flies swarming round something already dead, until the cloud thinned and dispersed, to reveal fallen, thrashing horses, men scrambling to their feet in full armour, dead horses, dead men. For once Joiauz hung back, unable to make himself participate in the slaughter. The lancers were trying to scramble out of the way, but the Cosseilhatz were too quick for them; besides, they now outnumbered them three to one. It was open ground, there was nowhere to escape to, and no need to close to within the reach of a spear or a sword. Joiauz realised he had no way of calling his men off; they weren't looking at him, only at the next target. Five minutes later there were no more wedges, no more lancers, just a smear of shapes on the ground and the swarm reforming, nothing left to fly at; job done.

"Piece of cake," Luzir panted at him, reining in beside him.

Joiauz was too angry to speak. He nodded and spurred into a gallop, leaving Luzir staring after him. The Cosseilhatz were doing their usual leisurely sweep, shooting the dismounted lancers on the ground, target practice. There was no point trying to stop them. Nobody needed him for anything, so he turned and headed back to the ford.

Chauzida was riding toward him on a small black mare. Instinctively he headed him away from the battlefield, though there wasn't much point; it was obvious from the look on Chauzida's face that he'd seen everything Joiauz would have preferred him not to see. Stupid instinct, in any case. A prince of the Cosseilhatz who couldn't handle such sights would be like a fish who couldn't swim. Even so, he said, "You shouldn't be here. I told you."

"I've changed my mind," Chauzida said.

"What do you mean?"

"I've changed my mind," Chauzida repeated. "We aren't going to war. This—" He lifted a hand off the reins to wave at the battlefield, then quickly replaced it, like someone holding on to a rope. "Whatever the plan was, it's not worth it. Sorry."

To his great surprise, all Joiauz wanted to do was laugh. "I think it's a bit late for that," he said. "In case you weren't paying attention—"

"No war," Chauzida said firmly. "Do whatever you have to, to get us out of it. I've made up my mind. Finally."

"Don't be so bloody stupid." All the anger seemed to come at once. He was amazed at how much of it there was. "You don't give me orders, you're just a stupid child. You can't begin to understand. You've just proved that. God knows I've tried to teach you, train you, so that one day you'll be fit to be trusted with doing the job you were born to, but you simply won't listen, you've always got to know best. Well, let me make it perfectly clear. You don't know best. You don't know *anything*. You're just a child."

He drew breath, waiting for Chauzida to speak, but he knew there could be no reply. "Go back to the camp," he said. "Wait in the tent. I'll be back as soon as I've seen to things here, and then I'll—" He'd what? Explain? "We'll talk about this properly. Look, I'm sorry I shouted, there was no call for that. Go on, I'll be there directly."

Chauzida turned his horse and rode away; slowly to begin with, then suddenly bursting into a furious gallop. Joiauz watched him for a long time. He thought; I'm not his father, if I'd wanted a son, I'd have got married. And some things have to be done.

That evening, Semplan returned from his mission to the north. He was deeply apologetic for having taken so long; he'd been taken ill, so he hadn't actually reached the court of king Raffen, but he had news that would change everything. Calojan had got there first, and the Selbst had sent him twenty thousand men. Accordingly, this would not be a good time to provoke a war.

When Joiauz told him about the battle, he went quite pale.

WHEN THE PROTOCOL department of the High Chamberlain's office heard that King Raffen would be arriving with the Selbst army, their first reaction was stunned disbelief, followed by manic activity, accompanied by bitter reproaches. A king was due in the City in just over twenty-four hours; they'd had no notice, nobody had seen fit to tell them anything, the intelligence file on the king and his people was woefully inadequate. How they were supposed to do their job under such conditions was completely beyond them. Where, for example, was His Majesty supposed to sleep? Was this an official State occasion, in which case he would have to be quartered in the palace, or semi-official, in which case he and his suite should be given the use of a suitable government property for the duration of his stay—a minor palace, Temple manse or imperial hunting lodge, except that there weren't any available, unless His Majesty wouldn't mind a leaky roof and floors covered in pigeon droppings. If, however, it was an official military occasion, the proper thing would be to pitch him a pavilion on either the Artillery Fields or the Golden Spire green—easier said than done, because the pavilion was folded up in a warehouse somewhere and would undoubtedly reek of mould until it had been aired for a fortnight.

"He's a barbarian," Queen Gesel observed. She'd taken to sitting in on her husband's less important audiences, and nobody had found the courage to object. "His people live in wooden huts, don't they? I'm sure you can find him a hut. Or a shed."

The Chamberlain tried to explain; it wasn't a question of what the royal visitor was used to, or even of what he'd feel comfortable in. Such a visit required a display of imperial prestige proportionate to the status of the visitor's nation, which meant juggling the respect due to a valued ally with the proper show of superiority, as demonstrated by opulent and magnificent accommodations and furnishings. Putting a king in a shed, even a huge shed decked with the finest tapestries, would amount to an act of war.

"So he can sleep in a tent but not a shed," Gesel observed. "Oh well, I expect you know what you're doing. You'd better carry on and see to it."

The Chamberlain looked helplessly at Sechimer, but all he got was a bleak, mirror-like stare. "I know," Gesel said, "why don't you put him in the Orangery? That's sort of outdoors and reasonably spacious. You can borrow some chairs and tables and things from the palace, he'll be perfectly comfortable."

The Chamberlain opened his mouth but didn't speak; it was, in fact, an inspired suggestion. Florian IV's vast and monstrously vulgar folly was indeed timber-built, but inside it was decorated with a degree of gaudy splendour that couldn't fail to inspire the deepest awe in a barbarian heart, while its location in the centre of the palace grounds made it a perfect compromise between a State and a military occasion. If it was a spur-of-the-moment idea, it implied that Her Majesty had a genius for protocol. The Chamberlain preferred to believe that she'd thought of it much earlier, possibly in consultation with treacherous officials, and her earlier comments were designed to be annoying, in which she'd succeeded.

Eighteen hours of furious work on the Orangery were, in the event, completely wasted. King Raffen preferred to stay with his men in their camp outside the City walls. This scandalised the Chamberlain's people, but there was nothing they could do about it. The king, in fact, seemed to know his way about the place; it had improved a lot, he said, since the last time he was there—decent latrines, a well, proper wooden houses. Remarkable, he said, what a difference a war made.

"I won't be going with you this time," Sechimer told Calojan, on the way to the Selbst camp.

"Oh." Calojan frowned, just for a moment. "Well, I can't say I blame you."

"It's my wife." Sechimer put his hand between the collar of his breastplate and his neck; he wasn't wearing the usual scarf, and the rolled edge was chafing. "She didn't make a fuss or anything like that, but—"

"You don't need to justify yourself to me," Calojan said. "Anyway, we have no idea what's going to happen. If you're not there, it's one less thing for me to have to worry about."

King Raffen met them at the camp gates. He wasn't quite what Sechimer had been expecting. He was a big man, tall and broad-shouldered, with long black hair halfway down his back in a ponytail and a short black-and-grey beard. He was wearing a City worker's blue coarse wool jacket over a gilded mailshirt. He gave them a tired but cheerful grin, which told them he was far too busy for social calls but far too polite to tell them to go away.

"We weren't expecting you," Calojan said.

"Really?" Raffen raised an eyebrow. "It's how we do things. An army this big, naturally the king goes with it. Isn't that how you do it?"

Calojan carefully didn't look at Sechimer. "Sometimes," he said, "not always. Will you be commanding your men, or—?"

"Well, naturally. I may not be much use but I'm definitely not ornamental. It's what's expected of me."

"Excuse me for asking," Sechimer said quietly, "but do you have any military experience?"

Raffen raised both eyebrows, then laughed. "Oh yes," he said. "It goes with the big house and the gold hat. I've been fighting wars of one kind or another since I was thirteen years old. It's all right," he added, "I know your man here is the greatest military genius of all time, so I'd be a bloody fool not to do exactly what he tells me. But my people are used to taking their orders from me, so it'll make it easier if I lead them. If that's all right with you, of course. After all, you're paying."

"That's fine," Calojan said. "It's how I used to work with the Cosseilhatz, and we never had any problems."

"Out of interest," Sechimer said, "who have you mostly fought against? I'm afraid I don't know very much about your part of the world."

"Well, let me see," Raffen said. "Apart from the usual family bickering—you'd probably call it civil war, but basically it's a way of life back home—we've had a few spats with the Sceaf, to the north, and a bunch of really unpleasant people called the Cure Hardy, who turned up in ships about ten years ago and took quite a bit of getting rid of. Of course, I was just a chieftain back then, commanding a thousand or so. But I know what it's like at the sharp end, trust me. And I know how to take orders, which is what really matters, isn't it?"

On the way back, Calojan said to Sechimer, "That man missed his calling."

"Excuse me?"

"He's wasted as a king. He should be on the stage. I don't think I've seen a better actor since Carausio played Florian in *The Ascent*."

Sechimer frowned. "You think he's an impostor."

"No, he's their king all right. You could tell, from how their people looked at him. But he was definitely putting on a performance. Very good one, too. I'd guess he's one of those actors who really thinks himself into a part. The best way, if you ask me."

"He seemed perfectly sincere to me," Sechimer said. "Listen, if you think there's something wrong—"

"It's not that." Calojan rubbed his eyes, as though he'd got grit in them. "It's just that I've got used to being able to read people, and this one—" Suddenly he laughed. "This one's in a foreign language. But his people fight like lunatics and they're all we've got, so it doesn't really matter, does it?"

"If you want, I'll come with you," Sechimer said. "I promise I'll do as I'm told and not get in any trouble."

"No. You stay here. Please."

That evening, the imperial orchestra staged Maestulf's *Masque of the Sun*. The performance was in honour of the Selbst, who were unable to attend. Queen Gesel thoroughly enjoyed the show; afterwards, she happened to meet her brother, Aimeric de Peguilhan, at the reception. At first they both seemed rather awkward, but after a while the coolness seemed to thaw, particularly once Aimeric's companion had gone home, and they talked for over an hour in the palace arboretum, until it was time for the evening service in the chapel.

"You don't have to come," Gesel said. "I know you think it's all nonsense."

"I'd like to," Aimeric said.

"Why?"

"I've never heard the palace choir. I believe they're very good."

She gave him a despairing look. "Go home," she said, "or wherever it is you go, you don't have to pretend with me. It's all right, really."

Aimeric looked so sad that she smiled. "It wasn't me," he said. "Really."

"I understand that now," Gesel said. "In fact, your innocence has been proved beyond a shadow of a doubt. Sechimer's had the finest scholars in the empire working on the manuscript, and they all swear blind it's genuine. So, the prophesy's genuine too, and therefore it can't have been a devious plot to get Sechimer to marry me and install you as the imperial brother-in-law. You're in the clear. I haven't forgiven you, because there's nothing to forgive."

Aimeric didn't say anything, which was probably just as well.

"Also," Gesel went on, "it'd be monstrously unfair of me to be angry with you, even if you had arranged it all, bearing in mind that I'm happier now than I've ever been. The simple fact is, Sechimer and I love each other very much. I really can't imagine what he sees in me, but there it is. There comes a point when you've just got to stop fighting and let happiness win. Heaven knows, nobody could've fought harder over the years than I have, but I think even Calojan would have to admit defeat, in my shoes. You do see that, don't you?"

Aimeric nodded. "I'm so pleased," he said. "It wasn't just for me, you know. Not any of it."

She laughed. "Actually," she said, "your Orsella's not nearly as bad as I thought she'd be. She's very clever, and I've never met a woman who's so well-informed."

"She's certainly that."

"I had someone talk to her about religion," Gesel said. "Apparently, she genuinely understands the arguments in the Revelationist heresy, which is more than the Abbot of the Studium does. You should bring her to the palace some day, she can explain it to him."

Aimeric's eyes became very wide and round, but he said, "All right, if you're serious."

"I'm always serious, Aimeric. You know me."

She went to the service; Aimeric went to the *Supervening Necessity* in Longwall Street and won seventy-three solidi betting on a cock-fight, his first win since he'd left the University. All in all, he couldn't help thinking, things were looking up.

CALOJAN HAD ISSUED general orders to the commanders of all units; avoid battle wherever possible, evacuate and withdraw rather than engage the enemy. The imperial messenger network, though nothing like as efficient as it had once been, was still the fastest and most reliable system of communications in the world. The orders reached all of the main field armies except for the Seventeenth Mobile Reserve, a defence-in-depth unit comprising two battalions of lancers and one battalion of auxiliary mounted archers. Hearing that the enemy were about to move down into the Sorus valley, thereby directly threatening two large and unfortified towns, the commander of the Seventeenth advanced against the Cosseilhatz.

They weren't hard to find. Colonel Mastheric had fought in seventeen engagements in the Sashan war, nine of them as battalion commander. He'd seen the Cosseilhatz at close quarters, and made a detailed study of all general Calojan's campaigns. He had excellent scouts and a full set of the latest military maps. When his intelligence officer reported that the enemy were heading up the main cart road to Lanthano, he decided that the opportunity was too good to miss. Five miles from Lanthano, according to his maps and local information, the road passed through some notorious marshes. The causeway that carried the road was no more than thirty yards wide. If he could block the road in front of and behind the advancing enemy and bottle them up on the causeway, their speed and manoeuvrability would be useless and they would present a stationary target for his archers and his substantial detachment of field artillery.

He needed to move quickly. He sent half a battalion of lancers to skirt the edge of the marshes and come out behind the Cosseilhatz, to close the far end of the causeway. They did everything he asked of them, riding through the night to avoid detection and using the early morning mist to cover themselves as they made their final deployment. Mastheric gave them until mid-morning, when the mists began to clear, then advanced with the rest of the lancers to occupy the near end of the causeway. He held back his horse archers as a reserve, keeping them out on the right flank in case they were needed to hurry to the relief of the units at the far end.

The Cosseilhatz commander brought up his main force to charge Mastheric's lancers, only to be beaten back in confusion by volleys of rocks and scorpion-bolts from the imperial artillery, positioned in rear of the lancers and shooting over their heads. The Cosseilhatz wheeled, passed swiftly through their wagon train and launched a ferocious attack on the lancers at the far end. Anticipating the usual Cosseilhatz arrow-storm, the lancers dismounted and formed a five-rank shield-wall; the first rank kneeling, the second standing, the third holding their shields over the second rank's heads. So powerful were the Cosseilhatz bows that even this formation suffered casualties, but not enough to weaken it sufficiently to permit the Cosseilhatz to attack; as soon as a man in the front three ranks fell, another stepped forward from the fourth rank to take his place. Thanks to his insights into the Cosseilhatz' method of operations, Mastheric knew that they only carried enough arrows for half an hour's continuous barrage. He'd gambled that if the shield-wall could hold for roughly that length of time, the Cosseilhatz would stop shooting and try a charge with swords and lances. He was proved right; the Cosseilhatz charged, and the shield-wall braced itself to withstand them. As soon as the onslaught began, Mastheric despatched his horse archers to the far side, while moving his field artillery in closer so that they could resume their bombardment of the enemy wagons, a move which he hoped would prompt their commander to withdraw forces from the fighting at the far end.

Everything was going to plan—the dismounted lancers were holding out against considerably superior numbers and the reinforcements were making good time around the marshes—when a substantial unidentified force was observed heading across the plains, apparently directly at the horse archers. Mastheric quickly reconsidered his position. It was possible that the new arrivals were a Cosseilhatz rearguard or flying column; it made sense that they should have separated a substantial part of their forces before advancing into such a potentially dangerous position as the causeway, to deal with just such a situation as they now faced. If this was indeed the case, both the horse archers and the lancers would be exposed to attacks in flank and rear; without the horse archers, he knew he would have little chance of surviving an encounter with the enemy in the open. Relectantly, therefore, he sent word to the far end to disengage in good order and allow the Cosseilhatz to pass through, while taking up the best defensive position they could achieve in the circumstances.

It was embarrassing, to say the least, when the unidentified unit turned out to be imperial light cavalry—six squadrons of Permian auxiliaries, sent by sheer coincidence as a routine troop rotation, word of whose arrival had somehow failed to reach him before the battle. Nevertheless, the engagement could be regarded as a genuine victory; once the far end of the causeway was unblocked, the Cosseilhatz withdrew the way they'd come without making any attempt to engage or harass the imperial forces, Mastheric was left in possession of the field, Lanthano was saved (Mastheric immediately ordered its evacuation, and the civilian population eventually found shelter inside the walls of Beal Blemye) and the enemy suffered casualties in excess of four hundred men and a substantial, though not quantified, number of civilians.

At this point, Calojan's orders not to engage the enemy reached him, and Mastheric felt they left him with no alternative but to withdraw. This he did, evacuating the remaining towns and avoiding any further contact with the Cosseilhatz, until he reached Beal and added his forces to the garrison. Although his victory at Lanthano ultimately achieved nothing in purely strategic terms, it had a significant effect on imperial morale; the Cosseilhatz were, after all, mortal and fallible, and could be defeated by an intelligent commander in the right place at the right time.

"It was a disaster," Joiauz shouted. "It was a complete disaster, and it's all my fault, and don't any of you dare say otherwise."

There was a long silence. Then Luzir said, "You weren't to know."

"We should have known," Joiauz replied bitterly. "We should have found out. *I* should have—"

SAVAGES

"Anyway," Autet said sharply, "it's over, we got away relatively lightly, and we've learned a lesson. Now I suggest we stop beating ourselves up about it, and make the arrangements for the appeasement service."

After a defeat, the first priority was to apologise to the dead. There was a ceremony—there was always a ceremony, for every occasion and contingency. Nothing was ever the first time, or the last.

Although he'd taken no part in the action, it was Chauzida's job to make the apology. For the occasion he was dressed in the appropriate regalia; the iron crown, a wolfskin, a necklace made of the finger-bones of dead enemies. In his hand he had to carry the royal bow of the Cosseilhatz, which was now so old that nobody dared string it. Nearly all the dead had been abandoned in the retreat, but the few bodies they'd been able to recover were laid out on trestles. Properly speaking they should have been covered in meadow flowers, but because of the time of year—nothing was in flower apart from silkweed and purple hyssop—they had to make do with a few symbolic blooms arranged to cover their wounds. Chauzida rode up to the rows of trestles, dismounted about ten yards away and shuffled the rest of the way on his knees. He repeated, "I'm sorry," three times. That was it.

With that out of the way, the Cosseilhatz were free to start coping with the damage. The worst of it had come from the stone balls thrown by the artillery. They'd broken the backs of at least fifty wagons, mostly Blue Flower, smashed the strakes of three dozen more, stoved in the bows and tongues, killed or crippled the oxen. The men worked on them in a sort of dull silence, while the women sobbed; the children stood about, unable to play, knowing something was wrong but not what it was. Chauzida saw a little boy screaming and thrashing as his mother tried to drag him back to the wagon; he was clearly terrified of it, so presumably he'd been on board when a stone hit it. He saw a girl, about nine, sitting on the tailboard. She was very pretty, with long, straight hair and a perfect oval face, but when he walked a step further, he saw that her right arm was missing except for a red-bandaged stump. He saw an old woman lying on her back on the grass, her eyes closed, her mouth moving without making words. A man was sitting patiently on a wheel while his ten-year old son tried to pull a foot-long splinter of wood out of his back. There was no provision in the ceremony for Chauzida to apologise to them, so he said the words under his breath.

He expected to see Joiauz leading the repairs, but there was no sign of him, so he asked and was told he was in his tent, with the council. Rather than disturb him, Chauzida looked around for some way of making himself useful; he ended up carrying buckets of water from the spring, which made his back and arms hurt. He didn't mind that; it helped to have some physical pain, to share with the wounded and to go with the terrible aching feeling inside. Some time in the middle of the afternoon, he saw men leaving Joiauz' tent and concluded that the council was over. He walked over and found Joiauz sitting in front of a chessboard. There were seven pieces on it; four red, three white. Joiauz looked up and acknowledged him with a nod.

"They say Calojan does this," Joiauz said. "Each piece stands for a squadron or a battalion, and it's supposed to help you see the broader picture. I can't say it helps me very much."

Chauzida stood without saying anything. Joiauz moved a white knight, then put it back where he'd taken it from. "Was there something?"

"If you're not going to let me decide things," Chauzida said, "there's not much point in me being king. Why don't you take over instead?"

Joiauz gave him a look that hurt him worse than all the pulled muscles. "Can't," he said. "Can't be done. A king can't just hand over to somebody else. You're it, till the day you die."

"But you won't let me do what I'm supposed to. So where's the point?"

"They attacked us," Joiauz said violently. "We were riding along a road. They blocked the road and attacked the wagons with rocks. They never gave us a chance to get the wagons out of the way, or get the women and kids off the wagons. They just started shooting rocks."

It hadn't happened that way, but there was no point in telling him; he'd chosen to speak a lie, well aware that both of them knew it wasn't true. Why would anyone do that? "Do we really have to go any further?" Chauzida said. "Can't we just stop here? Then we can send people to talk to Calojan about a truce or something. We can sort something out."

Joiauz shook his head. "Sorry," he said.

Chauzida thought for a moment. Then he said, "It's you doing all this, but it's me that has to apologise, because it's my fault. I don't think that's fair."

"No," Joiauz said, "it isn't."

"Uncle—"

"I'm busy," Joiauz said firmly. "I don't have time right now. Later, you can whine all you like, all right?"

Chauzida knew that was meant to hurt him, but for some reason it didn't, like an arrow that lodges in your shield. "If I was to go to the chieftains, Luzir and Semplan and Autet, and said I want to stop the war, would they listen to me?"

"Of course not."

"Because I'm just a kid."

"Because the war can't be stopped now. It's too late. There's nothing anyone can do about it. If you weren't so stupid, you'd have understood that by now."

He could see Joiauz was upset, and he didn't want to make things harder for him than they already were. "I'm sorry," he said. "It was just seeing all those people—"

"Of course. It's only natural. It's the first time you've lived through anything like this." Joiauz still sounded angry, which didn't make much sense. Chauzida turned to leave, then heard Joiauz say, "I'm sorry. Really." For a moment he didn't understand that either; then it sank in, and he walked out without looking round.

SEMPLAN HAD HAD a bad day. His middle son (sixteen, brave as a lion, stupid as a rock) had contrived to get himself shot in the early stages of the battle. The arrow had hit him on the right thigh. The heavy quilting of his chausses had taken most of the sting out of it, and as far as anyone could tell, the wound was clean; the arrowhead had come out like a cork out of a bottle, and there hadn't been too much bleeding, but the sight of his son's blood had bothered him far more than his own. For his part, he'd been smacked on the head by a splinter from one of the stone balls. He'd been out of it for a while, and now he had a murderous headache, which really didn't help; also, being a scalp wound, the cut on his head had bled ridiculously, and all his clothes were damp and sticky and smelt of raw iron. Then he'd had a long and difficult council meeting, with Joiauz going all to pieces; he'd kept trying to blame Semplan for not going on to king Raffen and talking him out of the imperial treaty, while at the same time trying very hard to pretend that the empire's new alliance didn't really matter and hadn't actually changed anything; also, there was some sort of undercurrent he couldn't quite grasp, as though he'd arrived late and missed something important, without knowing what sort of thing it was. Just to make everything perfect, a scorpion bolt had pierced the side of his wagon and buried itself in the cedarwood trunk he kept his spare clothes in, effectively nailing it shut. He had no idea how he was going to get into it ever again.

He was sitting in his tent, staring sadly at his best boots (full of blood, and the seam of the left one had split half its length; the leather, not the thread) when his wife appeared in the doorway. She was all over blood, too, from changing the boy's bandages.

"The king wants to see you," she said.

Her voice sounded odd. "Oh for pity's sake," Semplan said, "I've just come from there. Now what does he want?"

"No," she said. "The king."

His head chose that moment to throb like a fiddle-string. Not Joiauz, then. Quite right; Joiauz was the regent, though they'd all tended to overlook that recently. Chauzida? "Where is he?"

"Here."

He looked, and there was the boy, standing diffidently behind his wife's shoulder. "Your Majesty," he said, standing up and wincing as he put his weight on his bare feet; there was a stone or something else sharp under the rug. "Please come in. Can we get you some tea?" he added, but Chauzida shook his head. Semplan's wife gave him an agonised look and withdrew, drawing the tent flap across after her.

It was, of course, the first time he'd been alone with the boy, and he didn't have the faintest idea how to talk to him. "You're sure you wouldn't like something? Tea? Milk?"

"No, thank you."

"Please, sit down." There was just the one stool, and he was standing directly in front of it. He took a long step back, turned his ankle over, swore instinctively and stumbled back two paces. Whatever the protocol was for a private audience with an under-age king, he was sure that wasn't it.

"No, please, you sit down," Chauzida said. "Are you badly hurt?"

"What?" Chauzida remembered; all that blood. "No, it's not nearly as bad as it looks, just a bump on the head." At which point he had another of the dizzy spells, and just managed to get himself onto the stool rather than the ground. "I'm sorry," he said. "What can I do for you?"

The boy sat down cross-legged on the ground, looking up at him, like a dog. "Can I ask you something?"

"Of course."

The boy hesitated, took a deep breath. "Who's really the king, me or my uncle?"

"You, of course. Your uncle's just holding the fort for you until you're old enough to take charge."

"So really it's him, not me."

Oh dear. "No," Semplan said. "He's sort of standing in for you, that's all."

"That's not the same thing as holding the fort, is it?"

"I guess not," Semplan said. "All right, he's sort of representing you, as though you were somewhere else. But you're the king, not him. Why?"

"So if I told you to do something," Chauzida said, "and my uncle said do something different, which one of us would you listen to?"

Even on a good day, he wouldn't have wanted to answer that; and this wasn't a good day. "I don't know, to be honest. I guess it would depend on the circumstances, and what each of you wanted me to do. I'm sorry," he added, "but it's not the sort of choice anyone's ever had to make, if you follow me."

Chauzida seemed to have understood, which was a mercy. "How about the other chieftains?" he said. "Would they say the same thing, do you think?"

"I expect so. I mean, we all respect Joiauz very much, he's a wise man and he's definitely got the best interests of the Cosseilhatz at heart." He wondered if he'd made that too complicated for a boy to understand, but apparently not. "But you're the king. When you come of age—"

"But if it was something really important," Chauzida said. "And you knew my uncle was wrong. You'd—" He hesitated—"you'd be able to obey me and not him. I mean, it wouldn't be against the law, or anything like that."

"No, I guess not. Well, there isn't really a law, as such. It's more what we've done in the past, adapted a bit to suit the present situation."

Chauzida nodded. "Precedent," he said. "Is that the right word?"

"That's it." Semplan took a deep breath of his own. "Is this about the war?" he said. "Only, I know you aren't happy about it, but really, Joiauz is quite right, it's all gone too far now, we can't turn back. Even if we gave up and went home, Calojan would have to come after us, and there'd have to be more fighting. Pressing on is the only way any of us can see of finishing it."

"Oh, I understand that," Chauzida said. "My uncle explained, and I know it's what you all believe. No, it wasn't that."

"Ah. So, what—?"

"I'd rather not say, if that's all right." Chauzida stood up. "Thank you for talking to me. I hope you feel better soon."

Semplan felt he had to say something. "Really, your uncle's only doing what he thinks is for the best."

"I know," Chauzida said. "And I do understand why he thinks that, and it's all for the Cosseilhatz and not himself. But I don't think he's right."

It was too embarrassing for a man with a bad head to cope with. "I'm sorry you feel that way," Semplan said. "But for now—"

"It's all right for now," Chauzida said. "Anyway, thanks again. You've been very helpful."

Well, Semplan thought, as the tent-flap fell back after him, that's certainly the best-mannered king we've had in my lifetime, though God only knows what that was really all about. Still, he really will be king one day, and it never hurts to get in with the man in charge. Then his head started swimming again, and matters of state rather lost their significance for a while.

THE DEPARTURE OF three quarters of the City garrison to fight in the Cosseilhatz war was precisely the lucky break Teudel had been longing for. Fewer kettlehats on the streets meant that he could walk about in daylight, visit his old friends, pick up the threads of his former career and, in both a figurative and a quite literal sense, start making some money.

Even in the short time he'd been out of it, though, the business had changed. Nobody wanted gold solidi, his speciality; there were rumours that the Mint was about to devalue, which would shave the margins down to practically nothing. Instead, everybody was after Vesani or Mezentine silver, in bulk, either plated or small-flan (a coin that was just that bit smaller than the real thing; you wouldn't notice when you picked it up in change, but there was a fraction less silver in it; melt down a thousand genuine coins and make them into a thousand and fifty). Since Teudel didn't go in for plated stuff, he found he had no choice but to do small-flan work, which wasn't his style. The Vesani dies were works of art, which made them awkward to copy, and the Mezentines designed theirs so as to make reducing the size and getting away with it as difficult as possible. Furthermore, silver is harder than gold, so he had to make the dies from best-quality hardening steel, which wore out his tools. Even then, a set of dies only lasted fifteen thousand strikings or so, which meant the purchasers couldn't afford to pay much for them and still make a profit. All in all, he decided, he could probably make a better living for less work digging ditches.

"Stop whining, will you?" she said in his ear, "You're all right. You've just been paid four solidi for a week's work. And you've got me."

He pulled away slightly. "How do you know how much—?"

"Don't ask. So." She slid out of bed and shook the tangles out of her hair. "Where are we going tonight?"

"I'm not going anywhere," Teudel replied, pulling the blanket back over himself. "I've got work to do."

"Suit yourself." She was getting dressed, which meant she was going to leave soon. "Give me some money," she said. "I think I'll go to the *Charity*."

"On your own?"

"Not for long." She was feeling in his coat pocket. "Is this all you've got?"

"Yes."

She counted. If she'd found them all, she was looking at thirty trachy. "They're genuine," he said, "if that's what you're thinking."

"Give me a solidus. I'll give you the change."

He sighed. "Feel under the collar," he said. "There's a little gap in the lining."

She laughed. "That's a funny place to keep your money."

"I'll have to think of a new one now."

"Actually." She hopped to put on her shoes. "You ought to think about making copper. No, really, listen. The material doesn't cost, you can use bits of water pipe, flattened out. And it's all profit."

"I'm an artist."

"See you tomorrow? At the *Restitution?*"

"If I've finished this job by then."

She'd taken two of the four solidi. He smiled; they were brass, trial pieces he'd made to show customers, no use to him any more. Would they notice at the *Charity?* Quite possibly. Ah well.

The real coins—five, not four—were in the toe of his left sock. He pulled it on and wriggled his toes so they would chafe. Flattened-out copper pipe didn't work any more; the gauge was wrong, and besides, there was barely any copper pipe left in the City. The government had taken it up and replaced it with lead, for the war effort. He dressed quickly, went into the other room, lit his work lamp and sat down at the bench.

He'd just reached a tricky bit—the curve of the wings of the angel on the obverse of the Mezentine double thaler—when the door burst open. His arms were grabbed and pinned to his sides, and he was lifted onto his feet. He opened his mouth to yell, and a rag was stuffed into it. Something very sharp was pressing into the side of his neck. Oh, he thought.

"Easy does it," said a voice he didn't recognise.

He didn't nod, because moving his head against the sharp point would've cost him his life. Another hand took a handful of his hair, he could feel knuckles against his scalp, and it made him shiver. A short walk to the door, down the two flights of stairs (an awkward business), out into the street. The open door of a coach was opposite the doorway. A powerful shove propelled him through it, and he landed on his knees on the coach floor. He heard the door slam behind him. Both doors were shuttered, and the shutters were up. He felt a jolt as the coach began to move. A man could be forgiven for worrying in a situation like that.

He spat out the rag and tried the doors; bolted on the outside, needless to say. Just possibly, he could smash a hole in the roof—not really, no, not with his bare hands. The floor, perhaps? He remembered the ship, the fear he'd felt then, and this wasn't like that. He sat down on the seat and tried not to feel utterly stupid.

It wasn't a long ride, and when the coach stopped and the door was opened, there was a familiar face waiting to greet him.

"Hello, Teudel," Orsella said.

The coach drove off, and he recognised where he was; the coachyard of the *Divine Covenant*, on the main south road. You got the mail coach here for Lonazep and all destinations to the Vesani Republic.

He wanted to yell, but he grinned instead. "Going somewhere?"

"Yes. Come inside."

"If you'd just sent a note—"

"This is serious."

Oh well. He followed her into the back dining room, which was deserted. He knew it well. There was a table on whose underside he'd scratched initials; his own and PL, whoever she'd been. "Well?" he said.

"I'm pregnant."

"Oh," he said. "Well, I'm sure Aimeric—"

"He had nothing to do with it. Teudel, you *bastard*."

All he wanted to do was laugh. He managed not to. Still, it was a joke. "Don't look at me like that," he said. "You know what to do. Get rid of it."

"Are you out of your mind?" Her face was white. "It's dangerous, you have to drink poison. I have absolutely no intention of dying because of you. Besides," she added quickly, "it'd be murder. I don't do that sort of thing."

He shrugged. For once, he felt quite calm in her presence. "No need for that," he said. "Just give Aimeric a big smile and tell him he's going to be a daddy. I imagine he'll go white as a sheet, but he'll come round, I'm sure. Anyway," he went on firmly, "I don't see that there's anything you need me for. Well, is there?"

She gave him a savage look. "I thought you might want to know."

"Under other circumstances—" He made a vague gesture with his hands. "As things stand, though, no, not really. I suggest you turn this to your advantage. Make Aimeric marry you. Sister-in-law to the ruler of the known world, it can't be that bad."

"You think I should do that."

It hadn't occurred to him that she might actually want his advice. "Yes, why not? Quite apart from everything else, think about the money. Young Aimeric's principal contractor to the imperial army. True, this war won't last for ever, but there'll be others, you can bet, and even in peacetime—"

"Teudel, I'm worried about this war." Something about the way she said it; he felt a cold uncertainty he'd never known before. "I think it could be very bad. I don't think we're going to win."

"Oh come on."

"Really."

He simply didn't know; were women in her condition prone to unreasonable fears, along with morning sickness and a craving for strange food? "We've got Calojan," he said, "and forty thousand bloodthirsty savages. Foregone conclusion. The empire always wins."

"It's not like the Sashan," she said. "It's completely different. The Sashan were *civilised*. If we'd lost, sooner or later things would've settled down, there'd still have been cities and houses and markets and trade. I went to Ummalas once, it was just another city; I sold some paintings there, for good money. These Cosseilhatz aren't like that. They live in tents. If they win, they'll just burn everything. There won't be anything left."

Teudel frowned. "What's brought this on?"

"I listen," she said. "And I think about what I hear. They're not like us at all. If they win—"

Teudel shook his head. "Won't happen," he said. "All right, even supposing the unthinkable happens and we lose half a dozen battles. So? Everyone crowds into the City, behind Florian's wall. What are a bunch of shepherds supposed to do about that? They'll lose interest and go away. Some time later—five years, or ten—we'll pull ourselves together and drive them out again. Or not; hardly matters, since the City's on the sea. We'll live by manufacture and trade, like the Vesani. Really," he said, trying to sound calmly reassuring, "great big things like that aren't going to affect us; particularly if you're married to the emperor's brother-in-law. You can bet that whatever happens, they'll still be dining off solid gold plate in the palace."

She looked at him for a disturbingly long time, then shook her head. "I want you to go to the Vesani Republic," she said. "I want you to settle down, stay out of trouble, sit tight."

He laughed. "Sure," he said. "Using what for money?"

From her sleeve she took a small square of thrice-folded parchment. "Here," she said. "No, don't look at it now. It's a bill of exchange on the Leucas brothers. Five thousand solidi."

Teudel had been knocked out with a club once, in a disagreement in a bar in Lonazep. He recognised the same feeling of dazed helplessness, of falling into darkness. "What?"

"My life savings. Take it. Buy a house. Try not to lose it on the lizard-fights. If the war goes badly, I'll come and join you. We'll come and join you." She looked at him, and in her eyes he saw a terrifying sincerity that made him think for a moment that he was back on the ship; sinking, going under the water, grabbing for something to keep afloat. "You will do this for me, won't you? Please?"

He made himself breathe in. "If you're so worried, go there yourself. Or I'll come with you, if you want. Why stay here?"

"I don't know." She shrugged. "It may be all right, maybe I'm worrying about nothing. Besides, if we win and I marry Aimeric, five thousand solidi will be neither here nor there. Please?"

He really didn't want to say it, but he felt he had no choice. "Do you seriously believe I'm fit to be trusted with all that money?"

"Yes. Yes, if it's for me." Suddenly she smiled, and it was as though he'd woken up from a disturbing dream and realised it wasn't real. "And your business is going to hell anyway, and you're a wanted man in the City with a price on your head, and you like living in the Republic, and the interest on five thousand will make you far better off than you've ever been in your life without touching a bent trachy of the principal, and you know perfectly well that if you steal my money, I'll have you hunted down and killed. So no, I'm not worried on that score."

He grinned. "A moment ago, you weren't a killer and all life was sacred."

"For you, I'd make an exception. Furthermore, if you're out there, you won't be here capable of making trouble for me when I'm the emperor's sister in law. That's the real reason," she added sweetly. "The other stuff was just pretend."

"Thought so." He reached for the parchment square and pulled on it gently; it came out of her hand like an almost-ripe apple off a tree. "You couldn't make it six thousand, could you?"

She stood up. "You're on the afternoon coach," she said. "The innkeeper's got twenty thalers for you, walking-around money. Write when you get there, care of the *Conscience* in Eastgate."

He nodded. "Good luck," he said. "Have fun."

"Any ideas for a name?" she asked.

"What? Oh, I don't know. My father's name was Totila. But I expect Aimeric'll have his own ideas. Probably something startlingly daring and original, like Aimeric junior."

"Unless it's a girl."

"Oh I hope not," Teudel said with feeling. "In case she takes after her mother."

"WHAT DO YOU know," Calojan asked, "about some people called the Goida?"

Raffen frowned. "The name rings a bell." He flipped the stopper out of his water-bottle with his thumb and swallowed deeply, twice. "I may have heard rumours, but I don't know if they're true."

"Tell me anyway."

Raffen hung the bottle on the horn of his saddle. "Well," he said, "they live away out east, but the Sceaf, who live to the north of us, reckon they've seen them on their eastern borders. I don't believe it myself, because the Sceaf have nothing worth stealing."

"And?"

"Oh, lots of wild stuff. Like, they have steel spearheads and bits and bridles, but otherwise they don't use metal very much. Their soldiers wear helmets made out of boar-tusks, sliced lengthways and wired to a leather crown."

"That's possible," Calojan said. "I've heard of something similar."

"Have you? Well, maybe it's true, then. Also, they have armour made of squares of horn, and they paint their faces with clay and white lead. They don't give a damn for anything made by anybody else, they smash it up or just leave it lying. Oh, and they kill everybody they come across, women and kids as well as men. They take a toe from every dead body they've killed, and they believe that if you die in battle, you're reborn as a swan. Apparently, that's a good thing. I don't suppose any of it's true."

Calojan nodded. "Strictly a nomadic race, then."

"A what?"

"Like the Aram," Calojan explained. "They move about all the time and herd sheep and goats. Not a seafaring people."

Raffen grinned. "Not unless there's a sea out that way nobody's told us about. Why?"

"Oh, just something I heard. But it was only a name. Probably someone got them mixed up with somebody else."

The Selbst weren't great ones for resting on the march, so it was evening before Calojan could reread the despatches he'd received from the coast; raiders, exceptionally savage, many civilian casualties, four towns burnt to the ground, raiders arrived and withdrew by ship; identified by a Vesani merchant as the Goida; request you send at least two squadrons of lancers immediately to secure against further attacks. Well, no hope of that, obviously. With any luck, the local prefect would evacuate the other coastal towns. If not, God help them.

Other despatches; the Cosseilhatz had occupied the Mier valley; they'd engaged a hastily-assembled rural militia at Ridishen and slaughtered the lot of them; they'd skirted round six towns without bothering them at all, but caught up with a retreating half-regiment of auxiliary infantry, pushed them into the ford at Seuno and killed them all; no prisoners. (I could have told them that, Calojan thought; you can't contain and control prisoners when you're as mobile as the Cosseilhatz, they'd get in the way and be a terrible security risk.) They were advancing, twenty miles some days, but the army always stayed close to the flocks and herds, so there was no chance of cutting off the non-combatants and using them as hostages. Besides, was there such a thing as a Cosseilhatz non-combatant? Hard to think in those terms when the fighting men rode right in among the wagons, chatting with their wives on the way to the next battlefield. They were at Dreunis; they were through the pass and out onto the moors above Caput Imperii; they'd bypassed Caput and its garrison and were on the West Road, headed straight for the City. They were sixty, forty, twenty miles away. They were here.

If there was anything positive, it was the attitude of king Raffen. The closer the enemy came, the more cheerful he seemed to become, like a man looking forward to his birthday. On the day when the enemy were reported at Cerauna, a small party of riders joined him; they'd ridden non-stop from Selbst, and when they arrived he seemed almost absurdly happy, so presumably they were close friends or family. He held a feast for them in his tent, to which none of the imperials were invited.

IT WAS THE first time Raffen had seen him since—

He allowed the surge of energy that the memory gave him to flow into his smile of welcome, broadening his mouth until he felt he could have swallowed the world. "Sighvat," he said. "Thank you so much for coming."

Sighvat looked at him warily. He looked exhausted, covered in mud and dust, his boots dull from being soaked in water. His two sons (what were their names?) hung back, like shy boys at a dance. "Your Majesty," he said.

"Oh, don't call me that." Raffen reached forward and took him by the elbow, led him into the tent. "I do have a name, you know. Anyway, how was the journey? Not too bad, I hope."

"It was fine," Sighvat lied. "But we'd quite like to rest now, if that's all right."

"Of course. You and your boys can have my tent, it's practically the only one we've got that doesn't leak. Sit down, get yourselves comfortable. I'll send someone to tell you when dinner's ready."

He could see the question in Sighvat's face, the one he couldn't bring himself to ask. He laughed. "It's fine," he said. "Really. Nobody's going to hurt you. I need you here because you're an experienced and capable soldier, that's all. I trust you to lead men. After all, I know what you're capable of."

He left the tent and went to persecute the cooks, who were sick of the sight of him already. Yes, they told him (politely the first four times, loudly the fifth), everything was just fine, it'd be ready on time, no, they hadn't forgotten the apricot stuffing, please go away. Finding he had no place to go to, he went to Calojan's tent and got under his feet for a while, until he was firmly but politely thrown out.

At the banquet, which by all accounts was a great success, he proposed a toast; to Sighvat. I owe this man, he said, more than I can begin to tell him. I won't bother you all with the details; suffice to say, Sighvat set me free. It was thanks to him that I started on a long journey, one which has brought us all here, to start what I trust will be a long and fruitful partnership with the empire. I can see from his face that he doesn't think he deserves the credit, but let me assure you, he does. So I'd like you all to stand and drink the health of my good friend and our great benefactor, Sighvat.

Afterwards, he'd called on him at the tent and, after a few awkward moments, they'd spent several hours talking strategy and tactics. Raffen explained exactly what he needed Sighvat to do in the battle; the biggest problem would, of course, be the Cosseilhatz horse-archers, and the imperials had demonstrated recently how you dealt with that. He needed a man he could absolutely rely on to command the shield-wall, make sure it held firm while the savages were riding up and down shooting arrows, then be ready to lead the counter-attack as soon as he saw the signal. Could he do that?

Sighvat thought for a moment. "I believe so."

"Of course you can. One thing I know about you, Sighvat, you've got guts. Right now, that's exactly what I need. Do this for me and—" He stopped. "Well," he said. "You know what I'm getting at."

Sighvat looked at him. "Is it really that easy?" he said.

"It should be." Raffen sat down, poured himself a drink of milk. "I have a special gift," he went on, "one that's granted to very few people. I don't think I'd ever have realised I had it, if it hadn't been for you and—well, what happened. My gift is, if I set my mind to it, I can be anyone I want. It's like a sort of magic; I can reshape the world, so things are how I want them, just by thinking, just by wanting it to be so." He settled the horn cup on the ground at his feet; soft grass, no rug. "Like, when I went to the City to work, they said they needed carpenters, I chose to be a carpenter. Two minutes later, I *was* a carpenter. Then they came to me and said, Raffen, we want you to be the king. Now I *am* the king. So," he went on, "if I choose to be the sort of man who can forgive you, that's exactly who I am. I just have to imagine such a person, and suddenly, that's me." He paused and smiled. "I reckon it's because whoever I really was died that day, and just by being alive I'm having to pretend, be someone else, every day of my life. I know this sounds stupid, but the first thing I did, after it happened; I swore an oath to myself that I wouldn't even think about trying to take revenge. What good would it do, I asked myself; couldn't think of one positive thing. So I made up my mind, from now on I'll be whatever I need to be, to get by; a carpenter, a king, an animal eating tree-fungus in the woods, it really doesn't matter. It's not really me, you see. That's all—" he paused to think of the words—"water under the bridge. And the result is—well, you can see for yourself."

Sighvat regarded him for a long time, then said, "Can I ask you something?"

"Sure. Go ahead."

"How did you get out of the well?"

Raffen laughed until it hurt. "Ah well," he said eventually, "I'm quite proud of that, though really it was just luck. And you were careless, you should've asked a few more questions." Then he told the story, for the first time. "Mostly luck," he said. "A certain amount of gumption, I'll say that for myself, but basically just luck."

"I'm sorry," Sighvat said.

Raffen gave him a big mock scowl. "Don't say that," he said. "I've thought about it, rather a lot, as you can imagine, and I've come to the conclusion that you were probably in the right. I did treat you very badly over the years. There came a point when it simply couldn't go on any longer; one of us was going to have to take out the other, and you acted first. That's all. So don't apologise, please. Apologising makes it sound like it was a mistake, and if it was a mistake, I shouldn't be here. Anyway," he said abruptly, standing up and straightening his coat, "that's quite enough about that, and we won't talk about it ever again. Agreed?"

Sighvat nodded. "Agreed."

"Wonderful. Well, sleep well. We've all got to be up early in the morning."

CALOJAN COULDN'T SLEEP, so he set out the chess-board. Knights for the Cosseilhatz, pawns and rooks for his own men. Something about the look of the board bothered him, no matter how he arranged the pieces. A shield-wall would have to be the key. Was it that he couldn't trust the Selbst to stand still, shields raised over their comrades' heads? He thought about it, and decided that wasn't it. Aside from the Selbst, he had five battalions of imperial heavy infantry, the very last of the home-grown regulars; two brigades of lancers, four hundred armoured archers; also about a thousand auxiliary light infantry, the sort imperial generals were accustomed to describe as salad. He knew exactly what the Cosseilhatz were going to do. Now all he needed to decide was where the battle would take place.

He spread out the big, good map, but the more he looked at it, the less it meant. Luckily, he didn't need a map this close to the City. He could close his eyes and see it, as though he was a bird flying very high up. He saw the Cosseilhatz column, a blurry sprawl like a swarm of bees. The rivers, mountains, woods, roads, bridges stood out clearly, as though they were the chess pieces (but the pieces stayed fixed and the squares moved around them). He didn't even have to think about how each feature could be used and how it could pose a threat. He could see the multiple alternate strategies, as clearly as pictures. Go along this road, and this is what will happen. Cut across toward that river, and this will be the sequence of events. Over-prepared, that was his problem; he was thinking about it as though each separate possibility had already happened and couldn't be altered. He poured himself a drink and tried to clear his head.

Back to the chess-board. He cleared it, and selected some pieces. To his mild surprise, he found himself picking up a king, a queen, the other king; he wanted at least one more, but there were only two. He tried a priest instead of one of the kings he needed, but that didn't seem right. Maybe it was simply that he only had red and white pieces to choose from.

Concentrate. Let these pawns be the shield-wall, and these rooks be the heavy regulars, to stop one end; the other end will need to butt up against something, rivers or a mountain. A wood would be nice, preferably a wooded hill; he glanced across at the map and found the place he was thinking of. A wooded hill, a river, flat ground, broken ground. He realised he'd made his choice. The battle would take place at Moisin, in two days time.

He leaned back in his chair. I've just made history, he thought; the decisive battle of the war would be fought at Moisin, at dawn, in two days. Around that battle, the future of the world will pivot; my choice, my action. My fault. Let the record show—

He asked himself whether the Cosseilhatz would fall for it. A simple process to arrive at an answer, straightforward and reliable as mathematics. He did the calculations and found that yes, they would. They would believe the wooded hill was hiding a substantial, decisive reserve. It'd be empty. They would believe four hundred archers wouldn't be enough. They'd be wrong. He reached out and nudged the white king with his fingernail until it fell over. A thousand years of human history will flow from here, he thought, like water from a leak. He shivered.

It still wasn't right, as though a significant piece was hidden behind something. He stood up and walked round the board, then realised that was ridiculous. He sat down again and considered each piece in turn. Something was wrong.

When I get back, he promised himself, I'll have to do something about Aimeric de Peguilhan. Aimeric was a knight, and he didn't like knights. It was somehow unfair that they could jump over the other pieces, and their angled attack was basically dishonest. He had, of course, left it too late, because Aimeric had been useful, a short-cut, an excuse for neglecting important details. It'd probably be enough just to scare the life out of him; he lacked ambition, he was being used by someone rather cleverer than himself. Who? Don't know. He pulled away from the frustration of a gap in his knowledge, tried to think about something else.

Two days. With a sigh, he pulled the map towards him and went over it carefully, closing his eyes every so often, then opening them again. It'd have been so much easier, he thought, and less bloody, and more productive generally, if Sechimer had agreed to let the Cosseilhatz have the empty land they'd asked for. But that had been the emperor's decision, not his. Curious, he thought. Both of us make decisions that change the world, but I have to go second, like it's some sort of game; like white always having the first move.

Only two colours; it was something to do with that—his fault, for only bringing with him one chess set, on the assumption that every game is between two players. He tried to imagine a chessboard designed for a three-player game; the board would have to be triangular, and you'd need to have triangles instead of squares, or they wouldn't fit; and in that case, how would the priests move?

Too tired to think clearly. He swept the pieces back into their box, and lay down on his bed.

SAVAGES

When the philosopher Saloninus was asked to name the unluckiest town in the world, he laughed and immediately said, "Moisin." It was generally agreed that it didn't take the genius of a Saloninus to reach that conclusion.

Moisin grew up on the river trade, as the loading point for lumber from the Blue Forest (in those days it was twenty times the size it is now) to be floated downstream to the City. At the height of its prosperity the river dried up, but the demand for building timber remained strong, so the people of Moisin built what was later to become a section of the eastbound Military Road. In its day it was the straightest, best-maintained road in the empire; which is why it was an obvious choice of route for the San Tan, those enigmatic destroyers of cities, when they launched their second great assault on the empire in the reign of Florian III. The people of Moisin saw them coming in good time and evacuated; when they came back, they had difficulty finding where their city had been, so thoroughly had the San Tan demolished it.

Realising that it was the road that had been their undoing, they decided to rebuild five miles north of it, in a wedge-shaped canyon in the shadow of Cone Mountain. It had never occurred to anyone that the Cone could be a volcano, so the eruption and lava stream that buried Second Moisin in the fifth year of Gaiseric IV came as a complete surprise.

Once again, the citizens had managed to get out in time, and they rebuilt four miles inland on the far side of the road, next to the dried-up river bed. Learned men say it was probably the eruption of the Cone that led to the subtle rearrangement of flow patterns that brought the river roaring back to life in the appallingly wet summer of the seventeenth year of Amalrich I. Third Moisin was swept away in a single night, though fortunately the townspeople were able to save themselves. They rebuilt on the top of the Hog's Back, a long ridge running parallel to the road; and in doing so they stumbled across the rich seam of porcelain clay which was to be the foundation of the city's prosperity for the next seventy years.

That happy time in Moisin's history came to an abrupt end during the First Collegiate War, when the Boule, heavily defeated by Florian V at Mauchart, retreated down the Military Road, forced entry into Moisin and were besieged there for nine months, until Florian's sappers succeeded in undermining the southern wall. The combination of the undermining and the deep excavations of the porcelain diggers resulted in catastrophic subsidence, which ended when a quarter of the city literally disappeared into the ground. By a miracle, the disaster took place on Ascension Day, when the vast majority of the townsfolk who'd survived the occupation and siege were assembled in the water-meadows below the city to give thanks for their deliverance.

Fifth Moisin was an altogether more modest affair than its predecessors. Built on a tongue of flat pastureland equidistant from the road, the river and what remained of the forest after four hundred years of systematic felling, it was principally engaged in the fullering trade; barges of nightsoil from the City arrived at the town docks, while drovers brought sheep for shearing at the great pens erected under the lea of the forest. Although the population had dwindled away by two-thirds since the heady days of the porcelain mine, the town was prosperous and comfortable, though regarded as something of a backwater. It's hard to explain, therefore, how it came to produce a man like the firebrand Absolutist preacher Vorteric, or why his doctrine of violent nihilism should have appealed so strongly to his countrymen. Be that as it may; on Midsummer's day in the eighth year of Lutimer II, the Vorterists rioted and burnt down the magistrate's house. A brigade of dragoons was sent from the City to deal with the uprising, and the result was the worst massacre of civilians the empire had ever seen. Eight thousand men, women and children lost their lives before Vorteric was finally taken and killed and the dragoons withdrew. The town itself was engulfed in flames; by morning, virtually nothing remained.

It was over five years before work on the construction of Sixth Moisin began, and when it was finished, there was nobody left to live in it. The survivors of the massacre had moved away or been deported to other parts of the empire, and so the authorities brought in settlers who'd been evacuated from the recent famine in West Scheria. Sixth Moisin was little more than a small market town servicing the local farming community, though the architect insisted on enclosing it in a fairly substantial crenelated wall—for old time's sake, he's reported to have said—and surrounding the wall with a formidable moat, linked to the river by a short canal. Sixth Moisin was about ninety years old when Calojan led his army up the Military Road, past the Hog's Back, and took up position to the west of the forest to await the arrival of the Aram Cosseilhatz.

"That's where he wants us to go," Joiauz reported to the council. "The question is, do we want to go there?"

Semplan stood up and threw a log on the fire. "I don't see why not," he said.

"I do," Luzir objected. "Think about it. If Calojan wants us to be somewhere, that's the last place on earth we should go."

Joiauz grinned. "In that case, we should never have crossed the Essa."

"Talking of which," Semplan said, "have you heard about the prophesy?"

"The what?"

"Oh, that," Luzir said. "I don't believe in that sort of stuff."

"What prophesy?" Joiauz said.

Semplan looked surprised. "I thought you'd have known by now. Apparently, it's all they're talking about in the empire right now. It's some really old prophesy that the emperors have tried to keep hushed up for hundreds of years, but somehow it's got out, and everybody seems to think it's coming true. They reckon a lot of things it predicted are happening right now, like the emperor getting married and stuff about the Sashan war. I was talking to some of the auxiliary deserters who came over to us last week. He reckons it's because of the prophesy that Sechimer decided to fight us."

"He didn't decide that," Luzir pointed out. "That was us."

"He turned down our demands, which led to war," Joiauz said firmly. "So, what does this thing say?"

Semplan frowned, trying to remember exactly. "If the great enemy of all mankind crosses the Essa, it will be utterly destroyed," he said. "Apart from its head, whatever that means."

There was dead silence for a moment. Then Luzir said, "Meaning us?"

Semplan shrugged. "It's an Imperial prophesy," he said, "so naturally we'd be the enemy, wouldn't we?"

"Obviously it's a fake," Luzir said. "To raise morale in a crisis."

Joiauz frowned. "Does it specifically say it means us?"

"Not in so many words," Semplan replied. "But they don't, do they, prophesies?"

"The Essa's only been the border this last two hundred years," Autet pointed out. "How old did you say they reckon it is?"

"I think Luzir's right," Joiauz said loudly. "It's a fake, to cheer people up, maybe to worry us. But it won't, because we're not that gullible. All right?"

"Sure," Semplan said quickly. "I'm not saying I believe it. Just thought I'd mention it, that's all."

Joiauz sighed. "Let's get back to the matter in hand," he said. "Calojan wants us to fight him at this place—what was it called again?"

"Moisin."

"Thank you. Well, do we or don't we?"

Luzir pulled a sad face. "To be honest," he said, "what choice do we have? He's sat himself down there with a city wall at his back. Either we fight him or we go round, and have him up our arses all the way to the City. Neither alternative is wonderful."

"You can say that again," Autet said.

"But," Luzir went on, "since they are the only two choices, I think I'd have to say fight. I mean, this whole venture's based on the idea that we can beat the imperials any day of the week, even with Calojan. Sooner or later there's got to be a battle. Do we believe we can win, or don't we? Simple as that."

"We can win," Joiauz said quietly. "I know we can. I've seen enough of the imperial army in action. Forget about that stupid mess on the causeway, that was my fault and I take full responsibility. We won't make a mistake like that again. In a pitched battle in the open, even with these Selbst on their side, they don't stand a chance against us. You can take that as a fact."

Semplan said quietly, "The king doesn't think so."

Dead silence. After it had gone on for a very long time, Joiauz said, "It's not up to him. Look, we've come this far. We all know this is the right thing for our people. It's this or go back over the Essa, and sooner or later the Goida will come and slaughter us all. I know we're all shit-scared of Calojan, with good reason. But he's just one man. We beat the Sashan for him when we were outnumbered three, four, five to one. This time, even with the bloody Selbst, we've got odds of three to one on our side. The closer we get to the City, the more chance there is of him slipping away and holing up behind Florian's walls, and if that happens, we might as well go home. I say let's get it over and done with, and Moisin's as good a place as any. Now," he went on, lowering his voice, maybe aware that he'd almost been shouting, "has anybody got any valid reasons against, that we haven't heard before?" He waited; they were looking at him, but nobody spoke. "Fine," he said. "We're agreed."

Joiauz went back to his tent. Chauzida was there, sitting on a footstool, eating an apple. He looked up, and for a moment Joiauz thought, he's guessed, he's figured it out. But Chauzida just sat there, munching.

Do I wait for him to finish, Joiauz wondered, but the thought made him feel sick. It would be like picking up a rat or a spider, something distasteful to be done at arm's length.

"Uncle?" Chauzida said, with his mouth full.

Joiauz picked up a cushion. He knew the theory, but he'd never actually done it or seen it done. You press the cushion over the nose and mouth, and they can't breathe. Yes, but how hard, how long for, do they struggle and thrash about, and how do you know when you've finished? A rather more ruthless man would've practiced beforehand; after all, this was important, he had to get it right.

"Uncle?" Chauzida said again. "Is something wrong?"

He wanted so much to explain—why it was necessary, because the Cosseilhatz desperately needed a strong leader, now more than ever before, because if this war wasn't won, the Cosseilhatz would cease to exist, wiped out by the other Aram or the Goida; because the king's uncle couldn't be king while the king still lived, it was unthinkable and impossible. Some part of him honestly believed that if he explained it properly, then Chauzida would understand, not mind, approve, forgive him. *Yes, uncle, I quite see that. Really, it's the only way.* I could make it look like he choked on the apple, he thought. Yes; how?

He lifted the cushion. He had to say something. "I'm sorry," he said.

"No, please," he heard Chauzida yell; but not to him. The boy was talking to someone else, someone behind him. He glanced round, and saw Garsio, Semplan's eldest boy, and two others whose names he couldn't immediately recall. He turned round some more. Garsio had a bow half drawn, an arrow on the string. The man next to him held an axe; and there was Semplan behind them, pale as milk, eyes wide.

"Please, don't hurt him," Chauzida said. "It's all right."

Semplan roared, "He was about to—"

"Yes. I know. But he's my uncle."

For the first time in his life, Joiauz had no idea what to do or to say. He dropped the cushion. He knew there was no explaining it away, no lie available. All he could think was, *how did he know?*

"Please," Chauzida said again.

Slowly, Garsio let the bow relax. Semplan said, "Joiauz, what the hell are you playing at?" He opened his mouth, but no words came.

"It's all right," Chauzida said, "he won't hurt me now. Please, just go. And, thank you."

Such a polite boy; always says please and thank you. "What should we do with him?" asked the man with the axe.

"Leave him, it's all right." There was an exceptional tone to Chauzida's voice; high, scared, a child, but a child in total command. The king's voice. It was enough to break a man's heart. "Thank you," Chauzida repeated; it was gratitude and dismissal. Semplan said, "Are you sure?"; deeply concerned, but leaving the decision to the king. "It's fine," Chauzida said. "And please, don't tell anyone."

"We should tell the council. They ought to know."

"Better not," Chauzida said. "Please?"

"We'll be right outside," Semplan said. "Just call, we'll be right here."

"Thank you."

Slowly, as if they were being gently pushed out by something irresistibly strong, they left the tent. Joiauz wanted to move—run away, find a knife and kill himself, there were various options—but he couldn't. He was pinned down by the look in his nephew's eyes, and he knew he couldn't do anything without a direct order from the king.

"It's all right," Chauzida said. "I understand. It's all right."

Which couldn't be true, could it? Joiauz swallowed, trying to moisten the inside of his mouth. He hadn't felt this cold since that terrible winter when the Essa froze and wolves came over the ice. There were so many things he could say, but where was the point? Chauzida knew exactly what he was thinking.

"I don't think you can be regent any more," Chauzida said. "I think I'll have to be king now. You'll have to tell them all. Is that all right?"

Joiauz nodded.

"All right. You'll have to tell me how to go about things for a while, there's such a lot I still don't know." Chauzida paused. "You can't lead the army in the battle tomorrow. You have to stay in the camp, with me."

So, no hope of getting rid of himself in a glorious death in battle. A good king would have let him. A better king wouldn't. How stupid I've been, Joiauz thought.

"Who do you think we should get to command the army?" Chauzida asked.

"Luzir," Joiauz heard himself say. "He had experience against the Sashan, he's smart and brave."

Chauzida nodded. "You'll have to call the council," he said. "They'd have to make Luzir the commander, wouldn't they? Is that how it works?"

"Not quite." For a moment, Joiauz was back in his mentoring-the-heir-apparent role, he'd recognised that tone in his voice. He thought; are we going to pretend this never happened? Then he realised he was being slow. A good king forgives and never forgets. And he tells the truth, but only to the people who really need to know. "I'll call the council and make a short speech telling them it's time for you to take over. They approve—just a formality—and you announce that Luzir will be in command. We can discuss it if you like, but if you've decided, you can just tell them."

"I see." Chauzida nodded. "Would you ask Semplan to send his son round and get the councillors?"

Joiauz hesitated. He needed to talk now, to explain, apologise, beg forgiveness, pledge the undying loyalty he now felt, the sheer admiration— But Chauzida wasn't going to let him; and that, apparently, was to be his punishment. And then it'd all be forgiven and never forgotten, not till the day Joiauz died. "Of course," Joiauz said, and did as he was told.

AT HIS FIRST council as king, Chauzida appointed Semplan as his chief adviser, with Joiauz and Autet as ministers of peace and war respectively; he made no other changes to the council. He also appointed Luzir commander-in-chief. Luzir said; "My understanding is that you don't want this war. Do you want me to pull out? There's still time."

Chauzida said, "I don't think we should be at war with the empire. But we didn't start it, they did. Also, now that they think we're dangerous to them, I don't suppose things can just go back to where they were. Sooner or later, they'd come after us, so we'd never be able to threaten them again. Most likely they'd gang up on us with the Chantat and the no Vei. As it is, we've got a chance to finish it now. Isn't that right, uncle?"

Joiauz nodded, but didn't speak.

"That's fine, then," Luzir said. "We'll carry on as planned in the morning."

"Yes, please," Chauzida replied. "Everyone knows what to do, don't they? In that case, maybe we should all go and get some sleep."

SIGHVAT SLEPT WELL after his long ride. He was woken up while it was still dark by someone nudging his toe. He grunted and opened his eyes.

"On your feet," someone said.

He started to sit up, but stopped dead as his throat came into contact with something sharp. It turned out to be a spear, resting against his windpipe. A hand grabbed his hair from behind, and he was guided out of bed, his movements strictly controlled between the pull on his hair and the sharp point. He didn't ask what was happening. He could guess.

They took him to the open area in the middle of the camp. The entire army was lined up in parade order, the men in full armour, leaning on their shields. A hand on the top of his head made him kneel. He looked for Raffen and found him in the front rank.

There was a long silence. Then; "Well," Raffen said, "here we are."

Maybe Raffen wanted him to say something; but where was the point in that? He squatted patiently on his haunches.

"Right." Raffen shook himself, like a dog waking up. "You all know the story. I bet you've been wondering, why's it taken me so long?" He paused, as if he was genuinely hoping someone would tell him the answer. "Let's just say it's high time it was sorted out, and leave it at that."

Sighvat twisted his neck, looking for his sons. He couldn't see them. Raffen must have guessed what he was thinking; he said, "They're in a tent over there. I don't propose to make them watch you die. They'll be fine." He smiled. "I may be a thief, but I'm not a murderer."

Sighvat looked at him. He wanted to say, thank you, but that would be ridiculous. He wondered what would happen, how they'd do it. He was still considering the issue when Raffen save a slight nod and a soldier drove his spear into his throat and out the other side.

Stone cold silence. Raffen studied the body carefully; it twitched a bit in the usual way, then lay still. He said quietly, "Is he dead?"

One of the soldiers examined the body and nodded. Raffen said, "Get rid of it," and three men dragged it away. How it was disposed of is not recorded.

Sighvat's two sons were given a horse each and told to go wherever they wanted. They were last seen heading towards the City. They were never heard of again.

Raffen cleared his throat. "Since we're all up and awake already, I'll go through the orders for the day. This is important, so listen carefully." He gave the orders. It didn't take long. There was dead silence until he'd finished and walked back to his tent. Then everyone began to talk at once.

IT RAINED TWO hours before dawn, which pleased Calojan; anything that made the going a bit softer for the enemy horses was a stroke of good luck. It stopped just before first light, which was even better.

As soon as he saw the sunrise, Calojan sent a messenger to the Selbst camp, just to make sure they were ready and everything was all right. Yes, came the reply, we're fine and ready to go. Calojan thanked the messenger and stood up. This time, he'd put on his armour (three hours ago; he liked to sit in it for a while in order to get used to the extra weight gradually). He took his swordbelt and buckled it on. Really, he ought to go now. Instead, he took a last look at the chessboard. All the pieces were back in the box, but a thought occurred to him, which made him frown. He picked up his helmet, tucked it under his arm, the way he'd been taught in basic training, and left the tent.

It was going to be a beautiful clear autumn day. A little mist hung on down on the lower ground, but it'd all be gone by mid-morning. It was crisp rather than cold, and the grass was wet. The general staff were waiting for him. A groom was holding his horse.

"Well?" someone asked him.

"Oh, you know," Calojan replied. "Quietly confident."

He could see his breath, a ragged white blur in front of his face; it made him feel uneasy, for some reason. In the distance, the enemy were clearly visible, their carts drawn up in streets and blocks, like a town. Their frontage seemed to go on for ever. For a moment, he believed he was about to fight the sea.

"What are they doing?" someone said. He glanced round. "Are they supposed to be doing that?"

He couldn't see anything from where he was standing. He looked to see who'd spoken. Someone else said, "Bloody fools, they're too early. They'll ruin everything."

The adjutant said, "Did you give the order? I thought they were supposed to wait till we advanced."

Calojan took three long steps forward, so he wouldn't have to peer round people's shoulders. He saw a shape, which made no sense at first, until he opened his mind to all the possibilities.

"Bloody savages," someone was saying. "They just can't do what they're told."

An understandable interpretation, but wrong. The Selbst were advancing, in column of march, straight at the centre of the Cosseilhatz. Calojan caught his breath. Three colours on the chessboard. Three.

He grabbed the nearest man to him and started to give orders, very fast.

RAFFEN STOOD UP in his stirrups to get comfortable, then sat down again. "There's been a change of plan," he said.

In the chilly air his words were visible; white and ragged, like bog cotton. They were looking at him. Then a boy said, "Excuse me, but why should we believe you?"

Raffen turned to Eyvind. "Who is this?"

Eyvind shrugged. A man next to the boy said, "This is King Chauzida."

"I thought—" Raffen stopped and shrugged. "That's your business," he said. "Right, why should you believe me? Well, because we're lined up in front of you in an incredibly vulnerable position, if you attack us now we're all dead. It'd take you about ten minutes. Also, it makes good sense. The empire's finished, we both know that. Why should we fight for the losing side? That's stupid."

The boy considered that. "In that case," he said, "why leave it to the last minute? Why didn't you join us earlier?"

Raffen smiled. "Two reasons," he said. "First, you'll observe that your enemy is stuck out in the open, where you can butcher him easily. If I'd declared for you earlier, we'd now be sitting under Florian's wall, wondering what the hell to do next, while their artillery shot rocks at us. Second, this way, the empire has just kitted out my entire army in body armour, helmets, shields and weapons, free, gratis and for nothing. Where I come from, only chieftains can afford this stuff. Does that answer your question?"

The boy was thinking about it. He clearly wasn't going to be rushed. Smart kid. "All right," he said. "I believe you. What do you want to do now?"

Raffen didn't let the relief show. "Well," he said, "if it's all the same to you, I think we'd rather leave the actual fighting to your people. After all, it's your war, not ours. We'll just hang back here and watch."

The boy frowned. "If it's all the same to you," he said, "I think it'd be better if you came with us."

Very smart kid. "If that's what you want," Raffen said. "Where would you like us?"

The boy looked sideways at an old man in a thick grey fur cloak, who said, "On the left, the river side. Stop them getting to the ford."

"We can do that," Raffen said.

"Actually," the boy said, "what I meant was, what do you want to do after we've beaten the empire? I think we ought to sort it out now rather than later."

"What, now?"

"Yes, please. I think it's probably quite important."

"Fine." Raffen smiled. "How about this? We draw a line. Everything north and west of the Sanarois is ours, everything else is yours. Would that suit you?"

The men on either side of him were about to speak, but the boy said, "Yes, I think so." That, apparently, was that. All done.

"In that case," Raffen said, "we might as well get on with it. Who do I take my orders from?"

SAVAGES

The man in the grey cloak said, "That would be me. Spread out your line between the end of our line and the ford, that'll mean they can't try and dodge across the river. Then their only option will be to try and get into the town before we can overtake them. No chance," he added, with a hollow grin.

"Understood," Raffen said. "If they do come our way, do you want us to just hold them, or try and push them back at you?"

"Hold them," grey-cloak said. "We'll be there directly."

"No problem. I didn't catch your name, by the way."

"Luzir," grey-cloak said. "Commander in chief."

"Splendid." Raffen smiled again, warm and cheerful. "See you after it's over, then. Nice meeting you all."

TRADITION DICTATES THAT the Cosseilhatz follow their king into battle. "It's all right," Chauzida told them, "I don't mind, so long as it's just riding along in front. I don't think I'd be much use in real fighting."

Luzir called out a dozen names. "They'll ride with you," he said. "Well before you get within bowshot, they'll give you a signal to slow down. The rest of the army will pass you, so you won't come anywhere near the fighting."

Chauzida frowned. "Isn't that cheating?"

Luzir laughed. "Well, if it is, we've been cheating for a thousand years. No, that'll be fine."

The riders of his escort were so tall and they rode so close that Chauzida couldn't see very much; just the tail of the horse in front and the scale-armoured back of its rider. Whoever he was, he had long black hair in a ponytail, that swung from side to side with the movement of the horse. "Don't worry," the man on his left said, "they won't stick around. Soon as they see us coming, they'll be off like rabbits."

He was concerned in case Chauzida was scared. "Thanks," Chauzida said, but he doubted if he'd made himself heard; they were cantering now, then galloping, and the horse they'd put him on was bigger and wider than he was used to; he had to concentrate just to stay on and not get his spine hammered up into his brain. He wished he had some armour or at least a helmet, so that if he fell off and the horses behind rode over him, maybe he'd stand a chance. He'd never ridden this fast before, but there was absolutely no way he'd be able to stop or even slow down. Maybe he'd fall off and be killed, and then Joiauz would be king, and that'd solve a lot of problems—

335

With a sinking feeling that briefly took his mind off the speed he was going at, he remembered that his uncle couldn't be king now, couldn't be allowed to be; capable and incapable of too much to be allowed to be. That was probably the moment when Chauzida realised exactly what he'd got himself into, the knowledge that here was a job that nobody else could do for him, no matter how much better than him they were, no matter how much they wanted to spare him. The moment came and passed, he rode over it and tried to fix his mind on the horse's arse in front of him, not getting too close, not falling behind (and his whole life from now on would be more or less doing that, in one shape or form) until the signal came and he could gently sink back into the anonymous body of his people, where he really belonged.

"NOBODY MOVE," A sergeant was yelling. "Anyobody breaks rank, I'll fucking kill him."

He meant it, too; and a sergeant of the regular imperial infantry is far and away the most terrifying thing in the universe, scarier than pain, mutilation, capture, torture and death. Transfixed by the threat, the line held, stayed, didn't break, didn't run, right up to the moment when they could see the horses' eyes, and the strings of flashing brass bells woven into their manes. Then they turned and ran, because no force on earth could stop them.

The sergeants ran too, so their backs were to the Cosseilhatz when four hundred archers stood up out of the low pocket of dead ground that Calojan had seen on his good map and recognised as the fulcrum on which the history of the world would turn. He'd told the four hundred archers; all I need you to do is loose three shots, and after that you can do what the hell you like. Of course, from where they were they couldn't see what was coming towards them, or they'd have run too. As it was, they stood up and loosed point-blank in one and the same movement, and their volley slammed into the front rank of the Cosseilhatz cavalry charge, and stopped them like a wall.

Only the front rank; the second, third, fourth ranks couldn't stop, so they rode over the downed, thrashing horses and the riders pinned under them; stumbled, fell, tripped, rolled, flew, impacted and compacted to build a living-dying barricade, all in the time it took for the four hundred imperials to nock their second promised arrow. The second volley tore into the stopped crash of the charge; the fifth and sixth ranks were frantically trying to pull round, to avoid ploughing into the mash, but there wasn't enough time or space. The third volley sailed over the tangle into the still-mounted rearmost ranks, who'd assumed they were safe. The four hundred dropped their bows and ran like hares. None of the Cosseilhatz were watching.

IT HAD WORKED, as Calojan had known it would (he'd seen it, in that last backwards glance at the chessboard, when he'd finally figured out what was wrong with the picture, and what he could do if his fears were realised), but needless to say, his four hundred archers had only engaged the dead centre of the Cosseilhatz lines, a very small part of the wave. The wings swept on—they couldn't have stopped if they'd wanted to—rushing like floodwater to engulf his tiny army and wash it away. He'd foreseen that as well, and given orders accordingly.

He didn't look as his two brigades of lancers charged. It was like throwing wisps of straw into a fire; they surged forward and were immediately consumed, there would be no survivors. The question was, would they be enough to slow the enemy down just enough to let the rest of the army cover the few hundred yards to the eaves of the wood, where the Cosseilhatz wouldn't follow?

The answer proved to be; yes and no.

ISNEL, LUZIR'S ELDEST son, took command when he saw his father die. It was purely instinctive, which was just as well. For most of his life, people had been telling Isnel that he was a disappointment, a nice enough fellow in his way but not a patch on the old man. If he'd had time to reflect on that, he'd have frozen or run away, and nobody would have slowed down the Cosseilhatz wings and drawn them back from pursuing the survivors of the imperial infantry into what was, beyond a shadow of a doubt, yet another of Butcher Calojan's fiendishly clever traps. In so doing, they told him later, he saved countless lives, secured a victory that could so easily have slid into a disastrous defeat, probably changed the course of history.

That the enemy's headlong flight to the woods was a trick didn't actually occur to Isnel until much later, when they were all congratulating him; at which point his blood went cold and he became very quiet for a long time. All he'd been thinking about was the king, who'd been in the centre, where the Cosseilhatz king always rides. Isnel was commanding the left wing, a job so simple even he could be trusted with it, when the archers stood up and he saw his father flying ridiculously through the air, landing in a crumpled ball and being trampled by two horses that could neither stop nor swerve. He saw that, realised what it meant; then he thought, Oh God, the king.

As soon as he'd stopped the charge and got the line into some sort of order, he led them back to where the archers had stood up, where the appalling mess covered the ground. The idea, he knew, would have been for the king to drop back into the fourth rank just as they came into range of the enemy; but the fourth rank of the centre had melted away, like ice on a stove, when the archers loosed their third volley. He yelled, "Find the king, find the king," until he could make them understand.

He looked at the wreckage on the ground, trying to figure out how it had happened. Enemy soldiers had literally risen up out of the ground, right under the hooves of the front rank; Calojan had stretched out his hand and crushed the best men of the Cosseilhatz, like they were dead leaves in his palm.

They found the king; he was sitting on his horse, perfectly still, boxed in on four sides by dead and dying men. When they called out, Your Majesty, are you all right, he'd just nodded. They saw how wide his eyes were, but he didn't say a word.

Much later, they realised that there had been no men lying in ambush in the wood; they knew, because they were watching, and only the men who'd run into it came out again on the other side. Somehow, that made it much worse. They really were fighting just the one man, and he'd beaten them.

"Well," Semplan said, at the brief, weary council they held that night, after a miserable day of killing wounded horses and burying dead men, "at least we've got that bastard bottled up in Moisin, where he can't do a damned thing. That's as good as killing him, really, if he can't get back to the City." Nobody said anything, so he continued, "And if you look at it in that light, we've done a good job today. All right, about half their infantry made it into the town, so what? We killed all their cavalry, and most of all, we've taken out the one man who stood between us and victory. I know he made bloody fools of us, but we're big enough to handle that. I say we won, and the hell with it."

Autet nodded slowly. "You're right," he said. "We did win. Just doesn't feel like it, that's all."

Chauzida said; "Excuse me, but does anyone know where the Sanarois is? I assume it's a river, but I've never heard of it."

It turned out that nobody else had, either.

SAVAGES

AFTER A BRIEF discussion, the Alliance agreed that the Selbst would stay behind and besiege Moisin, to make absolutely sure Calojan didn't slip out and get away, while the Cosseilhatz pressed on to the City. The news of this decision was waiting for Calojan when he finally arrived at the palace. It made him laugh.

He had, of course, left his remaining men at the gates of Moisin and ridden, alone and as fast as he dared go, straight back to the City. As luck would have it, his horse had gone lame; he'd managed to trade it and his armour for a miserable, half-dead creature in the courtyard of the *Integrity*, the third-to-last inn on the Military road before the outer suburbs. Not that the hold-up signified, in the end. It seemed that the enemy weren't in any hurry any more. They'd halted on the plain outside Moisin to hold funeral games for their dead; three days of feasting and athletic contests, with lavish prizes for the winners and heavy gambling on the outcomes; it was what they did when they'd taken a mauling and wanted to get rid of the misery. Over-simplistic, like everything the Aram did, but still, not a bad idea, at that.

NEITHER OF THEM spoke for a long time. Then Sechimer said, "Have a drink."

"You know what," Calojan said, "I think I will." He stood up and walked to the table, where the servants had put out an unopened bottle of wine and two silver goblets. Apart from the orange glow of the fire, there was no light in the chamber. "Well," he said, "one good thing at least."

"What?"

"At least we know now that the prophesy's a dud."

Sechimer looked at him. "What makes you say that?"

Calojan was trying to break the resin seal, but he couldn't. His hands had suffered terribly from the cold on the way back from Moison. They still ached, and he didn't have full use of his fingers. "Well," he said, "they crossed the Essa, and were they destroyed? I don't think so."

"Maybe the prophesy wasn't talking about them."

"Ah," Calojan said. "You think it hasn't come true *yet*."

Sechimer clicked his tongue. "Here," he said, "give me that, you're shaking up all the sediment." Calojan grinned sheepishly and handed him the bottle. "No," Sechimer went on. "I think the prophesy came true all right. I think the great enemy of all mankind is us."

It was clear from his face that Calojan hadn't considered that interpretation. "Fine," he said. "But they were the ones who crossed the Essa, not us."

"I don't think so." Now Sechimer was struggling with the bottle. "If you remember, the first military action was when our cavalry crossed the river on a punitive raid, and their civilians slaughtered them. So, we crossed first."

"Sorry, you're wrong there. The first crossing was when they went over after their stray sheep, or goats, or whatever it was. *Then* our cavalry—"

"I said the first military action," Sechimer replied irritably. "The men chasing the stray goats were a civilian incursion. That doesn't count. It wasn't official action. We crossed first."

Calojan held up his hands. "Fine," he said, "if that's how you read it. Seriously, though. Do you really see the empire as the great enemy of all mankind?"

"I'm coming round to that point of view," Sechimer said. "After all, what do we do? I mean, how do we measure our success? By battles won, enemies overthrown, nations dominated, sucked into the empire or wiped out. I ask myself, will the world be better off without us? And the answer—" He twisted too hard and the bottle cracked. He swore and shook his hand, which was bleeding. "Wonderful," he said. "The emperor, brother of the Invincible Sun and vice-gerent of Heaven, can't even open a bottle without smashing it. Sort of illustrates my point, don't you think?"

"I wasn't actually thirsty," Calojan said.

"I was." Sechimer wiped his hands on the nearest fabric, which happened to be the hem of the lorus, and sat down heavily in his chair. "But I've been thirsty too often for my own good lately. So, how bad is it?"

Calojan looked straight at him. "In theory," he said, "we have six armies comprising a total of seventy thousand men."

"In theory."

"In theory. In fact, we have a few thousand here and there, all of them cooped up in walled cities. So far, the Cosseilhatz have shown no interest whatsoever in trying to storm anything with a wall round it; they're scared stiff of artillery and they don't know the first thing about siegecraft, and it's not like our men are going to come out and attack them, so why bother?"

Sechimer was binding a handkerchief round his hand. "So what are they doing?"

"As far as we can tell, they're grazing their sheep. And our sheep, which are now their sheep, if you follow me. There's been no fighting, because all our people have left the countryside and scrambled into the towns. As you can imagine, that's not a satisfactory state of affairs."

Sechimer nodded slowly. "What can we do for them?"

"Nothing."

There was a long silence. "You're sure about that."

"Absolutely sure," Calojan said. "Right now, the forces at my disposal are the City garrison, five thousand regular infantry, six hundred lancers, and about four thousand auxiliaries; those people we picked up a while back, after they tried to raid us."

Sechimer frowned, then said, "I remember. There was a man called Ohtar. Thought we were the Sashan."

"That's them. Anyway, less than ten thousand all in, and we need that many just to cover the full length of Florian's wall. That's it. Nothing to spare for helping anyone."

Sechimer nodded slowly. "What about the other lot, the Selbst? What are they doing?"

"Not sure," Calojan replied. "The king seems to have gone back home, but the best intelligence we can get is that he's coming back with the rest of his people. They intend to settle."

"I see," Sechimer said. "Do you know if they share the Cosseilhatz' antipathy to siege warfare?"

"No idea. I doubt it, though. Of the two, I'd say the Selbst are the more dangerous, actually. The Cosseilhatz are better at wiping out armies to the last man, but I have an idea the Selbst might actually want to prise open a few cities and help themselves to the contents. And I wouldn't put it past them to figure out how to go about it. They're a resourceful lot, quick learners."

"Then we're screwed." Sechimer sounded calm, almost relieved. "It's all over, isn't it?"

Calojan looked at him. "I wouldn't say that exactly."

"Wouldn't you?" Sechimer was squeezing his improvised bandage. "Very soon, the cities will fall; either they'll starve or there'll be a plague—inevitable, I should think, all those people crammed into a tiny space—and that'll be the end of them. Then the Selbst will come for us. We'll probably kill tens of thousands of them, but we might as well not bother. We're finished, Calojan. The great enemy of all mankind has been destroyed." He grinned. "Bloody good prophesy, that. Wish I'd known of it earlier, I could've emigrated."

Calojan frowned at him. "Don't be like that," he said. "Come on, you used to be the admiral of the fleet. You know better than anyone that with the sea at our back, and the fleet intact, we aren't going to starve any time soon. We'll live by trade, like the Vesani, or the Mezentines. It doesn't matter if the only land we control is what we can see from the walls. No enemy has ever—"

"Breached Florian's wall by force, I know. Not yet." He shrugged. "Maybe you're right. But I think the Selbst want to see us got rid of. It's because of what we did to them, their people here, when we flooded their homes. I knew at the time we'd done something really, really bad. I believe they won't rest till the City's an empty ruin. If I was their king, that's how I'd feel."

"Yes, well." Calojan didn't want to listen to any of that. "You're forgetting, we still have one advantage. One thing in our favour that'll make them keep their distance."

"Really? What?"

Calojan said, "Me."

Sechimer opened his mouth, then paused, then smiled. "True," he said.

"Thank you," Calojan replied. "They all think I'm still trapped in Moisin with the remnants of the army. When they find out I'm here, ready to command the defence of the City, I imagine they'll have serious problems persuading their people to attack Florian's wall. And quite right, too," he added. "With ten thousand men, I could hold this city for ever against the whole world."

Sechimer looked at him, as though expecting to see *true* or *false* written on his forehead. "I don't doubt it," he said. "I take it you're planning on living for ever?"

"No," Calojan said, "just a very, very long time. And by then, everything will have changed. That's one thing you can bet on."

Sechimer sighed and leaned back in his chair. "I don't know," he said. "We've just lost getting on for three quarters of the land area of the empire in the course of a few weeks, and here you are talking about the future like there's going to be one, like you know what it'll be. I can't actually fault your logic, but it still seems all a bit too hopeful for me."

Calojan shrugged. "At the risk of sounding like something carved over a door, hope is all we have left. Well, hope, the walls, control of the sea and three hundred state-of-the-art warships."

"And you."

"Let's not forget me," Calojan agreed. "It's still an appalling mess, but it's better than nothing."

"True." Sechimer nodded decisively. "It's better than nothing. Which is just as well. Gesel's expecting a baby."

SAVAGES

Calojan had never found a way of reacting to those words without appearing hopelessly gauche, even in the best of circumstances. He tried, "Congratulations." It sounded all wrong.

"Thank you. Well, if you're right, the poor little devil may have something to rule over by the time he comes of age. I guess we'll have to wait and see, won't we?"

A little later, Calojan made his excuses and left. Instead of using the chaise that was waiting for him in the palace courtyard, he slipped out through the east postern and walked down the Barbican stairs into Cooperstown. In the past, he'd found it a good place for judging the mood of the City. When people were happy and confident, the narrow streets tended to be busy. Women with baskets in their hands or children in their arms processed slowly from stall to stall in the Pannier market, where country people from as far away as the Panoge gathered to sell their wares at ridiculously high prices, while men with no obvious legal livelihood sat on the grey oak benches outside the *Integrity* or the *Orthodox Virtues*, endlessly formulating complex schemes that would make them rich for ever. It was the sort of place where you could buy almost anything, where the flawless apples fetched in that morning from the orchard suburbs shone blood-red under a thin skin of skilfully-applied wax, where you might just get the bargain of a lifetime, and at least half of the change you were given could be relied on to be genuine. They said that Florian himself used to go down there with a hood pulled low over his eyes, to catch the mood and buy pancakes from a specially favoured stall—unlikely, since Cooperstown was open fields until the reign of Lusomer II, but people chose to believe it nonetheless. The pancake stall was still there, of course, with a giant gilded wooden Florian presiding over the griddle, while across the way and down a bit was the cobbler who made boots for Genseric IV-disguised-as-a-beggar, next door but one to the inn out of which Teudebert I was thrown for fighting while he was still the crown prince. All lies, of course, but they supported the City like the great oak tree-trunks driven into the sea-bed on which they'd built the West quay.

On a good day, you had to wait in line for a pancake from Florian's Choice. Today, there was no queue. The man asked Calojan, did he want honey with that? Five trachy extra.

"Five trachy? Get lost."

"Suit yourself."

He sat under the ancient plane tree (or the very old tree grown from a seedling of the ancient plane tree; it amounted to the same thing) and scowled across the deserted square at the empty benches outside the *Integrity*. Talking to Sechimer he'd almost managed to convince himself, but it wasn't quite so easy to believe, outside in the empty open air. Trade, yes, they could live by making and selling things; who to? The Vesani, the Mezentines, or maybe there were great islands out in the far sea where all the guttering was solid silver but they'd never seen an olive. I'm no good at peace, he thought, trying to picture himself leading a trade delegation, in tight new boots and clean fingernails, being polite to people. Here lies general Calojan, who won all his battles and lost the empire, dead from uselessness at forty-five.

A man was staring at him, and he winced. Just occasionally, he was recognised in public, usually by veterans. He never knew what to say. He stood up, and the man shot across at him like an arrow.

"Here," he said. "You want to earn a trachy?"

"One single trachy? Not really."

"You want to earn some money," the man explained patiently. "Well?"

Calojan shrugged. "Doing what?"

The man looked at him again, as though making sure. "Dunno if anyone's ever told you this," he said, "but you look a bit like him."

"Him?"

"Yeah, him. You know. General Calojan."

He pronounced it wrong; the O long, as in low, rather than short, as in ox. Calojan shook his head. "Nah," he said. "He's taller than me."

"Yes," the man agreed, "but who's to know if you're sitting down? And you could wear a wig."

"Why would I want to do that?"

The man gave him an impatient look. "We do this show," he said. "Four nights a week in the *Integrity*. Topical satire."

"Ah."

"You could do Calojan," the man said. "We tie you over a barrel and stick carrots up your arse—only pretend, of course—then we empty a piss-pot over your head and chuck you in the sewer. The punters'll lap it up. Forty trachy."

Topical satire. "I don't know," Calojan said. "I'm sort of busy right now."

"Work nights, do you?"

"Sometimes. Days mostly, though."

The man smiled. "Well, there you go," he said. "You do your day job in the daytime, right, and four nights a week you pick up an extra forty-five trachy, cash in hand, yours to spend. These hard times, you'd be mad to refuse."

"Forty-five trachy."

"All right, fifty. But that's it."

"And people will come to see that."

"Are you kidding? They got a Calojan lookalike down the *Orthodox Virtues*, they string him up by his balls and throw rocks at him, packing 'em in every night, and he doesn't look a bit like bloody Calojan. Not a patch on you," he added, "in a wig."

"Have you got a Sechimer as well? Only I know this man—"

The man looked horrified. "Don't talk daft, son. Look, that's my offer, take it or leave it. You'll be sorry."

Calojan frowned. "Four nights?"

"For starters. If it takes off, we could be looking at daily."

"Would it be all right if I thought about it?"

The man looked pained. "All right," he said. "But don't take too long about it. There's other Calojans, you know, be glad of the job."

SECHIMER FELL ILL. A cut on his right hand (he couldn't remember how he'd done it) went bad. His jaw started twitching; it was in the middle of a Treasury meeting, and nobody dared say anything, but he went straight to the court physician, who dosed him with archer's root to stop the spasms, and confined him to bed. The twitch moved into his neck, then down his back; sometimes the convulsions were so severe that he bent backwards, just like a drawn bow. His face was burning hot, but anything he drank seemed to go straight through and out onto the mattress. It got harder and harder for him to breathe. The physician doubled the dose of archer's root; it helped a little, but he knew that if he kept up the treatment at that level for too long, his patient would die anyway; they called it archer's root because its juice was used to poison arrowheads. Two days into the sickness, he started to sweat profusely. On the fifth day, he sent Gesel out of the room and told her he needed to speak to Calojan.

"Well," he said (each word had to be shaped, turned and finished, like a work of the finest craftsmanship) "what do you make of all this, then?"

"Lockjaw," Calojan replied. "Didn't they tell you?"

A spasm arched Sechimer's back into a hoop. Eventually, when he could talk again, he said, "Look what it's doing to me. My back is a bow, and I'm flooding the place out. Don't tell me it's a coincidence."

Calojan shookn his head. "Your trouble is," he said, "you're too damn slovenly when it comes to interpreting omens. Now me, I read a book about it, so I know about this stuff."

Sechimer breathed in and out, shallow and fast, four times. On the fifth breath, he whispered, "Enlighten me."

"Well," Calojan said, "I assume you're taking the back-bent-like-a-bow thing to mean the Cosseilhatz, right? And all the sweating and peeing is a somewhat far-fetched reference to when they flooded out the Selbst migrant workers. Yes?"

"Yes."

"Sorry," Calojan said, "but it just doesn't work like that. I refer you to Stauracius Hrabanus on the interpretation of portents, book three, I think it's somewhere around chapter seventeen. You're trying to read a causative portent and a portent of agency simultaneously into the same phenomenon." He shook his head. "Uh-huh. That's against all the rules. Therefore, it's not a portent at all, therefore you're just ill, with no supernatural overtones at all, therefore you stand a pretty good chance of recovery, providing you don't scare yourself to death with a load of self-inflicted mystical garbage. You know what? You want to pull yourself together, before you make yourself really ill."

"I remember now," Sechimer murmured. "The only time I cut myself recently was that bottle. When we didn't have that drink together."

Calojan frowned. "Are you saying you think the bottle was poisoned?"

Sechimer tried to shake his head; he stirred it a little, just enough to suggest direction. "Nothing like that. It just occurred to me, I'm going to die because I took the bottle from you. That means something, but I can't think what it is."

"Rotten bad luck," Calojan said. "That's all."

"Rotten bad luck." Sechimer tried to smile, but a tremor shook his face, ran down his spine and twisted him into an obscene arc. It was far worse than anything Calojan had seen before. He ran out of the room and yelled for the doctor.

They bled him, and gave him as much archer's root as they dared. When he came round, he asked for Gesel and a priest. Calojan escorted them to the door, and peered in as they sat down beside him. That's not Sechimer, he thought. That's some old man pretending to be him, but God knows who he thinks he's trying to fool.

The emperor died shortly after midnight. He was one week short of his thirtieth birthday.

AIMERIC STAYED AT the palace for a couple of days. The idea was that he would comfort his sister; in the event, they played game after game of chess, like they used to do when they were children. If he tried to raise the subject, she just looked at him, and he knew her too well.

"It's all right," she said, on the third day, "you can go home now. I'm going to be horribly busy with the funeral arrangements, and you'd better talk to the chancellor and the archdeacon about the regency council. Go on," she added, "I know you're sick to death of letting me win."

He hadn't been. She'd won the last seventeen games. "Will you be all right?"

"No, not for a very long time. But that doesn't mean you can't go home."

"Really," he said. "Will you be all right?"

She shrugged. "I'll pray for comfort and guidance," she said. "I know you think it's superstitious nonsense, but it helps me more than anything else. He was a good man, so I know it's all for the best."

He didn't know what to say to that, so he turned away and walked home. On the way he stopped at the Silver Moon, a small and unfashionable post-Resurgence temple on the corner of Old Stairs, and said a prayer for the soul of the emperor, and for his sister and his unborn nephew. As he stood up to leave, he tried to tell himself he'd felt something. From Old Stairs he'd intended to take Broad Street up as far as the Butter Market, but the road was closed and there were soldiers everywhere; riots, they explained, as if blaming the weather.

By the time he got home his feet were sore from walking, and all he wanted to do was sit down in his chair and have a drink. No chance. As soon as he opened the door she yelled at him, invisible.

"Why is it," she said, "that you're incapable of understanding simple instructions? Don't open the door when I'm working."

He knew all about that. When the ink or the paint of the gesso was wet, apparently, opening the door let in the wrong sort of dust; modern dust, whatever that meant. "You didn't tell me you were—"

"You haven't been home for two days, how could I? Shut the bloody door."

He did as he was told. "Where are you?"

"In my workshop, of course."

Half of upstairs—formerly two reception rooms and a gentleman's library—were now her workshop. She'd had huge holes gouged in the walls and glazed with clear glass, at six solidi a sheet, to make windows to let in the right sort of light. The doors were insulated with curtains so heavy it had taken two men to hang them, though apparently even that level of fortification wasn't proof against evil modern dust. "Can I come in?"

An audible sigh. "Hang on."

He heard the curtain rings graunch on the steel pole; then the door opened a crack and she peered at him. "What do you want?"

"I thought you might like to hear about what's going on at the palace."

She frowned, then opened the door a little more, enough for him to squeeze in sideways. "Well?"

There was a sheet of parchment on her desk, the corners weighted down with lumps of glass waste. Anything else left telltale marks, she'd told him. "What are you doing?"

"Saving your life. So, how's Gesel?"

"What do you mean," he said slowly, "saving my life?"

"And mine," she added, "and the kid's. Which is why," she went on, "I don't want you opening doors when the ink's wet."

It was a bit too much. He sat down. She went back to her bench, sat with her back to him. "I've got to get this finished," she said, "or it'll smudge."

"In what way are you saving all our lives?"

Maybe she hadn't heard him. "Did you find out," she said, "if Sechimer made a will?"

"What?"

"Did you find out—?"

"No. I mean, no, he didn't. I know that, because Gesel told him he ought to, and he was being stubborn about it. And once he was sick, he simply wasn't up to it."

"You're wrong," she said.

That made no sense. "No," he said. "Gesel told me, just before he got ill, Sechimer still hasn't made a will, he thinks it's bad luck. That's her exact words."

The sun in the window made her a black shape, surrounded by a burning aura; a bit like the Invincible Sun in an old, smoke-blackened icon. "Sechimer made a will," she said. "It's very important that you get that into your thick skull. Now, where would he have stored it?"

"How should I know?"

"I suggest you find out. But don't go around asking directly, for crying out loud."

He took a deep breath, which for some reason wasn't easy. "Orsella," he said, "what are you doing?"

"I'm writing Sechimer's will," she said, "what do you think?"

He felt as though he'd gone out onto a balcony with a girl at a dance, and suddenly she'd tried to push him over the rail. "Are you out of your—?"

"Aimeric." She had the knack of using his name as a term of reproach. "Please don't shout when I'm trying to do fine work. One slip and it'll be ruined, and there simply isn't time to start over again."

"You can't forge the emperor's will. It's—"

"Essential. For our survival."

He noticed a Mezentine brass table, basically a circular flat brass tray on a stand with four turned ebony legs. He hadn't seen it before. They cost ever such a lot of money. He'd never liked them much. He tried to believe that he was living in a world where the empire was on its knees, Sechimer was dead, there were riots in the streets and the woman he'd been trying to summon up courage to propose marriage to was forging the emperor's will. But all he could focus on was, now I'm the owner of a two-solidi brass table, lucky me. "Please," he said, "what are you talking about?"

Another long sigh. Still she didn't turn round. "Your sister is having a baby," she said. "That baby will be the next emperor. It's vitally important that Sechimer made a will appointing you the child's guardian."

"Why?"

He saw her hand fumbling on the bench for something. She found it; a tiny ivory-handled knife. He couldn't see what she did with it. "Because if Sechimer didn't make a will and appoint you as guardian," she said, "Calojan will step in, appoint himself and take power. Once he's got himself dug in, he'll make himself emperor—probably get the army to force him to accept the throne, he'll be oh-so-reluctant, but what can he do? And what's the first thing he'll do then?"

Aimeric felt as though someone else was talking through him. "Get rid of the legitimate heir."

"That's right," she said calmly. "And the heir's mother, and uncle, everyone who might be a rallying point for the opposition. Your unborn nephew, your sister, you. And me, probably, because I'm carrying your child. That's unless I do something about it. Which I'm doing right now, as fast as I can."

She simply didn't understand. "Calojan doesn't want to be emperor," he said. "Everyone knows—"

"You clown." Said without rancour, because it was simply a statement of fact. "Just think, will you, for once in your life. A nobody, the son of a dirty book merchant, works his way up through the ranks to be commander-in-chief. Everybody in the entire world recognises him as the greatest military genius ever. And you're saying, this man has no ambition. And you're prepared to bet your life on that."

"He's not ambitious," Aimeric heard himself say, though it did sound hopelessly naïve. "He's just a man who does his duty."

"Of course. It's his duty to save the empire. And, in order to do so at this desperate time, he *needs* to sieze the throne. Who else but Calojan could possibly guide the ship of state through these stormy waters? Grow up, Aimeric. It's him or us. Just count yourself lucky that on your side you've got the one person alive capable of doing this job. Otherwise, you'd be dead meat."

He felt like a man wrestling with a heavy object—a tree-trunk or a stone—that's too much for him to handle; he'd lifted it so far, but now his strength had run out and he was going to have to let go of it and drop it on his legs. He was sure she was wrong, but what if she was right? He stared at the back of her head—she was wearing her hair in a bun today, as usual when she was working. He thought; if she's right, it's got to be done. If she's wrong and Calojan doesn't want the throne, then no harm done, he won't care. He knew he was missing something, but he was too frozen with fear to see what it was. "The Golden Spire," he said.

"What?"

"That's where the emperors lodge their wills. I remember now. When Ruderic II died, they all went to the Golden Spire to find the will, and when they opened the box, mice had got in and gnawed the parchment and half of it was lost. I remember reading it in a book."

"Damn," she said. "By now they'll already have looked there. We'll need your friend the archdeacon. And," she added casually, "a miracle."

It was, the archdeacon said, a miracle; a genuine one, which would be certified as such by the next Ratification Synod in due course. When they'd gone to the cartulary to look for the emperor's will, they'd found nothing. Naturally they were greatly distressed, since the emperor's own brother-in-law had confirmed that such a document existed; he'd seen it, with his own eyes. So the archdeacon had done the only thing he could do; he'd prayed, and the Invincible Sun had come to him in a dream and told him where to look. Sure enough, the next day he'd returned to the cartulary and opened the box the Sun had shown him (a collection of trust deeds and conveyances relating to temple properties in the City, stored on an adjacent shelf) and sure enough, there it was. How it had got in there, he was at a loss to explain. What mattered was, the precious document had been found, and the regency council, the queen, her brother and a dozen other witnesses of unimpeachable integrity had all examined it and declared it was definitely and undisputably genuine.

The discovery couldn't have come at a better time. It was desperately important to know who would be the guardian of Sechimer's unborn child, since only he could appoint the negotiating team to meet the representatives of the Cosseilhatz-Selbst alliance, who suddenly wanted to talk about peace.

"WHAT IF IT'S a girl?" Raffen said.

They looked at him. "I don't quite follow," Chauzida said.

Raffen put down his empty cup and wiped his mouth with the back of his hand. "Well," he said, "if Sechimer's kid turns out to be a girl, and we've agreed a truce or a treaty or whatever, where does that leave us? A girl can't be a king," he went on, since they still didn't seem to have grasped the point, "so someone negotiating on her behalf can't be speaking for the king, so any agreement would be worthless. Well? Don't look at me like that, it's a valid point."

There was a long silence. A log shifted in the grate, stirring up a small fountain of red sparks. Then Semplan said, "Let's all hope it's a boy, then."

They'd been sitting there for hours. The dozen Cosseilhatz were clearly uneasy and distressed about something; Raffen reckoned it was the effect of being inside a solid-walled building for an extended period. He'd anticipated something of the sort, and accordingly insisted on holding the meeting there, in what had until recently been a way station on the Military road. The longer he could keep them cooped up in there, he figured, the more desperate they'd be to get back outside under the sky, the more prepared to compromise and concede. The danger was that they'd simply walk out, but he reckoned he could handle them. Not that his own people were in a much better state, though in their case it wasn't confined spaces that bothered them so much as the talks themselves. Sitting down and talking rather than getting up and doing something simply wasn't in their nature. Not that he minded. So long as he could keep his nerve and his cool, an atmosphere of anxiety and stress you could've made bricks out of was no bad thing.

Unfortunately, the Cosseilhatz king didn't seem bothered at all, or else he was an exceptional actor. He just sat there, perfectly still, in his too-big hand-me-down wolfskin, and listened. Raffen couldn't help liking him—he was so polite, for one thing—but even so, this was business.

"That's another thing," he said. "No offence intended, naturally, but am I the only one who thinks it's a bit odd to be sitting here negotiating with a child about who's going to go to the City and negotiate with another child who hasn't even been born yet? I'm starting to wonder. What the hell happened to all the grown-ups?"

He could feel the winces of his own people behind his back, but that was fine. Tension is contagious, and the Cosseilhatz were tense as wires, but still trying very hard indeed to keep their tempers. The fact that they were making the effort in the face of such boorish provocation told him that they needed him, or were afraid of him, or both.

"Is that a question," Joiauz snapped, "or are you just trying to be offensive?"

"Please, uncle." Oh yes, the boy was really rather exceptional. Possibly it was because he was the only one in the room who was being himself, instead of putting on a show. Joiauz subsided, angry but pacified. "I'm sorry," the boy went on, looking straight at Raffen, "I know it must seem very odd to you, but that's how we do things. Also, I'd sort of got the impression it's not so different in your country." He paused, glanced at Joiauz, who nodded; then he went on, "Only, my uncle was talking to some of your people, and apparently four out of the fifteen biggest chieftainships in Selbst are held by kids my age or just a little bit older, isn't that right? And I sort of got the impression that they don't have guardians or anything doing their work for them, they do it all themselves. That is true, isn't it?"

"It's not as simple as that," Raffen lied smoothly. "But what the hell, we don't mind if you don't. Shall we go back and have one more go at these frontier lines?"

Three more hours, and he had to admit, the boy had worn him down. That would've been irksome, if they'd been arguing over anything he cared about. As it was, it'd be a hundred years before his people could fill the territories the Cosseilhatz had already conceded hours ago. What they were really deciding was who was in charge and who was going to give way, now and in the future, and Raffen realised, surprised but not unhappy, that Chauzida had won that contest some time ago. No matter. He had no objection whatsoever to the boy being in charge. He was bright, sensible, level-headed and not trying to prove something, about himself or the world. You could have faith in someone like that.

So, when the struggle over some arbitrary boundary had reached total deadlock, he slammed his fists on the table, stood up and said, "Fine. If that's your attitude, I don't think there's much point in doing this any more. Let's just call the whole thing off."

Chauzida looked at him. "Excuse me," he said, "but that doesn't make sense."

"Not to you, maybe."

The boy glanced at his uncle again, then said, "I'm sorry, I don't understand. Surely we've agreed all the important things already. I don't mean to be rude, but it's like you're just making difficulties for the sake of it."

"You can think what you like," Raffen snapped back. "I think we've given way on one thing after another, and the more you get the more you want to take. I don't do things that way. The hell with it."

"I'm very sorry," Chauzida said. "I really didn't mean it like that. Please, sit down and we'll start again. I mean, it's really important that we get everything sorted out now, isn't it, so we don't have anything we can fall out over later. If there's anything you're really unhappy about, we can talk about it again."

The other Cosseilhatz were hard put to it not to shudder, but Raffen sat down. "All right," he said, "let's make it as simple as possible. Let's forget everything we've done so far. Where's that map?"

Maps made the Cosseilhatz uneasy; rather like the Sashan, who believed that pictures of gods are blasphemy. Raffen took the map and unrolled it, weighting down the corners with empty cups. The Cosseilhatz made themselves look at it, like respectable people confronted with pornography. "Here's the City," Raffen said. "Here we are. Up there's our country, and all this stuff here is imperial territory right across to the Essa." He got up, went over to the fireplace, scrabbled in the half-burnt trash that had fallen from the grate until he found a small bit of charred twig. "I'm going to draw a line," he said. "Do you have any really strong views on where it should go?"

Chauzida looked at him again. "May I?" he said, and held out his hand. Raffen gave him the charcoal. He hesitated for a moment, then lightly drew a faint line. It passed directly through the City. "How about that?" he said.

Raffen counted to ten under his breath, then said, "Fine."

From both sides of the table there came a soft, exhausted sigh. "You're happy with that?" Chauzida said.

"I think so," Raffen replied. "I think that's entirely fair."

"You're sure?"

"Sure." Raffen took the charcoal and drew over the line, pressing hard, until the charcoal started to crumble. "We need some ink or some paint or something," he said. "Anyone?"

Eyvind produced the writing set the imperial ambassador had given him. He opened it, unscrewed the inkwell lid, dipped a pen and drew over the line once again. "Settled," he said. "Now, I suggest we all take a very careful look at the map, so we can remember exactly where the line goes. Is there anyone here who can draw?"

Dead silence. "I can draw," Raffen said. "If you don't mind, I'll borrow this and make a copy. I'll show it to you so you can see it's just the same as this one, then I'll keep the copy and you can keep this. And then we won't talk about this subject again. Agreed?"

Chauzida smiled and nodded. Raffen lifted the cups and let the map roll itself up again. "In that case," he said, "we're nearly done. Just to get it straight in our minds, everything our side of the line is ours, we can move our people down here and settle and build farms. Everything your side is yours, you can graze your flocks wherever you want. That just leaves what we're going to do about the City."

Weary silence. Then Joiauz said, "Do we have to do anything? I say we leave it alone."

"Really," Raffen said.

"Why not? They can't hurt us, they've got no army. Even if they had one, without Calojan they can't hope to fight us and win. But if we try and take the City, it'd cost thousands and thousands of lives. Let them sit behind their walls and get on with it."

Raffen wasn't looking at him. Instead, he said to Chauzida, "Suppose someone stole all your sheep. He's bigger than you, he's an adult and you're just a kid, you daren't fight him now. So, you wait till you've grown up a bit, until you're bigger and stronger. You get someone to teach you to fight, and good weapons. Then, when you're ready, you wait until his guard's down, when he's peacefully asleep in his house. You go to his house and you kill him and take back what's yours. Well? Isn't that what you'd do?"

Semplan scowled at him. "We're not thieves."

"Oh, but we are," Raffen said, trying not to shout. "That's exactly what we are. What we're doing now is what a man called Sighvat did to me once—you know the story, I'm sure; if not, ask anybody, they'll tell you. The only mistake Sighvat made was not making sure I was dead, and look at him now. We can't make the same mistake. Trust me, I know all about it."

Dead silence. Then Chauzida said, "I agree."

"Now just a minute," Semplan started to say, but Joiauz grabbed his arm and squeezed it hard. Chauzida went on, "It's true, we are thieves. It's not a good thing to be, but I don't think we can be anything else. The Chantat and the no Vei and the Rosinholet are thieves too, and they're bigger than us, like he said. And the Goida. So, we've got to be thieves too. My uncle realised that, which is why he started this war. I can see now, he was right. Now King Raffen says we can't just be thieves, we have to be murderers as well. I think he's right, too. It's a terrible thing to have to do, but I don't think we have a choice."

Raffen leaned back until his chair creakled and beamed at him. "There you have it," he said. "I've known for some time that the City's got to be got rid of, it can't be allowed to go on. I realised that almost as soon as I set foot in the place. You know about this prophesy the imperials are so excited about? There's a phrase in it, the great enemy of all mankind. I think it means the empire. And one thing's certain, if we don't kill it now, while we've got the chance, it'll come back and kill us, just like I killed Sighvat." He leaned forward and looked straight at Chauzida. "I'm right," he said. "Aren't I?"

He realised as he said the words that it was a genuine question; that, if the boy said no, he'd have to think again. But Chauzida nodded, and said, "I think so, yes."

Another long silence. Then Semplan cleared his throat. "In that case," he said, "we need to think very carefully about how we're going to go about this. Does anyone here know anything at all about storming cities?"

Nobody spoke. Then Joiauz said, "Not me personally. But I know someone who just might."

"Of course," Hunza said. "As it happens, I'm an expert on siegecraft."

Somehow, without bringing anything in or even rearranging the few sticks of furniture, Hunza had managed to make the tent they'd put him in look like an embassy. Joiauz opened his mouth to speak, but Raffen got in first. "We've got spades and pickaxes," he said, "the Cosseilhatz have probably got buckets. Oh, and we've got a few woodworking tools, not many. There's a big forest about ten miles away, for lumber. That's it. That's all we've got."

Hunza smiled. "I will tell you how to build scaling ladders, siege towers, battering rams and catapults," he said. "I will also teach you how to sap and undermine, prop shafts and lay camouflets. In return, once the City has fallen, you will provide me with an army, so I can restore order in my empire. Is that acceptable?"

Joiauz remembered; something he'd forgotten to mention. He leaned forward and whispered in Raffen's ear. "Dear God," Raffen said, then shrugged. "Fine by me," he said. "According to the map, the old Sashan lands are all on the Cosseilhatz' side of the line, so it's no skin off my nose. If he wants to go there and be an emperor, let him."

"We agree," Chauzida said.

Hunza nodded. He didn't look in the least surprised, and not especially pleased. "In that case," he said, "send me your chief engineers and we can start immediately."

Joiauz and Chauzida looked at each other. Raffen said, "I'm the chief engineer. I'll get some paper and you can draw it all out for me."

IT WAS SAID of the imperial court, not without a certain degree of perverse pride, that there was a prescribed ritual for everything; for locking and unlocking the gates of the palace cistern; for accepting delivery of the day's vegetables; for watering the imperial hanging baskets; for changing the towels in the emperor's private latrine. The chamberlain was stunned, therefore, to find that there was no established ceremony for the investiture of guardianship of an infant emperor, let alone an unborn one.

"Marvellous," Gesel snapped. "Well, you'll just have to make one up."

The chamberlain tried to explain that court ceremonial wasn't simply invented. It had to grow, like coral, the practices and observances of successive generations gradually becoming stylised over centuries, precedents accumulating a fraction at a time—an extra step here, a further obeisance there—like the formation of stalactites. Only from this gradual organic growth could court ceremonial draw its authenticity and meaning. An entirely synthetic ritual would be worthless, a forgery, a fake.

"Rubbish," Gesel said. "Look, if you won't do it, I'll send for the archdeacon. He'll do *anything.*"

The chamberlain agreed that perhaps it would be best if the drafting was left to the proper religious authorities. Aimeric spoke to the archdeacon after Council, and a completed draft was on his desk the next morning.

"Just what the empire needs at this critical stage in its history," Gesel said, when he showed it to her. "More play-acting." But she read the draft, insisted on four or five major changes, and had the ceremony put into the court almanac for the day after next. "The sooner we get it done," she said, "the more chance we've got of beating Calojan. After all, that's the important thing."

Aimeric agreed. He'd given strict orders that the preparations for the ceremony should be kept secret from the military (hence no guard of honour, no march-past saluting the imperial balcony; a donation of two solidi a man for the entire army, yes, but they could learn about that on the day) and just for once, Imperial security managed to keep a secret. Of course, it helped that Calojan was nowhere to be found.

"That's impossible," Aimeric said. "He can't just have disappeared."

But he had. A succession of enemies had learnt the hard way that Calojan was never more dangerous than when you couldn't see him, and Aimeric assigned forty officers of the Household to tracking his last known movements. They reported back that he'd last been seen working late on overdue paperwork at the garrison barracks. That was four days ago.

"Well," Gesel said, "at least now we know for sure he's up to something. Get that clown of a chamberlain in here and tell him to bring the ceremony forward to tomorrow."

They had to cut it down a bit. They dispensed with the proclamation from the bell-towers of the seven temples, to make sure Calojan's agents learnt of the fait accompli as late as possible. They did without the presentation of twelve garlands by the daughters of the twelve thematic prefects. Much to the relief of the chancellor, they cut the scattering of specially-minted silver coins to the people in the Perfect Square. In the event, the ceremony involved a total of twenty people, was held in the palace cloister, and lasted half an hour.

"But at least it's done," Gesel said, "with a ceremony, so it's official. Now let's see him worm his way round *that*."

The investiture was announced by the tribunes' heralds, impromptu street parties were organised in wards right across the City, the soldiers got their money and were glad. Still no sign, however, of Calojan.

"That's bad," Aimeric said. He had dark rings under his eyes. "Quite apart from everything else, we desperately need him here for when the peace talks start. If we can't show them Calojan, we'll have nothing at all to bargain with."

The council agreed. It wasn't like him, the prefect said, say what you like about the man, duty always came first with him. Maybe, the chancellor said, he'd been murdered or abducted by the enemy. That reduced the meeting to horrified silence, as they contemplated the effect on the peace negotiations of the Selbst ambassador pulling Calojan's severed head from a goatskin bag. Or maybe he's changed sides, the prefect said. That'd be even worse.

Further enquiries and investigations; still no confirmed sighting of Calojan after he went to his office to work through the supply requisitions. Someone had a rush of inspiration, and checked the clerks' room;

the requisitions had been completed and filed, and the handwriting was Calojan's unmistakeably tight, elegant script.

"Well, that's something," the prefect said. "It means he hasn't defected. I mean, if you were planning to go over to the enemy, you wouldn't stop and do your grain requisitions first."

"I don't know," Aimeric said. "I think that's exactly the sort of thing he'd do."

THE COSSEILHATZ ARRIVED for the peace talks. Their column—ox-drawn carts escorted by cavalry and flanked on both sides by a white sea of sheep—was six miles long. They were a day late.

King Raffen arrived a day later, with five thousand soldiers; he'd left the rest of his army surrounding Moisin, four shifts of three concentric circles of armed men standing an arm's length apart, to make absolutely sure Calojan couldn't slip through and escape. As a mark of respect to Sechimer, Raffen and his men all wore a sprig of holly, the stem poked between the rings of their mailshirts just above the heart. Holly, Raffen explained to Chauzida when he asked, stays green in midwinter, when all the other trees have lost their leaves; it therefore stood for the immortal life of the soul, which never dies.

"Doesn't it?" Chauzida said. "I never knew that."

Raffen felt awkward. "Well," he said, "that's what we believe, traditionally. We believe that the souls of the dead live on. If you die in battle, you go and feast with Warfather in the Rainbow Hall. If you've lived a wicked and evil life, you spend eternity trapped inside the ice floes in the Great Northern Sea."

"Oh." Chauzida said. "What about if you lived a good life but didn't die in battle?"

"That's a bit of a grey area," Raffen conceded. "We think there's a country you go to. It's better than here, but that's all we know about it."

"I see," Chauzida said. "And that's what you believe."

"Well, not me personally," Raffen said.

The people of the City chose to regard the Cosseilhatz encampment as a vast and wonderful circus laid on for their entertainment. Because, from the designated viewing areas on the battlements, they could see women hanging out washing and children playing ring-a-roses and tag in between the lines of wagons, they seemed to reject the possibility that the Cosseilhatz were a hostile army. A committee of noblemens' wives started a subscription to buy blankets for the children, until it was pointed out to them that, first, until a treaty was signed the Cosseilhatz were the enemy; second, they had plenty of blankets already. Even then, the sentries intercepted at least two dozen attempts by well-meaning citizens to sneak out through the posterns with presents of food and religious pamphlets. Aimeric, meanwhile, was frantically busy at the factory, where he'd ordered the construction of a new range of mangonels and catapults, strong enough to reach the Cosseilhatz camp from the City walls.

"Take a look at this," Ermanaric said. He was the new chief steward, replacing Hosculd, who'd been arrested trying to defect to the enemy. "We think this may just be what we've been looking for."

They were standing in the gateway of the main yard of Number Seven, which had been cleared of goods and wagons. Ermanaric had brought with him a glass jar three-quarters full of yellow liquid and stopped with old rag, and a horn lantern. "If you wouldn't mind standing over there," he said. "We aren't quite sure about the next bit."

Aimeric moved quickly until he was a good ten yards away. "Is this all right?"

"Probably," Ermanaric replied cheerfully. "Well, here goes."

He opened the lantern and applied its flame to the cloth, which refused to light. Ermanaric swore at it and stuffed the cloth into the lantern, which put the flame out. "Sorry," Ermanaric called out, and fiddled with his tinder-box for a while trying to relight it; then he discarded the lantern, wound the tinder-box furiously, dumped the smouldering moss directly onto the cloth and blew on it until he'd managed to produce a feeble orange glow. Then he threw the jar across the yard.

It hit the ground and smashed. There was a loud rushing noise, like a lot of people running, and a black and orange flower of fire as tall as a man swelled and blossomed where it had fallen. Aimeric felt a wave of hot air brush his face. "Well," Ermanaric yelled happily, "what do you think?"

Aimeric was staring at the fire. It was burning furiously, though there was no wood or charcoal; essence of fire, divorced from any trace of combustible material. He couldn't help thinking of professor Carchedon's lectures on the quintessential nature of the soul, which exists separate from the body. A thick roll of black smoke curled off the apex of the flames. "What the hell," he demanded, "is that?"

Ermanaric joined him under the arch. The black smoke had dissipated, and the fire was now pure flame. "It's a sort of tarry stuff that oozes out of the ground in Scona," he said. "Distilled, of course, and we've mixed in pine sap and sulphur, and a few other bits and bobs. I was thinking, pour it into thick-walled pots and shoot it from catapults. A jar doesn't weigh much, so we could probably reach their camp from here with the catapults we've already got."

Ermanaric was only twenty-four; a long, thin man with ears that stuck out and severe burn scars on his hands and forearms; enough meat on him for one meal, as Gesel would've said. Quite brilliant, of course, in his way. "It doesn't seem to need any fuel to burn," Aimeric said. The fire was still roaring in the gentle breeze.

"It doesn't," Ermanaric said, "all it needs is itself, that's the joy of it. And," he added with a grin, "that's not all. Watch this."

He turned around and waved, and six men appeared, a bucket of water in each hand. Somewhat reluctantly they approached the fire and threw the water on it. Rolls of steam, but no other perceptible effect.

"You can't put it out," Ermanaric said happily. "Not with water, anyhow. You can smother it with sand, but it takes ever such a lot. Otherwise it keeps burning until it's all gone. Oh, and it lights on water, too."

That didn't make any sense. "It does what?"

"Pour the stuff on water and it floats on the surface. Set light to it, it burns. Just think of what that'd mean for the Navy."

Aimeric didn't want to think about it at all. "Where are you making this stuff?" he asked nervously.

"Back of Number Five. We're being ever so careful with how we handle it." Ermanaric had a new pink scar Aimeric hadn't noticed before, on the side of his face, just next to his left ear. Of course, he hadn't seen him for a fortnight. "After all, we don't want to burn down the City, do we?"

"Exactly what do you mean by careful?"

Ermanaric's list of precautions reassured him to a certain extent (though he couldn't help thinking of the Great Fire, in the sixth year of Botheric II, which started with a night-watchman's brazier and took out the entire commercial district). "All right," he conceded. "But how much of it have you made?"

"About forty gallons," Ermanaric said casually. "That's all the Scona oil we could get. They use it in perfume-making, of all things. I've ordered some more from the Vesani Republic, but it'll be six weeks at least."

Forty gallons. The glass jar had held, what, maybe a quart? Aimeric thought of the Cosseilhatz camp, wagons and tents laid out like stalls at a fair. A gallon would weigh around ten pounds, and the catapults on the walls threw a hundredweight stone two hundred yards. The camp was four hundred yards away. He felt sick. He asked himself (as he'd taken to doing lately); what would Calojan do? Well, that was easy.

"Good work," he said, in a rather high voice. "Now, I want you to find a supply of suitable gallon jars. Don't decant the stuff into the jars, don't do any tests for how far you can shoot them, don't tell a living soul about any of this. Do you understand?"

"Sure," Ermanaric said. "And when the Scona oil arrives—"

"Store it somewhere safe. Don't make any more of this stuff, for God's sake, not until I tell you. Got that?"

Ermanaric shrugged. "Understood. I'd quite like to do a bit more work on actually getting it lit, though. As you saw, we're still a bit primitive in that department."

"No," Aimeric said.

"That's fine," Ermanaric replied, apparently unconcerned. "So, do you want us to get back to the catapult project? We're working on a reinforced throwing arm, but the extra weight—"

"Forget about that for now," Aimeric said. "Let's just concentrate on spears and arrowheads for now." He paused, then asked, "A few other bits and bobs, you said. What, exactly?"

"Ah." Ermanaric grinned. "Well, there's sal draconis—the pure stuff, not the pink crystals—and Scherian vitriol, and flowers of petra eremia, just a smidgeon or it gets a bit unstable—"

Aimeric hadn't heard of most of the things, and the names just slid past him. Ermanaric stopped and laughed. "I know," he said, "it's a bit complicated; and the proportions have got to be just right, or it can get a bit funny. I'll write it all down for you."

"No," Aimeric said. "Don't do that. I don't want it written down anywhere, ever. That's very important."

Ermanaric frowned. Then he nodded and said, "Security, got you, yes. All right, how would it be if I wrote it down in code? Got to have a record of it somewhere," he added, "just in case something happens to me."

The red patches on his skin made it clear that a lot of things had already happened to Ermanaric; not so much a possibility, more a matter of time. "All right," Aimeric said. "But just one copy of the formula, and two copies of the key to the code; one for me, one for my sister." The fire was just starting to die down. "That's it. Understood?"

"It's your chess-set." Aimeric wasn't quite sure what that meant. "But you've got to admit, this changes pretty well everything, doesn't it? I mean, with this, if the savages try anything, we can mess them up real good."

Yes, Aimeric thought, so we can. And I was once a pacifist, in another place, at another time. "Until they figure out the range of our catapults," he said. "Then they'll just blockade us from a bit further away."

"Oh, I don't think there's any reason why it shouldn't be used in the field as well. I mean, just think what Calojan could do with a weapon like this."

Essence of empire, Aimeric thought, as he walked back to the palace. It destroys everything it touches, it can't be put out, even with water, and all it needs is itself (that's the joy of it). Gesel would approve, he had no doubt of that; she'd give the order herself, if the peace talks failed. It's a gift from the Invincible Sun, she'd say, it means we don't need Calojan any more, we can defend ourselves and take back the empire with this wonderful new thing—

He stopped, on the corner of Woodgate and Sheepfair, as if there was a barrier preventing him from going on. The thing was done now; it existed, and his duty to the City—no, no more lies, his duty to Gesel and her unborn child meant that he'd have to let it be used, if it came to it. Two copies of the formula, plus the contents of Ermanaric's head. The thing was alive, and couldn't be legally killed.

If it comes to it, he repeated to himself. Pray God it doesn't.

THE IMPERIAL REGENCY council proposed holding the peace talks in the great hall of the old wing of the palace. The Coalition refused. Instead, they proposed meeting in the open air, three hundred yards from the Bronze Gate. After two days of tight-lipped negotiation between the heralds of both sides, a compromise was reached, and the chamberlain was ordered to get the big tent out of storage again, and put it up two hundred yards (precisely) from the Gate. There was a further brief flurry of dispute when the Coalition heralds measured the distance and demanded that the tent be moved; it turned out that the imperial yard was three inches longer than the Aram yard, presumably because the Aram have shorter legs. The imperials refused to compromise, because imperial weights and measures had been ordained by the Invincible Sun Himself, and use of any other system would be sacrilege. Raffen then pointed out to Chauzida that the two-hundred yard stipulation was to make sure the meeting took place within long bowshot of the walls; he'd wanted to make it three hundred yards because that'd be out of range. The discrepancy between imperial and Aram units meant that if they insisted on Aram yards, they'd end up meeting sixteen yards closer to the wall, making life marginally easier for the imperial marksmen. The Coalition accordingly conceded the use of imperial measurements, conditional on the tent having four entrances instead of the two proposed by the empire. The chamberlain sent out for emergency seamstresses, the tent was duly modified, the Coalition observers grudgingly passed the entrances as acceptable. The peace talks were on.

It was naturally assumed that the archdeacon and the City prefect would be the main spokesmen for the empire. They were seasoned negotiators, universally regarded, even by their enemies, as the finest orators of their generation; they had all the facts and figures at their fingertips; their regalia and robes of office would dazzle and overawe the simple savages, who were known to be easily impressed by that sort of thing.

No, Gesel objected, absolutely not. The archdeacon and the prefect were pompous fools and not to be trusted; instead, she would lead the imperial delegation. The archdeacon pointed out that she was, with all due respect, a woman. She replied that she was also the outer casing of the emperor, whose unspoken thoughts and opinions could only find expression through her. The chancellor said that yes, strictly speaking, under imperial law that was perfectly true; however, the savages wouldn't talk to a woman, and that was that. Eventually, a compromise was reached. Gesel would lead the delegation, but wouldn't say anything directly to the other side. She would tell Aimeric what to say, and he would talk to the other side. The other members of the regency council would be present, but would take no part in the actual discussions.

The Coalition announced that they would be represented by King Chauzida, his advisers Semplan and Joiauz, and King Raffen of the Selbst. Aimeric objected that under imperial law, Chauzida was under age; therefore, any agreement made by him would be invalid and not binding on either party. Raffen replied that if that was the case, there could be no peace talks; the empire could change its laws, or stand by for an assault on the City. Aimeric asked him to be reasonable; the empire had respected the Coalition's views on women delegates, so a little reciprosity wouldn't hurt anyone. Raffen replied that the Coalition had no problem at all negotiating with women, and where had Aimeric got that idea from? At that point, Gesel pushed the archdeacon out of his seat, sat down next to Aimeric and said that in that case, she had no objection to the child, and could they please get on?

"It makes perfect sense," she added. "My child against yours, it makes it a fair fight. Right, what's first?"

Raffen smiled. "This is what we want. You give us all the territory we've already taken. You evacuate the City and go across the sea. You can take as much stuff as you can get on your ships. You have one month."

Gesel stared at him, lost for words. Aimeric heard himself say, "Why?"

"The empire is evil and must be destroyed," Raffen replied calmly. "When you've gone, we're going to dam the river, dig out canals and flood the whole place. All there'll be left will be a few towers sticking up out of the water. Well," he added with a smile, "you did it to us."

Gesel opened her mouth, then closed it again. Aimeric said, "I'm sorry, but that makes no sense. It's the biggest city in the world. You can't just kill it."

"We can try," Raffen said. "You can leave, all your people can be safe, you can even take your money with you, or we can smash down your walls and kill the lot of you. I know which option I'd prefer, but if you insist on dying, I can't do much about it." He stood up. "That's our offer," he said. "Take it or leave it."

Gesel looked at him in horror, then turned to Chauzida. "Your majesty," she said, "let's you and me talk. Like grown-ups," she added, with a passing scowl at Raffen. "The Selbst seem to have this ridiculous grudge. We've never done your people any harm."

"You killed my father," Chauzida said.

Aimeric cleared his throat. "I think you'll find that was the Sashan."

"You made him fight the Sashan. We had no quarrel with them. He died because of your war."

"The Sashan attacked us," Gesel said. "They started it."

"We didn't force your father to do anything," Aimeric said. "We paid him, he took the money. It was a business agreement."

Chauzida shook his head. "You can kill someone with money just as well as with an arrow," he said. "The empire kills people and destroys things. Sometimes it may not be your fault, but you're still the cause. Get rid of you, and it won't happen again. I'm sorry," he said, "but I think king Raffen is right. Please take your people and go. We don't want to fight, lots of our people will die, and all of yours. But we simply don't have a choice."

Aimeric was aware of something sharp poking him between the shoulder-blades. He turned his head and saw the archdeacon, frantically jabbing at him with the corner of his writing-case. The archdeacon handed him a note; he read it and dropped it on the floor. "A month isn't nearly long enough," he said. "Half of our merchant fleet is away, they won't be back for a week at least. Three months is the shortest possible time it'd take, just to get all our people out safely, let alone any property. For one thing, we need to negotiate with someone to find somewhere to go. We can't just turn up on the beach somewhere."

Raffen sat down again. "Why not?" he said.

"I'm sorry," Chauzida said, "but I think you're playing for time. In three months, you can buy in a lot more weapons and food, and that'd mean more of my people would be killed. I don't think we can agree. One month."

Raffen cleared his throat. "How about this?" he said. "You send a herald to Moisin and order Calojan to give himself up to us. You have one month to get him to come quietly. If he's in our hands by then, you get another month to finish clearing your people out."

Gesel started to say something, but Aimeric kicked her under the table. "Agreed," he said.

"Excuse me." Gesel had grabbed him by the back of the neck, like she'd done when they were kids. "I need to confer with my brother for a moment." She pulled him out of his chair and marched him out of the tent. "Have you gone mad?" she said.

"Gesel—"

"We can't give them Calojan, we don't know where he is. And if you think I'm going to stand by and watch them flood the City—"

He put his hand over her mouth. Her eyes went alarmingly wide, and for a moment he was worried she couldn't breathe. "Listen," he said. "We're not going to give them Calojan, or the City. We're not going to give them anything."

"So what—?"

"We're going to have to fight," he said. "But it's all right. Listen." And, as succinctly as he could, he told her about Scona oil. "In a month's time the new supply of raw oil will be in from Scona, we'll have gallons of the horrible stuff. We'll shoot it directly onto their tents and wagons. God knows how many of them we'll kill, but it's not like we've got a choice."

"Raffen—"

"The Selbst can't take the City on their own," Aimeric said. "And besides, Raffen won't want to see his people going up in flames, any more than Chauzida will. It'll mean we keep the City, just as long as we've got this horrible thing and they haven't." He took a deep breath and removed his hand. "God knows, it's not what I want to do. But if we've got to load all the people onto ships and dump them on a coastline somewhere, it's just not going to work. A lot of them'll die, and the rest won't be much better off. If Calojan was here I wouldn't even consider it, but as it is—"

"The hell with Calojan." Her eyes were shining. "We don't need him any more. Don't you see? If this weapon's half as good as you say it is, we can take the war to them, we can get back the empire, we can wipe them out for good. Aimeric, you idiot, why didn't you tell me earlier?"

He looked at her and shivered. "We'd better get back inside," he said. "Don't say *anything*. Just leave it all to me."

"You?" She gazed at him. "Are you mad?"

Well, now. What sane man would seriously consider launching burning Scona oil at children? You'd have to be out of your mind. "Gesel," he said. "Shut up."

TWO WEEKS. THE oil arrived, and Ermanaric tested scale models of the catapults, to give him an idea of the elevation and windage needed to hit the Cosseilhatz civilians. Raffen gave safe passage to three imperial messengers as far as Moisin. When they came back, they told Aimeric there was no sign of Calojan; not in Moisin, not anywhere.

Later that day, he met Semplan in the big tent. "My people spoke to Calojan," Aimeric said. "He says he'll surrender, but first he needs to make preparations for the defence of Moisin. I'm afraid he doesn't trust you not to attack the moment he leaves."

Semplan didn't say anything. The agreement, of course, made no reference to Moisin, or any of the other cities still holding out against the Coalition.

"Anyway," Aimeric went on, "the orders I gave him were to go straight to your commander at Moisin. Perhaps you'll be good enough to tell me when he shows up there."

"Of course." Semplan was a truly bad dissembler. In the City, he'd starve. "I'm pleased to hear he's decided to be reasonable."

"He wouldn't do anything that might jeopardise the safety of the empire, or its people. You know that as well as I do."

Maybe Semplan had difficulty with the word jeopardise. He nodded, stood up and left the tent.

Three weeks. Ermanaric reported that they now had a hundred gallons of Scona oil, and two hundred heavy-duty terracotta half-gallon wine jars. The only problem remaining was lighting the fuse reliably and safely, so it'd stay alight as it soared through the air and wouldn't erupt in flames while it was still on the catapult arm. But he had every confidence; which was just as well, since there were only seven days left before the Cosseilhatz withdrew their wagons to a safe distance and began the assault.

"I think he's just gone," the archdeacon said gloomily. "He's realised that there's no hope for the empire, and that the savages will want him dead. He's probably in Mezentia by now, giving lectures at the military academy."

"Well," the chancellor said, "at least we can be fairly sure he hasn't defected to the enemy. If he had, we'd be dead by now. At the very least, they wouldn't be demanding that we hand him over."

"They'd have told us if they'd killed him," the prefect said. "So, he's still out there somewhere. On the other hand, if he was coming home, he'd have done it by now."

None of them knew about Scona oil, and Aimeric was determined to keep it that way. So he'd made them into an evacuation subcommittee, to organise getting people on ships. Already, several hundred senators, assemblymen, distinguished landowners and clergy and their families were safe in the Vesani Republic, along with their best furniture and a significant proportion of the City's coined gold money. There were only a few more boatloads to go, and then they could start evacuating the common people. Aimeric hadn't pressed them on progress; if they'd found that uncharacteristic, they hadn't said anything. The archdeacon had tentatively asked whether he should find a place on a ship for Aimeric's mother; he'd replied that she had no intention of leaving while her daughter and grandson stayed behind (which was perfectly true). And what about Orsella?

"Later, perhaps," Aimeric said. Sore point. He had an idea she'd made her own arrangements without telling him—in fact, he'd be amazed if she hadn't—but she was still there and showed no signs of packing or spiriting away large sums of money. If she knew about Scona oil it wasn't from him; but he'd long since given up trying to figure out how Orsella knew things.

The archdeacon asked Aimeric if he could see him in private.

"With the general evacuation about to start," he said—he sounded nervous, almost guilty—"my colleagues and I believe that it's time we established the foundations of an effective government in exile, based in the Vesani Republic, to provide the necessary functions of governance when our people start arriving there. Accordingly—"

"You want to get out while there's still time," Aimeric said. "Of course."

The archdeacon flushed, pretended he hadn't heard. "Accordingly," he went on, "the regency council feels it would be appropriate if we transferred our seat of operations to the Republic as soon as possible. There will, after all, be considerable administrative and logistical hurdles to be cleared, and—"

"I said yes," Aimeric interrupted. "Go. Get the Navy to take you if there's no civilian ships." The archdeacon opened his mouth and closed it again. "I agree with you," Aimeric went on. "Time's running out. And it'd be a tragedy if our people got there and there was nobody to pay taxes to when they arrived. I'll stay here and look after things, it's perfectly all right."

The archdeacon gave him an odd look. "You're quite happy to remain here," he said.

"Yes. Gesel needs me and she's not leaving. And who's going to run the City if all its best and most talented administrators have flown the nest? Of course," he went on, "you'll need money. Can't expect you to set up a seat of operations out of your own pockets, can we?"

He could feel the suspicion, like a blind man's hand groping his face. Maybe he should've yelled and made a scene. Too late for that now. However, the offer of money managed to prevail over the archdeacon's instinctive wariness. They started talking about exactly how much money, and the interview didn't last much longer after that.

"At least I've got them off my back," Aimeric said, when he got back to the palace that night. It was very late, and he'd been talking all day. "I had to give them next year's highways and public works budget, but I don't suppose we'll be needing it."

Orsella laughed. "Not so very long ago, those men were your friends."

"Yes, they were, weren't they?" Aimeric shrugged. "I don't know. It was different then. The empire was there to be stolen from back then. Now it's going to die unless I save it."

"You've come a long way, Aimeric," she said, and he didn't think she was laughing at him. "Not nearly far enough and much, much too late, of course."

"You can talk," he said. "You came here to make money, no other reason."

She kissed him on the forehead. "Perfectly true," she said. "However, it may have escaped your attention, but I'm still here."

He closed his eyes for a moment. "Yes," he said. "Why?"

She frowned, as if working it out. "Because Calojan is still unaccounted for," she said. "And because there's still eight days to go. And because you're here."

"Those aren't very good reasons."

"Not individually, no. But put them together and it's enough to tip the balance. Also," she added casually, "I believe in the empire."

He stared at her. "You what?"

"Oh, not as a force for good and a light to enlighten the heathen. I believe the empire's not done for yet, not by a long way. There's still eight days to go. A lot can happen in eight days."

She knows, he thought; damn it, somehow she's found out about the fire oil, or maybe she knows where Calojan is. In which case, she'd have told me, surely.

"Bless you for your simple faith," he said. "I'm going to bed. I'm exhausted."

"HE'S DEAD," SEMPLAN said breathlessly.

They all looked at him, until he could bear it no longer. "It's true," he said, "I've seen it, I've got proof. Come and look."

They followed him out of the tent. Outside, someone had stuck a spear in the ground. On it was a head, the shaft shoved up into the windpipe, so that the head lolled forward, like a man dozing after a heavy meal. Raffen took a step forward, then stopped. "Is that—?"

Chauzida moved past him, turning sideways so as not to shove him out of the way. He pulled the head back a little by its hair so he could see the face clearly. "I think so. Uncle?"

"I'm not sure." Joiauz tilted the chin. "It's pretty beat up, and it's been dead at least a week, so it's sunk in a lot." He glanced at Semplan. "Where did you get this?"

"Moisin," Semplan said. "Two of our scouts brought it in just now. That's the point. It's got to be him, because our people got him. I mean, if it had been some bounty hunter or something—"

"Moisin," Raffen repeated, as though he'd never heard of the place.

"That's right," Semplan said. Joiauz was doing something with the head, pushing the left ear-lobe back. "A routine patrol caught him outside the town. The weird thing was, he wasn't trying to get out, he was headed back in. Anyway, they saw a man on a horse, he didn't stop when they shouted, so they shot him. And it's Calojan."

"It is him," Joiauz said quietly. "There's a scar, a small one, just behind the left ear. He got it from a little nick on the cheekpiece of his helmet; only a scratch, but it bled like hell. I was there when it happened. He made a joke about it; all those years he'd been in the wars, and this would be his very first scar." He let the head go; it drooped forward on the spear-shaft and fell to the ground. "That's him all right."

They looked at each other, then at the odd, almost comical object lying on the grass. "Well then," Raffen said abruptly, "that changes things. We don't need to wait any longer. Well, do we?"

"We gave them a month," Chauzida said quietly. "Even if they didn't give us Calojan, they had a month."

"Six days left," Raffen said. "The hell with it. What's six days?"

"It'll be another four days before Hunza gets here with the artillery and the siege stuff," Semplan pointed out. "We can't go before then."

"We'll give them their full month," Chauzida said. "We aren't liars. We don't need to break our word."

Raffen bent forward and picked the head up by the ear. "Unless anybody wants this for anything," he said. "I think we should let them know their general's dead. They can give it a state funeral if they want. They enjoy a good show in the City."

A GOOD SHOW was what they got. Raffen's men paraded it three times up and down the outside of the wall, on top of the longest pike they could find, to make sure Aimeric couldn't hush it up. Then they left it, in a cedarwood box decorated with gold and ivory panels, outside the Bronze Gate. It stayed there for several hours before some soldiers came and collected it.

There were no major riots in the City, mostly because Aimeric had imposed a curfew and put the entire garrison on the streets. The curfew didn't extend to the docks, where the lines of people waiting to get on ships clogged the roads so badly that the carts couldn't get through and the ships riding at anchor couldn't be provisioned for their next trip. There was no question of using troops to disperse the queues. Any suggestion that the regent was trying to stop people getting out would have started a panic that would've rendered the Cosseilhatz entirely superfluous. Instead, the carts had to go round to the palace landing-station, which was inside the palace walls and therefore clear of desperate crowds; there, the provisions were loaded on small boats and taken out to the ships by sea. It held everything up, of course; but it was patently obvious by now that only a tiny proportion of the population was going to get a place on a ship. Remarkably, most people stayed calm. It was inconceivable, they argued, that the savages could storm Florian's wall, so their ridiculous deadline was meaningless anyway. There was still plenty of time to get out, and the Empress would see they were all right. For some reason, they'd come to love Gesel more than any emperor in living memory; because she was rude to the priests and didn't take any nonsense, they said, or because they were sorry for her, losing her husband with a child on the way, or because she'd stayed in the City when all the big men had run away. The Empress cared about them, more than Sechimer ever had; hadn't he brought all this down on their heads by flooding the Westponds and driving the Selbst king mad with desire for revenge? He should've known better, they said, dealing with savages. They're so irrational.

SAVAGES

Two days left. A huge column of ox-drawn carts appeared on the skyline. When they came a little closer, the watchmen on the wall were able to make out the distinctive shapes of heavy artillery; the long necks of catapults and mangonels, the swaying blocks of siege towers. The viewing areas were immediately closed to the public.

"Siege towers," Ermanaric said happily. "Wooden structures covered in leather hides, hollow inside. What we in the trade call chimneys."

Aimeric let that pass. "What's the accuracy going to be like?" he asked.

"Oh, we'll be fine," Ermanaric said. "We've been working on it like mad, compiling windage charts. Aiming artillery is now a science rather than a branch of the dark arts. I can more or less guarantee we can hit a siege tower at three hundred yards."

There was something else he needed to talk about. The Cosseilhatz were starting to pull their wagons back, to clear the plain in front of the City so that the soldiers could manoeuvre. Once they'd done that, the women and children would be out of range. "How soon can you be ready?" he asked. "I mean, what sort of notice do you need?"

Ermanaric shrugged. "Half an hour," he said. "As long as it'd take for my trained engineers to walk from here to the Wall."

Aimeric hesitated. In half an hour, he could fill the sky and the plain with fire. The best possible target was wandering away. All he had to do was say the word. "That's fine," he said. "Keep your people standing by, just in case they decide to attack before the truce is over."

What would Calojan have done, he asked himself, as he walked away. Well, the right thing, naturally. Probably not this; he wouldn't have let the best chance of saving the City and ending the war slip away, doing nothing about it, standing idly by. He wouldn't have allowed himself the indulgence of mercy; he wasn't a coward, who was too scared of nightmares and guilt and looking at his face in the mirror to do what had to be done. Calojan would've taken the evil upon himself, put it on like the lorus and the divitision; swallowed it whole; taken away the sins of the world, like the Invincible Sun.

Just as well I'm not him.

They retrieved the tent the night before the truce expired. They wouldn't be needing it for further negotiations, since the Coalition had said quite categorically that there weren't going to be any. So; if the City survived, it'd be there for the next time they staged an open-air ceremony. If the City didn't survive, well.

The truce was set to end at dawn, but Semplan was up and about well before then, supervising the setting up of the artillery, which he had no idea how to use. The ground was soft and churned up by the wheels of the civilian wagons, which had finished pulling out the previous morning; the enormously wide iron tires that Hunza had insisted they fit to the wheels of the catapult limbers coped with the mud and the ruts up to a point, but when eventually they got stuck, they got very stuck. At one point, Semplan had half the army out pushing or hauling on ropes. It was broad daylight by the time the engines were lined up and ready to go. There were five hundred and six of them, nearly twice as many as the total strength of the imperial artillery at the height of the Sashan war, and ten times as many as were facing them on the City wall. They'd cut down a forest to build them, and Raffen had brought in twenty thousand of his people to do the carpentry. They'd dismantled an entire town to get stone blocks to use as ammunition; an interesting thought, Raffen had observed, using one Imperial city to smash down another.

"Well," Joiauz said quietly, "here we all are. We might as well get on with it."

He nodded to Semplan, who yelled the order to loose in a high, shrill voice. The catapult ropes creaked, like tall trees in a high wind, and then the ground bumped under their feet as the catapult arms swung through the air and slammed against the padded stops. The stones sailed up—they were slower in flight than Chauzida had anticipated, almost gliding, like birds about to pitch—and drew perfect hooped arcs through the sky, and fell short, about fifty yards from the wall.

Dead silence; then Semplan started to swear. "Can you crank them up a bit more?" Joiauz asked, but Semplan shook his head. "That's as tight as they'll go without pulling themselves apart," he said. "Nothing for it, we'll have to move them forward some more."

They all knew what that meant. Fifty yards further forward would bring them within range of the imperial engines on the wall. Hunza had promised faithfully that the Sashan pattern of catapult had seventy-five yards, easily, on the imperial model. Apparently not.

"Bring up the big shields," Semplan ordered. The proper name was *pavise*, according to Hunza, but nobody else would know what that meant. The shields were eight feet tall and five wide, woven from riven hazel. In theory, they could stop arrows. There weren't anything like enough of them.

"Where's that idiot Hunza?" Joiauz was yelling. "Get him here, right now. I want him to explain why his stupid machines are building the enemy a spare wall instead of knocking down the City."

Hunza was duly produced. "Simple," he said. "Your workers didn't follow the specifications I provided for them. If they had, the volley wouldn't have fallen short. I can't be blamed for your allies' incompetence."

"He's probably right," Autet said quietly. "The Selbst reckon they can do anything, but they've never built catapults before."

"It doesn't matter," Chauzida said. "We've got plenty of time and plenty of rocks."

"Yes, but we're going to have to move our machines within range of theirs," Joiauz said bitterly. "Which the Great King here assured me wasn't going to be necessary. There'll be people killed because of his mistake."

Chauzida looked at him. "Uncle," he said. "An awful lot of people are going to get killed because of all our mistakes today. I don't think shouting at each other's going to make it better."

"They aren't shooting at us," Autet said.

They all turned and looked. The catapults were lumbering painfully forward, with great clouds and swarms of men in front of them, hauling on ropes. They had to be well within range by now, but the imperial artillery hadn't loosed a single stone. "What are they waiting for?" Joiauz asked.

"No," Aimeric said. "Not yet."

The artillery commander rolled his eyes but said nothing. He'd already made his views quite clear. There was absolutely no case to be made against them, and Aimeric hadn't even tried. Of course they should have loosed their first shots much earlier, as soon as the enemy engines crossed the five hundred yard line, estimated maximum range for the wine-jar missiles. Having passed up that opportunity, of course they should have dropped firepots in among the crowded masses of Cosseilhatz and Selbst as they dragged the machines forward after their first failed volley. Now the hauling teams had done their job and scampered back to what they fondly imagined was a safe distance, and only the artillerymen remained. So, Aimeric thought, do it now, why not? If it's the thought of killing more people than you absolutely have to that's holding you back, then this would be a good time; there's only five or six men to each engine, you can burn wood instead of flesh and still make a war-stopping impression. Now would be the best possible time; except that—

"They're about to shoot," the guard captain said loudly. "You might want to get your head down, sir. Rock splinters can carry a long way."

"I'm fine here, thanks," Aimeric heard himself say; which was ridiculous, because a flying shard could break his head off his neck, and only a lunatic would take the risk. But he couldn't move, because he had to stay here where he could see; because it was all up to him now, and he had to see it for himself. The captain nodded briefly and dived into the open doorway of the guard tower. A few yards away, Aimeric could see a plain, unglazed pottery jar sitting in the padded spoon of the catapult arm, while an artilleryman stood by motionless, holding a burning torch. I can't do this, he thought. They have to shoot first.

"What the hell," he heard somebody say, "is that?"

He looked up, but he couldn't see anything. "What?" he shouted, but whoever it was must've assumed he was talking to someone else. "What can you see?" he yelled. "Answer me."

No reply; but none needed, he could see it for himself. A large body of horsemen had appeared over the crest of the ridge, from the direction of the Cosseilhatz camp. Aimeric frowned, because it made no sense. Why were the enemy deploying their cavalry for an assault against a fortified position? Was it some brilliant piece of strategy, or were they simply too lazy to walk?

The Cosseilhatz hadn't shot. The realisation hit him like a smack to the head, administered by an exasperated teacher. They were ready, their catapults were wound up and aimed, but the crews were running away. Why would they run at the sight of their own cavalry?

"THE KING," JOIAUZ was screaming. "Protect the king."

Admirable sentiment; nobody was listening. The problem was that nobody had any weapons; they'd left their bows and spears behind, assuming they wouldn't need them. As a result, there was no question of fighting back, even if anyone had found the suicidal courage to try. Instead, they were running, heading back to the camp. But they couldn't run nearly as fast as the lancers' horses.

From the wall, it looked like the moment when a dam breaks and the floodwater surges in, sweeping up everything in its path and turning it into flotsam, floating on the unstoppable water. The tide of lancers swept down on both sides of the line of catapults, engulfing the scattering crews, who simply disappeared, surging together at the end of the line to turn and flood the pitiful redoubt that had formed up around the Coalition commanders.

"Stop," someone called out. "That's enough."

Chauzida looked up, above the dead bodies and the hedge of spears. He couldn't see who'd shouted, but it seemed to have worked. The horsemen stopped and backed away. He couldn't see, because Joiauz was standing right in front of him, to protect him with his body, since he had nothing else. Gently, he pushed his uncle aside. "It's all right," he said.

Autet was dead; he'd seen him crushed under the horses' hooves. Raffen had been knocked down, but he hadn't actually seen him die. He had no idea where Semplan was; he'd been with the engines. He walked forward until he could go no further without climbing over the dead. "I'm Chauzida," he said. "I'm the king. Who's in charge, please?"

The solid forest of horses' legs and steel greaves parted, and a man approached, on foot, holding his helmet tucked under his arm. Chauzida recognised him. He was supposed to be dead.

"My men have surrounded your camp," he said, in a loud, calm voice. "I've got three thousand horse-archers drawn up round the tents and wagons. You will come with me and give your soldiers the order to stand down, or I'll have my trumpeters blow the signal and we'll shoot your families."

Chauzida looked at him. "We thought you were dead."

"Of course you did. And now you're coming with me." Calojan held out his arm. "You'll be quite safe," he said, "if I wanted you dead, you would be."

Naturally. "It's all right," Chauzida said, as Joiauz started to lunge forward. "Please stay here, all of you. I'll be quite all right."

"I'm coming with you," Joiauz said. He took a long stride forward, and a lancer clubbed the back of his head with the butt of his spear. He dropped to his knees. "Leave him," Calojan said. "Come on, I'm in a hurry."

Calojan wasn't bluffing. From the top of the ridge, Chauzida could see the cordon of horse-archers, one at the top of each lane of the lower half of the camp. They'd brought the women, the children and the old men out of the wagons and crowded them together in bunches, for ease of execution. He tried to work out how long it would take the soldiers, drawn up in battle formation three hundred yards away, to get there and kill the imperials; four, five, possibly even six volleys, if the imperials stood their ground. At that range, against targets packed so closely together, it was hard to see how they could miss.

They were walking towards the Cosseilhatz line. A few yards behind them rode a dozen lancers, no more (but eleven more than it'd take to kill me, Chauzida thought). He could feel the anger rising from his people as they watched the imperials watching their families, but he knew they wouldn't dare try anything. In other words, checkmate.

"Who's in command of your army?" Calojan said.

"His name's Semplan."

"He's an idiot." Calojan shook his head. "The most basic rule, you don't leave your camp exposed and unguarded. If I were you, I'd pull his neck."

"He's probably dead already," Chauzida said. "He was over by the catapults."

"If he isn't, he deserves to be. I was expecting to have to cut my way through to the siege engines, and I was able to ride straight up to your wagons without anyone lifting a finger. The main body of your army was half a mile off, and looking the other way. There were no pickets, no sentries, no scouts, nothing."

"We didn't think we'd need them. We thought you were dead."

Calojan pulled a face. "The first thing they tell you at the academy," he said. "The worst words a general can ever utter are, I never expected that. Was this Semplan in the war? I don't remember him."

"He's new at the job."

"Get rid of him. What happened to your uncle, Joiauz? He was pretty competent, as I remember."

"There were problems," Chauzida said. "Political stuff."

"Ah." Calojan nodded sympathetically. "Soldiers should keep out of politics, the way sensible men stay out of burning houses. Well, I say that. I guess I'm not very sensible."

They walked on in silence; then Chauzida said, "Are you going to let us go?"

"I hope so," Calojan said.

They were close to the line now; much closer, and the Cosseilhatz would be able to hear them talking. "What have I got to do?" Chauzida asked.

"Agree with me. It's all I ever ask of anyone."

A lancer dismounted, stuck his spear in the ground, drew his sword and stood directly behind Chauzida, so close he could smell his sweat. Presumably the man was nervous, so close to the enemy, charged with the task of killing their king, should it come to that. Calojan didn't seem nervous at all. He advanced to within ten yards of the line, tucked his helmet firmly under his arm, and said, "Some of you know me, I'm Calojan. As you can see, I'm not dead. I have your civilians herded up where my archers can't miss. I also have your king. I think we can safely say I've won this round."

A man slid off his horse and walked forward; Garsio, Luzir's son. Chauzida couldn't remember what rank he'd been given, but it didn't seem to matter. "What do you want?"

"All right," Calojan said, "here's the deal. You pull back at least two miles and stay there until we've finished dragging your beautiful new catapults inside the City. When we've done that, we'll go inside and let the king go. That's all. By the way, this isn't a negotiation. I'm giving you your orders. Understood?"

"How can we be sure—?"

"Because I say so. And because the fewer of your people I kill today, the easier it'll be for us all to get along nicely for the next thousand years. Now please go away, before something goes wrong and we have a massacre on our hands."

Garsio looked at him, as if wondering if he was real. "You're supposed to be dead," he said. "They stuck your head on a pole."

Calojan grinned. "Didn't anyone tell you? I'm immortal. Which means I'm going to carry on beating the shit out of you people for ever and ever. I suggest you get used to it."

ON THE WAY back, Chauzida asked, "Is that true?"

"What?"

"That you're immortal."

Calojan laughed. It was a curiously friendly sound. "God, I hope not. I don't know, I might be. We'll have to wait and see."

"But you were dead. I saw it myself, your head on a spear."

Calojan shrugged. "Actually," he said, "that wasn't me. That was a quartermaster sergeant of the Seventeenth who had the misfortune to look a lot like me. I found him doing rude impersonations of me, at twenty trachy a time. So I had him cut his hair like mine and shave his beard, even faked the scar behind my ear. It's something we're very good at in the empire these days, fakes and forgeries."

"I'm sorry," Chauzida said. "I don't know what you mean."

"Good," Calojan said.

WHEN THEY TOLD the chamberlain they'd be needing the big tent again, he was not amused. He didn't say anything, of course, but the look on his face said it all.

"It comes at a price, of course," Calojan said, on the way to the peace talks. "To raise that many men in a hurry, I had to strip the garrisons out of all the major cities on the north coast. In practice, they're defenceless. I'm hoping that the Cosseilhatz haven't figured out yet what I've done, so they won't know they can just walk in there and kill a quarter of a million people if they want to." He shook his head. "I told the governors to get the civilians out by sea, as quickly as possible, but whether they'll be able to get everyone to leave or not, I just don't know."

Aimeric nodded. "You can see their point. I wouldn't want to do it."

"While we're on the subject." Calojan stopped. They were under the Arch of Gaiseric, between the Horsefair and the North Foregate. The escort stopped too, discreetly out of earshot. "I'm afraid you've got to go."

Aimeric opened his mouth, but no words came.

"Sorry," Calojan went on, "but I don't want you around here any more. You're a clever boy and you've been useful, but you're too stupid to see when people are using you. I suggest you go back to the Vesani Republic. You liked it there, didn't you?"

"You can't. Gesel won't let you."

"I've spoken to your sister." Calojan looked past him, as though he was no longer there. "She agrees with me. I'm going to marry her, by the way."

He couldn't have heard that right. "You what?"

"Strictly political," Calojan said. "That way, Gesel will know her child will be safe, and it'll give me more legitimacy as regent." He rubbed his eyes with his thumbs; he sounded exhausted. "If it's a boy, he'll succeed me when I die. If it's a girl, when she comes of age I'll divorce Gesel and marry her. It's all agreed."

Unbelievable. "Divorce Gesel and—"

"Her suggestion," Calojan said. "For all her unfortunate manner, your sister's a very intelligent woman, very practical. I think we'll work well together."

Aimeric felt his knees go weak. "I don't want to go."

"Of course you do. Go back to the University, finish your degree. Get drunk a lot and bet on the lizard fights. Oh, and take that bloody woman with you. I don't want to see her around the place when I'm in charge."

Aimeric shook his head. "You can't do this."

"Sorry," Calojan said. "But I can do what the hell I like."

"It's for the best," Gesel said, when he finally got to see her that evening. "For your sake, too. You're so naïve, Aimeric. People make you do things, and you can't see it. Look at that girlfriend of yours. She's got you wrapped round her little finger."

Aimeric tried to grab her arm, but she was too quick for him. He took a step back. "Is that what all this is about? You don't approve of Orsella."

Gesel shook her head. "It's about saving the City and two million people," she said. "I wouldn't expect you to understand. You never did care about anybody except yourself."

He went to the factory, but Ermanaric wasn't there. Soldiers had come and taken him away, they told him. They'd also seized all the Scona oil, the jars, the raw materials, everything. They'd made a real mess of the office, papers everywhere, the locked strongbox smashed open, all the ledgers and account books taken away; also, all the money in the big steel chest. They hadn't even given a receipt.

So he went home and told Orsella, who already knew. She wasn't angry or upset. She was packing, with the unhurried efficiency that only comes with long practice. One case—long, thin and flat, elegant but robust rust-brown pigskin with brass clasps—was already standing by the door. The other, a more conventional rectangular shape, was half-filled with clothes.

"We ought to take money," he said.

"Don't be silly." She considered a green velvet dress, frowned, dropped it on the floor. "It's bulky, it's heavy, and if we get robbed, it's gone for ever. Bills of exchange drawn on the Zeuxis brothers, however, take up virtually no space at all." She tugged the corner of a piece of paper out from under her sleeve, then poked it back in again. "I sold this house ten days ago," she said. "Just in case."

"You sold—"

"Your signature's so easy a child could do it. Or you, even." She frowned. "Don't glower at me like that. Either we were moving to the palace or getting strung up or thrown out; in any event, we wouldn't be needing this place any more."

He hesitated. "Are you going to leave me now?"

She neatly folded and packed a silk chemise before answering. "No."

"Why not?"

"Aimeric." Her not-now-I'm-busy voice. "I'm not going to leave you. After all, what good would it do?"

"But I've lost everything and you don't love me. So why stay?"

She tried the lid of the case; it wouldn't shut. "Lean on this for me, would you?" He did as he was told and heard a soft click. "You haven't exactly lost everything," she said, "thanks to me. You've lost everything except six thousand solidi with the Zeuxis brothers and five thousand with Boioannes and Tragus. Oh, and you also own a ship."

"Do I?"

"Everyone should own a ship," she said, "they're so useful for getting out of places. Unfortunately it's not here right now, it's on its way back from the Republic. I thought you'd last another couple of days. A rare example of miscalculation on my part."

"You bought a ship."

"Also," she said, "a nice house in the Republic and a sort of hunting lodge thing on Scona, though it'll be a cold day in hell when we go there. I hate Scona. Still, the price was right and it pays to diversify."

He stared at her, awestruck, as though in the presence of the Lady Moon herself. I don't deserve her, he thought; and all interpretations of that statement are equally valid. "You arranged all that."

"Of course I did. Someone had to, and you're so innocent, it never crossed your mind to put something away for a rainy day. I forged drafts on the business. When Calojan goes over the books, he's in for a nasty surprise."

Aimeric sat down on the bed. "Who are Boioannes and Tragus?"

"Second biggest bank in Mezentia. Good reputation, very solid. You get better rates with the Mursuphlus, but I think they're over-extended in textiles."

He looked round the room. Now he came to think of it, there was nothing in it he recognised, apart from one icon he'd brought from home. She's my whole life, he thought, or all of it I actually care about. If only I could be with her, nothing else would really matter.

"There," she said. "All done. I suggest we go now."

"Now?"

She nodded. "If I was your brother-in-law-to-be, I'd send half a dozen kettlehats, in the middle of the night. There's probably a passage for us on a grain freighter. Knowing Calojan, steerage. I've booked us on board the *Roebuck*, for the Republic. I know the captain from way back. We'd better get a move on."

He leaned across and lifted his icon down off the wall; the Invincible Sun handing a small model of the City to Florian. It fitted in his pocket. "Fine," he said. "Let's go. Thank you for taking me with you."

She frowned at him. "I do love you," she said. "Sort of. Also, the accounts in the Republic are in your name. Women can't have bank accounts over a certain amount, would you believe."

She let him carry the big case, so he could feel useful. They walked in silence as far as the Yarn Market; then she said, "You didn't tell me about the fire oil."

"I assumed you'd find out."

She shook her head. "For once, you did a really good job of keeping a secret. I only found out because Ermanaric didn't want his wife to know about the barmaid at the *Austerity*. Really, Aimeric, that could've been so useful. It could have kept us here, if you'd let me deal with it."

"I'm sorry."

"No, you aren't. Still, too late now. I don't suppose you happen to have the formula?"

"No."

"Ah well. I assumed not, or Calojan wouldn't be letting you go, he'd have killed us both instead."

It was a long way to the docks, but Orsella insisted that they walk; he wasn't quite sure why, but he knew better than to argue. Since Calojan's return, the queues had melted away. Nobody wanted to leave now, and it was quite likely that most of those who had would be coming back. Even so, Aimeric was surprised to find the dockside practically deserted; no dockers loading or unloading, no passengers sitting on their luggage, no officials nosing through bills of lading with impatient captains. They found the *Roebuck*, but there was no gangplank, and nobody to be seen on board. Eventually, after they'd stood around feeling helpless for a rather long time, they saw a tall, sad-looking man in a thick brown coat, identified by Orsella as the *Roebuck*'s captain.

"Sorry," he said, "but if you want your money back, you can forget it. I've lost enough on this trip as it is."

Orsella said, "You mean you're not sailing?"

The captain looked at her. "You haven't heard?"

"Heard what?"

"The Republic's gone," the captain said. "All gone, nothing left. Nothing but rubble and ashes."

ONCE AGAIN, CALOJAN'S prompt action forestalled any public display of panic. Soldiers on the streets put any thought of riots or demonstrations out of people's heads, and the curfew was brought forward by an hour. The Exchange was closed for business for three days, and the Stamp Office declined to put official stamps on any commercial documents until further notice, which effectively put a stop to financial speculation and prevented runs on the banks. Since the offices of chancellor, prefect and archdeacon were presumed to be vacant, Calojan assumed their powers and issued a package of interim measures to keep the economy working and money circulating until the full impact of the disaster was properly understood.

They had come, according to the best available accounts, quite unobserved and wholly unexpected. A number of sea-going vessels—some reports referred to rafts or floats, others to oversized flat-bottomed galleys; the number was somewhere between two and five hundred—appeared in the Gulf on the morning of the sixteenth Feralia. There was a heavy mist, which undoubtedly helped, but so far no convincing explanation had been given as to where the ships, or rafts, had come from, or how they managed to cross the Gulf in plain sight and land on the Crescent in plain sight, without the Vesani navy or coastguard doing anything to stop them. Once ashore, they attacked with unbelievable ferocity, killing and burning at will and without restraint. Most reports agreed that they didn't seem interested in looting, only in destruction; they herded people into large buildings, jammed the doors and set fire to them. When people tried to escape through the landward gates, they found them closed and barred from the outside; there was no reliable information about that, but it had to be assumed that there had been some sort of carefully co-ordinated support operation, with land forces moving in to block the gates. As a result, there were very few survivors, a couple of hundred at most; the crews of half a dozen ships that happened to be sailing out as the attackers came in, a handful of merchants and merchant-seamen who slipped past the massacre on the Crescent and managed to launch; a team of workers making repairs to the underground cisterns, who came off shift after it was all over and emerged to find the city in flames.

The only information available concerning the identity of the attackers came from a very unreliable source. A crewman on board a ship that passed the flotilla as it entered the Gulf had mentioned to a crewmate that he thought the rafts looked familiar; he'd seen something like them once, mnay years ago, on the great lakes far away to the north-east. Most unfortunately, that man couldn't be questioned by the investigating authorities. His ship reached the City a full day before the news broke, and the man in question had finished his service and was signed on to another ship, leaving immediately for Mezentia. Efforts to trace him had failed, so all that was known was what he'd said to his colleague, who freely admitted that, at the time, he hadn't been interested and wasn't really listening. About all he could remember was the name of the people who used the rafts on the great lakes. They were called, he was pretty sure, the Goida.

It WAS TOUCH and go for three days; on the fourth day, the imperial doctor sent by Calojan at Chauzida's request announced that king Raffen was out of danger and would probably make a reasonably full recovery. He left detailed instructions for his patient's care, refused to accept any reward and returned to the City under a flag of truce.

"Marvellous character," Raffen said, when finally Joiauz was allowed in to see him. "Incredibly clever and miserable as hell. Clearly he thought I shouldn't be treated and should be left to die, but I'm guessing he was under orders that failure wasn't an option. I reckon he pulled me through the fever by sheer force of personality."

Joiauz shook his head. "I told Chauzida not to bother asking, I thought they'd never agree to send us a doctor. But Chauzida insisted. He said it never hurts to try."

Raffen laughed, then winced; three broken ribs. "He's smart," he said. "What's better, from Calojan's point of view; a dead martyr or a live king under an obligation? Still, I'm not complaining. It'd be really frustrating to die right now, just when it's starting to get interesting."

"They told you, then."

"About the Goida? Oh yes. Heard it from the doctor, in fact; he'd got it from his assistant when she came in with some stuff he needed. I think Calojan wanted us to know right away."

Joiauz nodded. "He's pitching the idea that we now have a common enemy and we need to settle our differences and come together," he said. "I have to say, it's gone down rather well. You probably don't realise just how terrified my people are of the Goida."

"If it's them," Raffen said. "But yes, I had got the message. Anyway, let's not go into all that right now. My friend the doctor said I'm not to think about business for at least another three days, or it'll kill me. To be honest, I'm really glad of the excuse."

Joiauz frowned, but let it go. "We've finally got some numbers for you, if you feel up to hearing them."

Raffen looked straight ahead at the side of the tent. "Go on."

"Four hundred killed," Joiauz said, "another two hundred-odd badly injured. It could have been worse," he added, when Raffen didn't react. "After all, most of the artillery crews were your people."

"It could have been far worse," Raffen said, without perceptible expression.

"We lost a hundred and seventy-six," Joiauz went on, "including Semplan and two elders of the Grey Dove. I think we killed something like four imperials, though they won't give us a figure. They took all the catapults, apart from six that sort of fell to bits after the first shot. They're mounting them on the wall right now, as a matter of fact."

"It's a fair trade," Raffen replied, in the same flat voice. "They gave us third-rate armour, we give them jerrybuilt siege engines. That way, everyone gets what they deserve."

"What I'm getting at is," Joiauz went on, "the council has decided that any attempt to attack the City, now they've got all that extra firepower, would be suicidal. So we're giving up. We're going to negotiate a settlement."

Raffen yawned loudly. "Because of the Goida."

"Because of the Goida, and because Calojan's not dead after all, and because we don't want to get smashed to bits by rocks from our own engines. And because Chauzida says so."

"Ah well." Raffen folded his arms on his chest; the customary attitude of a dead body on a funeral pyre in Selbst tradition, though Joiauz probably didn't know that. "Not much I can do about it lying here. And not much we can do about it if you decide you've had enough. Peace it is, then."

"You don't want peace, do you?"

"Peace is all I want." A slight hint of vehemence, quickly controlled. "And there won't be any peace until that city is levelled and put back to pasture. But not to worry. I'm sure you people know what you're doing."

Joiauz was feeling uncomfortable. "I'd better let you get some rest," he said. "Chauzida would like to come and see you tomorrow, if you think you'll be up to it."

"Of course." Raffen let him get right to the doorway, then said, "Joiauz."

"Yes?"

"Is it true you tried to murder your nephew?"

Joiauz was perfectly still. "Who told you that?"

"Oh, I can't remember. Well? Did you?"

"Yes," Joiauz said.

"Ah." Raffen nodded sleepily. "And he's forgiven you."

"Yes, he has. Which is just like him, and a damn sight more than I deserve."

"Of course. You're both fools, you know. If I've learned one thing, it's that if you rob a man, you really do need to kill him too. And make sure about it. Shoving him down a well isn't enough, and neither is sticking his head up on a pole, apparently. Make really, really sure he's dead, it's the only way."

Joiauz pulled back the tent flap. "That's what you've learned, is it, after all you've been through and all the extraordinary things you've done?"

Raffen thought for a moment before answering. "Pretty much, yes."

"I'll see you around, Raffen."

Raffen smiled. "Count on it."

BETWEEN THEM, THEY had enough cash money to get to Lonazep. "Where the hell is Lonazep?" Aimeric asked. She told him and he went slightly pale. "All right," he said, after a long pause. "I guess we'll just have to walk from there."

"Maybe," she replied. "Maybe not."

The ship was a stone transport, built to carry huge blocks of granite from the Lonazep quarries to the four corners of the known world. There were only three corners now, and the City wouldn't be buying any more premium-grade building stone for a long time, so the ship's owners had diversified into second-hand clothes. It was a buyer's market—the captain had brought in a cargo of flour, dried fish and raisins, and in return he was overwhelmed with silks, furs, even one or two pieces of the genuine imperial purple, forbidden by law except for members of the emperor's immediate family. He packed the stuff up in bales and filled his hold and all the available space on deck. He wasn't sure where he was going to sell all that high-class merchandise, but he couldn't resist the bargain.

Aimeric and Orsella, therefore, slept on a bale of the finest Aelian silk. The barge was painfully slow. There would be no landfall between the City and Lonazep (a small settlement on the north end of the Boec peninsula; the south end, sixty miles away, was separated from the island of Scona by two miles of water). Orsella had made herself a sort of cabin by draping heavy brocades over bits of the rigging, and didn't want to be disturbed, so Aimeric spent most of his time leaning on the rail, staring at the sea. He asked the captain and the first mate if there was anything he could do to help, but they just laughed.

The harbour at Lonazep was small and wind-blasted. The buildings were mostly wood, bleached a uniform grey by the salt air. The harbour master came out to peer at them over the folds of a huge, fat scarf, but nothing he saw seemed to interest him. The crew started to unload, with the slow, efficient movements of men who know they have a lot of work to get through.

Aimeric looked down at his smart, expensive City boots, their shiny toes clouded with encrustations of white salt. "Well," he said, "we'd better start walking."

"Not just yet," Orsella said. She didn't seem particularly affected by the general gloom of the place. "What we need is a bar."

"Really."

"That way," she said, nodding, "assuming it's still there. I haven't been here in years."

It was still there. It was the only brick-built building in town. It was empty, apart from a huge bald-headed man, asleep with his feet up on a chair.

"Hello, Rainault," Orsella said.

The bald man woke up and rose to his feet like a startled bird. "Good God," he said. "You."

"That's right. Don't worry, I'm not stopping."

"Too right you aren't."

"I'm here to sell."

The bald man hesitated, then shrugged. "What've you got?"

Orsella frowned. "For pity's sake, Rainault," she said. "We've just got off the boat, we're freezing cold and starving hungry." This was news to Aimeric, but Orsella had a way of turning anything she said into the truth. He shivered. "Get us some bread and cheese and load up the fire. This is supposed to be a friendly, welcoming place."

Rainault scowled at her, but did as he was told. The bread was close-grained and incredibly dense, but nowhere near as hard as the cheese. The fire made the room uncomfortably hot.

"Well?" Rainault said.

"Take a look at these."

She put the long, flat case down on a table and unbuckled the straps. Rainault peered down, blinked a couple of times and rubbed his jaw, as though he'd been punched in the face.

"Dirty pictures," he said, in a faintly awestruck voice. "Not a lot of call for that sort of thing round here."

Orsella was smiling. "Not just any dirty pictures," she said. "Look at the signature."

A gleam in Rainault's eye suggested he'd already done that. "Genuine?"
"You know me."
Obviously he didn't. "All right," he said slowly. "What were you thinking of asking?"
"There's more," Orsella said. "Here, look."
She turned over one of the sheets. In faded brown writing, spiky and sloped, Aimeric could just make out—

Directly as a consequence of the making of this picture, my son was born on the 17th day of the seventh month of the third year of Ortheric II. In the circumstances, I believe it would be appropriate to name him Calojan.

"Calojan means 'little dog' in Old Permian," Orsella explained. "And the couple in the picture—"
"Yes," Rainault said. His face was expressionless, but his eyes were bulging. "How much?"
"I think you'll have no trouble finding a buyer," Orsella said. "The Mezentine government, for instance. They're probably looking round for a suitable coronation gift right now."
"Ten tremisses."
"Forty," Orsella replied. "And I'm only selling because we're cold and hungry."
Rainault turned the sheet over, pursed his lips so tight that they showed white, walked to the counter, opened a jar and sloshed big silver coins into the palm of his hand. "Nice to see you again," he said, with his back turned. "Where are you headed?"
"Scona," Orsella said. "We need a ride."
"I know for a chaise," Rainault said. "Twelve tremisses."
"Nine."
The back of Rainault's head moved up and down. "Give me an hour," he said.

So it was that, just over an hour later, Orsella and Aimeric found themselves in a small dog-cart with flaking paint and a tattered canopy, rattling slowly over the bone-dry ruts on the transpeninsular road. In two days' time, if they were lucky, they'd see the improbably tall, cone-shaped profile of Scona on the flat horizon. Once a volcano, always a volcano, the saying went, but it didn't stop forty thousand people living there.
Orsella was making charcoal sketches, though the bumps in the road made it difficult. Clearly, a large number of hitherto unknown masterpieces

by Calojan's father were about to reach the market. Aimeric, doing his best with the reins and the footbrake, was muttering something over and over again, under his breath; twenty parts Scona oil, four parts turpentine, one part sulphur, one part sal draconis—

ON THE FIRST day of the old moon in the sixth month of the regency of Calojan the Great, the empress gave birth to a boy. He was slightly under-sized, but healthy. He was given the name Roumain, after the regent's father. He had six fingers on his left hand.